D1572835

Love is
a time of enchantment:
in it all days are fair and all fields
green. Youth is blest by it,
old age made benign:
the eyes of love see
roses blooming in December,
and sunshine through rain. Verily
is the time of true-love
a time of enchantment — and
Oh! how eager is woman
to be bewitched!

THE GOLDEN WEB

With the ending of the Peninsular War, Major Alexander Lacey rides home to England to take up residence at Blakestone House, now a blackened ruin devastated by an inexplicable fire. His unexpected arrival is greeted with deep hostility from his neighbours; among them the wilful Lady Elisa Maytland. Then the major encounters a beautiful young widow to whom he had once lost his heart, and soon he seeks to rekindle the flame. However, past events begin to threaten his life as he attempts to unravel the mystery surrounding Blakestone House.

G. K. COLLIER

THE GOLDEN WEB

Complete and Unabridged

ULVERSCROFT
Leicester

First published in Great Britain in 1996 by
Robert Hale Limited
London

First Large Print Edition
published 1997
by arrangement with
Robert Hale Limited
London

The right of G. K. Collier to be identified as
the author of this work has been asserted by
her in accordance with the
Copyright, Designs and Patents Act, 1988

LP 17511

British Library CIP Data

Collier, G. K.
    The golden web.—Large print ed.—
    Ulverscroft large print series: romance
    1. English fiction—20th century
    2. Large type books
    I. Title
    823.9'14 [F]

    ISBN 0–7089–3682–2

Published by
F. A. Thorpe (Publishing) Ltd.
Anstey, Leicestershire

Set by Words & Graphics Ltd.
Anstey, Leicestershire
Printed and bound in Great Britain by
T. J. Press (Padstow) Ltd., Padstow, Cornwall

This book is printed on acid-free paper

To
Kate May Ruth Edwards
and
Thomas Robert Douglas Collier

For the great joy your birth has brought.
And to the proud grandparents of the
Collier, Edwards and Pearson families
with deep love and respect from your
children.

To
Kate Mary Ruth Edward,
and
Thomas Robert Douglas Collier

For the great joy your birth has brought.
And to the proud grandparents of the
Collier, Edwards and Pearson families
with deep love and respect from your
children.

1

AS the chaise turned off the pike road and plunged into the tree-deep lane, a strengthening wind seethed angrily amid the leaves and the noon day darkened. Ahead of them, a great, purple swell of clouds was massing upon the backs of the hills hunched on the near horizon. Scowling up at the louring sky, the post-boy whipped up his horses and the carriage lurched onwards, rapidly gathering speed. A few minutes later and the first random spots of rain spattered against his face. He cursed concisely beneath his breath, pulling down the peak of his leather cap; it seemed he was like to get a thorough soaking and with no hope of comfort at the end of this journey. Why the gentleman should wish to go to Blakestone House at all, he could not imagine.

A sudden, jagged streak of lightning briefly lit the western skies, followed after a few seconds by a deep rumbling of thunder. The horses needed no further urging as they leapt into their stride and the chaise rattled noisily on its way.

Eventually they emerged from the sheltering trees and bowled along between the neat hedgerows that lined the open pastures. The solitary passenger leaned forward in his seat and let down the glass, his eyes fixed on the rolling Downs.

Then he saw it. High up on the summit and just visible above the wildly tossing tree-tops, rose the grim ruin of a great and ancient mansion. In the blackened brickwork, rows of gaping, rectangular spaces that had once held gleaming windows, were open to the elements and behind them now moved only the billowing, black storm-clouds. Again an ear-splitting crack rent the heavens, as a javelin of blue fire was hurled quivering earthwards.

In this lurid light he could see plainly that the roof and upper floors had been completely destroyed. The house, once thriving with life, was like a shattered skull with hollow, sightless sockets, a haunting desolation that pierced his heart.

2

Suddenly the rain began to sweep down from the hills like a marauding horde, spears brandished and beat upon the chaise with a mighty onslaught.

The young man shivered as if unaccustomed to the English climate and closing the window, leant slowly back against the squabs of the cushioned seat, seeming to fall into a deep reverie.

Despite the buffeting wind and rain, the carriage continued on its course and began to make the ascent, doggedly following the narrow road that wound gradually up the sides of a very steep hill. When they were about halfway up and passing through a deep wood of beech trees, the chaise halted abruptly.

"Why the devil have we stopped?" demanded its occupant moodily, as he put forth his head.

The answer to his question became immediately apparent as his eye was caught by the sight of a magnificent black stallion that was impeding their progress. The great beast was rearing up on its hind legs, its hoofs flailing the air, while a slim, young woman in an umber-coloured riding habit stood holding tenaciously on to his bridle, unmindful both of the rain and her danger.

The gentleman muttered some unintelligible remark to himself and leapt down into the road, impatiently thrusting back his cloak over his shoulder as he advanced. In a few quick strides he had reached the lady's side and snatched the bridle from her hands. By dint of sheer strength and fearless determination, he mastered the nervous animal and expertly brought him under control. When he was certain that the creature was pacified, he turned to the young woman.

"Whose mount is this? Has he thrown his rider?" he questioned sharply.

"Certainly not!" she replied indignantly. "Sabre did not throw me. It was all your fault," she continued accusingly. "If you had not been travelling at that break-neck speed, you would not have startled him. It's lucky you did not run us down! What business have you here, anyway? This is private property, you know!"

The gentleman ignored her complaint and merely looked her up and down in a manner which caused her to bristle with annoyance.

"Do you mean to tell me that you are actually permitted to ride about the countryside on a horse that is clearly not a suitable mount for a young lady?" he enquired suspiciously. Then, looking swiftly about him, he added, "And without your groom?"

"I don't mean to tell you anything!" she retorted petulantly. "Except that you are trespassing and have no right to be here — and certainly no right to ask me impertinent questions!"

"On the contrary, I thought them extremely pertinent," the gentleman remarked evenly, "especially since you seem so reluctant to answer them. I can only suppose you are here without the knowledge or permission of your family. Am I correct?"

The young lady eyed him contemptuously. "Permission? As if I should need to ask permission to do anything I wish to do!" Then, observing that beneath his cloak he wore the splendid uniform of an officer of Hussars, she gave a scornful laugh. "It's only little toy soldiers like you who must wait for 'permission' — even to speak! So hold your tongue, sirrah!"

"I need do so only in the presence of a superior," he snapped curtly. "Now if you will excuse me, young lady, I must be on my way. Good day to you!" He clicked his elegantly booted heels and gave a cursory bow.

"Just a moment!" she commanded imperiously as he made to go. "In the absence of a groom, you will serve me as well. Help me on to my horse before you leave. I cannot mount unaided and it is your carelessness that has caused my plight."

At first he was tempted to refuse her insolent request but glancing back over his shoulder, he hesitated momentarily and then returned to her side.

"A little civility would not come amiss. However, it is my guess that you have not the ability to learn that in the brief time I can spare you. Besides," he grinned broadly, revealing perfect, white teeth, "you look like a fledgling fallen from its nest and I was ever tender-hearted." He gave a flick of his forefinger to the bedraggled feathers drooping sadly on her velvet hat, a stylish creation somewhat at odds with the rest of her rather plain mode of dress. "Come, little bird, hop on to my hand."

She lifted her chin disdainfully as she picked up the train of her skirt and placed her slender foot in his grasp. In a trice she was on the stallion's back and gathering up the reins. Nimbly she settled herself in the saddle and arranged her skirts to her satisfaction. Another arrogant toss of her proud head, a little kick of her heel and the huge horse bounded away into the dense woodland with his skilful rider seated easily on his broad back.

The seasoned cavalry officer stood staring after her with grudging admiration. She might be lacking in the social graces but in the saddle she was grace itself.

He resumed his seat in the carriage and they moved on again, this time without interruption. Some ten minutes later the chaise pulled up at an immense archway built into a high stone wall that stretched away left and right, marking the boundaries of a large park.

"Do you want to go any further, sir?"

called back the post-boy.

"Of course, man! Drive on to the house!" ordered his passenger peremptorily.

With a weary sigh and shaking his head at the incomprehensible ways of the gentry, he set his horses' heads towards the gateway.

The rain still fell relentlessly as they drove down the carriage road, the wheels crunching on the weed-strewn gravel and splashing through the deep puddles forming in the ruts and holes along the way. A tangle of overgrown shrubs intruded into their path and merged with the long, rank grass that lay in twisted mounds and knots at the edges of the drive. Nature was attempting to reclaim her own and so far she was succeeding. With the thunder continuing to roll and crash above them, they finally drew up on the top of the hill and looked towards the aged mansion.

It was a strange homecoming. A ruined, burnt-out shell of a house awaited him. The only welcoming light glimmering in the few remaining window panes, came from streaks of lightning intermittently illuminating the stark desolation of the scene. Now the carriage resumed its progress along the last half-mile stretch leading right up to the broken, crumbling steps that had originally given on to a grand portico. Only one of the fluted columns still stood and below it lay the lichen-yellowed remnants of the huge pediment which had once surmounted them.

When the chaise at last came to a standstill, the officer leapt lightly down and stood gazing around him. The entire east wing was gone, together with most of the west wing and the shattered stone walls bore streaks of melted lead and the sooty scorches of the fire that had wrought so much destruction. The empty, frameless windows which he had seen from afar, towered above him like open mouths screaming a silent despair, while the storm rampaged over the tumbled masonry in a frenzy of wild abandon.

"What now, sir?" enquired the post-boy, eager to be on his way back to the cosy inn and a nice, warming mug of grog.

"Would you care to step in for some refreshment?" invited the gentleman, raising his voice to make himself heard above the wail of the wind.

The unfortunate man stared at him in dumb surprise, almost completely convinced that his passenger was quite insane.

"No, thank you, sir. I'd rather be on my way, if it's all the same to you," he answered hurriedly. "Goodbye!" and with that he turned the carriage about and rattled furiously away with as much speed as he could muster. As he gave one last glance behind him, he saw the strange young man still standing on the ruined steps, with the rain and the wind raging all about him.

When the chaise had passed from sight, the officer wrapped himself tighter in his cloak and made his way along the scarred wall of the west wing until he turned a corner and came upon a stout oak door that yet defied the elements. He rapped as loudly as he could with the iron knocker and leant into the shelter of the wide lintel. A minute or so went by and then came the sounds of hastily drawn bolts and the door swung inwards.

"Major Lacey, sir! I did not look

to see you until tomorrow at the soonest. Come you in, sir! Come you in! Whatever possessed you to set out in such weather?"

"The truth of the matter is, Ned, I left early this morning when the day seemed set fair. There was nothing to keep me any longer in London," answered the major, handing his soaking mantle to the grizzle-haired batman. "How have you fared here in this ghoulish cavern? Did you manage to make it at all habitable?"

"You shall judge for yourself, sir. Follow me and I'll take you to the drawing-room," smiled Ned with a quick nod in the direction of a long, narrow corridor.

He preceded the major along the stone-flagged passage which, despite the mullioned windows set at intervals along its entire length, was almost as dark as night.

"Here we are, sir," he announced cheerily, "these are our new quarters and compared to some we've shared over the years, as cosy a nest as we could wish to call home."

Major Lacey ducked his head under the low doorway and entered the room, his keen gaze noting with appreciation the many comforts that Ned had provided for their sojourn, however long that might be.

A blazing log fire burned in the high grate that had obviously been recently cleaned and polished. The floor and the flagged hearth-stone were neatly swept and a copper kettle was just beginning to steam on the hob. Two spindle-backed armchairs were set one on each side of the fireplace and a frayed but well-beaten woollen rug lay between, its faded hues rekindled by the glow of the leaping, yellow flames.

The single diamond-paned window to the right of the fireplace overlooked what had been, in prosperous days, a flowered border but now alas, exposed a riot of sodden and flattened nettles and dandelions. Rose-patterned curtains hung from a polished-wood pole and these at least still retained something of their original charm and added a touch of elegance to the room. Underneath the casement, Ned had placed a small

12

oak table and two more chairs which reflected the gleam of firelight in their beeswax-burnished surfaces.

"Why! This is splendid, Ned! I see that a return to civilization has not diminished your skills! You could make a palace out of a pig-sty!" declared his delighted master. "You've already worked wonders here and in just a few days! I commend you!"

"Thank you, sir," grinned Ned, reddening with pleasure as he sensed the major's genuine approval of all his efforts. "Would you care to view the rest of your billet, sir?"

"Willingly. My expectations are becoming brighter by the moment! I am now ready to be astonished beyond belief."

"Then step this way, sir."

Ned escorted him further down the passage and threw open a second door. "Your bedchamber, sir," he informed him grandly.

"Ah, this is the old butler's pantry, an I mistake not. And the other was the housekeeper's room. Well, this is all excellent! We shall deal tolerably here, I'm sure, which is more than I dared hope." The major surveyed the room glad-eyed. "A veritable haven! Is that a real feather mattress I see?!" he cried joyously. "I wonder if I shall ever be able to accustom myself to such a luxury?"

"Not easily, sir, I'll warrant! You and I are too used to a bed of cold earth and a leather saddle for a pillow. I hope you've no objection to it, sir, but I've taken the liberty of setting my pallet in the strong-room adjoining. The plate is long gone and it's empty now, of course. But there's room enough for my bed between the shelving."

Major Lacey crossed the bare floor and pushing open the massive iron door, peered inside.

"It's rather cramped and cold, Ned. You ought to make your bed out here. There's plenty of space for us both if we move some of this furniture."

"Good Lord, sir! Haven't I slept like a babe in the snows of the Pyrenees? That's as warm as the Hotel Hades in comparison. It'll serve me well enough, don't you worry!" chuckled Ned reassuringly.

"Well, perhaps if we keep a fire in,

should it become necessary," mused the major consideringly, "we're certainly not going to be short of firewood. Yes, it will serve the purpose, I suppose."

"We're going to be as snug as can be, sir! No doubt of it! Now what do you say to a warming glass of my special? I've reconnoitred the area and made a foray into the village yonder, so we've plenty of provisions."

"A glass of your rum punch, is it? Well, why are we tarrying here? Let's to it!" replied the major eagerly, clapping Ned on the shoulder and propelling him back into the passageway.

A few minutes later they were both ensconced before the crackling fire, their glasses in hand and their feet propped comfortably on the fender. The major's tall, red shako and sopping-wet cloak were steaming on a chair beside the hearth. He had thrown aside his handsome, fur-trimmed pelisse and loosening the neck of his tunic, lounged at ease in the armchair, the flickering firelight gleaming on the rich frogging of his uniform and lending a ruddy glow to his curly, brown hair.

"Ah! Ned!" he sighed contentedly. "'Tis no small wonder I have managed to survive this interminable war. A glass of your special is a restorative worthy of universal acclaim! I do believe this is truly the panacea for all ills! The legendary elixir of the Gods!"

"Ay, there's many a body has tried to tempt me into revealing my secret recipe. Captain Rowland once offered me thirty guineas and four dozen bottles of his finest claret if only I would divulge it to him. But I stood firm. 'Captain', I said, 'there's not a man in the King's Army could prise it from me. Nor a whole lake of the best vintage those Frenchies could provide! I shall take the secret to my grave, so help me'. Oh, you should have seen his face!"

"Rowland offered to part with his precious claret?!" exclaimed the major, astounded. "Then that's more than he's ever done for any man! It were almost easier to believe the camel threaded!"

"And yet 'tis gospel truth, sir. When I refused to be swayed by such devilish inducements, he then tried to persuade me to enter his service. As if I would even consider deserting my post!"

"It is well for me you stood your ground. But your faithfulness is ill-paid, Ned. Look what I have brought you to." The major waved a shapely, sun-bronzed hand to indicate their surroundings. "I had half-expected to find the place uninhabited when I arrived. I am sure you can never have been so close to desertion as when you first beheld this English Jericho."

"Not a bit of it, sir! Today I am put in mind of the time we crossed the Garonne, just before the battle of Toulouse, do you remember? Such foul weather! We thought to see old Noah himself come a-sailing down the river! But when I took up residence here last week, the place looked none so grim. Haply the sun will shine again tomorrow and you'll see our situation will seem greatly improved."

The major smiled across at his honest henchman. "I should have guessed you'd look on the bright side, Ned! It has ever been your way. And how could I forget Toulouse? We very nearly drowned that afternoon, didn't we? I was obliged to

17

walk my horse across the last section of that damned pontoon, because every minute it threatened to break loose! It was like standing on a rolling barrel half-submerged in water! This seems but an April shower after that experience!"

"Ay, we've had some ticklish moments, sir, and no mistake! Lord! But Old Hookey led us into some rare brews." He smiled fondly, reaching for the kettle sputtering over the fire. "Things are going to be deadly dull from now on, I'm thinking."

"I'm inclined to agree with you," sighed the major, leaning back his head and closing his eyes wearily. "It will be an odd thing to have survived the war only to die of boredom in one's own bed."

"Well, if I know anything of you and I've known you since you were breeched, you will find something to occupy your mind. Don't think I haven't guessed the reason why we have come here of all places. It's no use your telling me it's idle curiosity because I won't swallow that humbug! You're convinced there was more to this tragedy than mere accident and that's a fact!"

The major opened wide his eyes again and regarded Ned in some amusement. "And what does the Oracle say about that, may I enquire?"

"Oh, I'll only predict that if there's trouble to be found here, you'll be the one to discover it, since trouble follows you as sure as night follows day!"

By the next morning the storm had moved away and the high, thin cloud that had remained in its wake, soon began to disperse as the sun grew stronger. Major Lacey spent the first hour after breakfast exploring his new surroundings. The damage was considerable. The outer walls were still standing but the once gracious apartments were almost all completely ruined except for the west tower and the section of the west wing which they now inhabited. The kitchens were largely unscathed but the stairs leading down to them were partially blocked with rubble and the cellars inaccessible. Two or three of the ground-floor rooms facing north had also survived the flames but were in a dangerous condition owing to the extensive damage to the ceilings and inner walls. By the time the major

19

had completed his tour of inspection, he returned to his quarters looking more like a grubby schoolboy than an officer in the respected King's Hussars.

Ned shook his head disgustedly. "You look as if you've just led a charge through one of Boney's cannonades. Didn't I tell you that your baggage hasn't arrived yet? If anyone comes calling, I'll be forced to disown you. As batman to a commissioned officer in a crack cavalry regiment, I have my reputation to consider."

The major gazed down at his somewhat besmirched finery and grinned unrepentantly. "Don't worry, Ned, no one will be the least bit interested in us. This place is as good as a hermitage. Who would want to visit such a lonely outpost? The only signs of life I've seen this morning are the crows up on the battlements of the West Tower."

He began to knock the dust and grime from his tunic until Ned protested impatiently that the soot was getting in his dough. The major put up his hands in a gesture of surrender. "All right, all right! I'm going," he said, backing to the door. "Ah, it looks as if we are soon to be in need of some more firewood, so I'll make myself useful," he offered, bending to pick up the log basket.

"Then have a care of your clothes!" warned Ned sternly, as he glanced up from his baking. "We're not in Spain now, you know!"

"No, but I'm beginning to wish we were!" called back the major mournfully as he strode down the passage, his once glossy Hessians ringing loudly on the stone floor.

He found the long-handled axe leaning against the wall just behind the outer door and seizing it up, swung it over his shoulder as he strode away into the sunny garden, whistling cheerily as he went.

Mindful of Ned's warning, he stripped off his tunic, hooking it on to a convenient branch and then addressed himself to his chosen task with a will.

So engrossed was he in his labour, that he was completely unaware that three riders had emerged from the woods behind him and were approaching the house. The moment they espied him thus occupied, they all three reined in

21

their horses and stared inquisitively in his direction.

"There! What did I tell you?" cried the young lady to the two gentlemen who rode beside her. "I'll wager that's the same man I saw yesterday, driving up to the house!"

The smaller of her two companions rubbed his jowl doubtfully. "I say, Harry, the fellow peels to advantage, don't he?" he remarked, noting the major's broad, muscular back and the strength of his arms as he sliced effortlessly through the huge logs. "Perhaps we ought to exercise a little caution."

"Hmph! Do you think me as spineless as you, Alfred?" sneered his elder brother contemptuously. "I'll soon send him packing, see if I don't!"

Then as he made to advance on his quarry, he turned with an air of bravado towards the young lady. "You had better remain here, Elisa, I have no wish to expose you to any — unpleasantness," he smirked arrogantly.

"Pooh! As if I cared for that! I'll not have anyone suppose me missish, least of all you, Harry Palmer!" she scoffed, a glint of anger in her green eyes. "Come, Sabre, on boy!" She tapped him with her whip and the stallion leapt eagerly forward, leaving the two gentlemen to gallop hastily after her.

The major glanced up at the sound of the horses' hoofs thudding across the stretch of greenery that had in times past deserved to be referred to as a lawn. Now, however, it resembled nothing so grand, being but an unkempt mass of grass and meadow flowers. He screwed up his eyes against the bright sunlight. It seemed he was to have visitors after all, one of them female. He frowned in annoyance, belatedly regretting that he had dispensed with his shirt that morning. Unhurriedly, he reached for his short jacket, shrugging himself carelessly into it as they rode nearer. Then, arms akimbo, he stood at ease astride the fallen logs and waited for them to come up with him.

It was the young lady who reached him first, pulling in her horse so sharply that the stallion reared slightly, his nostrils flaring and his great, black eyes rolling back in his head. She settled him again in a moment, never once losing her control of the highly-strung animal.

The major gave his visitors a cool appraisal, not at all put out at being discovered *déshabillé* by two elegantly arrayed gentlemen and a lady who, although not elegant according to his critical eye, was most certainly expensively dressed. Indeed, he managed to achieve a certain *hauteur* in his face and in his stance as he stood silently watching them, that belied the fact that he was very far from neatness and propriety himself.

Damp tendrils of dark brown hair clung to his perspiring brow, a smear of soot streaked his smoothly shaven cheek, his unbuttoned tunic revealed an expanse of naked flesh and despite the sumptuous silver lacing of his uniform, his clothes were not exactly immaculate.

Lady Elisa Maytland gazed at him with great interest. Her eyes, flicking over him from his bare head to his dusty boots, showed as little embarrassment as his own.

"Well, well," she murmured, having finished her scrutiny, "I wonder what the toy soldier has been playing at today?"

He continued to regard her meditatively, his deep-blue eyes as tranquil as a summer sea.

"Oh, I nearly forgot," she remarked with a wry smile, "you have to wait for permission to speak, do you not? I grant it. And you may begin by telling me what you are doing here."

"You have no business intruding on this property," intervened Sir Harry Palmer superciliously, as he edged his horse forward. "The house may be unoccupied but this is still a private estate, not a camping ground for itinerant vagabonds," he added, looking down his long nose at the major's state of undress. "Now take yourself off before I report you to the constable."

As the young officer continued to maintain a dignified silence, the second gentleman took heart, saying brashly, "I am Alfred Palmer and this is my brother, Sir Harry Palmer. We happen to be neighbours of Lady Cullan, the owner of this estate and mean to do our duty in evicting any interlopers from these premises. So if you wish to avoid a good thrashing, you'll do as my brother suggests."

He ended by tapping his riding crop menacingly in the palm of his gloved hand.

The major's deep-blue eyes suddenly sparkled like sapphires and his handsome countenance broke into a boyish grin that, together with his dirty face and ruffled hair, gave him a decidedly *gamin* appearance.

"Oho! So it's a fight you're after, is it?" he answered gleefully, his voice in his excitement betraying a slight Irish lilt. "Sure and it's a grand day for it!"

"It's as I suspected from the start! The fellow's a damned tinker!" drawled Sir Harry disdainfully. "That uniform is probably stolen from some poor, unsuspecting traveller!" He urged his heavy bay mare forward. "We'll show you how we deal with rogues like you in this part of the country!"

As he rode at the major with his whip upraised, Lacey, instead of cringing away from the blow that was aimed at his head, launched himself at the oncoming horse and grabbing the bridle in one hand

and the axe haft in the other, dealt his attacker a hefty poke in the ribs that sent him crashing to the ground. Then leaping agilely into the vacated saddle, he wheeled the mare about so suddenly that the other gentleman who had been rushing in behind, was forced to pull up short. His horse jibbed at the bit giving the major the opportunity to lean across and grab the rider's foot, tipping him instantly into a puddle.

"Now let's to it, my lads!" cried the major enthusiastically as he swung himself down again. "I haven't enjoyed a good mill in weeks!"

As Sir Harry staggered to his feet, the major put up his fists invitingly but his opponent was in no mood to oblige him. His cork had already been drawn by the fall from his horse and he was holding a handkerchief to his bloodied nose. His brother Alfred was still lying winded on the sward, while his mount trampled heedlessly on his expensive headgear. The lady had judiciously withdrawn to a safe distance and viewed the proceedings with lively amusement.

"You damned ruffian!" cursed Sir

Harry, his voice peculiarly muffled. "You've broken my nose! I'll have you know you can't lay hands on a gentleman and get away with it! I'll see you gaoled for this!"

"What? Are we not to make some sport for ourselves?" reproached the major, disappointedly looking from one to the other. "How about you, sir?" he asked, squaring up to Alfred who had just managed to retrieve his crushed and sullied hat. "I can give you a few inches, it's true but you look sturdy enough. We might make a very good match of it. What d'you say?"

"I say the devil take you!" spluttered Alfred, vainly attempting to straighten his high-crowned beaver. "I shall ensure that Lady Cullan hears of this outrage and has you taken up for trespass!"

"Oh, you need not put yourself to such inconvenience, sir. You have already exerted yourselves enough on Lady Cullan's part. I am certain she will be very glad to know that she has such excellent neighbours," replied the major, lowering his guard and smiling in a friendly fashion upon them all.

"Oh? Are you acquainted with Lady Cullan?" demanded the young woman, drawing closer and looking down at him with growing curiosity in her wide, green eyes.

"Of course he isn't!" mumbled Sir Harry tersely. "I'd lay my life on it that he doesn't know Lady Cullan at all!"

"That would be a foolish wager and irresponsibly wasteful. You see, I do know Lady Cullan," he stated simply.

"Who are you?" interposed Lady Elisa, staring fixedly down at him in frowning perplexity.

He returned her puzzled gaze, his own eyes dancing with laughter. "Why! I'm your new neighbour! May I bid you all welcome to this ancient pile of rubble that I now call home?!"

"But that's impossible!" she protested unbelievingly. "Aurelia never mentioned . . . "

It was at this interesting juncture that Ned decided to put in an appearance. He had been watching from the parlour window and had waited to see how things developed before venturing out. Now that hostilities appeared to have been abandoned, he finally intervened.

The lady turned her head at the sound of his footsteps, noting his shocked expression as his fulminating eye fell upon his master's unseemly appearance.

"You look an honest man," she observed, bestowing a dazzling smile upon him, "can you tell us who this gentleman really is?"

"Ma'am," answered Ned wrathfully, "I have never set eyes on this black gypsy in all my life!"

2

LADY AURELIA CULLAN and Mrs Margaret Wytcherley, were engaged in conversation with Sir Eustace Newbury and his young nephew Mr Thomas Greenwood, when Lady Elisa swept in upon them unannounced.

The gentlemen arose at once and bowed in her direction as she marched into the room with her long, swift stride. She eyed the cosy little group around the hearth, her glance darting in inquisitive interest to the faces turned towards her, until they finally rested on the exquisite countenance of her aunt's dainty companion, Lady Cullan.

"How delightful for you, Aurelia," she drawled derisively, "I see you have acquired a new swain to languish at your feet. One nearer in age to you this time," she added pointedly, noting with malicious glee the angry flush that stained Sir Eustace's unhealthy pallor.

"Good morning, Lady Elisa," he

greeted her coldly, his thin, saturnine features displaying a marked annoyance. "It is always such a pleasure to see you."

"Oh? Is that why you are become such a fixture in this house? I had supposed the attraction that draws you almost daily to our fireside, lay in the person of the black widow who now presides over it."

"Elisa!" cried Mrs Wytcherley, horrified at her niece's ill-concealed malevolence. "How many times must I ask you to curb that unruly tongue of yours! Lady Cullan is my guest for as long as she chooses to remain with us and I will not have you continually abusing her!"

"Oh, please do not quarrel over me, I beg you!" pleaded Lady Cullan, her beautiful eyes filling with bright, glittering tears. "I understand how dreadfully trying it must be for you, dear Elisa, having to share your home with another woman who is not even related to you. I know I ought to have removed to the Dower House by now but it is so lonely up there, I just cannot face living in such awful solitude." She dabbed with a wisp of lace at a crystal teardrop sparkling on the ends of her delicately curving lashes. "If only you realized how painful it is for me even to think of my poor, darling Lucius!" A sob broke from the trembling, rosy bow of her lips and she pressed the handkerchief to her soft, tragic mouth, turning her face away, unable to continue.

Mrs Wytcherley flew out of her chair and bent solicitously over her, putting a comforting arm about her drooping shoulders.

"There, there, my dearest! Do not upset yourself, I pray! You will make yourself ill again and Doctor Osgood will reproach me for allowing your spirits to fall so low. Come now, take a little sip of wine, it will strengthen you," she insisted encouragingly. "See, Mr Greenwood has kindly fetched your glass. Do please oblige him by accepting it from his hand."

The young widow peeped up over the crumpled square of fine cambric and seeing the deep concern on the young gentleman's face, managed to bestow a grateful smile upon him. Mr Greenwood was instantly smitten anew by the glory of those dazzling eyes.

"Thank you, sir. You are very kind, I'm sure," she murmured softly. "I do not know what you must be thinking of me. I mean to be so strong but somehow I cannot overcome my sorrows. Memories are a mixed blessing, are they not? Sometimes so sweet but more often yet, so very sorrowful!"

"Bravo, Aurelia!" applauded Lady Elisa admiringly. "You outshine Mrs Siddons herself! Your talents are wasted under this roof. Have you never thought of capturing a wider audience? You would be a great success in Drury Lane; I wonder that you have not considered the opportunities it must afford you. After all, actresses have been known to receive even royal favours. Only think of Mrs Jordan and sweet Perdita Robinson."

"That's quite enough, Elisa!" snapped Mrs Wytcherley furiously. "No doubt Harry Palmer has been telling you those tales! Your father shall hear of your abominable behaviour when he returns to us! I heartily wish he had never gone to South America without you! I declare you are the most . . . " Mrs Wytcherley compressed her lips tightly, remembering her visitors. "I shall speak to you later. Now kindly go up and change your dress. It is almost time for our luncheon."

"I see you are anxious to be rid of me, Aunt Meg. You prefer artifice to plain speaking, as do most of our acquaintances it seems. Have you never thought it odd that Aurelia still chooses to wear her widow's weeds? Lucius has been dead these three years now; it's time she cast off the role of grieving widow. Why don't you begin by tearing down that old ruin up there on the hill, Aurelia? Lucius must have left you some money, surely? Enough to refurbish the Dower House I should have thought. There's nothing left of Blakestone that's worth saving!"

"How could you, Elisa?!" shuddered Lady Cullan, eyeing her reproachfully. "It is all very well for you, you have no delicacy of feeling! You can never understand what misery I endure! That house shall remain untouched for ever. It is my darling's shrine, the place where last my eyes beheld him before . . . before . . . " She choked and hid her face against Mrs Wytcherley's generous bosom.

"Now see what you have done!" accused that worthy matron angrily. "You've made her cry again and you know very well what harm that does! Her constitution is not strong. I wish you would try to remember that when this wicked, teasing mood is upon you!"

"Then perhaps it might cheer her to learn that someone is bearing her dear Lucius company at Blakestone," answered Elisa airily as she turned to go.

"What do you mean?!" cried Lady Cullan, suddenly raising her golden head, her unhappiness momentarily forgotten.

"I mean that Blakestone House has a new tenant. He's already made himself quite at home amid the remains of the West Wing. He was chopping firewood when we came away."

"Don't upset yourself, Lady Cullan," intervened Sir Eustace. "This is probably another of her misplaced jests."

"Well, if you do not choose to listen, I'm sure it is of small matter to me. But Harry will tell you as much, should you care to ask him. He tried to throw the intruder out and received a broken nose for his trouble! I think perhaps Harry is deserving of your gratitude, Aurelia. His wound was received whilst acting solely in your interests. It was very noble of him, was it not?"

"Why do you persist in thus tormenting me, Elisa? What have I ever done to you that I must suffer such cruel persecution? Since Lucius first brought me to Blakestone as his bride, you have sought to injure me at every opportunity. I only ever wished to be your friend but you never could forgive me for marrying him, could you? You have never wanted to believe that we loved one another. That is why you won't respect my wishes and keep away from that house. You will not even try to appreciate my feelings. Don't you realize that to me it is hallowed ground? It is like . . . it is like having his sepulchre desecrated. You would not trample upon the graves in the churchyard yonder, would you? Of course you would not! Can you not then see how it hurts me to think of you and the Palmers disturbing his rest?"

"Stuff and nonsense! Such melodramatics cut no ice with me! Save them for the likes of Mr Greenwood. If I am not very much mistaken, his heart is quite melted by them." She cast a scornful glance at the young gentleman whose sensitive emotions were indeed wrung with pity for the sufferings of such a brave, angelic soul. "Besides, Blakestone House is hardly a sepulchre. Lucius may have died there but he is interred in the family mausoleum along with the rest of his ancestors. And you, Aurelia, hold the only key to that, so how can I possibly be accused of trampling on his grave?"

"Then you will not give me your word that you will never go there again?" pleaded Lady Cullan, her voice full of earnest entreaty.

"Why should I? Besides, now that gypsy has set up camp there, I daresay you will be glad that I like to ride about the place from time to time. You never know what mischief he might get up to!"

With this emphatic warning, she went from the room, leaving them all staring after her in amazement.

"Do you suppose her to be speaking the truth?!" gasped Lady Cullan faintly, her lovely face paling dreadfully. "Surely no one would dare to trespass on my land — not even gypsies?"

"I have heard nothing of gypsies being seen in the vicinity," replied Sir Eustace calmly. "It is most likely that Lady Elisa is deliberately trying to provoke you again. We all know how spiteful she can be when she chooses. I wonder at your fortitude, my lady. You bear her ill-manners so patiently. I am sure I would not."

"Alas, she was always a wild, wilful girl," complained Mrs Wytcherley bitterly. "Since my brother-in-law was widowed almost as soon as she was born, he has indulged her beyond what is to be considered acceptable. He gives way to her at every turn. How many times I have tried to remonstrate with him but he would not allow me to be the judge of what is best for her. When I came to live here after poor Wytcherley succumbed to a fever, I tried my utmost to stand in the place of a mother to that ungrateful child. But she nothing heeds me. I am at my wits' end and know not what I may do to chasten her. If it were not for Jocelyn's sake, I would pack my belongings tomorrow!"

"You are too good, Margaret, too kind an aunt ever to be able to impress your will upon such a spirited girl," sympathized Lady Cullan gently. Then she sighed regretfully. "And I have added to your burden, have I not? Elisa is quite right: I ought to have removed to the Dower House. I should have tried to manage alone. I despise myself heartily for my weakness but I regret to say I am not a person of strong resolve. You have made me so very comfortable here, I own I am now reluctant to change my circumstances. At least we must acknowledge that Elisa is a fearless creature. That stallion she rides about the countryside fills me with terror!"

"A highly-strung animal indeed," agreed Sir Eustace. "It is often a failing of these thoroughbreds, I have found. A nervous, skittish beast, far too mettlesome for my taste. I shouldn't wonder at it if that girl should one day break her neck! What can Lord Maytland have been thinking

40

of to buy such a savage brute for his daughter?"

"Oh, as to that, I can tell you precisely how it came about," replied Mrs Wytcherley sourly. "Elisa chose the horse herself. Jocelyn took her to Tattersall's the last time they were in London and allowed himself to be swayed by her sweet blandishments. She knows she stands uppermost in his affections and that he can never gainsay her. It cost him a vast amount to purchase it, you would be astounded if I were to name the exact figure. I only wish I might succeed in impressing upon him the folly of acceding to her every whim."

"I am sure we all wish it, ma'am," remarked Sir Eustace with a flicker of a smile. "That young lady thinks far too much of herself in my opinion. And this predilection she has for Sir Harry Palmer's company will not add to her credit in the neighbourhood. Difficult as it must be for you, that particular connection should be discouraged. I will not sully your ears with an account of his riotous behaviour in London but it is well known that, together with that brother

41

of his, he is set on pursuing a ruinous course. But you have woes enough and I do not mean to cause you further distress. I wish only to warn you. Come, Thomas, we must take our leave having already intruded far too long upon the hospitality of these gracious ladies. Good day to you, Mrs Wytcherley and thank you for receiving us so warmly. Goodbye, Lady Cullan." He bowed and pressed his lips to her small hand. "I hope I may look to see you at the assembly rooms on Friday next? And may I at least try to persuade you to stand up with me for one of the country dances?"

"I don't know, Sir Eustace. I seldom feel like dancing these days. Although my mourning period is long past, my grief is not. But thank you for your company this morning. It is always a delight to make new friends and I shall be happy to renew my acquaintance with your nephew, should we meet again soon. Will you be attending the assembly with your uncle, Mr Greenwood?"

"Indeed, I shall make a point of it, Lady Cullan," answered the young gentleman fervently, as he too bowed over her outstretched hand and earned for himself one of her brilliant smiles. This circumstance had the effect of reducing him almost to incoherency and his final farewells were lost in a fit of stammering.

Later, while the ladies at Dovecote Hall nibbled daintily at a cold collation set out for them in the dining-room, Lady Cullan determined to avoid entering into any further arguments with her kind neighbour's wayward niece. She was quite convinced that Lady Elisa's tale of gypsies at Blakestone House was in all probability another of her acts of provocation. These had become one of that young woman's chief delights ever since Mrs Wytcherley had taken Lady Cullan into her home on the fateful night of that dreadful conflagration. This temporary refuge had gradually become a more permanent arrangement. After living for so many years as companion and chaperone to a headstrong, unmanageable girl, whose doting father had allowed her all the freedoms generally due only to a son, Lady Cullan's sweet nature had come as a welcome respite to Mrs Wytcherley.

Aurelia was so kind and gentle, nothing seemed too much trouble for her.

She was perfectly content to sit for hour upon hour in quiet, comfortable silence while they plied their needles or sorted threads or read the latest novels from the circulating library. When they went to the village or into Brighton, they travelled sedately in the landau or the barouche. Not for Lady Cullan this mad careering about the district on a great brute of a horse. Such hoydenish behaviour was inexcusable but Elisa was not the sort of girl one could reason with, preferring to take no other counsel than her own and consequently setting up the backs of most of their disapproving neighbours by her total disregard for the conventions. Small wonder then that Mrs Wytcherley was reluctant to part with so amiable a friend and would not hear of her quitting them until Aurelia should feel ready to do so. Three years had passed in this way and only Elisa's abominable temper had marred the tranquillity of their days.

"Of course, the reason why Elisa has taken you in such aversion is that she is quite eaten up with envy," Mrs Wytcherley had once explained to Aurelia. "She doted on Lucius, you know, although he was much older than her. Well, ten years is a great deal of difference when a girl is only eleven, and that was her age when first they met. She was used to follow him about like a pet dog. He was kind to her, yes, but I daresay it was because he pitied her. She had few friends near to her in age at that time. I think he felt for her as an elder brother might feel towards his young sister. She, on the other hand, fancied herself head over heels in love with him, no doubt convincing herself that he returned her regard. A childish infatuation, that was all it amounted to; she misunderstood his attentiveness, believing it to be something deeper than mere friendship. She was scarce turned fourteen when you and Lucius were married and had no more control over her temper than when she was a babe."

Thus it was that the antipathy that had sprung up between the rivals upon their first becoming acquainted, had grown into a bitter hatred in Elisa's heart, one that had deepened after Lucius's death. It seemed as though she blamed Aurelia for his untimely demise and lost no opportunity to tease and insult her, often reducing the young widow to tears.

When they had finished their meal, during which the two antagonists had maintained an icy silence, Lady Elisa announced her intention of driving into the village.

"Well, I hope you mean to take the gig this time," commented her aunt sternly as she arose from the table. "That vehicle you had sent down from Bruton Street is totally out of place in the country, besides being highly dangerous. In my opinion, it is hardly to be considered a respectable conveyance for a young lady."

Elisa stamped her foot in sheer exasperation. "Why must I be forever listening to other people's opinions of what I should or should not do?! I never ask for them and it is wholly beyond my comprehension why anyone should presume that I wish to hear them expressed. Papa bought me that carriage because he knows I am perfectly capable of driving it. Now if you will excuse me,

I am going to put on my bonnet."

The door slammed shut behind her with a reverberating crash and Mrs Wytcherley winced painfully. "That girl! She will send me to an early grave!" she groaned despairingly. "She sets herself up for censure at every turn. I cannot hold my head high in the district since she left the schoolroom. Her behaviour is quite deplorable. What am I to do with her?"

Lady Cullan shook her beautiful head pityingly. "What indeed? I have never met such a rude, headstrong girl in all my life. I can see only one way out of your dilemma."

"Oh? And what is that pray?" enquired Mrs Wytcherley.

"You will just have to hope that someone will make her an offer. Then she will no longer be your responsibility."

"But who could be prevailed upon to wed such a graceless creature? Jocelyn would never countenance an alliance with either of the Palmers. He thinks them paltry fellows."

"No, that would not serve," agreed Lady Cullan, wrinkling her brow thoughtfully. "She needs a firm hand to control that wildness in her nature. Have you never considered that Sir Eustace might be a suitable match?"

"Sir Eustace?!" exclaimed Mrs Wytcherley in astonishment. "Surely you speak in jest? For you must know that he is very taken with you, my dear," she added coyly.

"I shall never marry again. It is impossible that I should ever feel for anyone else as I still feel for Lucius," she answered quietly. "But I believe that Sir Eustace would suit Elisa very well."

"But he is more than twice her age and has already buried two wives. Besides, I am certain he has taken Elisa in dislike. She has been dreadfully impertinent to him."

"All this is quite true. I am not suggesting that this could ever be a love match. However, you must allow that Sir Eustace, being a man of some experience, would know just how to deal firmly with an unruly girl. A younger man would find it difficult to restrain her when she is in one of her passionate tempers. Then there is the matter of the property. Lord Maytland has no male heir and one day, I trust it be not soon, everything will come to Elisa. I am sure you realize how necessary it will then be that she is guided by a man of good sense and strong principles. Sir Eustace's lands partly adjoin these and he has mentioned that he would like to extend his parkland. Perhaps that desire might be enough to induce him to view the matter in a fairer light. When Lord Maytland returns to England, you could at least bring the advantages of such a scheme to his attention. Each of you would benefit from the alliance. You, my dear Margaret, would be free to pursue your own interests and be rid of this irksome responsibility at last."

"Yes, there is a great deal of sense in what you say," mused Mrs Wytcherley, deep in thought. "Many great marriages are conveniently arranged. Now that I come to consider it, I can see that it might answer very well."

"It would be wiser not to broach the subject with Elisa until you have had the opportunity to discuss this with Lord Maytland. Forgive me if I pain you, but it has seemed to me that your niece determines to oppose your every wish, no matter how reasonable your request. She is quite likely to dismiss the whole idea out of hand if she thought you in favour of it."

"You are right, I know," replied Mrs Wytcherley despondently. "She will not recognize my authority. But she may be got to obey her father; we shall just have to wait and see."

The young lady who was the subject of this discussion, was at that very moment in the act of disobeying her aunt's instructions. The gig remained in the coach house, Lady Elisa having scorned that mode of travel. Instead she had ordered the greys to be put to the elegant perch phaeton with its pale yellow body slung high over the front wheels, a design which added greatly to its speed if not its safety.

This fact was ably demonstrated a few minutes later as the phaeton passed out of the gates and headed towards the village, taking the bend in the road at such a spanking pace, it seemed scarcely possible that the wheels could remain in contact with the unmetalled surface of the road.

However, Lady Elisa achieved her goal and drew up outside the rectory, having suffered no mishap.

Miss Stewart, the elder of the rector's three daughters, alone was privy to the arrival of the distinguished visitor, being engaged upon the pleasant task of plucking the fragrant flowers from the lavender bushes. These clung in misty, mauve clouds along the borders of the paved footpath that led from the garden gate to the rustic porch and the warm air was redolent with their heady perfume.

She gazed in great admiration at the skill displayed by the bold, young Jehu as she expertly handled the ribbons and having settled her leaders, leapt nimbly and fearlessly down from her high perch. She relinquished the reins into the care of the little tiger who had been sitting up behind her and approached the gate.

"Good afternoon, Celia. I hope you don't mind me disturbing your peace but I wanted to speak to you," explained her ladyship, unfastening the latch of the wicket and entering the garden.

She quickly saluted Miss Stewart's rosy cheek and linking arms, the two young ladies turned towards the house. "I have something particular to say to you, Celia. May I speak with you privately?"

Miss Stewart's clear, grey eyes surveyed her friend questioningly. "But of course. Father is gone to the church and Mama and the girls are driven over to Aunt Simpson at Shoreham. Come, we'll go and sit in the orchard and you shall tell me all your news."

She brought Elisa to the rear of the rectory through a pretty, little shrubbery that gave on to an expanse of smooth, green lawn, beyond which stood a grove of fruit trees. Some chairs had been set out beneath the shade of the apple branches which already showed an abundance of small, swelling fruits that promised a good harvest for the autumn. The well-stocked flower beds were ablaze with the brilliant blooms of full-blown roses, sweet bergamot, lilies and tall delphiniums, their colours a delight to the eye.

"Shall I have some refreshments sent out to us?" suggested Miss Stewart as she saw her guest settled comfortably into a seat.

"Not on my account, Celia, thank you. I have just partaken of lunch. Now, do you sit down here beside me and I'll tell you why I am come."

Miss Stewart dutifully obeyed and seated herself in a wicker chair close by. Setting down her lavender basket and folding her hands restfully in her lap, she waited expectantly.

"You will remember that I told you a few days ago that I thought someone had been up at Blakestone?"

Miss Stewart nodded. "Yes, I recollect your saying something of the sort."

"Well, I was right to feel suspicious. I rode over there yesterday to investigate matters for myself but I was caught in that horrid storm and had to abandon my search. However, as I came away, I met with a post-chaise travelling at a shockingly dangerous pace through the beech wood," she said peevishly. At this, Miss Stewart was obliged to subdue a smile. "It came upon us so suddenly," continued Elisa, "that poor Sabre was frightened out of his wits and I was forced to dismount in order to pacify him. As I struggled to calm him, a hatefully arrogant young man stepped down from the chaise and snatched the bridle from my hands."

"Good heavens! I hope he came to no harm!" cried Miss Stewart anxiously.

"No, he did not," replied Lady Elisa reassuringly. "In fact I rode him up there again this morning and he was in fine fettle."

Miss Stewart gurgled in amusement. "I meant the young man, goose! You are the only person who can control that horse, he won't let anyone else near him. I was concerned lest the unfortunate gentleman had been trampled upon!"

"He would have been well served if Sabre had kicked him! He almost ran us down! Yet strange as it may seem, no harm was done after all. For once, Sabre was perfectly obedient. I was surprised myself," she admitted frankly. "I have never known Sabre to behave so passively before, except with me or Jeremiah, our head groom. But then that odious fellow had the impudence to ring a peal over me!"

"And who was the mystery traveller?"

"That's just it: I don't know," replied Lady Elisa, puckering her brows. "As I said, I rode up there this morning with Harry and Alfred Palmer and what do you think? I saw the same man again and it seems that he is actually living at Blakestone!"

"Living there?! But that's not possible! How can anyone live there?! It's completely in ruins!" gasped Miss Stewart in astonishment.

"Not quite. A small section of the old west wing is still standing and judging from the smoke issuing from the chimneys, I would hazard a guess that he has taken up residence in what was once the housekeeper's room."

"But who can he be and what is he doing there? Why would anyone choose to live in such a desolate place? What does Lady Cullan say about it?"

"She didn't believe me when I told her," scoffed Lady Elisa. "That leads me to suppose she knows nothing of it yet. She'll be furious when she discovers the truth. You know what she is like about keeping the place sacred! However, this toy soldier says he is our new neighbour and claims a slight acquaintance with Aurelia. Perhaps he knew her before she was married," she added thoughtfully.

"When she lived in London? That's possible, I daresay. But why would he move into Blakestone House without her knowledge? Surely he would have sought her permission before doing such an odd thing? And why do you call him by that singular name?" asked Miss Stewart curiously.

"Because he exactly resembles a toy soldier I once cherished dearly," chuckled Lady Elisa. "It was the first present my father ever bought me. Not a doll as you would expect but a handsome, straight-backed soldier resplendent in all his regalia. I thought of that toy as soon as I saw him coming towards me. But this morning, all that finery had been sadly tarnished and he was not quite so prim and overbearing either."

"He is a military man then?"

"Apparently. An officer in a Hussar regiment. You must know what a set of vainglorious fellows they are! The pompous creature had the effrontery to ask why I rode without a groom in attendance! And he ridiculed my hat! It cost me five and twenty guineas too!" She sighed sadly. "Alas it is quite ruined by the rain! I must have looked a perfect quiz in it!"

"Do you mean that elegant velvet creation with the curled ostrich feathers?!" cried Miss Stewart aghast. "Oh, how very provoking for you! I remember it was I who persuaded you to purchase it when we were last in Brighton and it was so very becoming! Is it really beyond repair?"

"Quite. But I shall not repine. I should never have worn it again anyway. I never liked it as much as you did and I would feel a figure of fun in it now. I dislike pretty, girlish styles. They are ideally suited to Aurelia. I never met a more empty-headed, frivolous creature. But I digress. I came to enquire if your father had heard anything of a stranger moving into Blakestone. Has he mentioned such a thing to you, Celia?"

"No, he has not. But I am certain that he would have done, if he had known of it. And it does seem rather odd that nothing is rumoured in the village," she remarked in puzzlement. "You know how suspicious of strangers the local people are — and with good reason!"

Lady Elisa regarded her friend thoughtfully before replying in slightly lowered tones, "The smuggling fraternity, you mean? Well, I've heard that the trade is falling into decline since the war with France ended, so perhaps the need for watchfulness is not quite so necessary as it once was."

"Possibly," acceded Miss Stewart. "Yet Mama tells me that there are soldiers lately quartered at Shoreham, with orders to assist the Riding Officers."

"Yes, I had heard something of it myself. I suppose with so many soldiers returning from Spain, there will be a surfeit of young men only too willing to take arms against their fellow countrymen."

"Do I detect a note of sympathy for the smugglers?" questioned the rector's daughter, raising her brows in surprise.

"Many of the Gentlemen are forced to risk their lives in these daring enterprises," replied Elisa grimly. "How else are they to buy bread for their families? The price of a loaf has risen so high now, that the poorer folk are driven to desperation. A man can earn as much in one night's smuggling as he can in six days labouring in the fields. Is it any wonder that they are tempted to break the law?"

"Surely you don't condone criminal behaviour?"

"I do question the morals of some of our laws. Do you know that Mary Shaw's husband, Tom, was recently transported for poaching a pheasant on Sir Eustace's land? She is left with six mouths to feed and no man to help her."

"Yes, that was a harsh judgment and one that my papa tried to prevent. I didn't know that you were aware of the Shaws' plight?"

"I happen to know Mary and Tom very well," answered Elisa. "Oh, there's no need to look like that, Celia, I do hear what people say of me. But it doesn't bother me, I really don't care what anyone thinks. I am interested in Mary's affairs because I have known her since I was a child. I value our friendship far more than any of those stuffy, boring girls I have to associate with when I am forced to attend the assemblies." She arose suddenly in her usual impetuous manner, pulling on her gloves and saying briskly, "Well, I must be on my way. I have kept my horses standing too long as it is. Goodbye, Celia, and don't forget to let me know if you do hear anything about the stranger."

"I won't. Goodbye, Elisa. Forgive me if I offended you just now, I didn't mean to. I am very fond of you, you must know that and I don't listen to gossip. I happen to have realized that there is a great deal of misunderstanding brought about because you are so . . . well, so unconventional."

"I don't fit into the 'demure miss' catalogue, do I?" smiled Elisa, her eyes twinkling merrily.

"That you certainly do not!" laughed Miss Stewart, as she escorted her guest back to the sporting equipage that awaited her ladyship out in the road. "But things are never dull when you are around, so don't leave it too long before you visit me again."

3

THE following day, a modishly dressed gentleman came riding down the neat avenue of chestnut trees that shaded visitors to Dovecote Hall from the bright glare of the summer sun. Broad hands of golden-green leaves waved gaily in the breeze and the air was full of their gentle applause.

It was a glorious morning, the sky serenely blue and almost cloudless above the lofty tree-tops. Yet, despite the joys of such a perfect day, the gentleman could not help feeling a trifle apprehensive as he presently dismounted and approached the main entrance. A manservant came to answer the loud appeal of the door-knocker and the gentleman sent in his card. This was carefully placed on a salver and borne ceremoniously through the drawing-room and out into the garden where sat the ladies of the house: two of them busily plying their needles and the other occupied in reading the latest novel just sent down from London.

Lady Cullan glanced up enquiringly as the salver was proffered to her with a deferential bow. She picked up the card and scanned the inscription, her brows arching prettily. "Well? Who is calling on you today, Aurelia?" questioned Mrs Wytcherley with an amused smile. "Another of your admirers, no doubt. I think I might guess at the gentleman's name: it is Mr Greenwood, is it not? I knew he would call on you again, he was quite dazzled by your beauty! I was obliged to keep myself from laughing aloud when I saw the look on his face yesterday. I daresay he thinks himself hopelessly in love this morning. But there, he is very young and young gentlemen are generally disposed to fancying themselves in love on the merest of pretexts. You will just have to give him one of your gentle set-downs before he becomes too . . . why, Aurelia! Whatever is the matter, my dear? You look quite ill!" she cried aghast as Lady Cullan seemed to shrink back fearfully in her chair, the colour draining from her cheeks and her breathing becoming erratic. "Shall I send for Dr Osgood?"

"No! No . . . it's nothing. Just a sudden spasm that's all. I shall be well again directly, I assure you. I was simply taken by surprise. I never expected . . . I didn't know . . . oh, this is impossible!" She pressed a hand to her brow as if in desperation. Then collecting herself with a great effort, she said hurriedly, "Ask the gentleman to wait for me in the morning-room. I shall be with him in a moment."

The servant bowed again, no hint of the curiosity he felt registering upon his inscrutable features.

"I beg your pardon, Margaret, but it seems I have an unexpected visitor. Someone I must see privately. I'll explain later. Pray excuse me, won't you?" Lady Cullan rose agitatedly from her seat beneath the old sycamore and, still trembling visibly, hasted away.

"Good heavens!" exclaimed Elisa with great astonishment. "I declare I have never seen Aurelia so discomposed by a mere visitor. I wonder who this mysterious caller can be?"

"That is no concern of ours. You heard

what Aurelia said: the matter is private. Now where do you think you are off to?" demanded Mrs Wytcherley suspiciously, as Elisa got to her feet.

"I am just going indoors to fetch another book. This one begins to bore me. I cannot wonder at the author's not wishing to put his name to it. Why my godmother should suppose I would enjoy reading it, I do not know."

"Stay where you are, Elisa!" insisted her aunt adamantly. "I will not have you intruding upon Aurelia's privacy."

"I hope you do not mean to suggest that I might be tempted to spy on them?" cried Elisa in a wounded voice.

"I am sure there is no telling what you might be tempted to do next," replied Mrs Wytcherley scathingly, "so you will kindly remain where I can see you. Sit down."

Elisa regarded her balefully for a second or two and then with a careless shrug, threw herself back into her seat and pretended to peruse the slighted book with a renewed enthusiasm. However, an interested observer would have noticed that her eyes were seldom fixed for longer than a few moments upon its pages and were more frequently to be seen wandering in the direction of the house.

* * *

As Aurelia stepped hesitantly to the door of the morning-room, she took a deep breath and reached out for the doorknob. Then, schooling her features into a more natural and relaxed expression, she opened the door, ready to smile a polite greeting.

At her entrance, the gentleman leapt from the sofa where he had been sitting rehearsing his planned speech. Now they stood gazing wondrously at one another without moving and without uttering a single syllable. It was he who eventually broke the silence.

"You look even more beautiful than I remember," he murmured, abandoning completely his carefully worded phrases.

"Thank you, Alex," she answered quietly, her tone reflecting a coolness she was far from feeling. "You, I see, have changed a great deal since last we met. I should hardly have known you. You were a mere stripling when you went away and now, here you are come back to me a grown man. I certainly don't remember your being so very tall, nor so broad!" She attempted a light laugh but her voice shook woefully and she hurried into further speech in an attempt to appear at ease. "You have taken me quite by surprise, you know. When you did not answer my letters, I became convinced that something dreadful must have occurred. Lucius received news of your wound some weeks before he . . . before he died. When you did not come to the funeral, I feared the worst had happened. Why didn't you write, Alex? All this time I have been thinking you dead!"

He detected a note of accusation in her voice and taking her hand in his, drew her to sit beside him.

"I know. I meant you to think it. I never intended to come back to England ever again. Nor would I have done but the war ended and despite my efforts and those of the enemy, I have not managed to put an end to my existence after all.

66

So with Lucius gone to his rest and I still seeking mine, I am come back to see what I may do to help you."

He reached out a hand to her averted face and placing a finger beneath her downbent chin, turned her head towards him. Then looking steadily into her eyes, he said gently, "I have seen the lawyers, Aurelia. I know how badly things stand with you now. It was they who told me where you were living. I had thought you would be at the Dower House. I saw Lucius's will while I was in London. I could scarce believe that he had left you in such difficulties. What happened to place you in these straitened circumstances? I know my father left Lucius a comfortable fortune. What became of it all?"

She raised her head to free her chin and to escape the look of pity she read in his eyes. "There's no mystery to answer, Alex." This time her laugh sounded brittle. "We spent it. Every last penny; it wasn't difficult for either of us. And it didn't take us very long. Lucius and I shared the same tastes — expensive tastes. That's why I chose him instead of you. You were such an intense young man! Lucius was always such fun, nothing ever worried him: he enjoyed life to the full. I do not need to remind you how much he loved a wager; he never could refuse anything of that nature, no matter how ridiculous." She smiled fondly. "Oh, what a wonderful time we had; our hospitality was the talk of London society. We gave the most splendid balls, everyone came! And people still speak of the magnificent house parties we had at Blakestone before the fire destroyed everything." Her voice faltered and her hands twisted nervously in her lap.

"Can you tell me what happened that night, Aurelia? No one I've spoken to seems to know much about it. But I understand that you saw . . . that you witnessed the tragedy."

"I suppose you want to know what became of your inheritance," she replied bitterly. "Is that why you have come here at last, Alex?"

"How could you even think it!" he cried, stung by her unkind accusation. "I may have changed a great deal since I took my commission but I hope I am still

68

a gentleman! I did not come to burden you with my misfortunes but to see what I might do to ease yours. I only ask about Lucius because he was my brother and I need to understand how he came to such a terrible end. I always thought it would be me who would fill an early grave, because for a while I didn't care very much whether I lived or died. Without you my life seemed worthless to me."

"I'm sorry, Alex!" She covered her face with her hands and began to cry softly. He put his arm protectively about her and rested her head upon his shoulder, murmuring tender, consoling words to soothe her. He rocked her gently, like a child and laid his cheek against the shining, golden hair that was fragrant with the scent of sweet violets. How often in the night, with the stench of battle still in his nostrils, he had longed to hold her in his arms as now and have her perfume all about him.

"Hush, now, my dar — my dear. Please don't cry. I don't blame you for thinking so harshly of me. I was a selfish, unforgiving young bantam, I realize that now. I had no right to blame you for refusing my suit. I was not gracious in defeat, alas. I have been slow to learn that art. I always did have a fearful temper, I acknowledge it. Lucius knew that and he also knew that it would soon burn itself out." A little smile curved his mouth. "It's me darlin' mither oi've to thank for it, so oi have," he mimicked in a broad Irish brogue, "sure an' didn't she tell me so horrself? 'Alex', says she, 'you're the Divil's own son, so y' are'."

Aurelia stopped crying and smiled mistily up at him through long, damp lashes. "That sounds more like your old nurse! And as to your temper, I remember Lucius's saying that you were always spoiling for a fight."

"Did he tell you that? Well, I hope he also told you that it was he who led us into so many scrapes, the little schemer, leaving me to battle our way out of them! But I have long since regretted that last quarrel with him. I am sure he made you a far better husband than I would have done. After all, his mama was an English gentlewoman of impeccable lineage and he inherited her cool gentility. I am far more volatile and would have tried your patience sorely."

"At least you both have your papa's generosity. That is, I ought to say Lucius had it," she amended, drawing away from him again. There fell an awkward silence between them.

"He still lives for you, doesn't he, Aurelia?" he said sadly. Aurelia started and stared at him in sudden wonder. "I guessed it as soon as I heard you speak of him. Your heart won't let him die, will it?"

"No, never." Her eyes fell again. "I'm glad you understand that, Alex. No one else can. It will be so much easier for us to be friends if you realize how much I shall always love him. Now tell me," she continued in a brisker voice, "are you staying in the neighbourhood? I regret that my position is such that I cannot offer you any hospitality. I am only a guest in this house."

"Don't worry, I have my own accommodation. But whose house is this? It was used to belong to my grandfather but I seem to recall that Lucius eventually sold the house and some of the surrounding land."

"Yes. It belongs to Lord Maytland now. He bought it about eleven or twelve years ago. He is travelling abroad at the moment but his sister and his only daughter are living here. It is the sister, Mrs Wytcherley, who has been my good benefactress these last three years. I do not know how I would have gone on without her. She is unaware of my unfortunate circumstances and I would prefer it if you would keep my dreadful secret. I cannot bear that anyone should hear that I am nigh penniless. They all assume Lucius left me suitably provided for and I have not discouraged that belief."

"Of course. I will say nothing that would cause you any distress. But you are not alone now. You are still my sister-in-law and I see it as my duty to take care of you."

"I am only your half-brother's wife," she reminded him, "and I do not claim a sister's rights. How could I? Indeed, I thought you must despise me after all that has happened between us," she added in a small voice. "I quite expected that you had come to berate me. I know I deserve it. Lucius and I have ruined you as thoroughly as we have ruined ourselves. I have not forgotten the debt we owe you. You must know that I cannot pay back your loan. Lucius used the money to invest in some wild scheme that was supposed to restore our prosperity but nothing came of it. Oh, how you must hate us!"

"I could never hate you, Aurelia. What's done is done. I never expected to inherit a penny from Lucius anyway. It was his money to do with as he wished. I never imagined that anything like this would happen to him. And as to the money I lent him, I know that he would have returned it to me had he lived. We will speak no more of that. I would also like you to know that I do not mean to use the title. I prefer to keep the one I already have, at least as long as I remain with my regiment."

"You are very generous and considerate, Alex. I am so grateful for your kindness."

"Nonsense, it is nothing. I just wish I could do something more. If only Lucius had not left you so direly situated."

"Oh, I'll manage somehow. I do still have the Dower House," she answered lightly.

"So you do. And I have Blakestone. There, I suppose we are both amply provided for; still having a roof over our heads must count for something," he smiled cheerfully. "Ned and I have made ourselves very comfortable there already."

Aurelia gazed at him as if stupefied. "Blakestone? You are living at Blakestone?" she gasped incredulously.

"Yes. I arrived two days ago. I was greatly shocked to see the extent of the damage. It is far worse than I imagined."

"But you can't live there, Alex! It is out of the question!"

"Oh, Ned and I are used to all kinds of billets. Believe it or not, this is one of our best! We have made ourselves quite comfortable."

"But I tell you, you can't possibly stay there! You simply can't!" she insisted frantically. Then, observing his look of surprise, she quickly arose and walked away to the open window, gazing unseeingly over the garden. "Forgive me, Alex. I am aware that the house is no longer mine," she continued stiffly. "It is yours to live in or not, as you think best. It is just that I have a special regard for that old ruin. You will doubtless think it mere sentimental nonsense, as does everyone else, but I cannot help the way I feel. That house has become a part of me. It has been my home for only a few years, yet I grew to love it as much as Lucius loved it. And now, since this awful thing happened, it has come to mean so much more to me. It is well known by everyone in the district that I prefer to have the place to myself. I often visit the mausoleum and sit alone with my memories. Somehow, I seem to sense that Lucius is watching over me. Its very isolation, away up there in the park, makes it possible for me to feel close to him. I can't bear to have anyone else disturbing the peace that I find just by being there. The presence of other people seems an intrusion upon my most intimate moments of remembrance."

"But don't you think it is time you began to rebuild your life, Aurelia? You are only seven and twenty. A woman as beautiful as you ought not to shut herself away from society. You were used to be so light-hearted and carefree; it's not good for you to dwell continually in the past. Lucius would not have expected it of you. You said yourself that he enjoyed life to the full and that is what he would have wished for you. Don't bury yourself here: go back to London, it's where you belong. You may yet find happiness again. I'll help you to find somewhere to live, I have a little money of my own. Enough to set you up in a modest establishment, that is the least I can do for my brother's widow. And even if you will not accept for your own sake, do it for mine. I bitterly regret parting from Lucius the way I did and it would make me feel easier in my mind if you'd let me make amends by doing all I can to see you happily settled. You cannot wish to remain with the Maytlands for ever and the Dower House is too solitary a residence for a gregarious woman of your natural gaiety."

"It is good of you to worry about me, Alex, I really don't know why you should.

I treated you abominably once; you are not the only one to regret past errors."

"We were both very young and wisdom, like good wine, needs time to mature to make it palatable." He drew close to her and placed his hands on her shoulders, comfortingly. She half turned her head and smiled weakly up at him.

"It would not be very wise of me to let you persuade me. It would be selfish of me to take advantage of your benevolent heart. I must accept the consequences of my folly and live quietly here in the country. Mrs Wytcherley will stand my friend, I think. You go back to London, Alex. You still have friends there and you have your own life to live. The responsibility of supporting another man's widow would be too onerous, too great a strain on your meagre resources. I shall fend for myself, never fear. I cannot permit you to sacrifice your happiness for my sake. You may wish to marry: I am sure there must be any number of young ladies who would be only too eager to receive an offer from such a handsome young officer. I should think you look very fine indeed in your regimentals! Take my good advice and go back to London at once, I beg of you. It will bring me no pleasure to know that you are living in such a comfortless place for my sake. Please go back, Alex."

"And leave you here all alone? I cannot even think of it, Aurelia. I went away from you once before and always regretted it. I will not make the mistake a second time."

"You will not go? What can I do to persuade you that you must? What is left for you here? Nothing but a heap of broken bricks and a few acres of impoverished farmland. The rents will barely keep you from starving."

"I know. I saw Clifton, the bailiff, yester noon. He tells me that the farms have been neglected for years and our tenants can scarce make ends meet. I cannot believe that Lucius was so careless that he put not a single penny back into the land. I am going with Clifton tomorrow to see what may be done to improve matters. Though I doubt not that I shall find everything as bad as Clifton described."

He sounded suddenly weary and she eyed him anxiously.

"You won't sell the land, Alex? You won't let anyone take Blakestone from us, will you?"

"I might have no choice in the matter, my dear," he replied grimly. "I should not do it gladly but now that the house is gone, there seems little point in prolonging the moment. You must know that it would take more than the money we have left to put everything to rights."

"I do know! But don't sell yet, Alex!" she pleaded earnestly. "Not yet. Give me time to accustom myself to the thought of losing everything that binds me to Lucius. Especially the house we shared together, the place where our happiness once bloomed so gloriously." A heart-rending sob broke from her trembling lips, "Promise me you will wait a little longer before Blakestone passes into the hands of a stranger."

"Don't upset yourself, Aurelia," he answered soothingly, "it will take me several weeks to go over the details as thoroughly as I would wish. You may visit Blakestone as often as you did before I came back. You need not fear that Ned or I will disturb your peace, we shall have a great many things to occupy our time."

At that moment a knock sounded at the door and without waiting for permission to enter, Lady Elisa walked boldly in upon them.

"I was just wondering, Aurelia, if you and your guest would care for some refreshment? I thought perhaps you might feel a little awkward about offering hospitality in my father's house, so I am come to perform that service for you myself. My Aunt has fallen quite asleep or I am sure she would have come to you earlier."

Aurelia glared at her angrily. "I have already explained my position in this house, I did not need that you should feel obliged to do it for me."

Elisa ignored her outburst. "So you do know our new neighbour, Aurelia?" she continued smoothly. "I guessed you might." She glanced at him provocatively, her eyes bright with mischief. "Lady Cullan could not be brought to acknowledge your existence yesterday. No doubt she felt some reluctance to confess before our more respected neighbours, an acquaintance with a 'black gypsy'. But have no fear, your secret is safe with me. I can be very discreet when I choose. My lips are sealed."

"If they are not, they certainly ought to be. You have far too much to say for yourself, young woman. And I would thank you not to take too literally, words that were said in mere jest," replied the gentleman crossly.

"Oh? Was your companion trying to be jocular? I wonder that he should make the attempt, you are obviously a man who cannot share a joke."

"Pay her no heed, Alex. She loves to provoke. Your best defence is to ignore her completely, as I have learned to do," recommended Lady Cullan taking his arm and leading him to the door.

Elisa was quick to catch the intimacy in their glance and the use of the gentleman's given name. So they were more than just acquainted then? She frowned thoughtfully, studying Aurelia's half-averted face. How well did she know him?

"Aren't you going to introduce me to our new neighbour? We shall doubtless be seeing a good deal of each other if he means to remain at Blakestone. And as it seems that you are not after all of the Romany, sir, then perhaps you should tell me who you really are, if we are to avoid any further misconceptions, that is," she added pointedly, her challenging gaze falling to rest briefly upon their entwined arms.

"Very well, I have no objection to your knowing," answered Aurelia carelessly. "This gentleman is Lucius's brother, Major Alexander Lacey and therefore, my brother-in-law. Does that satisfy your curiosity?"

"Lucius's brother!" she gasped in amazement. "But how can that be? Why did Lucius never mention you? And why did you not attend his funeral? If you truly are his brother, surely you ought to have paid your last respects, especially since the circumstances of his death were so shocking?"

"I do not know the circumstances of his death. That is one of the reasons I am come here," replied the major coldly. "And at the time of my brother's interment, I was engaged in a struggle to avoid my own. Now if you will excuse me, Miss Maytland, I must take leave of my sister-in-law."

"Sir, you are addressing Lady Elisa Maytland," corrected Elisa haughtily, drawing herself up to her full height.

The major bowed slightly. "I am sorry, I had no idea you were a lady," he responded in a voice devoid of any particular expression but which nevertheless brought a flash of anger to Elisa's eloquent eyes as she watched them go.

While they waited for the major's horse to be brought from the stables, Aurelia apologized for Elisa's incivility.

"I shan't heed it," he smiled reassuringly, "I knew from the first moment I met her that she was an untrained filly. She needs a curb put on that sharp tongue of hers."

"When did you first meet her? Yesterday?"

"No, I ran into her, or almost that is, the day before. Up in the beech wood. She was quite alone, save for a splendid horse that I now think must have belonged to her father. She was having difficulty in controlling the animal and I had to help her settle the poor creature. There was a thunderstorm that day and the horse was frightened by the noise."

"I see." Aurelia appeared decidedly annoyed. "Do you know if she had come from the direction of the house?"

"I really could not say. But why do you ask?" he enquired, intrigued by her question.

"It's nothing. Only that I expressly forbade her to go," she muttered angrily. "I won't have her poking her inquisitive nose into my affairs, she is always spying on me."

"But what harm can she do up there? The damage is already done. Why trouble yourself about it? And why should she wish to spy on you? This is not like you, Aurelia. It seems to me that you are becoming too morbidly attached to that old wreck of a house. Perhaps it would be best to salvage what I can from the remains and have the building completely razed. It's in a dangerous condition anyway. Someone might get hurt, or worse, if they wander about the place. In fact, I'd rather you didn't go up there alone either."

Aurelia was staring at him with an odd look in her large, clear eyes. Surely it wasn't fear that had suddenly shadowed their china-blue depths? No, he must have been mistaken. "What is the matter, my dear? You seemed so worried just now. Are you afraid of something?"

She managed to recover her spirits and smiled brightly. "I'm only being foolish, Alex. It's just that I had not thought Elisa to be in any danger. But what you say is true. It might be that some accident could befall her if she persists in visiting Blakestone. I should be grateful if you would keep an eye on that reckless girl. If you see her there again, send her away. It is your property now, I no longer have the authority to compel her to obey my wishes. But you do. She'll listen to you, if you are firm with her. Make it plain that you don't want her trespassing on your land. Oh, they are bringing your horse, I must not keep you standing here." She stepped down on to the drive with him. "I'm so glad you came back, Alex. It's wonderful to see you after all these years but I still hope you will heed me and think again about staying at Blakestone."

"Have you forgiven me for causing you to believe me in my grave?" he asked softly.

"If you will, in return, forgive me for causing you so much pain when last we met. Will you remember that I was very young and very much in love with Lucius? If it happened now, I would not be so careless of your feelings."

He smiled back at her, his grip on her fingers tightening briefly. "Come and visit me soon, Aurelia. There is so much I still have to say to you. And you need not bring that red-haired vixen with you. It is perfectly proper to visit your long-lost brother-in-law. And I don't want her breaking in again upon our tête-à-tête."

Aurelia, having seen him ride away, wandered slowly and pensively back into the house where she found Elisa awaiting her.

"Why did you keep silent about having

a near relative, Aurelia? Everyone thinks you quite alone in the world. Or did you suppose that you would receive less sympathy if it were generally known?"

"Not at all. I had no knowledge of it myself until today. I thought him dead these last three years. Lucius had been informed that his brother had received what was considered to be a fatal wound. When I received no further news of him, I assumed he had not recovered from it."

"But why did Lucius never mention him to me? We were such close friends, yet he never once spoke of having a brother. It seems very odd to me that he should hide the fact."

"Why should Lucius confide in you? I knew of him, that's all that matters. Lucius wasn't trying to hide anything. If you must know, after Lucius's father died, Alex chose to return to Ireland with his mother. You must have heard that Lucius's own mother died when he was an infant. He had no friends in Ireland, so preferred to remain in England. They simply lived quite separate lives after that and seldom met. But now Lucius is dead, Alex has come back. The estate is rightfully his according to the terms of his father's will."

"He means to live permanently at Blakestone?" asked Elisa sharply.

"That seems to be his intention," answered Lady Cullan, at the same time putting an end to the conversation by turning away towards the garden. "So you won't be able to trespass on our . . . on his property any longer," she finished triumphantly. "Alex is determined upon that!"

"Then I shall have to persuade him otherwise," murmured Elisa under her breath.

4

IT was with a growing sense of dismay mingled with sadness that the major rode around the Blakestone estate accompanied by his bailiff, Mr Clifton. He could remember all too clearly the days of his early boyhood when these fields were tall and deep, rippling with wheat and corn. Now most of them lay fallow, given over to sparse, spiky grasses thickly peppered with ox-eye daisies and spattered with blood-red poppies.

The farm buildings they passed were showing signs of the years of neglect. Barns and cottages, once neatly thatched with combed straw gleaned from the harvested fields, were beginning to fall into a state of disrepair. The thatch was rotting and gaping holes were visible, no doubt letting in both rain and wind.

Even the few men at work in farmyard and meadow, seemed to reflect the general air of dilapidation which had crept into this previously prosperous landscape. Their coarse linen smocks and thick worsted stockings displayed patches and darns in plenty and their faces, though browned by the sun, showed pinched and weary beneath the battered slouch hats.

At last the major pulled in his horse as they reached the summit of the Downs. Before him sparkled the blue expanse of the English Channel, dotted here and there with tiny fishing boats bobbing amid the curving waves. Far below lay the little, fan-shaped cove with its triangle of amber and grey shingle delicately edged by the frothy, silver lacing of the surf.

"What happened to the yacht?" he enquired, turning towards his companion who was just reining in beside him. "Did Lord Cullan sell it?"

The bailiff looked surprised. "Do you mean the *Seabird*, sir?"

"Yes, of course, what else should I mean?"

"Then you haven't heard about the accident?"

The major shook his head. "What accident?"

"It was three years since, sir, the night before the fire. Did you ever hear tell of Sam Frant as lived over to Rottingdean? Well, he could sail these waters blindfold, so folk said and Lord Cullan took him on as captain of the *Seabird*. Went out regularly in her, day or night, when his lordship was in residence up at the house. No one'll ever know for sure what happened but it seems that poor old Sam must have taken her out on his own, the Devil knows why, it needing at least three men to sail her safely. However that may be, they found the wreckage washed up on a beach somewhere near Folkestone, I believe it was. Never found Sam though: his body must have been carried out to sea. There are some treacherous currents along the Kent coast, so the fisher folk d'say. A strange business it was, Sam being such a skilful sailor and all," he concluded, shaking his head slowly as if deeply perplexed.

"Did he leave any family?"

"No, none. But Tom Shaw did. He was a friend of Sam's and they often sailed in the *Seabird* together when an extra hand was needed. He was taken up for poaching just a short while before Sam drowned. Perhaps that's why Sam went off alone that night. Tom was accused of stealing a pheasant out of Sir Eustace's woods and got transported to Botany Bay for his trouble. And him a father of six small children too! It has left his wife, Mary, very badly placed indeed. She rents a cottage on your land: I'll point it out to you in a moment, we have to pass it on our way back."

"Transported, eh?" remarked the major frowningly. "That seems extremely harsh I must say. Some of our soldiers occasionally resorted to poaching, despite the dire warnings against it, hunger being their justification and probably that poor fellow's too."

"Sadly for him, Sir Eustace Newbury is a local magistrate and not known for his leniency, that's why it went so ill with Shaw. Even the rector could not persuade Sir Eustace to be merciful, though he tried heavens hard."

"I don't think I know this Sir Eustace Newbury," mused the major thoughtfully. "Has he lived very long in the neighbourhood?"

"Some eight years, as I recollect. He is a very wealthy gentleman: a banker, in fact. When Barhurst village was enclosed, he added several acres of the surrounding common land to his property and has built himself a large house about seven or eight miles inland. It lies over there," he said, pointing away to the right, "just beyond that ring of trees."

"Then his estate skirts our north boundary," observed the major, following the direction of the bailiff's extended arm. "So he and I are near neighbours, it seems."

"Exactly so, sir. That's why he has been pressing Lady Cullan to sell some of the Blakestone land to him. He is desirous of extending his parkland even further and is well aware that the woods on this estate are very fine indeed and would afford him some excellent shooting. The woodland on his more recently purchased land was sadly depleted during the war years, the oak trees especially. Of course, he had assumed that Lady Cullan was responsible for the property, since her husband's death. You must know that it had been generally thought that you . . . ahem, that you would not be returning to Blakestone."

"So I understand," replied the major with a slight smile. "I suppose my return could be described as rather topical at the moment, at least among my most immediate neighbours?"

"Well, sir, your presence at Blakestone House is proving to be the cause of a great deal of speculation. I must confess that I am myself more than a little curious to know what you mean to do, now that you are come home again. As you have seen this morning, there is much to be done to put matters right here. I have tried my best with what resources I had at my disposal but I'm afraid Lord Cullan . . . " He paused as if not certain how to proceed, then with an anxious eye upon the major's profile, added awkwardly, "That is to say, I formed the opinion that Lord Cullan did not choose to interest himself in the affairs of the estate."

"Then our opinions coincide, Clifton," acknowledged the major, grimly eyeing the vista before them as they rode back down the hill.

Encouraged by this reception of what he had feared might be taken as an impertinent criticism, Mr Clifton grew more daring.

"May I be so bold as to enquire whether you mean to take an interest, sir?"

The major's first instinct was to quell any such notions immediately and it was on the tip of his tongue to inform his bailiff in the plainest of terms, just how matters stood with him, when he suddenly remembered his promise to Aurelia. How could he take Clifton into his confidence at the expense of hers?

After a brief tussle with his conscience, he replied carefully, "I am not yet sure of my plans. I never expected to be placed in this position, as you may well imagine. I am a soldier by inclination, not a farmer and I am still not clear in my mind which course to pursue."

"I see," remarked Mr Clifton, sounding deeply disappointed. Since receiving the news of Major Lacey's arrival at the old house, he had entertained great hopes that at last he might be able to begin to make amends for all the wilful neglect of the last few years. None of his many schemes had hitherto been realized because of his late master's repeated refusals to discuss any of the proposed improvements. Now it seemed as if his hopes were to be dashed once more. "Does this mean that you are contemplating the sale of the property, sir?"

"I am considering the idea, yes, but it is not decided. I must have time to think before I take such an irrevocable step. And where better to think than at Blakestone itself? I could not have chosen a more secluded spot in which to assemble my thoughts."

"No doubt you will be seeking out Sir Eustace then, sir?"

"If what you tell me is still true, I daresay it is I who will be sought after. Well, I shall be prepared to receive a visit from him and at least give ear to what he has to say," answered the major, drawing slightly behind Mr Clifton as they approached a narrow track, edged on one side by thick woodland and on the other by a deep ditch that lay at the foot of a high hedgerow.

It was as they were proceeding in single

file along this rather gloomy pathway, that the major had the distinct impression that their progress was being closely observed. A prickling sensation at the back of his neck alerted him to this certainty rather than any physical presence in the dense undergrowth. It was a sixth sense that he had developed during the long years of campaigning in the Peninsular and one that he had learnt not to mistrust. His eyes, sharpened by experience, began to rake the darkest shadows and his ears strained to catch the slightest sound. At first he could hear only the creak of saddle leathers and the soft padding of the horses' hoofs on the grassy carpet of the byway as they ambled leisurely along. The leaves of tree and shrub seemed to owe their gentle animation entirely to the vagrant breezes and to no other more sinister cause and yet the feeling still remained that all was not well.

The sudden, *chackering* cry of a blackbird startled from its perch somewhere amid the boskage, drew the major's immediate attention and it was at that very moment that he spied the barrel of a pistol projecting from a deep thicket.

He had but a split second to note that it was apparently aimed at him, not at Clifton and throwing himself from the saddle, heard at once a resounding report as the weapon was fired.

At almost the same moment came the whine of a bullet that hurtled over his head and embedded itself in the trunk of an elm tree on the far side of the hedge.

"What the Devil?!" exclaimed Mr Clifton in great alarm, struggling to steady his terrified mount. Then swivelling about in the saddle gasped, "Good God! Major Lacey!"

Hastily he jumped down from his horse and ran to aid his master. "Are you all right, sir?!" he cried, anxiously bending over him.

"Get down, man! He may have another pistol ready!" urged the major in a hoarse whisper, reaching up a strong arm and seizing him firmly by the sleeve.

The bailiff tumbled headlong beside him without further ado. "Who was it fired the shot? Did you see?" he questioned fearfully.

"No, alas I did not," replied the major tersely, "more's the pity!"

"It must have been poachers ... a stray shot, surely?"

"In broad daylight? Oh no! Murder was planned here today, Clifton. I've been shot at often enough to know when I am being used as a target. That bullet was meant for me, of that much I am certain!"

"But that cannot be the case! Who would want to kill you? What purpose would be served?"

"I've no idea. It does seem ludicrous, I must say. But someone wishes me harm, whatever the reason!"

As he finished speaking, there came the sound of a horse galloping away through the woodland and then silence fell once more.

"Whoever it was, he is gone," declared the major, clambering out of the ditch and reaching down a hand to assist Mr Clifton to his feet. "Wait here a moment, Clifton, while I take a look over there. He may have left some clue as to his identity."

"Oh, do be careful, sir, he could have

had an accomplice," warned Mr Clifton nervously.

"I'll be vigilant. Wait here with the horses."

"It's lucky your horse did not bolt, mine was of a mind to do so had I not managed to retain my seat."

"Oh, Perseus is a seasoned campaigner like myself. It would take more than a bullet to frighten him. He's been trained to face cannon fire, haven't you, *mon brave*?" smiled the major, stroking the gleaming satin neck of his courageous charger. The powerfully built creature whinnied softly as if in answer and nuzzled his master's face affectionately. "Stand now, Perseus. I'll be but a moment." With that command, the major left him there untethered but perfectly still and disappeared into the thicket.

He cast about among the trees for some few minutes but could find no indication as to what manner of man his assailant might be. A couple of freshly broken twigs and a tuft of coarse black hair from a horse's mane were the only proofs that someone had been hiding there. At last he gave up the search and returned to Mr Clifton.

"Well, sir?" enquired Mr Clifton eagerly.

The major shook his head. "Nothing. Not even a button. I doubt I shall ever discover who it was, or why he — or she should be so desirous of putting me to earth."

"Oh, not a woman, sir! Surely not a woman!" responded Mr Clifton in shocked accents.

"Probably you are right," agreed his companion, "a woman would likely prefer to skewer me with some sleek little stiletto. That's more a woman's weapon. I suppose I shall just have to wait until the next attempt on my life to discover the culprit."

"Next attempt?!" cried the bailiff. "You don't believe he will dare such a thing again? Perhaps he did not actually intend to kill you, he may only have wished to frighten you."

"A warning shot across my saddlebow, you mean?" laughed the major, as he swung himself up on to his horse. "You may be right. If that was indeed his purpose, then he may be satisfied that he has achieved his ambition so easily. It certainly was not an excess of bravery propelled me so urgently into the ditch!"

They continued on their way without further mishap and eventually emerged into an open pasture bisected by a pretty little rill.

"That's Mary Shaw's cottage, sir," explained Mr Clifton, nodding towards the far corner of the field.

"Oh, yes, I remember the cottage. The gamekeeper used to live there when I was a bantling."

"That's right. Joel Martin: he married one of Lady Cullan's maids. I expect you must know that was the reason why none of the servants was up at the house on the night of the fire."

"No, I have heard nothing of it. Do go on," invited the major.

"Well, it happened that Lady Cullan gave all the servants leave to attend the wedding celebrations. Joel and Florence had been in service in Blakestone since coming there as children and her ladyship knew that everyone would want to see them wed. Very kind and thoughtful is Lady Cullan, bless her," added Mr Clifton fondly. Then his face fell as he recalled the fateful events that had blighted the joyful festivities. "The wedding feast was held at Barhurst. That's where Florence's family live. During the evening, Lady Cullan looked in to wish the couple happy and as she stayed to drink their health, so came Nick Tranter to raise the alarm. He'd been returning from a day's fishing when he saw the smoke of the fire as he climbed up from the cove. Upon reaching the top of the cliff, he could see that Blakestone House was burning fiercely and ran as fast as his sea-boots would allow, to raise the alarm in the village. Someone had seen Lady Cullan driving away in the gig on her way to Barhurst, so while Nick went to fetch her and the servants back, the rest of the villagers sent for the pump to be brought up and took pails, ewers and suchlike and hurried up to the house. However, there was very little that they could do, the flames having taken too great a hold. By the time the folk from Barhurst had arrived, the upper floors were well alight and poor Lady Cullan crying out that her husband was inside the house! Some of the men were for trying to find a way in through the west wing, that not appearing to be completely overtaken by the fire. But before they could attempt it, Lady Cullan spied his lordship up at a window. The brave gentleman called out to them not to be so foolhardy as to risk entering the building on any account, the stairs being all ablaze and in danger of collapsing. He said he would try to make his way to the servants' staircase to see if he might effect his escape through the cellars." Mr Clifton paused and heaved a great sigh. "That was the last time we saw him alive. They fought the fire all night and managed to save a part of the wing which you are now inhabiting, sir. Alas, everything else was lost, including a life. Lord Cullan's body was found on the following day, lying at the foot of the back stairs that lead to the cellars. He must have attempted to take shelter down there in the hope that the fire would not penetrate below ground. It was terrible. Lady Cullan was distraught with grief and Mrs Wytcherley took her home to Dovecote Hall. The poor soul has never been the same woman since. She was once so lively and gay; always beautifully gowned and often with a crowd of friends about her at Blakestone. Now she seldom goes out into company and wears only black. Oh, it's a tragedy, sir, a terrible tragedy!" he ended gravely.

"Is it known what caused the fire?" questioned the major quietly.

"No one could tell, sir. Lord Cullan was quite alone in the house at the time. It might have been a coal fallen from a grate, or a spark of wood. The damage was too extensive even to gauge where the blaze began."

They had reached the brook by now and halted while the horses slaked their thirst. The bright, pellucid water burbled merrily along its pebbled pathway with all the joyful abandon of a happy child let out to play. Winking stars of sunlight flitted like fireflies across its cut-crystal surface as with busy haste it bounded downward, staying for nothing.

The major, lost in thought, followed its meandering course with his eyes until his glance rested on the old cottage that crouched in a corner of the meadow, backed low against the darkling woods.

"Let us call on Mrs Shaw," he announced suddenly, "I think I should like a word with her."

"As you wish, sir," answered the bailiff cautiously, "although I ought to warn you that our visit may not be welcome. Mrs Shaw likes to keep to herself and has chosen to live in solitary seclusion. She and her children moved here only recently. Lady Elisa Maytland provides the means, she has always been very good to the family. Though why Mary should wish to live so far from everyone, I can't understand."

"Well, I don't mean to cause her any great disturbance, we shall only stay a moment or two. Come along."

With that he urged his horse into the water and crossing the brook, cantered away towards the cottage.

At the sound of their arrival, a troop of children as ragged as the campions that crowded at the door, came hurtling pell-mell out of the house to see who the intruders might be. They pulled up short at sight of the major astride the big roan horse and stared in silent wonder as he approached them. The youngest, who looked to be about four or five years old, retreated to hide behind the apron of an elder sister and dared advance no further until her siblings should lead the way.

"Good day, Peter," called out Mr Clifton, addressing a sturdy lad with a shock of black hair, "is your mother at home this morning?"

"She'm out the back a-doin' o' the washin', Mr Clifton, sir."

"Then run and tell her that Major Lacey has called to see her, will you, Peter? There's a good lad."

The boy scampered excitedly away, yelling for his mother at the top of his voice. At the sound of his vociferous appeal, a woman soon appeared in the doorway, wiping her hands on a spotless white pinafore. When she caught sight of her visitors she stopped in her tracks and after staring a moment at the gentleman on the roan horse, began to nervously push a few, flying strands of hair back into the confines of her muslin cap.

The major dismounted and tucking his riding crop under his arm, turned to greet his tenant.

"Mrs Shaw, is it not? Good morning to you. My name is Lacey, Major Lacey, your new landlord," he explained as she continued to watch him guardedly. "Forgive my intrusion, I can see you are very busy but I wanted to ask you if you had heard or seen a horseman come by within the last few minutes?"

Mrs Shaw said nothing. Her eyes, dark like those of her children, seemed over-large in the pale oval of her worn face. He thought he caught a glimpse of scared suspicion in their fathomless depths, that reminded him poignantly of the Spanish peasant women who had watched stoically as the English cavalry had ridden through their villages, expecting to have stolen from them the last meagre rations that the retreating Frenchmen had overlooked.

"Perhaps the children may have done so then?" he asked, glancing at them in friendly fashion as they crowded about their mother, protected and protecting. "Have you seen anyone riding past your door this morning?"

"No, we've not sin an 'orseman," replied Mrs Shaw abruptly. "Now go indoors childer an' finish yer chores. I'm sorry, sir, but I am busy as ye say, so if there's nothin' else?"

"Only one more question, Mrs Shaw, if you will allow me," he interrupted with an apologetic smile. "If you did not see a rider, then perhaps you may have heard a shot fired from over yonder?"

"Yes, I heerd a shot but that's not t' be wondered at. No doubt 'twas one of yer own keepers a-shootin' of a magpie."

"Perhaps you are right," nodded the major. "Well, I'll not disturb you further." He turned to go and as he did so, noticed the imprint of a horse's hoofs in the soft earth beneath his feet. Observing the reason for his sudden distraction, Mrs Shaw bit her lip anxiously and when the major half turned towards her she opened her mouth to speak.

Before she could utter an explanation, another figure appeared from the dark aperture of the doorway and gently set her aside.

"Good morning, Major Lacey," said Lady Elisa Maytland coolly. "Why are you troubling Mary with your foolish questions? She has troubles enough of her own as you would soon see, if you'd take the time to look at the sad state of this poor place she has to call home. 'Tis a pity her landlord can do no more for her than plague her with his idle curiosity."

"Lady Elisa," he acknowledged frigidly. "I think a man who has just been deliberately fired upon might well be forgiven for attempting to discover the identity of his assailant. I confess I am a little more than idly curious to know who it is wishes me dead. I perceive that you are habited for riding, perhaps you may have noticed something?"

"No, I have rid up through the wood myself this morning and so far as I am aware, it was a solitary exercise. Perhaps one of your keepers took you for a black-hearted gypsy, intent on mischief?" she suggested laughingly, eyeing the dirty marks of the ditch upon his clothing.

"I might have guessed you would find this amusing. You are a woman of a perverse humour as I have already discovered. However, I am not come to provide you with entertainment, so if you will excuse me, I will be on my way. Good day to you."

He moved away towards his horse

and taking the reins from Mr Clifton's grasp, swung himself up into the saddle. "One last question before I go, Lady Elisa. How did you know it was in the wood that I was nigh murdered?" he questioned, regarding her closely as she made to answer him.

"I overheard Mary's saying that it must have been one of your keepers fired the shot. I assumed you had indicated to her, that it was in the wood the incident occurred. Does that answer your question to your satisfaction, sir?"

"It might, we shall see. Goodbye, my lady," he replied in a clipped voice, his face far from friendly and looking as if he would like to have said something more.

Noting this, she smiled sweetly up at him, remarking teasingly, "I see you have managed to recall that I am a lady, Major Lacey. I am glad I did not need to remind you of it again."

"No, madam, I have no such recollection, I merely remember that I am a gentleman. Come, Clifton, let us go."

"Oh, m'lady, do ye think he suspects somethin'?" asked Mary worriedly, as she watched them ride away. "If 'e means to remain at Blakeston', we'll 'ave t' be a deal more watchful."

"Don't fear, Mary, the major will not present us with the least difficulty. Leave him to me, I'll take care of him."

When the two men had regained their path, the major turned to Mr Clifton, saying rather irritably, "Why is it that I constantly meet that woman riding about my property?"

"Lady Elisa, I suppose you mean?" answered Mr Clifton, puzzled by his master's evident annoyance.

"So she calls herself," muttered the major ungraciously.

"Well, sir, she has been used to roam these woods quite freely since she was a small girl. She and Lord Cullan were on intimate terms for a number of years. Almost like brother and sister you might say. Lady Elisa has always been welcome at Blakestone."

"I can't think what can have induced my brother to encourage the chit. I had not thought him such a fool. She's hardly more than a child now and not a very prepossessing one either!"

Mr Clifton smiled, understandingly this time. "She is rather an unconventional girl, sir. It is popularly believed by those who know the family well, that her father, Lord Maytland, was desirous of being succeeded by a son. Alas, fate thwarted him of that ambition and Lady Elisa alone stands to inherit his fortune. In consequence of this, he has brought her up as if she were indeed the longed-for son and heir. He has actively encouraged her to indulge in all the pursuits normally enjoyed by young gentlemen. There is scarce a fellow in the entire neighbourhood can equal her in matters of sporting prowess. She can ride and shoot with the best of them. And on the hunting field there are few braver."

"Small wonder then, that she is so unladylike! The man must be wanting in sense to have had such feather-brained notions. Why could he not have been content to remain the father of a dutiful daughter and spared the rest of us the inconvenience of having to endure the results of his ridiculous folly?"

113

5

LADY CULLAN promptly returned her brother-in-law's visit and arrived at Blakestone House accompanied only by her coachman. The major met her at the door himself and gave her a brief tour of his humble quarters. She allowed them to be surprisingly comfortable but far too primitive for her fastidious tastes.

"I have just come from the Dower House," she explained, laying aside her bonnet and seating herself in the chair he drew forward for her. "It is solely in the charge of Albert and Tilda now. Since your Aunt Sybil passed away, the house has been closed up and I have set them to watch over it for me."

"Albert and Tilda? Are they still here? Then I shall ride over to see them. They must be grown very old. Tilda was in my grandmother's service was she not?"

"That is so. She has lived at Blakestone for sixty years and more, I believe.

114

They have nowhere else to go and seem perfectly content to remain at the Dower House. Of course there is nothing for them to do these days. Everything of value has been removed and all else is left in holland covers. Tilda and Albert are both very frail and so I must visit them frequently. Mrs Wytcherley's cook is very obliging and always keeps a little something aside for me to bring them."

"I see Mr Clifton is not mistaken in his good opinion," smiled the major as he handed her a cup of freshly brewed tea. "He said you were kind and thoughtful and you are." Aurelia blushed prettily at the compliment so warmly expressed and her hand trembled slightly as she accepted the proffered cup.

"Did he say that indeed? Then it is more than I deserve. You must know that Mr Clifton's task has not been an easy one, thanks to our extravagance. There was never very much money to spare him. Alas, we gave matters of the estate little consideration. It is a miracle he has not sought employment elsewhere. I do not know how I would have gone on without him: he has been running Blakestone single-handed since Lucius died. I am deeply indebted to him." She paused to drink her tea before continuing. "As all our other servants were of an age to find work in new households, I felt it to be my duty to care for Albert and Tilda. If you are intent upon visiting them, I pray you will wait until I call again in a day or two. Their eyesight is failing and they are very hard of hearing, I fear you might startle them if you came unannounced. I am their only visitor and they are used to me and know when to expect my arrival. I think it will be less of a shock to them if you came in my company."

"Whatever you think best, Aurelia. I shall be guided by you. If you tell me when you mean to go there again, I will be certain to go with you."

"I shall look forward to it," she answered happily. "I wonder if I might also prevail upon you to accompany me to the assembly rooms on Friday? It is time you met some of your neighbours and I am sure they are all eager to meet you. There are several very agreeable young ladies who will, I know, be delighted to have the opportunity to stand up with you for some of the dances. Will you come?"

"If you particularly wish it, I will. I would do anything to oblige you, Aurelia," he replied seriously, "you have only to ask, you know."

"Thank you, Alex, I shall not forget it," she murmured softly. "I am truly grateful for your regard."

Her vivid blue eyes met his fleetingly before she set aside her cup and arose from her chair. Nevertheless, the look was enough to cause his heart to lurch wildly and he caught his breath. She was so lovely! The pale gold of her hair and her smooth, white skin glowed luminously against the black silk gown and the delicate black lace fichu that she wore about her shoulders. The widow's garments seemed to give her an ethereal beauty that somehow placed her beyond his reach and made him feel almost reverent. He gazed at her adoringly as she put on her silk-trimmed bonnet, deftly tying the ribbons in a coquettish bow beneath her left ear. When she was ready, she slipped her arm through his with the old familiarity and catching up her trailing skirts, allowed him to escort her to the waiting carriage.

"Goodbye, Alex. I'm going to visit the mausoleum now; I have some flowers I wish to place there."

"Would you like me to come with you?"

"No, I thank you," she smiled sadly. "I prefer my own company when I go there. You do understand, don't you?"

He took her hand and pressed it to his lips. "Of course, I would not dare to intrude and I promised you that you were free to come here as often as you desired, without fear of disturbance from me."

"Bless you, Alex, for your sweet solicitude," she murmured gratefully and he handed her up into the carriage. As he watched her drive away, he wished for the thousandth time that fate had been kinder.

He had not long to wait to see her again. She came two days later to take him up in the carriage with her and together they drove to the Dower House, situated about a half-mile further down the hill from his own dwelling.

It was built in a narrow dene that opened at one end on to the pebbled beach and was clustered about on all sides by tall fir trees standing shoulder to shoulder like some old imperial bodyguard. The wind soughed unceasingly in the heaving branches, echoing the sound of the thirsty sea sipping and swallowing the shingle.

Major Lacey alighted from the carriage and turned to assist Lady Cullan. For a moment they stood silently side by side, staring up at the grim façade of brick and stone. Although the day was fine, the house seemed cold and dark, silent too, save for the wind and the intermittent banging of a shutter broken loose from its fixings. There was an air of neglect about the place, apparent in the peeling paintwork and the dirty window panes. It was now merely a relic of the past, every feature reminiscent of a bygone age.

Lady Cullan drew her shawl closer about her and hurried him towards the house. "Come, follow me. Let us go inside." She stepped hastily up to the door and felt in her reticule for the key. "Here, you take this, Alex. You may keep it if you wish, you will need it if you want to visit the house again. Open the door would you? There is no point in knocking, they won't hear us and the bell does not work."

The lock was stiff but the release gave way at last and the heavy key turned with a loud click. Seizing hold of the circle of twisted iron set just above the lock, the major shouldered open the massive oak door. It swung inwards with a grating rasp of ancient hinges that set the echoes shrieking.

The hall was deep-shadowed and dim after the brightness of the morning. As his eyes adjusted to the gloom, he could see oak panelled walls, a wide, galleried staircase also of dark, polished oak and a bare, boarded floor.

Aurelia closed the door behind them and taking his hand, led him along a narrow, low-ceilinged gallery, the sound of their footsteps thudding hollowly as they walked its length. Here and there, the wooden panels, blackened with age, showed lighter squares of a warm, golden colour, where once framed portraits had hung. The air smelt stale and musty. He felt particles of dust tickling his nose and smothered a sneeze. Surely it must be years since anyone had used this entrance to the house?

"Here we are. This is the staircase to the kitchens. Tilda and Albert have one or two rooms down there for their use," Aurelia informed him as she lightly descended the steps, lifted a latch and preceded him into the nether regions of the house.

Albert, who had once been a footman up at Blakestone, stood in front of the kitchen fire stirring a pot suspended from a chain. His tall, spare form was now bent almost double with age and his shiny, bald pate glistened with tiny beads of perspiration in the light of the flames.

Tilda was seated in a ladder-back chair facing the open doorway that overlooked a walled garden. An apron full of pea pods was on her lap and she was shelling them slowly but determinedly, despite the handicap of gnarled, rheumatic fingers.

Aurelia touched Albert's shoulder gently and he stopped stirring the contents of the cauldron and peered round at her, the fire hissing and spitting as he held the dripping ladle in mid-air.

"Oh, 'tis 'ee, milady! I never heered 'ee knock. Tilly m'dear, why didn't 'ee telled me 'er ladyship were come!?" he shouted in the loud voice of the very deaf.

His wife looked up from her absorbing occupation and greeted Lady Cullan with a toothless smile. "Good marnin', milady. I never see'd 'ee come in. And 'oo may that be as 'ee've brought wi' 'ee t'day?"

The major strode eagerly forward. "Hallo, Tilda! Do you remember me? Perhaps you will if I remind you that I used to steal your blackberry and apple tarts from the kitchen table when you set them to cool and Albert here would chase me all the way down to the beech wood but never once caught me."

Tilda and Albert gaped in amazement, screwing up their eyes the better to concentrate on his face, peering fixedly at this tall gentleman who stood in the middle of their little kitchen, somehow making it seem even smaller.

"It's never master Alex!" cried Tilda, gathering up her apron and struggling stiffly and awkwardly to her feet. The major leapt forward to help her and she set aside the peas and stared into his face. "Let me look at 'ee," she said taking him by the elbows and drawing him towards the light from the door. "Gracious goodness! I do b'lieve it is 'un! How big an' tall 'ee've growed! I 'ardly 'ould've knowed 'ee."

"It's good to see you again after all these years, Tilda. And Albert too! I thought there was nothing left to remind me of the old times but seeing you has made me feel at home at last!"

He hugged her to him and then set her gently back in her chair.

"How are you, Albert?" he said, warmly shaking the old man's hand.

"Fair to middlin', sir, fair to middlin'," replied Albert grinning broadly and gripping the ladle upright like a sceptre. "We heered ye'd gone off to fight they Frenchies."

"'Tis said they 'ud done for 'ee," interrupted Tilda. "Folks 'ave said as 'ow 'ee weren't never comin' back yere no more. We thought 'ee dead along o' yer pore brother as 'aunts th' old place.

Lor' but 'tis a sight o' yers sin we've see'd 'ee!"

"Indeed it is, Tilda. In fact it is nigh on fifteen years ago that I left Blakestone with my mother."

"Fifteen yer, is ut? Seems like yesterd'y. An' now ye's a pore orphin an' no 'ome ter come back ter," mourned Albert, shaking his head sadly. "'Tis a vale o' sorrer an' no mistake."

"Major Lacey is living at Blakestone, Albert. In Mrs Evelyn's old room. He and his valet have made it quite cosy, you know."

"Ye bean't livin' theer, sir?!" cried Albert in horrified astonishment. "A'n't nob'dy telled 'ee th' old 'ouse be 'aunted?"

"Now, Albert," commanded Aurelia sternly, "you know very well that is all nonsense. There are no such things as ghosts. I have lately visited Blakestone House more frequently than anyone and I have never seen anything that looks the least bit spectral."

"Ay, but 'tis only they as 'ave the gift can see 'un. Jem Purdy 'as the seein' eye an' 'ee do swear 'twas 'is lor'ship rose

124

up out o' the ol' ruin on the very spot wheere's 'ee died. 'Tis often the way wi' them pore souls 'as dies afore theer time. They jest can't rest ye see, sir."

"Jem Purdy will swear to seeing anything when he has had his fill of rum," replied Aurelia tartly. "I would prefer you not to repeat these foolish tales which are only the product of his drunken visions."

"Lady Cullan is quite right, Albert. There are no such things as ghosts. I have seen too many men die before their time and helped to bury some of them. But not one of them ever left that plot of earth where they were finally laid. So let's hear no more talk of hauntings. Besides, it is very distressing for Lady Cullan as I'm sure you will understand."

Albert and Tilda exchanged knowing glances. It was obvious they were not convinced but they said no more on the subject and the rest of the brief visit passed in pleasant reminiscences.

When they eventually took leave of their retainers, Tilda seemed reluctant to let them go.

"Won't 'ee stay a minut' more, master

Alex, sir? It's sich a pleasure jest to sit and prattle wi' 'ee; an' Lady Cullan a'n't 'ad a chance to g' over th' rooms. She allus likes t' inspec' th' rooms, doan't 'ee y'r Ladyship?"

"Thank you, Tilda, not today. But I shall come again on Thursday as usual. Goodbye."

They left the old lady and her husband to finish cooking their meal and returned to the waiting carriage. As they reached the old oak door, the major had to fumble for the handle in the gloom and once again the door swung open to the sound of screaming hinges. He stood aside to allow Aurelia to pass through ahead of him and as he did so, he could not resist a compulsion to look back over his shoulder into the eerie darkness behind him. What sort of life must that faithful old couple lead in such dismal surroundings? His eyes wandered to the ancient staircase carved in oak by some long dead craftsman in the days' when Henry Tudor, the seventh of that name, succeeded to the throne of England. Small wonder that Tilda and Albert imagined ghosts could appear! All this dark oakwood was oppressive and he was certain that he could hear mice scuffling behind the wainscoting. A board creaked above his head and he glanced up suddenly.

"What's the matter, Alex?" asked Aurelia impatiently. "Why don't you lock the door?"

"I beg your pardon," he apologized, stepping swiftly out into the bright, fresh air and pulling the door to behind him. "What an odd sort of place this is, I am not at all surprised that you cannot bring yourself to live here. In fact, I am all the more determined that you shall not do so. I am amazed that you even bother to take such an interest in the house, apart from visiting Albert and Tilda."

"Well, they are far too old to be climbing all those stairs to air the rooms, so I have taken that task from them. I like to keep an eye on things here anyway, as I know I shall have to live here sooner or later. Lord Maytland may return at any time and then I must leave Dovecote Hall."

"But you said there is nothing of value here?"

"Nothing of great value, it's true. But several pieces of furniture remain and there are those who will steal anything if they think it will make them an easy profit. We've all slept sounder in our beds since Shaw was taken up."

"Tom Shaw? I understood from Mr Clifton that he only took a pheasant."

"He poached a pheasant, Alex, from Sir Eustace's land. And that was not all. It was well known that he was also a free-trader."

"Was that charge ever proved against him?"

"No, his kind are too clever for that! They take care to hide all the evidence and have accomplices in every village and hamlet for miles around. Yet I dare to think Sir Eustace has succeeded in showing them that justice will prevail in the end."

"By the example of Tom Shaw being transported for the sake of one small pheasant?"

"Sir Eustace is of the opinion that such a severe punishment will deter Shaw's friends from attempting worse crimes."

"That seems like using a hammer to crush an ant."

"We are speaking of evil villains, Alex, who would stop at nothing to ensure that their trade flourishes. However, I hear that there is a new officer at Shoreham who is said to be very zealous in the performance of his duty. They will not find it so easy to smuggle goods ashore now, I think."

They climbed into the waiting carriage and as it turned up the hill towards Blakestone, the major glanced back over his shoulder for one last look at the house. As he did so, something caught his sharp eyes. A sudden movement among the closely grouped fir trees. Was it the shadows or was someone following them?

"What's wrong, Alex?" asked Lady Cullan nervously. "What are you staring at?" She sounded suddenly frightened and anxious not to alarm her unnecessarily he smiled reassuringly saying, "Nothing at all. I was just thinking how totally unsuitable this grim place is for one as lovely as you. I really could not allow you to live here alone, we must see what can be done to find a happy solution."

On the Friday evening of that week, Lady Cullan was seen to enter the assembly rooms upon the arm of a dashing young soldier. She had insisted that he wear his uniform for the occasion and despite his reluctance had managed to cajole him into giving her his promise to do so.

Their arrival caused no little stir. Lady Cullan did not generally attend the assemblies now that she was widowed and her appearance in the company of such a splendidly dressed cavalry officer, set her neighbours' tongues a-wagging.

"So that is her brother-in-law?" whispered Miss Stewart to her companion. "You did not tell me that he is very handsome!"

Lady Elisa cast a scornful glance in their direction. "I did not need to. I am certain he will not hesitate to tell you himself, the strutting peacock! Just look at Aurelia! See how she simpers like a bird-witted milkmaid! Oh, there is Sir Eustace just entered the room; he will not be best pleased that his place at her side has been usurped by a younger man — and one who can boast a uniform. He has been paying court to Aurelia these three years past. Let us draw nearer so that we can hear what he says!"

She gripped Miss Stewart's arm firmly and dragged her across the room, paying no heed to her embarrassed protestations.

As they came within earshot, they heard Aurelia performing the introductions and Sir Eustace's decidedly cool acknowledgement.

"I am pleased to make your acquaintance, Major Lacey. I had no idea that Lord Cullan had so near a relative. I do not recall your mentioning a brother-in-law, my lady?"

"Did I not? How very remiss of me, Sir Eustace. As a matter of fact, Major Lacey and I have known each other since I made my entrance into society. I was a green girl when first we met, was I not, Alex?" she trilled, peeping up at him with an intimate smile. "We are old friends."

Sir Eustace's thin lips became a hard line in the unnatural pallor of his face. "Then you are to be envied, Major," he murmured, his hooded eyes sliding from the young officer's pleasant, open countenance to study, with keen interest, Aurelia's animated expression.

"Lady Cullan," he continued, still watching her intently, "may I have the pleasure of partnering you in the next dance? I know that you seldom allow we unfortunate gentlemen an opportunity to enjoy that happiness but I never give up hope."

She hesitated slightly before replying, then slipping her arm through the major's and unfurling her fan with a coquettish flick of her wrist, said, "How very kind of you, Sir Eustace but I have already engaged to dance with my brother-in-law. Pray do excuse me. Come, Alex, they are about to make up the set."

She made to move away to the centre of the room and as she did so, her eye fell upon Elisa's prying gaze. Guessing the reason for her proximity, she turned back to Sir Eustace.

"Why do you not ask Lady Elisa instead, Sir Eustace? I see she is without a partner and would no doubt be most grateful to receive an invitation."

With that barbed remark, she glided triumphantly on her way.

Sir Eustace put up his quizzing-glass and surveyed Elisa through it, contempt on his curling lip and in the angle of his high-arched nose. He raked her with a penetrating stare: her curled red hair, cropped fashionably short at the back of her neck; her unsymmetrical features: eyes too large, short, *retroussé* nose and generous mouth and finally her slim, almost boyish figure, clad in a simple muslin gown, its plainness unrelieved by a single piece of jewellery or even a knot of ribbons.

Having finished his brief appraisal, Sir Eustace let fall the glass, swinging it idly on its ribbon and turning on his heel, stalked majestically away.

Elisa flushed furiously at his deliberately insulting behaviour, her ready temper threatening to boil over as she made to hurl some fierce invectives in his wake. Miss Stewart, anticipating an unpleasant scene, quickly stepped into the breach.

"Don't, Elisa," she said, firmly propelling her away. "It is exactly what would amuse him the most. I dislike him as much as you do and his manner just now would have provoked a saint but don't, I beg of you, give him the satisfaction of seeing you censured for it." Elisa continued to glare across the room at Sir Eustace's aquiline profile. "As if I would want to partner that ageing roué, even if he asked me! I would sooner embrace a dancing bear! How dared Aurelia suggest it!"

"To anger you, of course. When will you two call a truce? There is nothing to be gained by this open warfare. I pity your aunt, it must be an appalling strain on her nerves. I do not envy her."

"It is she who invited that woman to stay with us and must suffer the consequences. I made it quite clear from the beginning that I could not tolerate that bubble-headed ninnyhammer! What an idiot Lucius was, marrying such a vain, silly creature. She brought him nothing but trouble and all for the sake of a pretty face. She is like a painted china doll — and with as much sense in her head! Oh, why did he do it when he could have . . . " She stamped her foot angrily, blinking back a tear.

"When he could have married you? Is that what you were about to say?" replied Miss Stewart quietly. "I know you loved him, Elisa, but I don't think it was the kind of love that would have stood the test of time. He wouldn't have made you happy. There was a weakness in Lucius that I don't think you allowed yourself to see. His affections were never deeply engaged. Lucius loved to please himself. Sir Eustace is the same . . . "

"No! Never say so!" expostulated Elisa hotly. "You did not know Lucius as I did. He was so kind, so good to me . . . no! Don't dare to compare him with Newbury, I won't have it!"

"Very well," agreed Miss Stewart calmly, "I shall be silent on the subject. Let us speak of something else."

"By all means," answered Elisa distantly.

"I have said too much already. Perhaps you would prefer to choose a topic."

"Then tell me, do you know who that gentleman is: the one wearing the scarlet regimentals?" asked Elisa, her annoyance quickly forgotten as her attention was captured by the stranger who had that moment entered the room. "Oh, he is speaking to your mama!"

Miss Stewart studied her mother's companion. "He is quite unknown to me," she answered wrinkling her brow. "I wonder where Mama can have met him? Shall we intrude upon their conversation?"

Elisa nodded and they hurried across the room to gain Mrs Stewart's side. "Here comes my eldest daughter, Captain Rowland. You two have not yet been introduced, she did not accompany her sisters to Shoreham. Celia, do you come and meet Captain Rowland. Ah, and this is our neighbour, Lady Elisa Maytland."

The young ladies greeted the stranger politely while Mrs Stewart continued the introduction. "Captain Rowland is but lately come into the county; we met only a few days ago at your Aunt Simpson's house. He is quartered at Shoreham now and so I hope we may persuade him to dine with us at the rectory when he can be spared from his duties."

"I should be honoured, ma'am," he bowed, "and I would need no persuasion, your lovely daughters are inducement enough. Any invitation that would further my acquaintance with them would be accepted with alacrity, I assure you."

He took Miss Stewart's hand, a look of admiration in his dark eyes.

Elisa observed with astonishment the slow blush that crept into Miss Stewart's cheeks, her usually cool composure obviously deserting her. She glanced at the captain's face to try to discern whether he was aware of the effect he was having on the rector's daughter and wondering if he was similarly affected.

Elisa concluded that he was. His eyes never left Miss Stewart's pretty countenance as she engaged him in polite conversation and he appeared to have forgotten Elisa's presence. She continued to study him thoughtfully while his attention was so wholly occupied. He had sun-browned skin like Major Lacey and his eyes, set beneath thick, dark brows, seemed to twinkle merrily. When he smiled, as he did now at some remark of Miss Stewart's, it was reflected in the eyes which seemed to smile also, crinkling attractively at the corners.

When he eventually realized that he had not included Elisa in the conversation, his apologies were profuse and he begged her pardon several times before he was convinced that he had not offended her.

"Please think no more of it, Captain Rowland, I am quite accustomed to being overlooked. The only time my presence is felt, is when I lose my temper, which I do frequently. Hence this warning beacon on my head." She grinned impishly, indicating her flame-coloured curls.

"Then I am fortunate not to have roused it," he laughed, "I would have received my just deserts if you had fired up at me. I take it as an act of generosity that you did not choose to do so and therefore am encouraged to believe that I may yet have the felicity of being counted among your friends."

She held out her hand and he took it willingly. "I have too few of that rare breed to pass over such an application, Captain. Miss Stewart is one of them — and the dearest. If you are fortunate enough to gain her friendship, you will be blessed indeed, for a kinder, more faithful companion does not exist."

Miss Stewart's blush spread to the roots of her hair and she knew not where to look. Such effusive praise from Elisa was seldom heard and she wondered why she had chosen this moment to express it.

"What a pretty compliment, Elisa," beamed Mrs Stewart delightedly, "and one that is truly deserved, even allowing for a mother's natural partiality."

"Mother, please!" muttered Celia in a whispered aside, beginning to wish the conversation would take a new direction, preferably away from her. She stole a glance at the captain's face and in catching his eyes, thought to read understanding in their warm depths.

"Perhaps, Miss Stewart, you would consider honouring me with the pleasure of your company and allow me to lead you into the next set? Will you take pity on a stranger whose acquaintances in this part of the country are very few?"

"Go on, Celia," prompted Elisa encouragingly, "I don't need you to chaperone me, I will stay and talk to your mama."

"Well, if you are quite sure you won't mind my leaving you for a little while?"

began Miss Stewart uncertainly.

"I am three and twenty and perfectly capable of playing the wallflower without it causing me the least distress, I assure you. Now don't keep Captain Rowland on tenterhooks any longer or he will think that you do not want to dance with him."

"Yes, do go along, Celia," urged her mama. "Elisa and I shall keep each other company."

When they had gone, Elisa turned to Mrs Stewart, a mischievous glint in her eyes. "I think she likes him, do not you? I have never seen her so covered in confusion! He is rather charming though," she added confidingly. "How did you meet him?"

"At Shoreham, when I took the girls to see their aunt. My brother-in-law is a comptroller in the customhouse, as you may already know, and he was introduced to Captain Rowland at a meeting at the Ship Inn. The captain has orders to assist the Riding Officers in the pursuit of their duty. Mr Simpson was very impressed by the captain's determination to end the smuggling along this coastline. I must say he seems a very capable young man; I should think he will prove to be a nasty thorn in the side of the smugglers in this locality. Oh, look! I do believe Captain Rowland has found that he is not such a stranger after all."

Elisa peered over her shoulder to see for herself what had interested Mrs Stewart so suddenly. She saw the captain vigorously shaking hands with Major Lacey, clapping him on the back like a long-lost friend. Their faces were wreathed in smiles and it was apparent that they were quite delighted to see one another.

The mystery was solved some time later when the captain returned Miss Stewart to her mother's side and explained his joy in discovering an old comrade among the crowd. "Major Lacey and I knew each other in Spain. He is the very best of fellows and I am happy to have run into him again. We fought some hair-raising campaigns together and it is the greatest stroke of good luck that I should find him here tonight. He tells me he is living close by in the burnt-out remains of his ancestral home! Trust

Alex to perch himself amid the ruins. I could never imagine him adapting to civilization: he is a born soldier. I am so glad you suggested that I come here this evening, Mrs Stewart. It has proved to be a most enjoyable event for me. I have renewed an old friendship and, as I venture to hope, have embarked upon some new and equally valuable ones."

"Well, for my part, I will say that I shall always be happy to welcome you to the rectory if you should care to call on us, Captain Rowland. What say you, Celia?"

"Why, yes, of course," stammered Miss Stewart bashfully, "that is, if Captain Rowland can spare the time."

"I shall make the time, Miss Stewart," he promised solemnly, well pleased with this auspicious start to the evening.

Not so Sir Eustace. He had been forced to spend his time in listening to the vague prattlings of Mrs Wytcherley, who had foisted herself upon him in the mistaken understanding that he would be glad of her company while Aurelia was occupied with her brother-in-law.

"How perfectly splendid Major Lacey

looks in his uniform," she observed admiringly. "We ladies always have a weakness for a man dressed in regimentals. It is very gratifying to see Aurelia enjoying herself so much. I could never have thought it possible; the dear soul has been dreadfully miserable these last three years, I had begun to doubt that she would ever be happy again. It has done her a vast amount of good to see her brother-in-law after believing herself to be utterly alone in the world. She thought him dead, you know; it has come as a great surprise to her that he is come back to Blakestone. He is actually living there, Sir Eustace! Though why he should choose to do so when it is all a dreadful ruin, I cannot conjecture. It seems a very odd thing to me. I am sure nothing would induce me to live in such a place, not for all the wealth in the world! They say it is haunted," she added in an awed whisper.

He looked at her sharply, his heavy brows drawing together and making his face seem more thunderous than ever.

"Has he said anything to you, madam? Concerning the reason for his unexpected return to Blakestone, I mean?" he enquired abruptly.

"Why no, Sir Eustace. I hardly know him, we have had no conversation to speak of, we have only exchanged pleasantries. It is Aurelia alone who has his confidence. But I daresay he is come here to deal with the business of the estate. I know he has seen Mr Clifton because I heard him mention it to Aurelia."

"Is she very fond of him?"

Mrs Wytcherley looked askance at him. Did she detect a note of jealousy in the tone of his voice?

"I think they are on friendly terms," she answered carefully, "but they have known each other a long time, you heard her say: it is only to be expected that she would appear easy in his company."

Sir Eustace merely scowled and Mrs Wytcherley thought it judicious to change the subject. She had the distinct impression that Sir Eustace was not best pleased.

6

MRS STEWART was as good as her word and within the week, Captain Rowland received an invitation to dine at the rectory. He was glad to have the opportunity to develop a closer acquaintance with the Stewart family, especially one particular member, whose sweet countenance was already indelibly imprinted upon his memory.

The younger girls were the first to greet him having elected to take their work into the parlour, the window of which cosy apartment happened to command a clear view of the front gate and the road beyond. As soon as they heard the sound of an approaching carriage, they rushed to the door and after some slight wrangling over who should be the first to open it, admitted the eagerly awaited visitor into the house.

Mrs Stewart, alerted by the noisy altercation in her hallway, rescued the gallant captain from his admirers.

"Girls! Is this a proper way for young ladies to behave? What do you think your papa would say if he were to hear you?" admonished their mother quellingly. "Good evening, Captain Rowland, I hope you had a pleasant journey."

"Good evening, ma'am. Splendid I thank you. I took the coast road for a mile or two and consequently feel that I have benefited greatly from the fresh sea air."

"Am I to take it that you are speaking of the stimulation of your appetite, Captain?" she smiled, as he bowed over her hand.

"I am not sure it is polite to confess to being ravenous but honesty compels me to be candid. I could eat a horse!" he confided in a stage whisper.

"I'm afraid that I did not include that dish when I planned my menu, the horses were all needed on the farm today which left me with only a saddle — of mutton," she answered merrily, "I hope that will suffice."

"Mama!" intervened her youngest daughter pleadingly, her round, chubby face pinkly glowing. "May I take Captain

Rowland's hat and cloak? May I, Mama?" Miss Kate Stewart was thirteen years of age and still as boisterous as a puppy, hanging on to her mama's arm with both hands and bouncing up and down excitedly.

"Don't let her, Mama," insisted her second daughter plaintively, "she only wishes to do so because she knows perfectly well that I came into the hall with that intention myself. Tell her to go up to the schoolroom, she ought not to have come down without Miss Dean's permission anyway."

"Miss Dean said I might bring my book downstairs if I was very quiet and did not disturb Papa while he is writing his sermon," argued the indomitable Kate.

Her sister Abigail, who at fifteen considered her wishes should rank higher than those of a mere child, looked to her mother to make this point clear.

"Ladies, may I make a suggestion?" proposed Captain Rowland, unfastening the strings of the light cape he had worn to keep the dust from his best dress uniform. "Miss Abigail, my cloak. Miss Kate, my hat." He bestowed these items upon the girls with a flourishing bow for each of them. "And Mrs Stewart, my arm," he finished, offering this capable appendage for her convenience.

"Thank you, Captain. How very diplomatic of you," congratulated Mrs Stewart approvingly.

"I was brought up with a brother and two sisters of my own, ma'am," he explained with a grin, "the experience has left its mark."

"Really? Then I should like to hear more of them. Let us go into the sitting-room. My husband will be joining us very shortly and Celia will be down in a moment; she must be nearly ready by now. I have never known her take so long at her *toilette*."

They entered a door that opened upon a charming room overlooking the garden. It was a warm evening and the glass doors were set wide allowing the sweet air, scented by roses and honeysuckle, to drift into the house.

"Good evening, Captain Rowland," came a voice from the veranda and Lady Elisa arose from a rustic bench placed just out of view beyond the window.

"Lady Elisa! What a pleasant surprise, how do you do?"

"Very well, thank you. Mrs Stewart has kindly offered me a place at her table tonight; my aunt is gone out with Lady Cullan."

"I have another surprise for you, Captain," beamed Mrs Stewart, "but I need say no more about it. My girls are about to announce him now I think."

Kate came running into the room crying, "Mama! Mama! There is another gentleman come! I do not know who he is. Shall I let him in? Prewett is helping cook, so she will not mind. Shall I, Mama?"

"I will come with you, Kate. Excuse me a moment, Elisa, Captain Rowland." She hurried out into the hall just as a knock sounded at the front door. They heard a man's deep voice as the visitor entered and Mrs Stewart's answer. Then Major Lacey was ushered into the room.

"Alex! I had no idea you were joining us! This is wonderful indeed! So this is your other surprise, Mrs Stewart?" he exclaimed delightedly.

"I thought you would be pleased. My husband called upon the major a few days ago and invited him to dine, so as you are old friends I determined to have you both sit down with us. Major Lacey, you are already acquainted with Lady Elisa, I think?"

"We have met, ma'am," he confirmed and bowed to Elisa. "Good evening, my lady."

"Major Lacey," Elisa answered with a slight inclination of her head.

Their cool greeting was in stark contrast to the warm welcome that followed as Miss Stewart almost ran into the room.

"I am so sorry, Mama. Forgive me for keeping you all waiting, I did not realize that the hour was so advanced. Elisa, I am very glad you could come. Major Lacey, Captain Rowland, I am so pleased to see you both again."

The captain was captivated anew by the sweet, shy smile that had drawn him to her on the occasion of their first meeting.

"Miss Stewart." He took her hand, returning the smile and hoping she

150

would meet his eye. She did oblige him with a glimpse into the clear, grey pools that sparkled up at him with unconcealed pleasure. "How lovely you look, you quite take my breath away," he murmured softly, his own eyes glowing with admiration.

"Thank you, Captain," she answered, a little breathless herself and immediately dropped her gaze.

She had received the reward for all the time and energy she had expended on her appearance this evening. Her hair alone had taken two hours to dress; the maid had never known her to be so exacting. However, the final result had been worth all her pains. An intricate top-knot of twisted plaits, shining clusters of ark-chestnut ringlets over each ear and three tiny curls to soften the smooth sweep of her brow.

Her new gown of olive-green sarsenet with an over-dress of gold net, revealed the feminine curves of her neat figure and its short, puffed muslin sleeves displayed rounded, graceful arms. The only jewellery she wore was the gold locket and chain that her papa had given her for her eighteenth birthday six years ago. Celia could not help thinking that this much-loved treasure would have appeared to greater advantage if the neckline of her dress had been cut a little lower but alas, Papa would never permit it: fashion was not a word he included in his vocabulary.

"Would you like to go out into the garden?" suggested Mrs Stewart, smiling upon them all. "It is such a fine evening and it is very warm indoors. I shall be with you again in a while; I must see how dinner is progressing. I will send Prewett with a tray of refreshments directly. Celia, I entrust our guests to your care while I am gone."

"Yes, Mama," complied her daughter willingly.

"What a delightful prospect," remarked the captain as he fell into step beside her.

"It is lovely, is it not?" agreed Celia, viewing the lawns and flower beds with an appreciative eye.

The captain's dark eyes twinkled merrily at this completely ingenuous remark. "Yes, it is lovely, very lovely,

Miss Stewart," he answered, smiling down at her. "This is the sort of night we dreamed of when we were far from home, eh, Alex?" he continued in a louder voice. "A beautiful English garden: is there anything in the world more peaceful? I sincerely doubt it."

"A sequestered spot indeed," concurred the major, stepping after him, "but for real solitude, you will not do better than Blakestone House. Wait until you see it, Hal. Especially on a wild night when all is black as pitch and the air is full of the roar of the breakers pounding against the cliffs."

"You make it sound positively desolate," grinned the captain. "I admit I am curious to see it but I think that I shall probably prefer this tranquil plot. Will you be my guide, Miss Stewart? I should like to explore it thoroughly."

They went on down the steps and strolled leisurely across the lawn, Miss Stewart pointing out the plants and shrubs that were her particular favourites. Major Lacey and Elisa followed in silence a few paces behind, only speaking when the captain or Miss Stewart addressed some remark to one or both of them.

When the others entered the rose arbour, Elisa declined to go with them: she was sure that Celia would prefer to show this part of the garden to Captain Rowland alone.

"Celia! I am going to sit on the seat under the apple trees. I shall await you there," she called as they disappeared from sight.

The major paused uncertainly. Courtesy demanded that he should bear her company but inclination argued against it. She did not look to see if he would follow her and appeared perfectly content to be by herself. In the end he compromised with his conscience and remained within her vicinity, pretending an interest in the flower borders.

From the orchard behind him came the pure, cascading notes of a throstle high in the branches of a pear tree and a gypsy wind wandered in over the wall with the tantalizing tang of brine on its breath. Then all was still again, nothing stirred. The sleepy sun stretched its long limbs across the lawn, lovingly caressing the leaves and flowers with a soft Midas touch, until the whole garden blushed a deep, rose-gold that spread slowly up from green grass to mossy bough and mingled with the turquoise sky.

The major sighed gently. Hal was right: surely there was no finer place on earth than an English garden on a summer's eve. If only Aurelia were here with him.

He heard Mrs Stewart calling them from the veranda and as he turned his eyes from the glory of the gloaming sky, he was suddenly aware that Lady Elisa was watching him attentively. In the roseate light her hair was a rich, golden-red, gleaming bright as a flame against the dusky shadows of the orchard. She did not possess Aurelia's translucent beauty, nor her graceful elegance but if she would follow Aurelia's or Miss Stewart's lead in matters of dress, she might be a taking little thing perhaps. That Quakerish gown of pearl-grey crepe did nothing to enhance her looks.

"I was about to ask you what occupied your thoughts a moment since," she remarked in her usual abrasive manner as she came up with him, "but I see from your expression now that your answer would no longer be of interest to me." With that, she turned abruptly and strode briskly back towards the house.

He stared after her in astonishment. What a peculiar girl she was: quite unlike any other woman he had ever met. There was nothing gracious nor gentle in her nature that he had yet observed. She had none of Aurelia's feminine traits. It was hardly surprising that there was a strong antipathy between them; they were completely opposite in character.

When they were presently seated at dinner, civility compelled him to make some attempt to converse because he had been placed next to her. However, conversation between them was desultory; he found it impossible to draw her out on any of the subjects he introduced and it was with considerable relief that he eventually transferred his attention to Mr Stewart who had requested his opinion on the merits of the burgundy that had just been brought to the table. By the time this theme had been thoroughly explored, Elisa was fully occupied by Mrs Stewart and the major now felt justified in avoiding any further intercourse.

The rest of the evening passed pleasantly enough, Miss Stewart being prevailed upon to play the pianoforte while Lady Elisa and Captain Rowland sang some Italian songs in duet, he in a fine baritone and she in a surprisingly sweet soprano.

Mrs Stewart demanded that the major play his part. Nothing loath, he acquiesced with her wishes by performing a selection of Irish ballads, one or two of them in the vernacular, much to the amusement of his hostess, who enthusiastically beat time to the lilting rhythms with her fan and both feet.

The party eventually broke up when Mrs Wytcherley and Lady Cullan called to take Elisa up into the carriage with them, as they returned from an evening spent playing whist with some near neighbours.

Although Mr Stewart pressed both gentlemen to stay and broach another bottle with him, the captain reluctantly declined, pleading the excuse that he must be on duty early in the morning and would therefore require a clear head. He finally departed with a firm promise to visit the major at his ruined 'castle' as soon as opportunity permitted.

Mrs Stewart and her daughter went off to their beds leaving the major to drink a parting glass with the insistent rector.

They retired to his study to enjoy it, Mr Stewart settling himself in an aged but extremely comfortable leather armchair, his legs stretched out before him and his feet resting on a low footstool. When they were both seated, the rector lifted his brimming glass in a salute.

"Your health, Major." He tasted the wine and then set aside his glass. "Well, young sir, what do you mean to do about Blakestone?"

"I wish I knew," smiled the major ruefully. "Things are in a very bad way as you guessed. It was extremely negligent of me not to have come sooner but I really had no idea that my brother was in such difficulties. He never mentioned it in his last and only letter to me while I was in Spain. On the contrary, he seemed in high gig. He told me that he was invited to invest in a scheme that would make him a very wealthy man. That must have been nothing but a pipe-dream because our solicitor tells me he knows naught of the matter. There is no record of any such investment among Lucius's papers that he has been able to trace. To speak truthfully, I have almost beggared myself in settling with some of my brother's more insistent creditors. Now there remains only the matter of the estate to be decided and then I shall know how to go about clearing the other debts."

"Did he not mention the nature of this investment?"

"No, he gave me no indication as to what it might be. The trouble is, I put up the blunt for it, whatever it was," he answered in a self-mocking tone. "I could not refuse to send him the money. I had parted company with him in a manner which I later regretted and when he sent me that letter, I saw it as an olive branch. He had never asked me for anything before and it seemed churlish to refuse him my help. Especially as, at the time, I doubted that I would ever have a use for the money."

"I see," muttered the rector, rubbing his long chin thoughtfully. "Then you know nothing at all of his business interests?"

The major shook his head and picked up his glass. "As I said, that one letter was the only communication that passed between us during the seven years that I have been abroad with my regiment."

"In that case you will not be able to throw any light on the matter," sighed Mr Stewart disappointedly and got suddenly to his feet.

"I'm sorry, Mr Stewart, I don't think I understand you," replied the major, nonplussed.

"No, indeed, how should you?" murmured the rector, as if preoccupied with weightier problems.

He had crossed the room to stand at his desk and taking up a pair of spectacles lying there, he perched them on the end of his nose, opened a drawer and began searching through its contents. After some few moments, during which time the major watched him in puzzled curiosity, he eventually appeared to find the item he was seeking and returned to his seat.

"Do you remember that I spoke to you

the other morning concerning one of your tenants, a Mrs Shaw?"

"Yes, certainly. I have already instructed Clifton to send someone over to the cottage to make the necessary repairs."

"Have you?" said the rector, peering over his spectacles and eyeing the major keenly. "Well, well, that is good news indeed," he went on, looking pleased and not a little surprised.

Major Lacey smiled understandingly. "I told you that I would do what I could and I meant it. But I am afraid that it will not be sufficient to make a great deal of difference. A substantial investment is required to enable the estate to be administered properly and as I have confided to you this evening, I just do not have the necessary resources to make it viable. However, I can improve Mrs Shaw's accommodation and, I hope, that of some of the other tenants also."

"Excellent! It will be much appreciated, I am certain. Now, speaking of Mrs Shaw, there is something here that I want to show you. You have heard that her husband Tom was taken up for poaching?"

"Yes, Clifton told me of it. I understand that you tried to persuade the court to offer clemency?"

The rector heaved another deep sigh. "I did all that was within my power but alas, it availed him nothing. They would not even permit his wife to visit him before the sentence was carried out. I myself was refused entrance to his cell and only succeeded in obtaining an interview by mere chance. I went down to the quay on the day that the prisoners were being taken to the ship and happened to see the officer in charge of them. I had some small acquaintance with him and so managed to enlist his help in my endeavour to speak a few words of comfort to Shaw ere he was taken aboard. As soon as he saw me, he seized me by the arm and drew me roughly aside, at least as far as his hateful chains would allow him. Then he whispered in my ear, 'Tell Cullan I think they are on to him! He and Sam must be warned!' 'What do you mean?' I asked. 'Of what should I warn them?' He pulled up his sleeve and, looking swiftly all about him as if he were afraid of being observed, he took a piece of paper from inside his shirt cuff and pushed it into my hand. 'Just give this to Cullan, sir! It's life or death!' Before I could question him further, the guards were ordered to march them away again. He called out to me to tell Mary that he loved her and that he would come back to them. That was the last I was to see of him and so far as I have heard, he has not been able to keep that final promise to his family."

"What did my brother say when you gave him the message?" asked the major, listening avidly to this extraordinary tale.

Mr Stewart shook his head sadly. "I regret to say, I was unable to deliver the message. By the time I was able to return home, it was too late."

"Too late?" the major reiterated quietly, the eager look on his face giving way to one of obvious sorrow and he slumped dejectedly back against the chair cushions. "But what of the paper he gave you?"

"I still have that," answered the rector, looking down at his palm wherein lay curled a small piece of thick, blue paper.

"May I see it, please?"

"You may keep it if you wish; though what possible use it could be now, or ever was for that matter, I cannot conjecture."

He passed it across to Major Lacey and watched him examine it. The major turned it over in his hand, then turned it again and finally held it nearer his face.

"But this is only a blank piece of paper!" he exclaimed in astonishment.

"Not quite," replied Mr Stewart, bringing the lamp a little closer. "I came to that conclusion myself at first but I have had many opportunities to study it in detail. If you look here, where the paper has been folded." He took it from the major's hand and held it against the light. "See this circular mark at the bottom? Look carefully."

The major obeyed and bent his head towards the lamp. "Ah, yes, I see now. There is a number writ here but it is very faint. Let me try to make it out." He screwed up his eyes in an effort of concentration. "It is a two and, I think, a nought. Twenty?"

"Yes, that is right. I have studied it with a magnifying glass and it is undoubtedly the number twenty. Though what that implies, if anything, is beyond my comprehension."

"It might have told us something more but I see the paper is torn across the top. I wonder what is so significant about a torn scrap of paper, that Shaw was very insistent that my brother should have it?"

"He said it was life or death," the rector reminded him grimly, "and before I could deliver the message, Lord Cullan was dead. What is more, Sam Frant, Shaw's closest friend, drowned at sea. One other inexplicable event also occurred at the same time as Frant met with his accident: Daniel Prescott disappeared on his way home from Barhurst village inn and was never seen again. Prescott was a near neighbour of Frant's and they were often to be seen in company with one another, drinking in the tavern by the fishing huts."

"Good God!" muttered the major in shocked accents.

"I have long since begun to believe that these accidents had very little to do with the Almighty's will," admitted Mr Stewart. "Yet there is not a shred of evidence to the contrary. I should never have doubted that they were anything but coincidences if it were not for my encounter with Tom Shaw."

"Yes, that was remarkable," agreed the major, "and I confess I am now even more suspicious of the circumstances of my brother's death than I was when I came here."

"Oh? You had suspected foul play before you heard my story?"

"It had struck me as a peculiar event that Lucius should have been completely alone in the house at such a moment. Mr Clifton has since explained that mystery but one other thing still remains to puzzle me."

"And what is that?" prompted Mr Stewart, his attention riveted on his companion's face.

"When I returned to England, I went directly to London to settle my business with the lawyers. It was there that I discovered the extent of my brother's debts. I was shocked to say the least. Mr Stewart, you are a man of the utmost discretion as I know, you will keep my confidences?"

"You may rest assured of that, Major Lacey," asserted the rector quickly. "Our conversation will not be repeated to anyone, I give you my solemn promise, so help me God."

"Thank you, sir. I am assured of it. Therefore I will tell you of all that I discovered in London. It seems that about five years ago, my brother, desperate no doubt to stave off his many creditors, mortgaged the property. Yes, Mr Stewart, you may well frown, it was a foolish decision and one that ought not to have been necessary. However, it was done and provided a brief respite from his financial embarrassments. Alas, within two years, the bank threatened to foreclose and things were looking very bad for him indeed. Then, only a week or two before the fire, Lucius redeemed the mortgage in full. How he was able to do this and where the money came from, the lawyers have no idea, they had not the chance to enquire of him."

"Well bless my soul!" gasped Mr Stewart, looking and sounding astounded. "But surely Lady Cullan . . . ?"

"She is in ignorance of the whole affair.

Lucius did not confide his troubles to her. She did not even know that he had mortgaged the house. I must say I do not blame him for that: to have shared such a burden with her would have been unthinkable," he said feelingly. "And I will do everything I can to prevent her ever knowing of it. I adjure you to do likewise. I trust you have not told her of your meeting with Shaw?"

"No, I could see no purpose in doing so. She had enough grief to bear and I only had my suspicions. There was no proof that any other party or parties, were involved in her husband's death. You are the first person to learn my secret."

"Thank heaven for your good sense, Mr Stewart! I would not have Lady Cullan suffer any further distress. As to her knowing aught of the repayment of the mortgage, I am convinced she does not. Having decided to tell her nothing of his actions at the time, I doubt very much that Lucius would have confessed to it when it was no longer necessary. She has certainly given me no indication that she is yet aware of that particular piece of folly. I mean to look into this, Mr

Stewart. I am determined to find out the truth. If Lucius was killed deliberately, I want to know who is responsible. Tom Shaw would have been the man to speak to about this, if only he were not on the other side of the world. Do you think his wife might be able to assist me?"

"I don't know. I did ask her if she knew if her husband was in some kind of trouble before his arrest but she denied any knowledge of it. She has always maintained his innocence. Mary insists that on the night Tom was supposedly poaching on Sir Eustace's land, he was in fact aboard the Seabird with Sam."

"Did Lord Cullan know of this?"

"At the time of the trial, Lord Cullan was in London. Frant's evidence was dismissed by the court because of his friendship with Shaw and because Sir Eustace's keepers swore that Shaw was caught with the creature's blood upon his hands. He is supposed to have discarded the bird as soon as he realized they were on to him. The keepers found the bag containing the carcass, concealed in a hollow tree nearby."

"And the gun? He must presumably

have shot the creature?"

"Not a trace. But Sir Eustace's men claimed that Shaw had ample time to rid himself of the implements of his trade."

"What did Shaw say in his own defence?"

"He denied the charge completely. He told the court that he had been returning from Blakestone Bay where he and Sam Frant had moored the yacht after a night's fishing. As he returned home, he took a short-cut across Sir Eustace's land and upon entering the copse on the edge of Longacre field, a sack tied at the neck with string, dropped in his path. He looked about him to see who it was had tossed the bag down but could see nothing in the darkness. Wondering what it might be, he picked up the bag and felt something wet and sticky on his hands. The next thing he knew, the keepers were upon him with their dogs and he panicked. He sped off into the wood as fast as he could and stumbling across the hollow tree, he wedged the sack inside and ran on. The dogs caught up with him first, poor fellow and that sealed his fate."

"What of the night's fishing? Surely their catch would have proved his case?"

"Perhaps it might have established his whereabouts for part of the night. But whether it would have been helpful to his case is irrelevant. They had caught nothing all night. There was no proof that he had been fishing, only his and Sam's word for it."

"What sort of man is Tom Shaw, in your opinion, sir?"

"I thought him quite a likeable fellow. Not very talkative: kept himself to himself. He worked hard to provide for his family and was always willing to take on any task to earn enough for their bread. He told me he was determined that they should never have to 'go on the parish'. Tom had a fierce pride in his strength and ability to keep his wife and family from want."

"Did he always make his money honestly?"

Mr Stewart peered at the major over the top of his spectacles. "I assume you may have heard rumours of the smuggling that occurs all along this coast? Well, I daresay there is hardly an able-bodied man in the district who has not run such risks in order that he might supplement his meagre income. This long war has meant difficult times for the labouring man in these rural regions. It is only the people who own large areas of land who have continued to flourish." He smiled sympathetically at the major's droll look. "Men like Sir Eustace Newbury, for instance. Since so many of the villages have been enclosed, the poorer folk can no longer feed themselves but must hope to earn enough from their employers to enable them to buy their bread. Unfortunately, the price of corn is rising faster than their wages and more and more of them are being forced to seek parish relief. It is hard to condemn those who have turned to smuggling rather than see their families starve. Which of us can say that we would not be tempted to do the same in like circumstances?"

"Quite so, Mr Stewart. But there are some who do it for less worthy reasons and have no qualms about using violence against anyone who tries to prevent them. But I see that it grows late, I must not keep you any longer from your bed. Oh, just one more question if you would oblige me. What do you know about Daniel Prescott, the man you mentioned earlier, who mysteriously disappeared?"

"Ah, yes, that was a strange business. He and Sam Frant were seen together a few hours before poor Sam was drowned. They were at a tavern in Barhurst and, according to report, were engaged in a heated conversation. It had something to do with your brother's vessel. Prescott was heard to insist on being allowed to accompany Frant down to the bay where the yacht was moored. Frant refused him several times and an argument developed which finally ended with Frant leaving the premises alone. Prescott finished his drink and followed some minutes later. That was the last anyone ever saw of them."

"My curiosity craves to be satisfied, Mr Stewart. How I wish I could have had the chance to speak to Tom Shaw. Alas, he has been placed quite beyond my reach but I'll not let that deter me."

"Have a care then, Major Lacey," warned the rector. "It has occurred to me that this could be dangerous ground on which we are treading. You said yourself that there are those who are not averse to using extreme methods to gain their own ends."

The major seemed much struck by this observation. "You could be right, Mr Stewart," he mused absently, staring into the glass in his hand as if it might contain some vital clue to these mysteries.

"What are you thinking now?" prompted Mr Stewart gently.

"I was just considering the implications of your last remark. When I first arrived at Blakestone, I had not thought in those terms. I merely wished to satisfy myself that Lucius's death was just an unfortunate accident. But I have lately begun to wonder if my life is as much at risk here in England as it ever was in Spain. I can't explain exactly why that is so but since I came to live at Blakestone, I have had the strangest feeling that I am being watched and followed everywhere I go. Even tonight as I rode here, it seemed that some malevolent presence was dogging my heels . . . " He stopped and gave an apologetic smile. "Forgive me, sir, I am not usually given to such strange imaginings."

The rector eyed him thoughtfully. "I am sure you are not. In fact you strike me as a singularly level-headed young man. My advice to you is that you act upon these — shall we say warnings? — and keep your wits about you. And if ever you have need of help, remember that you may call upon me at any time."

"Thank you, sir. But let us hope that I am mistaken as well I maybe."

7

ON the day that Captain Rowland chose to visit Blakestone House, it was very far from being the bleak place that he had been led to envisage. It was a stiflingly hot afternoon and as he turned into the lane that curved up the hill, the sun was burning into his back. Perspiration trickled slowly down his spine and he ran a finger under the black stock wound about his neck, in a vain endeavour to get some air to his skin. His hand brushed against the silver gorget and sprang away again immediately, for it was like fire to the touch. He was beginning to feel as if he were back in Spain.

When he reached the beech wood, the leafy canopy above shielded him from the sun's fierce rays but it was scarcely cooler. Not a breath of wind stirred anywhere and the air lay thick and heavy beneath the silent boughs. Even the birds seemed drugged by the heat and dozed amid the branches, watching with one eye opened as horse and rider slowly paced through the crumbling leaves littered below.

He looked about him with great interest. How densely the trees were clustered on this lonely hillside. The road which he had left only a few minutes ago was already lost from sight. A whole battalion could remain hidden in these woods without fear of discovery; it was the perfect place to carry out an ambuscade.

Suddenly a horseman appeared on the path a few yards ahead of him, startling the captain from his reverie and instinctively he laid his hand on the pistol that hung from his saddle.

"Alex!" he exclaimed with a relieved laugh. "Must you burst upon me in that alarming fashion?"

"Did I take you by surprise?" smiled the major, as his old comrade thrust the pistol back into its leather case.

"Well, I haven't yet got used to the fact that I am now living in a peaceful country. I was just that moment thinking what an excellent spot this would be if I were planning to take the enemy unawares. Then you leapt out of nowhere."

"Not quite. This path does lead somewhere, believe it or not. It's rather overgrown admittedly, especially at this time of year but follow me and I'll show you the way." He turned his horse about and rode back along the path that, after about ten minutes, brought them within sight of the house.

"That's it, Hal. My new quarters. The ancient home of the Lacey family." The major nodded towards the broken walls of his inherited property. "What do you think of it?"

Captain Rowland looked dumbstruck. "It's . . . it's . . . er . . . picturesque."

Major Lacey grinned. "I'll settle for that, you need pay me no further compliments. Come, let me perform the duties of a host. I'll begin by finding you something to slake your thirst. You have had a long, hot ride from Shoreham."

"I'll not deny it. And who knows? By the time I've washed the dust from my throat, I may begin to see just why you find this place so attractive!"

They rode on towards the house and

as they came in sight of the west wing, Ned came out to meet them.

"It's been a good while since we last saw you, Captain Rowland. How are you, sir?"

"Pretty crisp, Ned," replied the captain cheerily as he swung himself down from his horse, "despite this intolerable heat. I must say you are looking as stout as ever."

"Never better, sir. Here, let me take the horses. You'll find something to drink over there on the terrace — if I can still call it that," he added disparagingly.

"Thank you, Ned. I suppose there's no chance that I might sample a glass of your special?" he enquired hopefully.

"I thought you'd find it a little on the warm side today for a bowl of the brew, sir. Far too hot in my opinion. A nice, cool jug of lemonade's what you'll be wanting. Isn't that right?"

Captain Rowland eyed him warily. "Lemonade?" he echoed faintly, a comical expression of doubt and dismay on his face.

"That's the very thing, eh Hal? 'Twill lay the dust at least. Ned and I drink little else these days, do we, Ned?" intervened the major bracingly.

"Oh, indeed, sir. We live very frugally now as you can see for yourself," averred Ned dolefully as he led the horses away.

"Of course, I suppose you must," murmured the captain, gamely hiding his true feelings for fear of embarrassing his friend. He cast another glance about him as he followed in the major's wake. Poor Alex! That he should be reduced to such straits! The place was practically derelict. And to be forced to serve lemonade to his guests was surely beyond enduring!

"Sit yourself down, Hal. You'll find it a little cooler on this side of the house. Oh, and watch your step, be careful of those broken bricks. That's it. Now here's your glass, drink up." The major handed him a tall glass brimming with a pale, sparkling liquid, then lifted his own glass in a toast. "Your health, Hal."

Captain Rowland, with a puzzled look, tasted his drink. He frowned and sipped a little more.

"I see you two have been having some sport with me," he said accusingly. "This

180

isn't lemonade at all. It's good French champagne!"

"The very best, Hal," laughed the major as he pulled up a chair and sat down in the shade. "We brought it back with us. Several cases, in fact."

"Trust you cavalry men to be invited to take the comfortable route home when the army disbanded," complained the captain. "You had an easy ride to Boulogne, feasting all the way. My poor foot soldiers tramped each long, weary mile to Bordeaux."

"I might have guessed you'd make straight for Bordeaux," laughed the major. "I'd lay odds that was the fastest march in the history of the infantry!" He lounged back in his chair. "Ah, what halcyon days — and nights — they were! Wine, women and song: with the compliments of King Louis. We revelled in it, I can tell you! We were feted in every town and village across southern France. Mmm . . . those beautiful dark-eyed m'amselles! You should have joined the cavalry, Hal."

"What?! Exchange my brave, scarlet coat for one belaced with more fripperies than a ballet dancer's petticoats? Never! Besides, the ladies, bless their lovely eyes, adore a gentleman in scarlet regimentals. Did you not see how Miss Stewart smiled at me the other evening?"

"Yes, I did, you lucky dog! But perhaps, if we were invited a second time to dine at the rectory, I shall try what a tunic, resplendent with fripperies, can do to win such delightful favours."

"Oh no, my friend. This time the cavalry has come too late to the field: the prize has gone to the gallant infantry. You will have to see what you can do to capture the little redhead. I am sure you cannot be impervious to her charms."

"The Maytland girl? You speak of charms? Hmph! I must needs wear several about my neck if ever I should get within arm's length of her!"

"Do you not admire her?" asked the captain in genuine astonishment. "She is a bright, vivacious girl in my opinion. I imagined that you two would get along famously."

"If you had not been so intent upon encouraging Miss Stewart's smiles, you might have realized that vivacity was notably lacking on our side of the dining-table. I have seen more animation in one of Mr Maillardet's mechanical curiosities. I should rather have had one of those as a dinner partner. At least I could have derived some amusement from the experience and certainly enjoyed as much conversation."

"Dear me! What a rare bird the young lady must be! The first woman who has failed to respond to Alexander Lacey's famous Irish blarney!" mocked the captain, feigning amazement.

"Oh, she responded, Hal, believe me! But not favourably, it has to be said. Yet, I find we are in accord on one important issue: she dislikes me as much as I dislike her!"

"Why have you taken her in such aversion? What has she done to deserve your disapprobation?"

"I find it difficult to feel a fondness for a woman who has not only levelled insults at my head but a pistol as well," replied the major frankly.

"What do you mean?!" exclaimed Captain Rowland, sitting bolt upright in his seat and staring at his friend in astonishment.

"Oh, yes, Hal. Lady Elisa has some charming arts. I've yet to discover why she has used them on me but I hope to solve that mystery when she and I are better acquainted. Meanwhile, keep this to yourself, there's a good fellow."

"I will if I must but you can't leave it there! Tell me everything."

The major briefly described the events that had taken place in the woodland on the morning of his ride with Mr Clifton.

"Are you quite certain it was Lady Elisa?" frowned the captain. "Perhaps her presence at the cottage was merely coincidental."

"Whoever lay in wait for me that day was of a very light build: I could see that from the condition of the ground. Also, a horse had been tethered to a branch beside the broken stump of a tree, which indicated that the rider had need of a mounting block: usually a woman's requirement. Then while we were at the stream, I noticed that the grass showed signs of having been recently trampled and I followed that track directly to Mrs Shaw's cottage."

"That could be explained, surely? If Lady Elisa freely admitted that she had been riding through the woods, she might well have approached the cottage from that direction."

"Very well; I'll admit that there is a slight chance that someone else could have been in the vicinity at the same time, though I have my doubts."

"But why should she have done it? What possible reason could there be?"

"I don't know. In fact, when I saw her at the rectory the other evening, I had convinced myself that I must be mistaken: that her presence at the cottage was purely by chance. It all seemed so preposterous. Why should she wish to harm me? We don't care for each other, it's true, but that's hardly a reason to put a bullet in me. And yet she is such an odd creature: her mood changes so swiftly. When she was sitting in the orchard at the rectory that night, I was sure that she smiled at me as if she meant to say something pleasant for once. However, as she drew near me, her expression altered and the Devil seemed to be at her shoulder again. The smile became a scowl even before a word was exchanged."

"Well, she did tell me she had a sudden temper but I refuse to believe her capable of attempting to murder you."

"All the same, I mean to keep my wits about me when I find myself in solitary places. The rector told me a disturbing tale that has much occupied my thoughts since I left his house."

"Indeed?" remarked the captain, his curiosity aroused. "This begins to sound more and more intriguing. You really must explain."

"Then I had better tell you all that I have discovered from the moment of my arrival in London."

Captain Rowland listened with growing interest as the story unfolded. When the major finally finished speaking, Rowland gave a low whistle.

"What an extraordinary business! I must say I find it all rather fascinating. So many unanswered questions. What will you do now?"

"I mean to start looking for some

answers, my friend."

"But where will you begin? All your principal players are gone."

"True, alas. But I shall not allow that to deter me. I shall commence by asking my sister-in-law some questions. She might know something that will at least give me a clue to this mystery."

"Well, if there's anything I can do to help, you have only to ask."

"My thanks, Hal. As a matter of fact, there is something you might be able to do for me. I have been wondering if there was a particular reason for Tom Shaw's being kept in solitary confinement during the period of his imprisonment. The rector said no one was permitted to visit him, not even the man's own wife. Do you think you could make some discreet enquiries when you get back to Shoreham? Perhaps someone may recall the event: it was only three years ago."

"He was held at Shoreham was he?" mused the captain thoughtfully. "Then I think I shall have a word with Sergeant Roach; I understand he has often escorted prisoners to and from the courts. I'm certain he told me that he had been carrying out his duties in Shoreham for some five years. I'll see what I can discover. Now, in return, you can tell me something. Do you happen to know a gentleman called Sir Harry Palmer? He lives not far from here, just the other side of Barhurst village, at High Dean."

"Harry Palmer? Well, I don't know him exactly but I have met him. It was the day after my arrival at Blakestone. He and his brother rode over to welcome me — with a horsewhip!" chuckled the major, relishing the memory. "We had a bit of a skirmish and I haven't set eyes on either of them since."

The captain laughed gaily. "I ought to have known! But one day in the county and you must be at your brawling! I'll swear you enjoy tapping the claret as much as I enjoy drinking it. Did you plant them both a facer?"

"No, they proved to be poor sport, alas! But why are you interested in them?"

"Well, you are aware of the reason for my presence in Sussex? I have been appointed to aid the Riding Officers in their efforts to prevent contraband being landed on these shores. When my predecessor handed over to me, he told me that the Revenue men had sighted several smuggling vessels along this stretch of coast over the last few years. Unfortunately they have little chance of catching them; these smuggling ships are designed for speed. They are carvel-built with pine planks, much lighter and sleeker than the oak Revenue cutters and their other advantage is their greater firing power. Our only hope of stamping out the trade is to seize the goods when they are landed. However, that is not an easy task either. It is virtually impossible to determine where the landing points will be until it is too late. Someone based here on shore is able to signal the incoming ship and bring her into safe waters. Once the contraband has been unloaded, it is got quickly away before the Preventives are able to come up with them. Now, in order to effect such a rapid escape, a large number of pack animals is required. The only people in this area who could supply these horses would be farmers — or landowners. A few months ago, one of the Riding Officers came unexpectedly upon a party of smugglers as they were transporting their ill-gotten gains along a dark country lane. He was overpowered and knocked unconscious. When he regained his senses, he found himself tied across the back of one of the horses in the caravan. In the light of the early dawn, he could see that this horse had a wound on its right shoulder. He also noticed that the right foreleg had a patch of white hair on the fetlock. Luckily for him, the horses, when they had been stripped of their loads, were left in the care of a youth and it was he who eventually released the officer in some remote spot far from habitation. The poor man was left to walk several miles to the nearest village, his arms still tied behind him. Afterwards, by the greatest stroke of good luck and a deal of perseverance, he came upon that same horse at the smithy in Barhurst. He enquired of the blacksmith as to the name of the owner and was informed that the horse had been brought in by one of Sir Harry Palmer's grooms. When Palmer was later questioned about the matter, he grew quite violent and threatened to have the officer dismissed from his post."

"I can well believe it," smiled the major. "I thought him an evil-tempered bully and regretted that he should have broken his nose so easily, without the least effort on my part."

"So you did manage to tap his claret?" grinned Captain Rowland. "I thought as much!"

"No, it really was an accident. He did it while I was helping him from his horse," explained the major innocently.

"You mentioned a horsewhip, I think?" remarked the captain. "What did you mean?"

"Well, for some cause or other, the fellow took exception to my presence here. He seemed rather eager for me to take myself off again. Though in fairness I ought to mention that he didn't know who I was at the time. If you want to learn more about him, why don't you enquire of your charming Lady Elisa Maytland? She seems to be very well acquainted with the Palmers. She was with them on that occasion and appeared to be as desirous as they for my immediate removal."

"They are her near neighbours, I suppose. I daresay they might have thought you were trespassing on the property. However, I think I shall keep a close watch on those two gentlemen, especially on dark, moonless nights. Now who is this? I think you have another visitor, Alex."

Lacey glanced over his shoulder to see Ned coming towards them with a tall gentleman following close behind him. He got to his feet and went to meet them.

"Good afternoon, Sir Eustace. What an unexpected pleasure," greeted the major politely. "Captain Rowland and I were just enjoying a glass of champagne. Will you not join us?"

"Thank you, Major Lacey," replied Sir Eustace willingly, "I should be delighted."

"Ned, bring another glass would you? Please take a seat, Sir Eustace, while I fetch a chair for myself."

He rejoined them after a minute or two and sat down beside Sir Eustace. "Ah, I see Ned has filled your glass. Our hospitality may seem decidedly primitive but the wine I need not be ashamed of: your health, Sir Eustace."

When they had drunk the toast, the major set aside his glass saying, "Now what brings you to Blakestone House on such a sultry afternoon?"

"You correctly surmise that I have undertaken the journey for a purpose other than the promotion of neighbourly feeling," answered Sir Eustace after sampling the champagne. "I am come on a matter of business, which I dare to think may be advantageous to us both. It has not escaped my notice that you live in somewhat insalubrious style," he murmured deprecatingly, casting a critical eye over the rubble that lay scattered all about the place. "It is this circumstance that leads me to suppose that you may well be amenable to the suggestion that you sell your interest in the property. If this should indeed be the case, then I am here to make you a handsome offer for the entire estate. What do you say to that, sir?"

"I am very grateful for your interest, Sir Eustace, but I have to consider very carefully before I take such a drastic step. I may yet find some value in the place."

Sir Eustace's pale eyes narrowed sharply. "Indeed? You amaze me. I should suppose there is nothing left here of any value to you whatsoever," he continued, watching the major with a cold, unblinking stare.

"That depends entirely upon one's point of view. My conception of what is valuable may be quite distinct from yours."

"I doubt it, Major Lacey. I imagine our opinions on that particular subject would lead us to the exact same conclusions. Perhaps I ought to mention that your late brother reposed a great deal of confidence in my judgement. We bankers are rather like physicians, you know. We become intimately acquainted with our clients whenever any ill befalls them. All their symptoms are revealed to us and we are then required to make a prognosis. I think I may say without fear of contradiction, that I have become quite an expert in that field of 'medicine'. You really will have to sell sooner or later, as I am sure you do not need me to tell you. My offer still stands but do not wait too long to give me your answer. Now that the war is over, I anticipate that there will be a considerable fall in the price of land. You will do well to heed my warning. Do you understand me?"

"Perfectly, thank you. Naturally I shall give the matter some thought. But may I remind you that you are not my 'physician', Sir Eustace, and can know nothing of my expectations. I have no fears for my health in the immediate future, so you need not concern yourself."

"I can only wonder at your confidence, Major," he replied slowly and deliberately, eyes as watchful as a snake about to strike. "I hope such self-assurance is based on something more substantial than mere bravado."

The major met his look challengingly. "It is very firmly founded, sir, on one very sure commodity, have no doubt about that. Is that all you have to say to me?"

Sir Eustace stiffened suddenly, the pale features grew strangely livid and his eyes burned in the shadowed, hollow sockets.

He gradually mastered whatever emotion had caused such an odd disturbance of complexion and twisted his lips into a grim replica of a smile. "There is one other matter that I would wish to make clear to you. It occurred to me quite recently that you were perhaps unaware that Lady Cullan and I are not merely neighbours but dear and intimate friends. Indeed, it is my intention to make her my wife. I but await her convenience before publicly announcing the happy news of our betrothal. I think that concludes my business. Good afternoon to you, Major Lacey. Adieu, Captain Rowland." He uncoiled his spare, almost cadaverous frame from the chair and took up his hat. "Do not trouble to call your servant, he is no doubt still engaged in attending to my horses. I will find my own way to my carriage."

As soon as he had turned the corner of the building, the captain threw an amused glance in his friend's direction. "Well, Alex, it seems to me that you have succeeded in alienating every one of your neighbours in less than one month. First Lady Elisa and the Palmers and now Sir Eustace Newbury. Whatever happened to the legendary Hibernian charm? Or is it only the rough soldiery who can appreciate that devil-may-care quality that endeared you to them? Now, don't glare at me like that, Alex, I am only quizzing you! I've no desire to goad you into throwing your castors. I rather like the natural arrangement of my features."

"I'm sorry, Hal, I'm not angry with you. It's that impudent fellow whose lights I should like to darken!"

"I didn't know he was engaged to your sister-in-law. Though I wouldn't be surprised to hear that she was to be married again. She's an absolute stunner! A diamond of the first water."

"And too sweet a girl to espouse herself to that supercilious vulture! She'll be furious when she hears of this. She isn't engaged to him, or anyone else for that matter. She's still in mourning for her husband. She told me herself that she cannot give her heart to another man while she still grieves for Lucius. What insufferable insolence to make such a claim! I've a good mind to call him out!"

"Whoa! Just a moment, my hot-headed friend! Not so hasty. It's all very well to quarrel with your neighbours, most people do, it's a universal *raison d'être*. But you are contemplating murder! Sir Eustace is old enough to be your father and looks in remarkably ill-health to me. So go and take a damper, that's my advice. That fighting spirit of yours is all very fine on the battlefield but remember we are now in the peaceful meadows of merry England. It won't serve you well here."

"Don't concern yourself, I shan't kill him: as much as I'd like to! You're right though. There is no place for me here. As soon as I have solved this mystery surrounding Lucius's death, I'm off again. Perhaps I'll go to America. Some of your infantry regiments have been sent there. I may change my coat for a scarlet one. What do you think?"

"I think you're a fool, Alex. You should be thanking God that you have come home safe again: we all should. There are thousands who didn't. We've got a second chance to do something else with our lives other than fighting to the death. I certainly don't mean to soldier on for the rest of my days. The moment I can get my hands on my inheritance, I'm selling out of the army. That's why I have taken this posting. I have no desire to fight the Americans when I am on the verge of gaining my own independence. I've had my *victoire de gloire* and now I'm for settling down at my own fireside with a pretty little wife to bear me company. Who knows? I might even set up a platoon of Rowland's Own Infantry."

"You forgot to mention your wine cellar," reminded the major with the glimmer of a smile.

"So I did. Well, perhaps I'll first lay down a good cellar and then set up my nursery."

"That's if your wife has no objection to sharing a house with the other love of your life."

"I shall be sure to choose one who is prepared to be accommodating. I suggest you do the same."

"Don't imagine I haven't given it some thought, especially since I came here. But I don't hold out much hope of a happy ending to my daydreams. They are of the impossible kind," replied the major broodingly.

"Ah! So that's the way the wind blows is it?" murmured Captain Rowland, eyeing his friend sympathetically. "No wonder you did not wish Sir Eustace joy."

"Nor will I — ever!" he scowled blackly.

"Perhaps it is time to tell the lady exactly how you feel, before it is too late?" suggested the captain seriously.

"She already knows how I feel. Has known for years. You see, Hal, I once asked her to be my wife."

"Oh, I see. Well then, I can understand your feelings. You will not wish to place yourself in such a position again. I can't say that I blame you."

"You credit me with too much sensibility. I should not hesitate to ask her again if I thought there was the slightest chance that she would accept me. But she has made it abundantly clear that she wishes only for my friendship. She entertains no stronger emotion for me, alas. My brother still holds all her affections even from beyond the grave." He gave a low, mirthless laugh. "I do believe that champagne is making me maudlin! There's a lot more to life than mere loving."

"Yes, but there's nothing more worthwhile as I think you'd soon discover. Don't let one disappointment blind you to that fact. You're only eight and twenty, Alex. You haven't yet experienced all that life has to offer, so don't throw in the towel."

"Not I! You know me, I'll always come up to the mark, come what may," answered the major briskly, seeming to shake off his melancholy as he tossed down the last of the champagne. "Now, you've had the dust laid, so let me show you just how beautiful Blakestone really is. Come, follow me and I'll give you a different view of things."

"I'm entirely at your disposal and feeling decidedly mellow, so point out Paradise by all means," acquiesced the captain happily.

As they walked along, carefully avoiding the many obstacles strewn all about, the captain gave a grimace. "I hope you spoke the truth to Newbury just now, Alex. This place needs a great deal of money spent on it. What was that sure commodity you referred to so confidently?"

The major laughed. "That? Oh, I was naturally referring to one Alexander Lacey, his unfailing confidence in himself. That was just a bit of blarney to put that supercilious old Devil in his place."

"Well, it certainly put him out of countenance. I thought he was about to have an apoplexy."

"Yes, I thought so too. I must have got right under his skin with that remark. I daresay he is too used to having his own way."

By this time they had reached the corner of the house and the major directed him to look to his feet as the ground was uneven and scattered with stones and blackened timbers. Then, clambering over a pile of rubble, he turned to lend a hand to his friend. "Where in heaven's name are you taking me?" demanded the captain as he scrambled up after him.

"Save your breath, Hal. You will need

it for the climb. Up with you!"

They began to ascend a twisting stone staircase set inside a circular tower. The rough-hewn steps were lit by long, narrow apertures set at intervals in the outer wall and through which could be caught glimpses of the surrounding woodland. When at last they reached the top, the captain found himself high above ground level and standing on a platform of very thick stone about twelve feet in diameter. A crenellated wall encircled the platform and leaning against this parapet, he saw spread before him a breathtaking patchwork of meadows and woods, threaded through with the curling blue river that shone like a smooth satin ribbon tossed carelessly down in their midst. Then out and up swept his gaze, to the wide, open Downs and the gleaming, white chalk slopes that skirted the bay. The sea was a glittering sapphire that melted into the misty haze of the horizon until water became vapour and vapour, soft, azure sky.

"What a magnificent view!" cried the captain appreciatively. "I can see for miles!"

"Wonderful, isn't it?" enthused Lacey, resting beside him. "That's Seaford Head you can see there and over that way lies Eastbourne."

"This is certainly a superb vantage point," remarked the captain walking around the whole circumference, admiring each new aspect.

"That's probably why my ancestors chose this particular site. This part of the house was built in the days when invasion by sea was a common occurrence."

"It must have been useful in this latest war, when England was under threat of the French invaders. I wonder if it was to be used as a beacon? I know there are several along this coastline. Dieppe is none so far from here, just a few hours away in a fast ship."

He began to look about him for some sign of a brazier having been set there. There was nothing now to indicate that the tower had served any useful purpose in recent times, just a heap of bricks piled against the wall beside the staircase.

"What are these bricks for, Alex? Are they kept here for you to hurl down upon your disgruntled neighbours?"

"They might be. Let me look," he smiled, crouching down to examine them and idly picking up a few then tossing them aside. "They seem to be scorched, so must have been brought up here from another part of the house; the fire never got this far. What's this?" He reached down to touch a black substance spilt on the floor of the tower and rubbed it between his fingers. "I thought so. This is oil. I wonder how that came about?"

"Maybe it is a gruesome reminder of the times when your ruthless forebears used to pour boiling oil upon their visitors," grinned the captain, bending down on one knee beside him and inspecting the dark stain on the stone-work. "You're right. It is oil and spilt quite recently, too, by my guess."

"From a cauldron freshly brewed, no doubt? Well, don't look at me. I may have quarrelled with my neighbours but I haven't declared war on them."

"I'm glad to hear it. But there must be a plausible explanation. Why would anyone take the trouble to bring all these bricks up here?" pondered the captain.

"Perhaps this tower was used as a

look-out point during the war," the major suggested helpfully.

"Possibly. This is oil from a lamp and a lamp lit here at dead of night would be seen for miles."

The major straightened himself and wiped his fingers on his handkerchief. "Now what are you thinking in that suspicious mind of yours?"

The captain stood up and looked out over the sea, his brow wrinkled thoughtfully. "I was merely speculating. You must admit there is something a little odd about this."

"I do think it strange that someone should bother to carry heavy bricks up those steep stairs. But it could be just by chance that they have been placed on this particular spot. Why should anyone take such trouble to cover a patch of oil?"

"Someone who did not wish it to be known that a lantern had been brought up here I should imagine. Suppose that a ship was waiting out there to receive a signal that would bring her safely in to shore. This tower would be extremely convenient for such a purpose, would it not?"

"Do you mean to suggest that my house is being used by a band of smugglers?" laughed the major, highly amused.

"If it was used for that purpose," continued the captain unperturbed by his friend's humorous view of the situation, "then your sudden appearance at Blakestone would be seen as very inconvenient. You said that the Palmers were most insistent that you leave immediately."

"Are you seriously expecting me to believe that Elisa Maytland and the Palmer brothers are a gang of villainous smugglers?" laughed the major, giving way to his amusement. "Is that why she shot at me?"

"Of course not. But I think you are mistaken in believing it was she who shot at you. I think it may have been her presence in the wood that saved your life. Your assailant probably fled when he heard her approach."

"Saved my life?" scoffed the major. "She would sooner have helped him load the pistol for a second shot!"

"You are being unfair, I'm sure.

However, I doubt that she was aware of the murderous attempt on your life; she probably thought the shot was fired by a gamekeeper as she implied and took no notice. Alex, I want you to be extremely vigilant from now on. This may be just an odd fancy I have taken into my head but I don't think you should ignore my warning. I have a strange feeling that Blakestone House may hide a great many secrets."

8

AT the earliest opportunity, Major Lacey rode over to Dovecote Hall intent upon seeing Aurelia alone. He was shown into the drawing-room where he found Lady Elisa awaiting him.

"Good afternoon, Major Lacey. I understand that you wish to see Lady Cullan?"

"I had hoped to find her at home," he admitted coolly, "but if she is gone out I shall not wait. I will call again at a more convenient moment."

"There is no need for you to hurry away, Major," smiled Elisa blandly. "I do not mean to inflict my company upon you. As a matter of fact, I was just about to go out myself. Aurelia is resting but I shall inform her of your arrival."

"Please don't disturb her. Another time will serve as well. My business will keep for another day."

"Of course you will not disturb her,

Major Lacey," insisted Elisa sweetly. "Aurelia will be quite rested by now and I am certain she will be utterly inconsolable if I should allow you to depart without seeing her. I shall not know how to comfort her."

"Really?" he replied dryly. "Inconsolable, you say? In that case of course I cannot consider leaving. I would not wish to render her distraught nor you distracted."

"I had not believed you capable of such consideration! But I am ready to be astonished. As to my being driven to distraction, you need not concern yourself. I am well acquainted with Aurelia's histrionics, it is I who must frequently give audience to them and I have long since ceased to be impressed."

"Speaking of consideration, I believe you mentioned that your departure was imminent? I would not wish to detain you."

"So I did and so it is. I shall send Aurelia to you directly, Major," she promised, her eyes sparkling with amusement and with that she whirled gaily out of the door.

He sighed in exasperation as she disappeared from view. If ever a child were in need of discipline, it was that one! Not that she was a child exactly, despite her childish behaviour but that was probably the result of having an over-indulgent parent who chose to absent himself indefinitely from his only daughter. Well, was that to be marvelled at? Who would not wish to distance himself from such an ungovernable romp? Where was Maytland hiding himself anyway? Did not Aurelia mention South America? "If she were my daughter, I should wish myself at the South Pole," he muttered beneath his breath as he idly turned the pages of an album lying open on a side table. The book contained several fine watercolours and some excellent sketches executed by a skilful hand. One page in particular caught his interest. Here, depicted in soft washes of blue and green, was a view of the coastline precise in every detail, just as he and Captain Rowland had observed it from the top of the tower. He looked for the artist's signature and found the initials

'E.M.' neatly inserted at the bottom right-hand corner of the page. So she was in the habit of climbing the tower, was she? Perhaps there was a simple explanation for the spilt oil after all? She might have taken a lantern up there to light herself back down the stairway. But why bother carrying bricks up all those steps? Or had someone else done that?

His musings were interrupted by Aurelia as she quietly entered the room with all the dignity that was so lacking in the girl who had just left it.

"Alex, I'm sorry to have kept you waiting. I did not expect to see you here today. I thought you would be busy with the estate. Mr Clifton tells me that you have set some work in hand."

"Did I disturb you? Lady Elisa was certain you would be pleased to see me. And I dared to hope you might."

"Not at all, you know I am always happy to receive you. Won't you please sit down?"

Gracefully she seated herself on the *chaise-longue*, leaning an elbow on the scrolled armrest and holding out a hand to him as he came towards her. He pressed her fingers to his lips and gazed rapturously down at her exquisite countenance. She blushed prettily and her long, curling lashes veiled those brilliant eyes.

"Don't look at me like that, Alex," she murmured softly. "It quite breaks my heart, you know."

"Does it? I should not wish ever to cause you pain, Aurelia and yet if I can make you feel something for me, I cannot completely regret it."

He sat beside her, admiring her perfect profile as she silently turned away from him. Then, with her face still averted, she said calmly, "I told you how it is with me, Alex. I esteem you greatly but I cannot pretend a deeper emotion. Please do not hope for me to change my mind on this subject, I will never do so."

"Is it because you still love Lucius — or because you have accepted Sir Eustace Newbury's offer of marriage?" he asked with unexpected asperity.

She stiffened suddenly and slowly faced him, pale but outwardly composed. "Did he tell you that? Yes, I see that he did. I suppose he fears you mean to snatch me from his grasp?" She gave a scornful laugh. "Well, I am not yet his property, despite his ambitions."

"Then you are not engaged?"

"No, I am not. I have told him that I cannot agree to it while I still grieve for Lucius."

"Surely you told him that you can never agree to it?!"

"I ought to have done so but I confess I did not." She bit her lip and eyed him anxiously, "Now you are angry with me but you do not understand. How could you? You are a man and can do whatever you wish and go wherever you choose to go. It is different for me. I am forced to remain here and conform to the dictates of society. I must be a respectable widow. Do you know what that means, Alex? It means that in future I must sit with the dowagers, wear a cap, drape myself in purple and black and never have any enjoyment at all!"

"But you can go back to London. You don't have to stay in the country. I said I would help you find somewhere to live and I meant it."

"Some dingy little house in Cheapside?

No, I thank you! Oh, it's no use, Alex! You could never enter into my feelings. You don't know what my life was like before all this happened! I was someone then: I had an enviable position in society. How can I go back to London and be nothing? I couldn't bear it! You don't realize how people will gloat when they know what misfortune has overtaken me. They would enjoy sneering at me, whispering and laughing — and what is even worse they would delight in giving me the cut direct!"

"Well, people who behaved like that would not be worth knowing anyway. Your real friends would always be civil to you. They are the people whose society you would seek and take pleasure in."

Aurelia turned her shoulder petulantly. "I said you wouldn't understand. You never really cared for the excitement of London society, so how can I expect you to appreciate just how much I have had to give up? If I married Sir Eustace I could have it all again."

"Do you love him?" he asked bluntly.

"No, of course I do not! How could I? I have told you that I shall never love anyone but Lucius. If I cared for Sir Eustace at all I would not even think of becoming his wife, not while I feel as I do. But he doesn't love me either: he only wants to buy me. I am to be another exhibit to place in his house along with the paintings and handsome furnishings. So you see, we should both gain something from our marriage."

"Could you really pay the price that such a union would demand? I cannot believe you would make such a choice!"

"Only a man may speak of choice!" she snapped. "A woman has not that freedom. I have but a single question to answer — 'what is my alternative?' In either case the cost to me is great. The one thing I cannot afford is to let opportunity pass me by. Whatever decision I make, it must be mine and mine alone."

"You desire me to be silent on this subject? Very well, it shall be as you wish. I see that I have no influence with you. I am merely sorry for my presumption," said he irascibly and rose to his feet. "I shall not keep you any longer, I am sure you would prefer me to go."

"Please don't think too badly of me, Alex," she begged, "I do not want to quarrel with you. Please try to understand. You are my very dear friend and it means a great deal to me that you have offered me your friendship. I wouldn't want that to be spoiled now or ever. It is because I value you so much that I have been at pains to explain my feelings to you. Sir Eustace has been very kind to me, has long been one of my most sincere and constant admirers. Now why do you scowl at me in that horrid fashion? It really is most unfair of you. You told me yourself that you had wished me to believe you were killed and so I did. You cannot expect that I should have made no plans at all for the future. After all, you are aware of my situation: what was I supposed to do? I am alone in the world and have no one else to turn to, I must look to my own resources."

Her eyes were brimming now with tears that slowly began to spill on to the soft curve of her pale cheeks and suddenly he felt a dreadful remorse. He sat down again and tried to comfort her but she turned her back on him and leaning her head on her forearms, sobbed uncontrollably.

"Aurelia, Aurelia," he murmured, deeply moved by her obvious distress, "please don't cry like that! I am an insensitive brute to have judged you so harshly. I did not intend to hurt you. What a stiff-necked fool you must think me! It is I who am at fault. I have no right to speak as I did. Of course you must do as you think best. I ought not to have tried to interfere in your life, it is none of my business. Please forgive me and dry your eyes. I am so very, very sorry."

"Then you aren't angry any more?" she asked in a tremulous voice.

"No, it was just that I have taken Newbury in dislike and I allowed that to goad my temper."

"Are you jealous of him, Alex? There's no need to be, truly. I am grateful for his kindness but I don't love him in the least."

"That is what makes the thought of your marrying him so hard to bear," he said grimly. "But I promise to say no more on that head. Come, let us shake hands like the good friends we are and let the matter rest."

He held out his hand and she placed hers in it. "I am glad we are friends again, Alex. I do so hate to quarrel. It makes me feel dreadfully out of sorts for days."

"I would not upset you for worlds. Please try to put it out of your mind. I swear I won't mention the matter again. I never intended to flare up at you like that."

She smiled pityingly at him. "Oh, Alex, you haven't changed so very much after all. You still think you are able to bring the world to heel by sheer strength of will. Some things cannot be altered. You remind me of those waves out there, continuously hurling themselves at the rocks. But it is they who break over and over again before they are dragged forcibly away. Don't waste your efforts in such fruitless endeavours."

"You need not worry. I do not mean to force myself upon you."

"That was not my meaning. I have done my best for you, now let us talk of something else."

"Willingly. Perhaps we could speak of

Lucius: there is a subject of which I am sure you will never tire," he retorted, unable to hide the trace of bitterness in his voice.

"Lucius? What more is there to be said? He is dead. Life moves on whether we wish it or no. It has no respect for feelings."

"There is much still to be said. I have refrained from asking you too many questions before because, as I have already told you, I do not like to cause you pain. But one of the reasons why I came to Blakestone is to learn all I can of the events that led to my brother's death. Was he in some kind of difficulty before the night of the fire?"

She sighed deeply. "Very well, if you must know all. Naturally he was greatly distressed by the financial ruin with which we were faced but he told me that he had one or two schemes in mind for effecting our rescue. We were not completely insolvent, you know."

"What schemes?"

"I have not the least notion. Lucius never explained them to me. He was a very considerate husband: he never bothered me with such tedious details. He always assured me that there was nothing to fear, that he had everything in hand and that we should soon come about. I trusted him implicitly."

"I am glad to hear that he felt so optimistic. Though for the life of me I cannot imagine how he managed it. I wish I shared his secret."

"What do you mean? What secret?" she demanded instantly.

"Why, the secret of his optimism in the face of such obvious disaster. I stand now in his shoes and can see no cause for hope of any kind. Did he not confide in you at all?"

"I have already said: I knew nothing of his plans. I have no head for business, such things bore me to distraction."

"What connection had he with Tom Shaw?"

"Tom Shaw? What has he to do with anything?"

"Lucius knew him quite well, I believe."

"Have you been talking to Elisa? Don't heed her nonsense! She and the Shaws are as thick as thieves.

Her friendship with that family has done nothing for her reputation in this neighbourhood. She disgraces her father's name by championing their cause. Everyone knows what sort of people they are! Lucius occasionally employed Shaw to help when he took the *Seabird* for a voyage along the coast. Sam Frant recommended him for his sailing skills, that is all. We had nothing else to do with him."

"What did you mean when you said that Lady Elisa is championing their cause?"

"She is spreading the lie that Sir Eustace has been unjust. She is constantly maligning his character, trying to destroy his good reputation among the populace and openly speaking against him to anyone foolish enough to listen."

"Of what does she accuse him?"

"Of having wrongfully arrested Shaw. She has the temerity to suggest that the evidence against him was fabricated by Sir Eustace's own men. Though why they should bother to do so she fails to explain! As if a man of Sir Eustace's standing in the county would trouble himself with the likes of Tom Shaw, except in the role of magistrate!"

"I believe I recall your saying that Shaw was a free-trader. You seemed certain of it."

"Yes, that is why I disapproved of Lucius's decision to employ him aboard the yacht. The man is of an ill reputation and I could not be easy knowing that Lucius had put himself at risk."

"At risk? Why should he be at risk?"

"Because the fellow was untrustworthy. How could I be anything but anxious knowing that Lucius had such a man with him when he put to sea? I was glad when Shaw was taken away. I did not like him."

"He seems to have been harmless enough, according to Mr Stewart. And while it is in my mind, I should like to know if Lucius had any dealings with a man called Daniel Prescott."

Her face grew pale and she dropped her gaze to her hands gripped tightly in her lap. "I don't know anything about the man except that he was of Shaw's ilk. I tell you these people are malevolent creatures, they make me feel afraid. Who knows what dreadful crimes they are prepared to commit?" She shuddered and wrapped her arms about herself as if she were cold. "They are unspeakably evil," she ended in an almost inaudible whisper. For a moment she seemed occupied with some dark thought but looked up suddenly and stared intently at the major's face. "Why do you ask me all these questions? Why are you so interested in Tom Shaw? Surely you cannot suppose he had anything to do with Lucius's death?"

"No, how should I? I merely wish to know something of him. You yourself made some mention of Shaw when we visited the Dower House and I have spoken to his wife. She is one of my tenants: her cottage is quite close to Blakestone. Mr Clifton made some reference to Shaw when he told me of the fate of the *Seabird*. I became curious to know more of that unhappy incident. Does it not appear to be a strange coincidence that such a catalogue of catastrophe should occur all at once?"

"I do not consider Shaw's punishment a catastrophe for any but his own family.

As to the rest, it is all very tragic but trouble often comes in company. We must bear with it as best we can. It seldom remains in one place for long."

"I am happy you are able to view your situation in that light. Now may I crave your indulgence for a moment more? I would like to know what Lucius was doing alone in the house on that night. Why did he not go to the wedding feast with you?"

"He had meant to accompany me," she answered, "but he had been out all day trying to discover what had happened to the *Seabird*. She had disappeared from her moorings the night before and he was worried that something dreadful might have happened to Sam Frant. He arrived back at the house late in the evening having discovered the awful fate of the yacht and her captain. He told me to tell no one until the wedding celebrations were over and sent me on ahead to Barhurst with apologies for his absence."

She halted in the telling of the tale and closed her eyes as if in pain. "I'm sorry, Alex. I don't want to think of it. Lucius here all alone and after such a terrible shock . . . his face so pale and drawn . . . I ought never to have left him!" She pressed a hand to her eyes and moved away from him. "I'm . . . I'm feeling a little tired now. Can we talk of this at another time? I think I'll go to my room, will you excuse me?"

"Certainly. It is time I went home. Thank you for bearing so patiently with all my questions. I hope you will understand why I had to know? Oh, one more thing I ought perhaps to mention to you. I also have received an offer from Sir Eustace — he wants to buy the estate."

"Indeed? And have you accepted his terms?" she enquired in a tight, subdued tone. "No doubt they are extremely lucrative?"

"I did not invite him to name them. I have told him I will think about it. Though I doubt there is much value in Blakestone land these days, certainly not enough to cover my brother's remaining debts. So you see, we are not so very differently situated, are we? We two must consider our future in the light of opportunity. I hope we both make

226

the right decision."

Having taken his leave of her, the major rode homewards, his mind very much occupied with the thoughts arising from this disappointing interview with his sister-in-law. He could scarcely bring himself to accept the fact that she was seriously contemplating becoming Sir Eustace's wife. How could she even consider it? The man was old enough to be her father! If she had fallen in love with him it might have been easier to understand but by her own confession that was not the case.

It appalled him to think that she of all people should find herself in such extremes that she needs must commit herself to so hideous a course. If only Lucius had managed his affairs more wisely! He had not taken his brother for such a prodigious fool. How could he have been so ill-advised as to squander a small fortune in so short a time? Really, it was too bad of him. He ought to have had more consideration for his wife and the privileged position he held. The fortunes of all the people living on this estate were entirely dependent on the landlord's good husbandry and yet it appeared that Lucius had not made the slightest effort to make any improvements at all. Nothing had been done since the death of their father.

The major heaved a deep sigh of exasperation. This was a damnable situation to be in and he could not help wishing himself well out of it. At least he had felt of some use in Spain. His duty then had been clear and simple and he had performed it with zeal but now . . .

He cast a weary eye over the surrounding acres of his property. Clifton was in the right of it: these fields were in desperate need of proper cultivation. If the soil were improved and the new ploughing methods adopted, they ought to be able to increase the yield tenfold. But where was the use in making idle plans? There was not enough money left in the family coffers to make any great changes here. It was a depressing thought but it seemed that the only course open to him was to accept Sir Eustace's offer with good grace and have done with it all. It was odd that Aurelia had not pressed him to do so.

But she had not looked or sounded in the least bit delighted with this answer to their financial difficulties.

Surely she must have realized that if Blakestone fell into Sir Eustace's hands and she became Lady Newbury, she would also regain possession of the entire estate including her old home for which she apparently held such an inordinate affection. Her prospective husband might even be persuaded to rebuild Blakestone House if he really were as plump in the pocket as rumour would have it.

The young officer scowled blackly. What had he to offer Aurelia but his undying love and devotion — and all the uncertainties and discomforts that attended a soldier's wife when she must follow the drum? Small wonder that she preferred to accept Sir Eustace's proposal!

He was suddenly jolted from these miserable cogitations by a piercing scream that shattered the silence of the afternoon. Immediately, he was on the alert and when the distressing cry came again, he lost no time in urging his horse into a gallop. Owing to his preoccupation with his troubles, he had not noticed how far he had wandered but now observed just how close he was to that same secluded track that had so lately been the setting for his own ambuscade.

Turning towards the woods, he heard a woman's voice raised in anguish and he spurred Perseus on to greater effort.

It was as he had surmised. Ahead of him lay the grassy track hidden behind the tall hedgerow and there, about halfway along its length, were two men holding a struggling youth between them while a woman fought frantically to free him from their clutches. They did not seem aware of the approaching horseman and the major was able to come up with them in a trice, flinging himself from the saddle before anyone knew of his arrival. He seized the nearest fellow by the collar and spinning him about, delivered a flush hit to the jawbone that sent him toppling backwards into the ditch where he lay as one dead. His companion, having a little more time to recover from the surprise attack, instantly sprang into action and grabbed the major in a bear hug that imprisoned both his arms. Finding himself in the powerful grip of a heavier opponent, the major knew he must resort to tactical manoeuvres if he were to regain the advantage. He struggled violently against the tightening embrace that threatened to squeeze the breath out of him. In so doing, he forced the man closer to the edge of the deep ditch before his own efforts to escape seemed to tire him and his struggles grew weaker. Now he felt the muscles in the brawny arms slightly relax and it was then that he drew back his right elbow and dealt the rogue a vicious blow in the stomach. He heard a great gasp of pain and for an instant the hold slackened on him and curling his foot about the man's ankle he shouldered his weight back against the stocky frame behind him. For a second, the fellow teetered on the sloping bank but he had been hurled off balance and unable to regain his foothold, he pitched sideways into the ditch.

With a loud bellow of rage he was up again in a moment, though at a grave disadvantage, his superior height availing him nothing now that he was standing in a muddy ditch. This unfortunate position was impressed upon him when the major's gloved knuckles hooked him under the chin ere he could gain the top of the bank. A stunned look glazed his eyes as he swayed precariously on his heels before crumpling silently to the ground, the beautifully timed blow having found its mark and been landed to a nicety.

"Well, you need not fear that they will cause you any more harm," began the major, turning to address Mrs Shaw whose terrified face he had recognized the moment she had stared wildly up at him as he had ridden to her assistance.

To his astonishment, the narrow path was deserted and there was no visible sign of either the woman or the boy. The major looked up and down the track but could see no one. It seemed that they had both vanished into thin air.

A low groan from the depths of the ditch drew his attention back to the two ruffians still lying in a huddled heap and he noted with satisfaction that they would be some little while regaining their scattered wits. The regimental boxing champion had not forgotten his old skills despite being sadly out of practice these last few months.

He decided that they would recover without any help from him and calling Perseus to his side, leapt up into the saddle and rode off with not a backward glance.

Emerging into the open meadow that lay on the other side of the wood, he espied the lone figure of a woman hurrying across the stepping stones that bridged the stream. Wheeling his horse about, he followed in Mrs Shaw's wake, catching up with her just as she was about to enter the cottage door. She paused on the whitened step and with one hand on the latch peered anxiously over her shoulder.

"One moment, please, Mrs Shaw," he called, swinging easily down from Perseus's tall back. He let fall the reins and left the stallion to amble away towards the water's edge. Warily and with a troubled look on her face, Mrs Shaw gave a tiny sigh and pushed open the door, standing aside to allow him to enter the cottage ahead of her.

He removed his hat and ducking under the low lintel passed into a small, dark room lit only by a single leaded and glazed window. A table and two rush-bottomed chairs stood in the centre of a cleanly swept floor and set against a wall was a large cupboard with a few shelves above which contained some plain blue plates and cups. In the chimney corner were placed a few simple, three-legged stools and on one of these sat a small girl watching an iron pot suspended from a massive hook hanging over a fire burning with fitful flames.

"Leave that now, Amy. I want ye t' go and find me some kindlin', there's a dear girl."

Obediently, the child trotted out to the rear of the cottage and disappeared into the woodland.

When she had gone, Mrs Shaw drew forward a chair and invited the major to sit down. She then settled herself in the other and politely enquired whether or no he would take a dish of tea with her.

"No, I thank you. I would rather you gave me some answers. Who were those two men and what were they about when I came upon you just now?" he questioned bluntly.

Again came that look of uncertainty and fear that he had observed in her face before.

"Please, don't be afraid of me, Mrs Shaw. I mean you no harm, I assure you. I only want to help you, if I can. And perhaps you can be of help to me also. I wish you might trust me with your confidence. Was that your son I saw back there in the wood? What did those men want with him? Is he all right?"

She shifted her dark gaze from his face to stare into the smouldering fire and it seemed that she had decided to keep her own counsel. Her lips were firmly compressed as if she was determined to keep her tongue between her teeth. Then she leaned forward and lifted the heavy brass poker from the hearth and began to coax the reluctant fire into vigorous life. When she was content with her efforts, she set it down again and without taking her eyes from the leaping flames answered in a low, steady voice, "'T'ain't me son. 'E be Sam Frant's nephew."

The major looked at her in some

surprise. "Frant's nephew? But I understood from Clifton that the unfortunate fellow had no family living?"

"They wasn't close. Sam's sister married a blacksmith as lived over t' 'Astings way. Their lad's a fisherman. 'E visits me from time to time. Brings me a few things — for the young 'uns, d'ye see? 'E's a good boy. My Tom liked 'un too. Poor Tom." She stopped to brush a work-worn hand over her eyes, "I s'pose ye've heerd about Tom?"

"Yes. I'm sorry. It must be hard on you and the children."

"What's 'ard, sir, is the punishment they've give to a innocent man," she replied in a tight, constricted voice. "Tom weren't no poacher, that I can tell ye. If yer brother 'ud come t' court t' speak fer Tom, 'e could've saved 'im." She faltered, pulling a handkerchief from the pocket of her grey stuff gown and blew her nose. Then in a brisker tone she continued, "Well, ye'll not want t' b'lieve us no more than Sir Eustace wanted t' listen t' the honest truth. But I shouldn't blame ye. Ye don't know nothin' of us and 'ow should ye, bein' as ye've bin away fightin' for the king? I ought t' be thankin' ye for comin' t' our rescue just now. Indeed, I do thank ye very kindly, sir. They would've took poor Eli if ye 'adn't 'appened to come on us and I couldn't 'ave saved 'im by meself. I dursn't think what would've become of the unfort'nate soul if it weren't for you. I was that frighted, I didn't know what t' do." She pressed a hand to her mouth and gave an almost imperceptible shake of her head. "Oh, it don't bear thinkin' on."

"What did they want with him? What has he done?"

"'E's done nothin'! It's what they think 'e knows, that's the worry!" cried she in great agitation.

"Oh? And what does he know that is of such great interest to them that they would risk kidnapping him in broad daylight?"

Mrs Shaw fell silent, twisting her handkerchief in her fingers.

"You may confide in me, you know. I really do want to help you," he insisted urgently. "Perhaps I ought to tell you that I have already spoken with Mr Stewart. He told me all he knows about your husband's situation. I am come home on purpose to discover everything I can concerning my brother's death. It seems to me that there may have been some connection between Tom's arrest and the accidents that befell Frant and Lord Cullan. If you know anything at all about these tragic events, I beg you to tell me."

Still she did not answer and appeared to be in a state of indecision, kneading her knuckles in her lap and rocking her thin body back and forth in her chair. The major put his hand into his coat and pulled out his pocket book. He opened it and carefully removed a strip of paper. "Would you at least look at this and tell me if you have seen this paper in your husband's possession before his arrest?"

Mrs Shaw stared blankly at the wisp of paper lying in his open palm and eyed him in utter amazement. "But 'tis just a bit o' paper! Why would Tom trouble 'isself to show me that? It's nothin' important is it?"

"Your husband thought it so. He begged the rector to give it to my brother as a matter of great urgency.

In fact, he told Mr Stewart that it meant life or death to Lord Cullan."

"'E did?" She shook her head in bewilderment. "I don't know what it means, truly I don't. Didn't Tom say anythin' more?"

"Yes. He said that he loved you and would do his utmost to come home again to you and the children," he answered softly. "Have you heard any news of him since his transportation?"

She looked away and briefly shook her head. "No. Tom never learned to read nor write, sir."

"I see. Yet he may find someone to write to you on his behalf."

"Mebbe but I don't pin no 'opes on it."

"I'm sure he will return one day, Mrs Shaw," he reassured her quietly and put a comforting hand on her shoulder. "I will not intrude upon you any longer. I never intended to cause you any more grief. God knows you have had enough. But please believe that I will do all within my power to assist you if you should desire it. If those men should dare to trouble you again, you must send me word at once. Do you understand? I mean what I say. I will not have any tenant of mine living in fear on my land."

"Yes. Thank'ee, sir. I'll do as ye say, though I doubt they will trespass on yer property again after the drubbin' ye gave 'em."

When the major had gone, a face appeared at the cottage window. It was a grimy visage topped by an even grimier woollen hat pulled low over the bright, mischievous eyes.

"Gone then, 'as 'e?" enquired the urchin. "Is it safe for ol' Eli to come in then?"

"Yes, it's safe enough now," sniffed Mrs Shaw, wiping her eyes and nose surreptitiously.

"Good. I'm starved!"

The boy strode in through the unlatched door closely followed by little Amy and taking a tin from the dresser, helped himself to a large piece of oaten cake. He handed half to Amy and stuffing the rest hungrily into his mouth, he sat astride the vacated chair and munched away cheerfully as though nothing out of the ordinary had happened to him all day. When he had finished eating he wiped his mouth on his grubby sleeve and sighed happily.

"That's better! My stomach was rumbling so loudly I thought he might hear me out there. By the way, those villains have taken themselves off now. I don't think they will dare show their ugly faces here again. Not while the fighting major is around to blacken their lights. Oh! Did you see how sweetly he milled down his man!"

The boy clenched his fists into a ball and swung his arms energetically, prancing about the room like a pugilist in the ring. "I wish he would teach me how to throw my castors like that!"

Mrs Shaw gave a rather watery smile. "Don' ye dare go near that young gen'leman," she warned, "I've enough to worrit me without takin' fright over yer mischief. I was that scared when those two rascals leapt out on us! I wish ye wouldn't take such risks! Suppose Major Lacey 'adn't come along o' us when 'e did, what then?"

"I shall just have to be more careful now, shan't I? They won't catch me so easily again," said he with all the optimism of youth. "I wonder who they are? They aren't from this part of the country, of that I'm certain. Neither are they customs' men; I know all of them by sight. And how did they know about Tom? That's what I should really like to find out."

"I can't understand none of it. Even that Major Lacey's bin askin' questions about my Tom. 'E showed me a bit o' paper that Tom was s'posed to 'ave give to the rector on the day 'e was took away."

"What sort of paper?" asked Eli, his eyes gleaming with sudden curiosity.

"I dunno. Just a bit of paper. It didn't 'ave no writin' on it, or nothin'. It looked like it 'ad bin tore off somethin'. Funny thing is, the major told me that Tom 'ad asked the rector t' give it t' is lordship urgent like. Life 'n death 'e said 'twas."

Eli frowned deeply. "Life and death? How I wish I might see that paper! I wonder if it is a clue to what Lucius was up to?"

"Ye aren't the only one t' wonder about that. The major says 'e wants t' know if Sam and Tom 'ad somethin' t' do with 'is brother's death. Oh, where will it all end!?" she wailed miserably.

"There now, Mary, don't cry. We'll get Tom's name cleared soon. Meanwhile we must do what we can for you and the children. In fact, that's what I came to tell you. There's a ship coming in on Thursday night."

"S' soon? Oh dear, I don' like it! I d' feel uneasy sin' those men come 'ere t'day. They've frighted me, I don't mind tellin' ye. They're bad 'uns, I know it. Theyn't like the Gen'lemen, so jus' ye be careful and keep yer wits about ye from now on!"

9

WHEN the major made his way back through the woods, he tried his best to catch a glimpse of Frant's nephew, hoping that he might still be hiding somewhere in the vicinity. However, his search proved fruitless and eventually he had to give up all hope of finding him on this occasion. He felt certain that the lad could have some vital information about his uncle's disappearance and the loss of the *Seabird*.

This mystery seemed to deepen at every turn. Mrs Shaw had obviously not trusted him enough to tell him all that she knew. Her answers to his questions had been reluctant to say the least. She had told him nothing that would shed any light on the matter. If only he could persuade her to be more open with him. Had she known the identity of the men who had accosted her? What had they really wanted with that boy? He would

244

give a great deal to know.

It occurred to him that he might be able to enlist the rector's help in tracing the lad's whereabouts; he knew most people living in the locality and was as eager to solve the mystery as the major himself.

Accordingly and regardless of the inclement weather, Major Lacey set off the very next morning to visit the rectory. A grey veil of misty rain hung over the entire landscape obscuring the distances and quickly coating horse and rider with clinging WEB s of fine moisture. As he rode along the top of the Downs, a flotilla of squalling gulls eddied above his head, their bodies shaped like Cupid's ready bow, gleaming white against the leaden sky. On a freshening wind came the sound of pounding waves surging up the beach, intermingled with the rattling gasps of the shifting shingle. He drew rein and turned to face seawards, removing his hat to prevent its being tumbled from his head. It was exhilarating to feel the wind and rain on his face and to breathe in the bracing scent of salt and seaweed. The water was a cold, grey-green and the boiling spume a dirty yellow as it plunged upon the pebbled shore. His thoughts drifted back to other days like this when he and Lucius were schoolboys and had cajoled their father into taking out the small dinghy to row about the bay. He remembered with a smile the excitement of riding on the back of the bucking sea, the spray soaking them to the skin as it broke over the bows of their brave little craft.

Even as he was picturing the scene again in his mind's eye, a longboat hove into view around the headland and began to make its way swiftly along the edge of the bay. The major watched it for several minutes, noting the speed of its progress. Despite the heaving waves, the boat seemed to skim through the water with the same ease of motion as that displayed by the graceful gulls overhead.

Soon it was lost from sight as they rounded the point and Major Lacey decided it was time to be on his way also. Taking the ancient chalk track that snaked across the backs of the cliffs he began to descend the slope, keeping the sea to his left as he negotiated the steep path, slippery now with the rain.

He began to think that it would perhaps have been wiser to have taken the more direct route to the village. This was hardly a day for riding about the fields and he realized too late that he was going to cut a very peculiar figure when he eventually arrived at the rectory. He could well imagine how oddly Mrs Stewart might view his appearance, wet and mud-splashed as he undoubtedly was.

Ahead of him, the path cut across a narrow dene and as he carefully guided Perseus down into it, he glanced towards the beach which lay only a few yards away. To his surprise he saw the longboat being hauled up on to the shingle above the line of the tide. Why had they chosen to put in here of all places? There was only a small, deeply shelving beach at the foot of these cliffs and with the tide almost up as it was at this hour of the day, it seemed an unlikely spot to have chosen for a landing. He lingered a moment longer to see what they were about. As he watched them drag the boat clear of the water, his attention was captured by a man in a distinctive, scarlet cap who was directing their efforts. His shouted instructions were all but lost above the din of the crashing waves but there was something vaguely familiar about his height and build that struck a note of recognition in the major's observant mind. If he was not very much mistaken, that was the same fellow whose brawny arms had nigh crushed the breath out of him but yesternoon.

His curiosity finally got the better of him and he abandoned completely his planned visit to the rector. This might prove far more interesting. If he could discover what these men were doing here, he might also discover the reason why an attempt had been made to abduct Frant's nephew.

The major slipped quietly from Perseus's back and hid him in the shelter of a cluster of hawthorn bushes with their additional camouflage of rose briars. Then he climbed swiftly to the top of the ridge and looked over the edge of the escarpment to the beach below. By now the boat had been made secure and just as the men were trudging up towards the mouth of the dene, another figure joined the group appearing as if from nowhere. He must have been standing in the lee of the cliffs, just beyond the major's line of vision and had only now decided to reveal himself. It was impossible to guess who this might be because the newcomer was wearing an all-enveloping hooded cloak. The men were obviously expecting him and stood aside as he approached, allowing the red-capped seaman to step forward. A few words were exchanged between them before they all turned aside and disappeared from view. Several minutes passed before they reappeared, this time carrying what looked like a large box or chest wrapped in oilskins. This was taken to the boat and heaved aboard in such an awkward fashion that the major surmised that it must be extremely heavy. There followed an indistinct dialogue that ended abruptly when a shower of loose chalk clattered down the cliff face. In his eagerness to see what was happening, the major had pressed too near the crumbling edge of the precipice. He knew that they had seen him and with a muttered exclamation of annoyance, stepped hastily backwards.

At the same moment a pistol ball thudded into the grass at his feet, sending up a cloud of white dust. Next came the sound of furious shouting as three of the men ran towards the chalk path and he quickly realized that, unarmed as he was, it would be useless to engage the enemy. An orderly retreat was preferable to certain capture, or worse, so without further hesitation he sprinted away to his horse and swinging easily into the saddle, galloped away to the shelter of the wooded valley.

As he made to cross the winding lane at the foot of the hill, he noticed a black chaise drawn up beneath the overhanging branches of the trees. Checking Perseus, he cast a cursory glance at the door panels to see if they bore a device that he might recognize. There was nothing visible to indicate its ownership and he was about to press on when, completely without warning, the coachman stepped out from behind the carriage, a heavy flintlock pistol in his hand. It seemed that the altercation on the slopes above him had alerted him to a possible danger and he called out to the major to stand and hold. This peremptory invitation the gentleman declined to accept and urged his horse into the wood. The coachman immediately opened fire and the major felt an agonizing burning sensation in his upper arm. Desperately he clung on to the reins with one hand, gripping Perseus tightly with his knees as a wave of pain threatened to topple him from the saddle. He leaned low across the stallion's neck so as to present less of a target and gave Perseus his head. Away they sped into the depths of the wood, weaving surely in and out of the broad tree trunks until the road was lost from sight. It was only then that the major pulled in his horse and wheeling him about, looked back along the path. All was quiet now save for the sound of Perseus' gruff breathing and it appeared that he had managed to throw off his pursuers. He dared not wander too far into the dense woodland for fear of losing his bearings. The wound in his arm was bleeding heavily and already he could see the blood trickling down on to the back of his hand. It was imperative that he get some help to stem the flow before he grew too faint. Adopting a more cautious pace, he continued along the mossy path, intending to find another exit on to the road and hoping that he would not be so unfortunate as to run headlong into those murderous rogues again.

Meanwhile, the coachman had been about to set off in hot pursuit of his victim, when he was brought to a sudden halt by a sharp command in a tone that he recognized at once. "Leave him, Sprake! Come back here!" demanded the man in the hooded cloak, his voice harsh with anger. Then swivelling on his heel he turned to glare at the men gathering behind him. "You brainless fools! That was not our man! How many times must I tell you to be careful to do nothing that will draw attention to us? I want this matter dealt with quietly, do you understand me?!"

"But sir! He were spyin' on us!" protested the man who had fired the first shot.

"Well? And what do you imagine he could have seen that would have harmed us? All you have achieved with your stupidity, is to arouse his suspicion and that of others which would be far worse!"

"I'll swear that was the cove as set on me and Toby Kelly yesterd'y," broke in the man in the red seaman's cap, rubbing his bruised chin ruefully. "I reck'n 'e's already in this some 'ow. Seems onnat'ral t' me that 'e turns up agin t'day. 'Ow did 'e know we'd be 'ere this mornin'?"

"You may be right, Vose. I'll grant you it's a strange coincidence. It's crossed my mind that he might know more about this business than perhaps is good for him, especially now that our friend is on the loose. However, I can lay my hands on that gentleman whenever I care to, so let's not trouble ourselves any further with him. Get back to the others and take your cargo to the tavern. I don't want anyone else stumbling on us. I had thought to act undisturbed on a morning like this and to have the advantage of appearing to be going about our legitimate affairs. I have no wish to start rumours flying along the coast. You must be very careful from now on. This business is almost at an end. Vose! You and Kelly are to keep out of Major Lacey's way. He knows you by sight and may well try to interfere again if he sees you about the place."

"No fear of that," intervened the coachman with a leering grin. "I've sin to 'im for ye. I don't think 'e'll be botherin' us agin in a 'urry."

"You got him then? But not a fatal wound?"

"Couldn't rightly say, sir. I jest sin one o' 'is wings a-danglin' like. 'E were too quick for me. That 'orse was orf like greased lightnin' afore I could finish the job proper."

"Well, let us trust that it was enough to prevent him from meddling. But more importantly, Sprake, did you see anyone else lurking about? Anyone who might have been keeping a close watch on that man you just fired upon?"

"No, sir, I only sin 'im. Not a soul 'as come along 'ere 'ceptin' that fine genl'eman. An' my peepers is rackon'd t' be re-mark'ble sharp."

"Good! We may have nothing to fear then but we must all keep vigilant. His coming here has made matters very dangerous for us. Now why are you all still standing about like lost sheep? The tide will be in. Hurry! Sprake, get to your horses, I've wasted enough time here as it is."

While the three returned to their boat, the major was just emerging from the woods. He was beginning to feel very light-headed indeed. It was only to be hoped that he could fight off this dizziness that was threatening to overcome him, long enough to reach Blakestone. Ned would patch him up in no time as he had done before on several occasions.

Wiping the perspiration from his eyes with the sleeve of his coat, he trotted Perseus along the winding lane, grateful for the cooling rain and wind on his face. He had not gone far when another rider came galloping furiously along the lane behind him. There was hardly time to draw aside before the horse was upon him and seemed set to continue its mad career without a moment's pause. However, as it passed him, it was brought to a sudden plunging halt just yards ahead and then was turned immediately about to canter to his side.

"Major Lacey! I thought it was you. I see you are not put off by a little rain either. Are you just come from the village?"

"Good morning, Lady Elisa. Somehow I feel that I ought not to be surprised at meeting you. Especially on a morning such as this has been."

"Why, Major Lacey, surely you don't mean me to believe that you find my company distasteful?" said Elisa feigning astonishment.

"Oh no, how could you think that when you know how much I am entertained by it?"

"Well, I can certainly tell that you are in a strange humour at the moment. In fact you look quite . . . " Her voice trailed off as he swayed dizzily in the saddle. "Are you ill, Major?" she questioned anxiously.

He did not answer but merely stared at her as if trying to focus on her face. While he struggled to fight against the blackness that was closing in on him, a chaise came lurching down the rutted, muddy lane and at a signal from Elisa, drew to a halt beside them.

The window was let down and the occupant called out to her crossly, "What is the matter?"

"Harry, I want you to get down at once. Major Lacey is unwell and, if I am not very much mistaken, is about to cup the candle."

Sir Harry Palmer gazed frowningly across at the major's pale features. "He certainly looks rather whey-faced. What's the matter with him?"

"I don't know. Don't just sit there asking foolish questions, come down and help me get him into your carriage immediately."

"Must we? I don't want him casting up his accounts all over my new upholstery," complained Palmer peevishly.

"Be quiet, Harry! And do as I tell you!" snapped Elisa impatiently, slipping hurriedly to the ground and tethering her horse to a convenient gate post.

Between the two of them they managed to help him out of the saddle and as Elisa took his arm to steady him, she cried out in sudden consternation.

"Oh! You are bleeding!!"

"The deuce! So he is!" exclaimed Sir

Harry, looking startled.

"I suppose I must now hope that you chose vermilion for the refurbishment of your carriage," murmured the major with a weary smile.

"What has happened to you?" demanded Elisa.

"Someone shot me, ma'am. But fortunately, I have become inured to it of late, as no doubt you will be only too aware."

"Shot?" she reiterated, turning a little pale herself. "Did you see who did it?"

"Yes, I did as a matter of fact, so you need not be afraid that I shall accuse you." He paused briefly. "Not this time." Then turning to Palmer he said, "I would be grateful if you could convey me to Blakestone, Sir Harry. Ned will attend to me. And you may send an account to me for any damage I may cause to the furnishings of your carriage. Now if I may, I should like to sit down before I become an even greater burden to you."

No sooner had they got him into the carriage, the major, despite his valiant efforts to keep his wits about him, slipped quietly into oblivion.

"Harry, he's fainted," said Elisa calmly. "Take him to your house, it's nearer than Blakestone."

"My house? But I don't want him there! It's too dangerous. He might be well again tomorrow."

"I don't think so." Elisa put a hand on the major's brow. "He's burning. He is going to be very feverish for a while."

"Then let's take him to Blakestone. You heard what he said. That servant of his can look after him."

"But don't you see, Harry? We don't want him at Blakestone, do we?" explained Elisa with a sigh of exasperation. "This way we can get his valet to come to your house to take care of him until he's well enough to leave. Now do you understand? We can make use of Eli tomorrow night after all. Everything can be just as it was before he came here. There will be no need to alter our plans after all."

"By Jove, you're right! I never thought of it in that light. Yes! This is a stroke of luck!" cried Palmer excitedly. "We could keep him out of the way, I suppose. I could put him in the Tudor bedchamber, he won't trouble us up there."

"Excellent. Now give me your handkerchief and I will try what I can do to tie up this wound. I wonder what he has done to bring this on himself?"

"Then it really wasn't your doing?"

"Certainly not!" she answered indignantly. "But I might ask you the same question. What are you doing up here this morning?"

"I had a little matter of business to attend to, if you must know."

"Business? What sort of business would induce you to get up this early in the morning?"

"I had to meet someone — for some private conversation," he replied with a slight quirk of the lips that might almost have been a smile.

"I see," she muttered tersely, her attention focused on the makeshift bandage, "no doubt I could guess the nature of that particular meeting. Especially if it needs must be held in these solitary surroundings."

"Unfortunately they are not as solitary as I could wish," he muttered, lounging back in his seat and lazily watching her imperfect ministrations. "Don't you think your task might have been a little easier if you had divested the man of his coat?"

"Yes! It might if you had bestirred yourself to help me!" she snapped irritably. "But this will have to serve until he can be got to bed. Now look after him while I attend to the horses. I will meet you later."

"But where are you going? You don't mean to leave me to play nursemaid, surely?"

"Just see to it that the bandage does not slip. You can do that much, can't you? I'm taking his horse back to Blakestone and then I shall send his valet to him."

Ignoring his protests, Elisa rode away, the major's horse trotting obediently beside her.

When she arrived at Blakestone, she found Ned sweeping out the stables. He looked up in astonishment as she rode into the yard leading Perseus by the reins. Hastily he threw aside the broom and came hurrying to meet her.

"Where is he? What's happened?" he questioned anxiously.

"The major has met with an accident. A pistol wound to the arm. I don't think it is serious but Sir Harry Palmer thought it best to take him to High Dean, being that it was close by. You had better go to him at once."

"Yes, indeed I must. But first I shall have to pack a portmanteau. And Perseus will need to be looked to . . ."

"Don't worry. I shall see to it that Perseus comes to no harm. It will take me but a moment to put him in his stall and make him comfortable. In fact, you may trust me for that while you are occupied at High Dean. I will ensure that Perseus is cared for. You need have no qualms on that score."

"But, my lady! I could not ask you to do that!"

"Well, you do not have to ask me. I've just offered, have I not? I'm perfectly capable of taking care of him, you know," she answered huffily.

"Yes, of course, I'm sure you are," said Ned awkwardly, "it's just that, well, you are a fine lady," he finished in some embarrassment.

"Your master certainly wouldn't agree

with you. And I am sure he thinks me perfectly able to wield a broom," she added with a deprecating look. "If knowing how to attend to the needs of a horse is considered to be an unladylike accomplishment, then doubtless your master is in the right of it. Now go to your packing and I shall stable Perseus."

Without further argument, Ned strode away to make his preparations. He looked in on Perseus before he left and found that all was done properly, exactly as she had said. The young lady had been as good as her word and he could see that he would not have to worry about the stallion's well-being.

He led his own horse out into the yard and having secured the bag, set off immediately towards Barhurst eager to judge for himself the severity of the major's wound. There was no sign of her ladyship as he turned into the drive and he wondered where she had disappeared to. Perhaps he would find that she had gone on ahead of him to High Dean. What an odd, quixotic creature she seemed but no doubt she was something of an original.

Ned arrived at High Dean to discover that his master had been borne off to a bedchamber in the oldest part of the house. When he entered the room, he felt as if he were stepping back into the past. It looked as if no one had slept here since the Civil War. The ceiling was very low and the oak panelled walls were now blackened with age. A massive, four-poster bed dominated the centre of the room, making it look and feel even more cramped. The heavily carved tester was covered by a dusty, dark-blue canopy and each of the corner posts were draped with faded, blue damask curtains tied back with knots of twisted silk. Opposite the bed was a large, stone fireplace in which a hastily lit fire was smoking feebly. Someone had thrown open one of the small, leaded casements set in the thick stone walls, in a belated effort to air the room or perhaps to bring some light into this gloomy, forgotten chamber.

Ned hasted to the side of the bed and bending over the limp form lying so silently, began to examine the wound with gentle fingers.

It did not take him long to ascertain that the shot had passed cleanly through the flesh and that the injury was not life threatening. His fears assuaged, he closed the casement and quickly set about unpacking the portmanteau before stripping the major of his ruined shirt. By this time, the footman had arrived with a bowl of water and some towels. Ned glanced round at him as he approached the bed.

"You've taken long enough about it," he muttered curtly, "the water's nearly cold!"

"No need to be so blimmin' maggoty. You want t' try climbin' up all them stairs wivout spillin' the 'ole basin! I dunno why the young tight-purse put 'im in this 'ere room anyways. Ain't nob'dy bin in 'ere since Sir 'Arry's great-great granfer breeved 'is last on that theer wery bed."

Ned was already busy cleaning up the wound and paid him no heed. The footman drew closer to the bed and peered over Ned's shoulder. "Looks queer as a miller's mouse, don't 'e?"

he observed gloomily. "Last time I see a phiz like that it were on a corpse. If ye want my o-pinion, 'e's as good as worm's meat."

"I don't require it, thank you, nor your presence either, come to that. So kindly take yourself off and leave me in peace."

"Well, if that's yer attitood, then dannel ye! If a man's opinions ain't walued then theer's no p'int in 'is a-givin' of 'em. An' if yer goin' t' spit nails at me, then I'm orf," he retorted, bristling with annoyance. He stalked away to the door, pausing only to add, "An' if ye wants ony more 'ot water, ye can fetch it yerself!"

The door slammed shut, rattling the window frames and sending up a cloud of dust from the bare floorboards.

Ned grimaced angrily. He was not impressed by Sir Harry's brand of hospitality. Even Blakestone was preferable to this near squalor and the sooner they could remove there the better for both of them.

As soon as he had finished with the bandages, he dressed the major in a clean nightshirt and left him to sleep.

He busied himself with the fire, coaxing it finally into a cheerful blaze. Then drawing up a solid, ornately carved chair, he settled himself beside the bed to watch over his master's slumbers.

Time passed slowly; the only sounds that broke the silence were the hissing of the logs on the fire as the flames licked hungrily around them and the restless movements of the patient as he tossed feverishly upon the yellowed linen sheets. The room grew darker as the rain became heavier, drumming against the lattice and Ned's eyelids began to drop. Suddenly, there came a gentle tapping at the door and he sat up, instantly wide awake. Lady Elisa appeared in the doorway, bearing a tray loaded with dishes.

"My lady!" cried Ned in consternation, reaching for his coat hanging over the back of his chair and hastily shrugging himself into it.

"Pray do not disturb yourself," she reassured him calmly, "I am merely come to bring you something to eat. Sir Harry is an ill host and I guessed how it would be with him. I daresay no one has been sent to you to attend to your needs, so I have brought the major a bowl of gruel and there is a raised pie and a dish of mutton for you."

She set the tray down on a chest of drawers and came softly to the major's bedside. "Has he woken at all?" she whispered, leaning over him and peering anxiously at his flushed countenance.

"Not yet," replied Ned coming to stand beside her, "but I am not unduly concerned. He has come through far worse injuries than this. There was a time, when we were in Spain, that I feared for him. A musket ball nigh pierced his lung. But he has a strong constitution, I thank God. He'll be right as a trivet in a day or two."

"He still looks rather feverish to me. Are you certain he does not need a doctor?"

"Quite, thank you, my lady," insisted Ned firmly. "He's lost a little blood, that is all. Plenty of rest is the best cure for that. He doesn't need one of those leeches physicking him. Besides, I've learned a thing or two out in the Peninsular. Enough to know that he is in no danger from a wound of this nature."

"Very well. Do you go and eat your dinner while I sit with him."

"Thank you, my lady. I must confess that I am feeling the want of a good meal inside me." He drew up a chair for her and she seated herself with a nod of thanks. For several minutes she watched the invalid in silence. Now that he was no longer scowling at her, he looked quite different. She studied his face, trying to catch some fleeting resemblance to Lucius but could find none. Lucius had been fair, his features pale and delicate; as graceful of limb as the hero of a Raphael painting.

There was nothing beautiful about the major's appearance. His was a strong, commanding face: broad browed with heavy-lidded eyes beneath, a proud length of nose and a square, determined jaw. Yet it seemed gentler in repose and in the immensity of this ancient bed, his tousled head propped against the mound of pillows, he looked somehow younger and more vulnerable. She glanced about her, noting the thick layers of dust on floor and furnishings and the darkness of the shadowed room with the rain beating angrily against the dirty window panes. A pang of remorse pricked her conscience. They ought not to have brought him here. The man might not be dying but he was certainly hurt and deserved better treatment than this. Harry only kept three indoor servants these days and they were so poorly paid it was not to be thought wonderful that they hardly bestirred themselves to keep the place respectable. She smiled to herself, imagining her aunt's expression if she could see where her niece was spending the afternoon. High Dean could never be described as respectable while Sir Harry remained its owner. Well, she did not care what became of her reputation, that was in shreds anyway and could scarcely be repaired now. Besides, she could not leave the major entirely in Harry's careless charge. She had caused him to be brought here and must see that he was made as comfortable as possible in these miserable surroundings. Had she not done as much for his horse? But it was well that Ned was here to wait upon him, at least he was sensible and reliable. She need not fear to place the major in his capable hands. Her attention was drawn back to the subject of her musings. He seemed restive and perspiration beaded his skin. Elisa arose and taking a cloth from beside the basin, dipped it in the now cold water and having carefully wrung it out again, lay it over his burning forehead. He opened his eyes and she found herself looking directly into them. They were brighter and bluer than seemed natural, two brilliant circles of colour fringed with dark lashes. Still he stared fixedly up at her and as she slowly removed her hand from his brow, he seized her cool fingers in his hot grasp and pressed them to his lips. Elisa's heart gave a sudden lurch and she felt a strange, inexplicable pain that robbed her of breath while she gazed at him in astonishment.

His eyes never left her face as he pleaded earnestly, "Aurelia! I knew you would come. You won't leave me again, will you? Promise me you will not?"

Elisa stiffened suddenly, a flash of anger in her green eyes. Now she understood! This was the reason for Aurelia's agitation that day in the garden. Had Lucius known that his own brother was in love with his wife? Was this the real reason for their estrangement? She had never quite believed Aurelia's explanations. No wonder Lucius could not bring himself to mention his brother's name. Her suspicions were confirmed, she had always believed Aurelia's protestations of love were merely theatrics. That woman had never really cared for poor Lucius.

Elisa eyed the major contemptuously. He deserved no consideration at all. Harry was right: this room was perfectly suited to their needs and she hoped the major would be forced to remain here for days. Whoever was responsible for giving him this wound was to be congratulated. She almost wished she had thought of it herself. Except that she was like to have put it right through his black heart!

She pulled her hand free of his clasp and stepped back out of his reach.

"Aurelia! Don't go! Stay with me!" he begged, his hand held out to her imploringly.

"Your master's wound is troubling him," she said coldly, striding towards

272

the door. "You had better contrive to calm him."

"Aye, that it is," sighed Ned frowningly. "But it's an old wound that's causing him such pain, I'll warrant."

10

THE major's fever abated during the night, thanks to Ned's unremitting care and by the following morning, the invalid was declaring himself well enough to eat a hearty breakfast. Ned was by now sufficiently acquainted with Sir Harry's household to realize that sending down to the kitchens for a nourishing meal would serve no good purpose. Finding his own way downstairs, he eventually discovered the cook engaged in the preparation of her master's own repast. This surly, red-faced dame, grudgingly pointed him in the direction of the pantry. She informed him brusquely that she had not the leisure to prepare meals to feed extra mouths and that if those clutch-fisted misers upstairs wished her to do so, then let them provide the means.

As quickly as he was able, Ned escaped from her monotonous plaints and hurried away to the more peaceful, if somewhat inhospitable, surroundings of the Tudor wing. He was rewarded for his effort and fortitude by the sight of his master demolishing with apparent relish, every morsel of the dishes set before him.

Ned grinned delightedly. "There's little ailing you today, that I can see. Didn't I tell the young lady that all you needed was rest? I knew you'd not be counted out: your constitution is as robust as my own."

"What young lady?" frowned the major, handing Ned the tray of empty plates.

"Lady Elisa Maytland. She sent me to you yesterday when she brought Perseus back to Blakestone."

"Did she? That was good of her, I suppose."

"I thought so. She said she would look after him while we are away."

"I had not credited her with such nobility."

"So she told me," smiled Ned, setting down the tray on an old wooden chest at the foot of the bed. "And I must admit that she is like no other lady that I have ever seen. Even I could not feel easy seeing her in this house yesterday and apparently unaccompanied. It cannot be thought quite proper, I am sure."

"She was here?" questioned the major, astounded.

"Indeed she was, sir. And in a bachelor's establishment! I hope that Sir Harry's servants are more discreet than they are industrious. Heaven alone knows what the gossips would make of it, should it become generally known."

"From what I have heard, that has never troubled her so far," muttered the major, settling himself back against the pillows. "What did she come here for? Hoping to view my cold cadaver, no doubt."

"The young lady came to bring us sustenance. She knew we should get little of that in this ramshackle household. I had to beg our bread this morning, or I fear we should have been left to starve. Our hosts seem to have forgotten our presence."

"I asked Palmer to convey me to Blakestone. Why he brought me here to this mouldering mausoleum, I cannot conjecture."

"I believe it was nearer and they were concerned for your wound. How did it happen, sir? Who shot at you this time?"

The major's blue eyes twinkled with amusement. "I confess I am grown weary of it myself, Ned. My self-esteem is at a very low ebb, you know. I was never so unpopular in my life! It is only with the greatest trepidation that I dare show my face in the neighbourhood." Then, growing serious again, he continued, "I cannot help thinking, that in some peculiar way this is all connected with my brother's death, though quite how it is I do not yet know. But I'm convinced that cork-brained girl is involved in the mystery. The very first day that I arrived at Blakestone, she crossed my path; from that moment onwards she has hovered at my side like some fell omen."

"Now you are beginning to sound fanciful. It was the fever induced that in you yesterday: I hope it is not returning."

"What do you mean?" demanded the major indignantly.

"Well, you wandered in your mind a little when the fever was upon you and began to imagine that Lady Elisa was the very same person who haunted your last sick-bed."

"Ooh," he groaned, putting a hand to his head in a gesture of dismay. "Did I speak her name?"

"You did indeed, sir and implored her to stay with you," sighed Ned, shaking his head despondently. "I knew how it would be the moment you insisted on coming back. It was no use telling me all that flummery about having put her from your mind. I've seen the way you look at her."

"I thought I had buried the past. I was sure I could meet her again without fear of renewing false hopes. But the very sight of her face and the sound of her voice, breathed new life into me. I only wish I may not have provided that odious girl with the means to torment a lady who deserves to be left in peace."

Their conversation was interrupted by Sir Harry's appearing at the door.

"Good day to you, Major Lacey. I trust that you have had a comfortable night? I regret my having been prevented from visiting you sooner but I have many demands upon my time as I am sure you will appreciate. How do you go on this morning?"

"Very much better, thank you, Sir Harry. I shall not trespass on your hospitality any longer than necessary, be assured. Ned and I will be on our way this day noon."

"Nonsense! I will not hear of it, sir. You cannot possibly be well enough to travel yet. You must allow your wound to heal properly. Please feel free to remain for as long as you like. You need not fear to incommode us; Alfred and I are frequently called away on numerous matters of business, so you shall almost have the place to yourselves. You need not hesitate to order what you will, my servants are instructed to oblige you in every way. It will be far more pleasant here than at Blakestone House: that is no place for a man in your state of health. No, no, you must make this your home until you are restored to full vigour, I insist upon it."

"You are too kind, sir," replied the major, exchanging a merry look with Ned. "But I must not encroach upon your good nature. I assure you I shall be perfectly able to make the short journey to Blakestone today."

"You must not even think of it! Perhaps tomorrow morning, if you should have regained your strength by then. I will not have it bruited abroad that I compelled a sick man to leave his bed and in such weather! Dear me, no. I could not permit it."

"Truly, Sir Harry, I am excellent well . . ."

Sir Harry held up an admonitory hand and shook his head, "Let me hear no more of your going today. You cannot mean to set forward in your weakened condition. A man who has lost so much blood would find the slightest effort far too exhausting, believe me. My brother and I are in perfect accord on this subject. He would have come himself to assure you of it but for the fear that too many visitors might tire you. I shall send Higgs for your tray: I do not wish your man to be put to the least inconvenience. He must be allowed to remain at your side for as long as you are confined to your bed. You may instruct Higgs as you will, he is to wait upon you for the duration of your stay at High Dean. Now, I shall leave you to refresh yourself with some sleep, you still look a trifle grey about the gills to me. I suppose it is not to be wondered at. Such a perfectly dreadful accident!" With that, he hurried from the room, leaving them to stare after him.

"Well!" exclaimed Ned, scratching his head in bewilderment. "I could scarce believe my ears. Make this our home, he says. Does he think we live in a cow byre? Just look at this room!"

"To be fair, Ned, it is not dissimilar to some of the rooms at Blakestone, though not to be compared with our own cosy quarters, I hasten to add. And Blakestone does have the excuse of having been struck by a disaster. I must confess that I am astounded by his concern for my health. It was very much against his inclinations to allow me into his carriage yesterday, let alone his house. What is the meaning of it, I wonder? Why this sudden change of heart?"

"I'm sure I couldn't guess, sir."

There came a scratching at the door and the manservant appeared, coughing and wheezing horribly as he set down a bucket of coals.

"I've bin sent f' yer breakf'us tray. An' I'm t' say that all yer meals is to be took in this 'ere room, bein' as the gen'elman ain't s' sprightly a-owin' t' the hinjury o' that there limb. If ye wants hanythink else, ye've t' ring the bell. There ain't no p'int in a-comin' dahnstairs, 'cause there ain't no fires lit t'day." He gave another choking cough and sniffing loudly, picked up the tray of crockery. "'Owso'mever, I 'opes that afore ye rings that bell, ye'll give du' con-siderwation t' them dooc'd stairs and t' me rheumaticks — vich same ain't nowise 'elped b' this con-founded rain."

Having ended his soliloquy, for such it appeared to be in that it was dolefully muttered to the ambient air without particular attention to either of the persons present, he shuffled from the room leaving Ned to close the door after him.

"Very obliging, ain't he?" grinned the major, catching Ned's twinkling look.

"Sir, I was overwhelmed," replied Ned with an answering smile. "With hospitality such as this, my only wonder is that the house is not overrun with visitors."

"Well, even such meticulous observance of etiquette cannot induce me to spend another night in this house. I'll rest this arm for a while longer and then we'll slip quietly away. No need to trouble our host to see us off, I think, otherwise we shall be letting ourselves in for another jawing. Do you think you could ride over to Mr Stewart's and ask for the loan of his gig?"

"I'll go as soon as you are washed and shaved. It won't take me long. I doubt we'll be missed. That long-faced fellow won't shift himself to discover why the bell does not ring."

Their departure was not so swiftly accomplished after all. The rector and his wife had taken the gig to Shoreham and were not expected back until after the dinner hour. Ned was obliged to return to the rectory later that evening and by the time he eventually drew up in the lane just beyond the gates of High

Dean, night had fallen.

The major was already awaiting him, having left the house via the back stairs and out through a rear door. He handed the portmanteau up to Ned with his sound arm and climbed into the gig. Ned chirruped to his horse and they set off at a trot towards the Downs.

Upon reaching the coast road some twenty minutes later, they travelled steadily uphill with the rain and wind in their faces. The two carriage lamps, one on each side of the gig, served only to briefly reveal the dark road ahead before it abruptly closed again behind them as they drove on through the enfolding mystery of night.

As they approached the crest of the hill, they could hear the crescendo of the windblown waves repeatedly attempting to scale the cliff face.

"Blakestone will be a bleak place tonight, sir," commented Ned, peering through the gloom.

"It will seem a cosy haven after that dismal room," replied the major cheerfully. "Listen to the surf, Ned. Isn't it grand?"

Ned turned his head towards the sounding sea and at that very same moment, saw a bright, blue flash of light burst in the great void of darkness.

"Did you see that!?" the major cried excitedly. "There's something out there in the bay!" Hardly had he finished speaking, when another light appeared, this time high above them. A gleaming, golden light that shone like a glittering star and then was gone, only to burn briefly a minute later and, as suddenly, die.

"By Jupiter! That can only have come from the tower at Blakestone! It seems that Hal may have been right after all. Someone is signalling to a vessel offshore. Oho! Now we shall see something, Ned!"

"What do you mean to do, sir?"

"We are going behind enemy lines. Turn around, Ned. We passed a gate a few minutes ago: the one that leads into Deepdene field. There is an old flint barn that will serve to conceal the gig while we climb down to the bay. Hurry!"

"But, sir! You cannot engage upon such an undertaking in your condition!" protested Ned vehemently. "This notion of yours is foolhardy. You surely don't really mean to clamber about these cliffs at dead of night and with that wound in your arm?"

"I only intend to do a little reconnaissance, you need not fear that I shall lead you into danger. Look! There's the gate: pull up here while I unfasten the latch."

Very much against his will, Ned obeyed the command. He knew the major far too well to argue any further against his rash decision. These last months of inaction had driven his master almost to distraction and now he was ripe for any mad adventure.

When the gig had been safely concealed in the barn, the two men retraced their path to the top of the Downs and began to make their way across the soaking grass to the very edge of the cliffs.

It was so dark that they could see nothing and had to tread extremely carefully. Heavy rainclouds still obscured the moon and stars and there had been no repetition of the flashing lights, neither was there any sound save that of the restless sea.

"There's no one here," whispered Ned.

"If it is a smuggling vessel, they may be making a landing further along the coast."

"No. That second light we saw was certainly a signal for a landing here tonight. Come, we will go down to the beach. Follow me closely, Ned, I know a short cut that will save us having to go back along the road."

"I don't like it, sir," complained Ned reluctantly, "I would not care to climb down there, even in daylight."

"You're right, of course. I should not ask you to take such risks. You stay here and keep watch from above. I'll go down alone and don't worry that I shall come to any harm because I could find my way to that beach blindfold."

"We might just as well be," grumbled Ned, "but if you're set on going down there, then I'm coming with you."

"Very well, old friend, but be sure to tread exactly where I tell you."

Together they began to make the descent, the major leading and guiding Ned's feet at every step. The wind was blowing on shore but not so fiercely that it endangered their lives. However, it drove the rain at their backs until their coats were saturated and their boots caked with sticky chalk. It was with considerable relief that Ned eventually felt the crunch of pebbles under his feet and realized that they had finally gained the safety of the beach. He was just about to voice his gratitude to a benevolent God, when the major grabbed him by the sleeve and drew him into the shelter of the rocks clustered at the foot of the cliffs.

"Hark, Ned! Did you hear that?!"

Ned strained his ears and eyes until, against the incessant gasping of the deeps, he could also discern the unmistakable rattle of feet on the shingle, though nothing was yet visible.

Then a small gap in the clouds gave a hazy glimmer of moonlight and suddenly before them rose the almost spectral shape of a sleek ship. She was painted black, rigged fore and aft with dark sails and lay at anchor only a few yards from the shore, riding the waves in the manner of a gigantic, predatory seabird her long bowsprit extended beak-like against the dim skyline.

"I knew it!" whispered the major

excitedly. "That blue flash we saw was the powder igniting in the pan of the spotsman's pistol. The ship must have been offshore as we came along the road and they may have thought our carriage lamps were giving them the all-clear. Look! The beach is swarming with men!"

As he finished speaking, Ned could see for himself that a mass of dark shapes were running along the shingle while others waded out through the foaming surf. The loud splash of heavy objects hitting the water, drifted across to him as the sailors on the cutter quickly tossed their cargo over the side. His eyes having become adjusted to the surrounding darkness, Ned now espied several barrels and bales bobbing about on the waves. These were swiftly recovered by the men standing waist-deep in the oily-black seas and hoisted up on to broad backs to be borne rapidly away to the shore. Others arrived on the scene, this time leading a caravan of ponies and donkeys and as the tubmen emerged from the water, a keg on each shoulder, willing arms relieved them of their load while they plunged back to the ship for more contraband.

A phalanx of men soon formed on the shore, passing bales, kegs and barrels down the human chain to be strapped on to the waiting animals. The larger barrels were already roped together in pairs as they were hurled from the decks of the cutter and within minutes of entering the water were being strung across the ponies' backs.

Within the twinkling of an eye, the first of these heavily burdened beasts were staggering away inland, soon followed by the rest of the caravan. The entire operation had taken less than ten minutes, owing to the strength and speed of this highly disciplined gang of men who had not uttered a single syllable between them. Whilst the last of the laden ponies was led from view, the cutter had also slipped away, tacking back and forth across the bay, her sails billowing as she ran upwind to vanish into the thick, black veil of night.

"Come, Ned, follow me! We are going to track these smugglers," hissed the major urgently. "I want to see where they go. We may yet discover who is behind this. Someone is using my house and my land to carry out this trade and I mean to find out who it is and how long it has been going on. I wonder if Lucius knew of it? That fellow Tom Shaw was involved in smuggling, wasn't he? Oh, I would give a great deal to know who organized this landing tonight. It has to be someone who knew neither of us would be at Blakestone. Come, we can go now, they are quite out of sight. Be as quiet as you can on this curst shingle, I don't want them to know they have been seen."

Keeping low against the cliff face, they darted between the rocks strewn along the beach, creeping silently towards the estuary and a path that snaked through the fields and on to the woodlands beyond.

Ahead of them they could still hear the muffled sounds of the ponies' hoofs as they climbed slowly along the chalky incline, their iron shoes wrapped in sacking.

They did not take the coast road but crossed over it and disappeared through a little coppice that grew to the side of an open field. Once through these trees, the caravan began to disperse, each group of animals being taken in a different direction.

"What shall we do now?" muttered Ned.

"Follow them," replied the major, nodding towards the men who had turned into a narrow track that continued to lead upwards. "If I am not mistaken, I think they are making for Blakestone."

It seemed that this string of ponies were those carrying the bulkier loads that would perhaps be more difficult to conceal, such as the large 'ankers' of overproof brandy which each held some eight gallons of liquor.

On and up they climbed until they reached the road that wound through the beechwood, leading eventually to Blakestone House itself.

Just as they were about to enter the wood, there came the haunting cry of an owl. Twice it echoed, first loudly and then soft and low. As the last notes trembled into silence, the men quickly drew their animals into the safety of the trees.

The major signalled to Ned to follow him and together they slipped soundlessly across the road, creeping furtively between the beeches until they reached the shelter of a bushy thicket. Crouching down, they peered into the darkness, wondering what would happen next.

At first, all they could hear was the pattering of rain on the leaves above them, amplifying the solitude. The absolute stillness of the men and ponies close by, seemed to add tension to the deep silence. Drops of water spattered continuously upon and around them as they waited, cold and uncomfortable in the eerie darkness.

Now came the soft rustling of foliage and out from the crowded trees stepped a slightly-built figure wrapped in a thick, seaman's jacket.

"Dicer!" hissed a voice urgently. "It's me — Eli."

One of the men at the head of the line came to meet him.

"What's the pelter? The jig ain't up, is it? 'As someone peached?"

"Soldiers. On the pike road. Hurry! We must hide everything up at the house. There's no time to waste. We'll not be able to get it away tonight. Come with me."

Quickly and without further discussion, the men hastened up the hill with Ned and the major keeping a wary distance behind them.

When at last they arrived at Blakestone, they turned along the ruined east wing and made their way to the far corner where a second tower had once stood.

The major now had to exercise extreme caution as it had become necessary to cross the open ground that lay in front of the house. He decided it would be safer to approach the building by leaving the cover of the woods at a point nearest to the west tower. It was still dark enough to conceal their advance and the moon favoured them by remaining in its thick bed of clouds. This happy chance enabled them to attain their goal and they came to the shelter of the west wall without being detected. Keeping well within its shadow, they edged along the front of the house until they gained the steps of the broken portico. From this vantage point, they could see across the ruined interior of the east section and although it was too dark to see clearly, there was no doubt that the men were busy unloading the ponies.

Putting a warning finger to his lips, the major began an advance upon the unsuspecting 'Gentlemen' with Ned following at his heels. Carefully, they picked their way over the broken masonry using the remnants of shattered walls to cover their stealthy approach. When they had gone as near as they dared, they hid themselves behind a heap of fallen debris and listened intently.

As before, when the men had been on the beach, there was no snatch of conversation to overhear. They worked in total silence and only the occasional grating of stone or brick revealed their presence. It was difficult to make out what was happening but there was a great deal of activity going on somewhere in the vicinity of the north-east corner of the ruined building.

After a few minutes more, even these slight sounds suddenly ceased and all was quiet again. The major deemed it safe to take another look and slowly straightening himself, peeped cautiously over the pile of rubble. At first he could see nothing, neither man nor beast. Then something caught his inquisitive eye. About twenty yards in front of him, the unmistakable form of a tall, shrouded figure gradually rose up out of the ground until it had gained its full height. It seemed to turn slowly towards him and he ducked down again to avoid detection. However, curiosity got the better of him and he quickly stole another look but to his utter amazement, there was nothing there. The figure had vanished as rapidly as it had appeared.

He stared about him in bewilderment. Where could it have gone? Surely he had not imagined it? But there was certainly nothing visible anywhere and all was still and silent as the grave. Was this perhaps the phantom of which Tilda and Albert had spoken? Of course not! Such superstitious nonsense! There was bound to be a logical explanation.

"Did you see anything, Ned?" he whispered softly, as Ned peered over his shoulder to discover for himself what it was that had absorbed his master's interest so completely.

"Not I. It's too dark to see anything much tonight. But I heard 'em, sure enough. Do you think they are gone away now?"

"I believe so. Let's take a closer look. But tread with caution."

Warily they picked their way over the damaged walls towards the tumbled ruins of the east tower. The major hunted about for some sign of the smugglers or their contraband but all to no avail. It was as if they had been swallowed up in the darkness.

"I think they have probably gone on down the hill, in the direction of the Dower House. I doubt if they would risk going back the way they came if the Preventives are about. Let's go back for the rector's gig, I'm too weary to follow them any further tonight. But we can be sure they will be back for their goods and I intend to be waiting. Meanwhile, we'll leave our investigations until the morning when we shall be able to make a proper search."

"I'm glad to hear you speak so sensibly at last," scolded Ned, "you must have windmills in your head to have embarked upon this enterprise on such a night — and you just out of your sick-bed. You'll stay right here while I go and fetch the gig. And don't you even think of leaving the house while I am gone!"

With this admonition, Ned departed in haste, leaving the major to make his way back to the more welcoming comfort of undemolished rooms.

Ned retrieved the gig from the barn and set off once more towards Blakestone. It was mizzling now and he sat hunched beneath the hood of the carriage, longing for some dry clothes and a warm bed. He rather wished that they had remained another night under Sir Harry's roof, at least his master would not have been tempted into such nonsensical folly. It had proved impossible to recognize any of the smugglers and they were none the wiser for all the trouble they had taken to follow the men. Every one had escaped into the darkness, as doubtless they always did, for they were too well practised for this to have been anything other than a routine procedure.

He was pondering over the night's

wearying events, when he suddenly pulled the horse to a halt. In the light of the lamps he thought he had seen something moving at the side of the road.

"Who's there?!" he cried sharply, eyes searching the shadowy hedgerow. No answer came but he distinctly heard a low, moaning sound. Nervously, he called once more, "Speak! Who is it and what are you doing there?!"

Still no word was uttered and this time Ned climbed down from the gig to investigate for himself. He walked a few steps back along the road until he almost stumbled upon a man lying face downwards in the long, wet grass that edged the lane. Bending over him, Ned stretched out a tentative hand and turned the man on to his back. The stranger groaned again as though in great pain and leaning closer, Ned could see that the pale features were streaked with mud. He fumbled in his pocket for his handkerchief and began to wipe the mire away.

"Are you well enough to walk a few yards to my carriage? No, I think not, my unfortunate friend," muttered Ned to himself, rising to his feet and hastening back to the gig. He took up the ribbons and backed the vehicle towards the inert figure still lying silently in the grass. Once more he jumped down and lifting the man by the shoulders, heaved him to his feet, half dragging and half carrying him to the waiting gig.

After a great deal of strenuous effort, Ned managed to haul him up on to the seat and propped him as gently as he could into a corner. It was now that they were sitting in the circle of light supplied by the carriage lamps, that Ned saw the man's face was horribly bedabbled with gore. A deep gash was visible in the grizzled hair just above his brow and blood was oozing down his face, to mingle with the mud from the grassy verge.

"Good Heavens, man! What has happened to you?!" cried Ned aghast. "You had better come home with me, I think," he continued decisively, aware that his words went unheeded. "You need to have that wound dressed immediately."

He set the horse into a brisk trot

and proceeded on his way, dividing his attention between the road ahead and the unconscious figure beside him.

As he neared the steep incline that led to Blakestone, he heard the sound of tramping feet approaching from the direction of the post-road. A group of soldiers led by an officer on horseback, came marching round the bend in the road and drew to a halt in front of him, barring the way. Ned pulled in the horse once more and waited for the officer to come up with him.

"The deuce! It's you, Ned! What brings you out so late and in such weather?"

"It's a long story, Captain Rowland, sir," sighed Ned wearily. "I begin to think this night will never end. I suppose you are searching for those smugglers?"

"How do you know that?" questioned the captain sharply. "Have you seen anything of them?"

"Too much, I fear! As this poor soul may have done also." He nodded towards the fainting man slumped against him. "I found him lying in the road; he's had such a vicious blow to the head, I doubt he'll last the night. What with him — and the major wounded . . ."

"Alex? Wounded?! How?"

"He was shot in the arm by a complete stranger just yesterday. But don't fear, he's well enough. You know his mettle: the major's a prime 'un! And as to your smugglers, they were last seen circling back to the coast road, up yonder."

The captain ordered his men to face about. "Thank you, Ned. We shall see if we can head them off."

"You can but try. Though I doubt you'll catch up with them: they had wind of you lads some while since."

"I guessed as much," muttered the captain, frowning with annoyance. "Farewell, Ned. Tell Alex I shall call on him tomorrow as soon as I am able. I should like to learn all that you know of this night's work."

"Goodnight, Captain. Good luck."

The soldiers marched smartly out of sight along the road and Ned gave a cursory glance at his stricken passenger before moving on towards Blakestone. He shook his head, sighing dismally, "It looks as if you'll be needing more than luck to help you through the rest of this plaguey night. But come, let's get on before any other misfortunes befall us; this is surely an accursed place, damn me if it ain't!"

11

UPON arriving at the house, Ned was obliged to summon the major to his assistance and between them they lifted the seemingly lifeless body from the gig and brought him into the warmth of the parlour.

Gently they laid him down in front of the fire and set a cushion beneath his head.

"He's still breathing, Ned," confirmed the major, straightening himself and staring down at the sick man whose face was half-concealed by the bloody clout which Ned had tied around the dreadful injury. "I wonder who he is? I don't remember seeing him before."

"Nor I. Though I doubt his own mother would recognize him just now. We'll see what he looks like when we've cleaned him up."

"There's hot water on the hob. I'll stable the horse. Or do you think I should ride into the village and rouse the doctor?"

Ned shook his head, "No, we'll not disturb him: I can manage. Let us see if this poor devil survives the night."

"You know best about these matters, Ned. I won't be above a moment or two. We'll put him in my bed for tonight — that chair will serve me just as well until we can rearrange our accommodation."

"Oh no! If anyone's to give up their bed it had better be me. You need your rest more than I after losing all that blood."

"There's no meat here for argument. I had plenty of rest last night, so I'll sit up with this fellow and you'll get a proper night's sleep — and that's an order Corporal Parrish!"

By the time the major returned to the house, Ned had already washed and neatly bandaged the stranger's wound. Together they undressed him and got him to bed. "There, that's all we can do for him tonight. Get you to your rest, Ned, I'll watch him."

"I want to take a look at your arm

first. After tonight's exertions, I'll not be surprised if that wound has opened up again. And there's no use in your issuing any more orders because I won't obey 'em, so don't trouble yourself to remind me of my rank!"

The major merely grinned at Ned's stern face and meekly submitted to his expert ministrations.

"Yes, it's as I suspected. It's bleeding afresh. You had no business clambering down those cliffs with a wound like this," scolded Ned, busy with more bandages. "I did warn you but you would go following after those desperadoes with no thought in your head for the possible consequences: just as you have always done for as long as I've known you."

"With you hurrying close at my heels, just as you always do," interspersed the major, laughingly.

"How else are you to be kept out of trouble?" grumbled Ned.

"Can I help it if it follows me about?"

"You could make a little more effort to avoid it. By the way, you seemed to understand more than most about that business on the beach. How did you know

306

what was going forward on that stretch of coast tonight? You'd better have a good answer because I met Captain Rowland as I returned with the gig and he is coming to question us about it in the morning."

"Thank you for the warning. To own the truth, Ned, I am not unfamiliar with the dealings of the smuggling fraternity. I have participated in a little free-trading myself in bygone days. When Lucius and I were boys, we struck up a friendship with one of the local fishermen: Nick Tranter, remember? It didn't take us long to discover that fishing was not his only means of earning a living. We thought it would be great gig to go with him and help the Gentlemen hide the contraband; we were sure we could find them some wonderfully secret places where no one would ever think of looking. Of course we had some rare sport evading the Revenue men and it was all a marvellous adventure. But it finally came to an end when we were sent away to school. So there you have it, Ned, that's how I learnt about the spotsman and that trick of his with the 'flash'. The spotsman has the task of guiding the ship to the men waiting on shore. He has to be fully conversant with the waters and the coastline; he must know its every contour like the back of his hand — especially by night. When he has brought the vessel to a prearranged position, usually at a convenient stretch from the shore where he can command a good view of the coast, he indicates their arrival with that distinctive light we observed. He does this by using a pistol from which the barrel has been removed. The pan is filled with powder and when the hammer is released, the powder ignites and flares with a bright, blue light that is quite unmistakable even at some considerable distance.

"Meanwhile, someone ashore will have been keeping a close watch on the Preventives, relaying their movements to the men waiting to unload. As soon as they are certain that they can work undisturbed, they signal back to the ship that the coast is clear and a second light indicates which landing point has been chosen.'

"That's when the crew must trust to

the spotsman's skill, for with all speed he has to bring the ship as close to the shore as he dare — and this on the blackest of nights! So you see what thorough preparations have to be made if they are to bring the contraband quickly and safely ashore. The Preventives are constantly on the alert but are few in number and have miles of coastline to cover. Their best chance to capture the smugglers is to take them by surprise, though with so many, sharp eyes following them about, that is no simple endeavour."

"It's very well for you that your father knew nothing of this," frowned Ned disapprovingly, "he'd not have been best pleased to discover that his sons were about such mischief! You might have been thrown into prison — or even killed! I don't know which would have pained him the most." He returned to their hapless guest who lay without moving a muscle, barely having the strength to draw breath. There was nothing more that could be done to his comfort and so they left him undisturbed.

When the glorious, golden-gowned morning, dripping with diamonds, came trailing misty muslin draperies through the trees, Ned and the major were already abroad as had been their habit for years past. Together they broke their fast before deciding what was to be done about the stranger.

"I think he looks a little better this morning, Ned. What think you?"

"He does seem to have a more natural colour in his face today. I believe he has made some improvement."

"I'll ask the doctor to call later. If he gives it as his opinion that the poor fellow should not be moved, then I'll make up a pallet for myself in here. Perhaps the doctor may know who he is and if he does, we shall be able to inform any relatives he may have in the vicinity."

"You ought to remain here for a while. Captain Rowland intends to call on you this morning," reminded Ned. "I expect he has several questions he would like answered."

"Yes, I daresay he may," smiled the major, "Hal will be furious at being outwitted by those smugglers last night. When he arrives, we will make a search of the ruins. Between us we must be able to find an answer to the sudden disappearance of such a large quantity of brandy. Where on earth could they have hidden it in such a short while? It cannot have been spirited away."

"Indeed not," laughed Ned, "it's somewhere about and you may be certain that they'll be back for it as soon as they think the coast is clear. Now I must be on my way. I promised Mr Stewart I would return his gig first thing this morning."

"Would you give him my thanks for the use of it, Ned? You had better mention to him that we have a badly injured stranger staying with us: he may be able to help in identifying him. Someone may be suffering a great deal of concern for his safety."

"I'll do that, sir. I shall be back within the hour," promised Ned shrugging himself into his coat. "If he regains consciousness while I am gone, try if you can give him a little warmed milk and brandy."

It was not long after Ned's departure that the major heard a horse approaching. Ah, that will be Hal, he thought to himself and made his way along the passage to greet the captain's arrival.

However, it was not Captain Rowland who dismounted at the door but Lady Elisa Maytland. Her riding habit was heavily splashed with mud and beneath the fashionable shako hat that she wore at a dashing angle on the side of her head, her coppery curls were decidedly dishevelled.

He opened his eyes wide with surprise as she came towards him, the fluffy plume adorning her hat fluttering gaily in the breeze. Why should she wish to visit him and in such obvious haste?

"Good morning to you, Major Lacey. May I come in?" she began in her usual brusque fashion.

"I suppose it would be useless explaining to you the indecorum of visiting a bachelor's establishment without the protection of a duenna?"

"It would. Though I doubt you would have troubled mentioning it if I had been Another and blessed with angelic blue eyes and golden tresses. Now, may I come in? Or must I stand shivering on your doorstep for the sake of your outraged sensibilities? I had not thought you such a milk and water fellow."

"That's doing it a little too brown," he drawled, "I know exactly what you think of me, though you may be certain that it bothers me not at all. And if you imagine that such singularly unamusing allusions will impress your wit upon me, then let me disillusion you at once for it is quite otherwise. But come in by all means. If you do not care for the proprieties, I am sure it is all of a piece to me."

He stepped aside and she swept past him, head erect, the train of her skirt sweeping behind her as she marched briskly along the flagged passageway.

"This is the reception room where I usually receive my guests," he said sententiously, as she paused at the door and purposely stood back waiting for him to open it for her.

"I know. I am as familiar with this house as . . . "

"As you are with High Dean?" suggested the major smoothly. "You see I have remarked your familiarity."

Her face flushed with sudden rage. "Then keep your remarks to yourself!"

she snapped furiously. "I remember, that you were not so prudish when you mistook me for Aurelia!"

It was his turn to colour. "If you mean to sully that lady's good name you need remain no longer in my house. I shall not trouble to show you out. You know where the door is."

"I haven't come here to quarrel with you," replied she, adopting a more conciliatory tone and making a visible effort to swallow her anger.

"Then why have you come?" he demanded churlishly.

"Shall we sit down and discuss that in a civilized manner?"

For a moment it seemed he meant to ignore her request as he continued to stand glaring balefully at her. Then, "If we must," he muttered stiffly and finally opened the door.

She bestowed on him a frosty smile and entered the room.

"How perfectly charming," said she gazing all about her with apparent interest. "You have improved it beyond all recognition. This was fallen into a dreadful state of repair since the house was abandoned to its fate."

"It is all Ned's doing, you must save your compliments for him. "But you did not come to admire my domestic arrangements, so let us dispense with such banality."

"My, my, your years in Spain have utterly destroyed your social skills, Major. Or did you never bother to develop them?"

"I shall admit only to having developed a strong and, as I begin to think, a lasting antipathy for your company, my lady, so please state your business and kindly leave me in peace. I have several important matters to attend to this morning and can spare you only a few minutes of my time."

This deliberate set-down did not have the desired effect. He had hoped to make her understand that he had no patience with the childish antics of an ill-bred termagent with nothing to recommend her to any person of sense. Instead, she suddenly fell into peals of laughter and it was he who now felt at a disadvantage.

"You must excuse me but I seem to have failed to appreciate the joke," he continued, eyeing her with a patent dislike.

"I'm sorry," she gurgled, her amusement beginning to subside under his quelling gaze, "it is unforgivable of me, is it not? But please don't glower at me like that, you can have no notion how difficult you are making it for me to refrain from laughing when you are trying so hard to look pompous. It really doesn't suit you, you know."

His blue eyes glittered dangerously but she merely smiled serenely up at him. He was about to speak the reproof that sprang so readily to his tongue, when she prevented his doing so by continuing suavely, "It won't do, I am determined not to be offended, try what you may. Besides, there is nothing you can say to me that has not already been said a hundred times and far more eloquently. Now if you will but remove that straw from behind your right ear, we will be able to converse easily and sensibly."

He eyed her suspiciously before crossing towards the mirror hanging above the fireplace. A quick glance into its somewhat spotted surface and he managed to retrieve the offending item that clung tenaciously to his thickly curling hair.

"I was engaged in making up a palliasse when you interrupted me," he explained rather irritably, "we had need of an extra bed owing to the arrival of an unexpected guest."

"Indeed? I am amazed that you can accommodate guests in so small a space. You cannot have more than two or three rooms fit for habitation at best. Or is it a fellow officer who has come to stay? Captain Rowland perhaps?"

"No, not Captain Rowland although I am expecting a visit from him at any moment, so if you would state your business?"

"Yes, you are anxious to be rid of me, that much is plain. Well then, I came to see how you did. I met Sir Harry this morning and he told me that you had left his house in rather mysterious circumstances without taking leave of your hosts and without informing any of the servants. We were naturally concerned for your health and, as I usually exercise my horse at this time of day, I promised him that I would call on you to ensure that all was well."

"I find nothing natural in your determination to interfere in my affairs. If you must know, I quit the house because I did not wish to further inconvenience Sir Harry or his household. Anyway, he was gone from home when we left and I could not await his return as time was pressing and I was determined to return to Blakestone. You may tell him that I am perfectly recovered and that I thank him for his hospitality, it was quite without equal."

"You did not then find the journey back to Blakestone in the least debilitating?"

"Not at all. In fact it was extraordinarily exhilarating," he replied, eyeing her keenly. "Did you think it might be otherwise?"

"That's what I came to discover for myself. Your condition when last I saw you had given me cause for concern. But I am glad to see that my fears were unfounded. I should have been sorry to find you at all indisposed. You were a little foolhardy to leave High Dean so precipitately but thankfully no ill has befallen you after all. There, you see?

It is possible to be civil if we but make the effort."

"Was my welfare the only reason for your calling on me at such an early hour?" he questioned deliberately.

"Not entirely," she answered returning his gaze with seeming candour. "I had given Ned my word that I would take care of Perseus and I would not be neglectful of my duty. But now that you are safely returned, I shall consider myself released from it."

"I suppose I ought to thank you for looking after my horse during my indisposition," he replied stiffly.

"Not if it pains you so much. And judging by your present expression, I can see that it does," she remarked with some annoyance. "Well let me relieve you from any sense of indebtedness. My concern was solely for the horse. Fortunately he cares naught for the proprieties and accepted my assistance graciously."

"Is that what you expected of me? Then I am sorry to disappoint you. I had sooner you had not troubled yourself. You certainly overstepped the mark when you came to High Dean yesterday. Did you stop to think what gossip you might have given rise to? I am no dumb animal conscious only of my own comfort; there are other considerations which, although you may be unable to grasp them, are not quite beyond my powers of understanding."

"You mistake, sir! My intellect is not so impaired, I assure you. We merely differ on the importance we attach to such things. You choose to live caged about by convention — I do not. That is entirely your decision but pray do not think to inflict it upon me!" came the rejoinder, uttered with considerable asperity, anger blazing in the flashing, green eyes as she faced up to him like a ferocious kitten.

His own swift temper now sprang into being and without warning he took a sudden step towards her, "Then you must accept the consequences!" he said with a grim smile and catching her up in his arms, kissed her hard on the mouth.

This sudden assault on her person was so unexpected that at first she was shocked into submission. Now she struggled to free herself from his embrace and surprise became fear because she felt his power was so much greater than hers. Finding her strenuous efforts so easily frustrated, a burning rage mounted in her breast giving her added strength and pushing with all her might against his chest she twisted her face away from him.

"How dare you!" she exploded furiously. "How dare you touch me, you vile, despicable oaf!"

He gave a low laugh and freed her at last. "Perhaps that will teach you the need to conform to the rules governing social behaviour."

The next moment she had sprung at him, fingers extended, scoring his face so viciously with her nails, that the blood welled up instantly leaving long, red scratches on his cheek. "And let that teach you to keep your hands off me!" she spat irefully, her voice harsh with unsuppressible hatred and her eyes smouldering up at him defiantly.

"You little wildcat!" he cried, seizing her wrists in a vice-like grip. "There's only one way you'll ever learn to behave.

Your father should have taken his whip to you years ago! You've had your way for far too long. Now get out of here before I decide to correct the omission myself!"

"As if you'd dare!" she sneered contemptuously, breaking away from his loosened grasp.

"Oh, wouldn't I?" he muttered threateningly and with a light in his eyes that signalled danger.

"You would live just long enough to regret it," came the hissing reply. "And this time I should shoot to kill!"

They eyed each other steadily, the air almost crackling with tension.

"So it was you that day in the green lane," he said without a trace of surprise in his voice. "I guessed as much!"

"You needn't flatter yourself that you thwarted my plans, I never meant to kill you then. I could have put a hole through your head at any moment of my choosing when you entered that path." She lifted her chin and eyed him triumphantly. "And if you come near me again that's exactly what I shall do, believe me!"

"Don't be so dramatic, child," he

322

scoffed carelessly. "Anyone would suppose it was the first time that you had ever been kissed."

She turned away from his mocking eyes and a look of stunned amazement altered his expression. For the first time since he had met her, she looked mortified. Well I'll be damned! he thought incredulously. Is her reputation undeserved after all?

He stared at her averted face curiously. Was it possible? Could this seemingly bold and free-spirited virago really be so unsophisticated? Surely not! Her behaviour was hardly that of a virtuous woman. Had she not come to Sir Harry's house quite openly and with no female attendant to lend her countenance? She had even had the effrontery to enter into a man's bedchamber according to Ned's account of events that had occurred while he himself lay unconscious. What was worse, she had discovered his true feelings for Aurelia and in his eyes that was an unforgivable intrusion of his privacy. Were these the actions of a respectable, unmarried woman? Certainly not in his opinion!

She was standing with her back to

him but he could see that she was still trembling with the violence of her emotions. Since he had vented his own spleen upon her with such energy, his temper had cooled a little and he was in control of himself again. He even felt a little guilty that he had allowed his anger to get the better of him. Yet it was her own fault; if she had not behaved with such brash arrogance he would not have been goaded into that rather regrettable act. To punish her by humiliating her, now seemed a crass revenge. What had it proved? Only that he had the greater physical strength. Was that really so glorious a triumph? It was his turn to experience a deep sense of shame.

"I think you had better go home," he said quietly. "We can have nothing more to say to one another. I don't even care to know why you attempted to murder me. I shall assume it was a further example of your eccentricity."

Elisa spun round to face him, fists clenched at her sides. "I hate you!" she cried in a choked voice. "I shan't care what happens to you now! You are the rudest, most conceited and selfish creature I have ever had the misfortune to set eyes on! I should have left you to bleed to death yesterday! I wish I had!"

He stared at her in amazement, shaken by the vehemence of this renewed outburst. She rushed past him and wrenched open the door.

"I hope they kill you next time!" she shouted, slamming the door with such violence the whole room reverberated with the shock. The sound of her rapid footsteps could be heard stamping down the flagged passageway and then the outer door slammed shut too.

The major was left staring at the closed door, feeling as if he had just been hit by a tornado. The woman must be quite mad! She ought not to be let out in any society, especially his! He seemed to have the same effect upon her as a full moon had on a lunatic!

Only a few minutes after her departure, Captain Rowland appeared at the door.

"Come in, Hal, I've been expecting you this last hour and more. Ned warned me that you were coming to see us this morning."

"Well, I should certainly like to hear

what you have to say about the tricks that were played on us yesternight," he began seriously. Then pausing suddenly, exclaimed, "Good grief, Alex! What have you been doing to your face?"

The major shrugged carelessly. "Oh, just an accident that's all. I scratched myself on a rose briar out there in that garden wilderness." He turned abruptly away and led the captain back to the cosy little parlour.

"That's not the only damage you've done to yourself, I hear," continued the captain following after him. "What's been happening? I know about the landing at Blakestone Bay; one of my men saw a signal light that seemed to come from that tower of yours. We marched over here as quickly as we could but they must have had word of our approach. I met Ned driving along the road and he confirmed that there were smugglers operating in the vicinity. What do you know about it?"

"Not as much as I would like to but sit down and I'll tell you all that's occurred during the last two days."

As briefly as he could, he explained

the sequence of events that had led to his being away from home until late the previous night. When he had finished, Hal eyed him thoughtfully.

"Do you suppose there might be some connection between the men who shot at you and this gang of smugglers?"

"It's certainly a possibility. Unfortunately, I did not manage to recognize anyone except that young man who spoiled your sport. His name is Eli and he is Sam Frant's nephew, according to the information I had of Mrs Shaw. It might be worth your while to track him down. One of the men involved in giving me this," he indicated his injured arm, "was the very same fellow that I came across in the lane near Mrs Shaw's home. He and his accomplice appeared to be trying to abduct young Eli. Apparently he has some information that they require him to share with them, though what that might be Mrs Shaw was definitely reluctant to impart to me."

"Then I shall seek him out as soon as I can. And what of this stranger Ned stumbled upon? May I see him?"

"Of course. But he's still unconscious,

alas, so you'll get nothing out of him yet."

They went along to the major's sleeping quarters and found the sick man just as he had been left earlier that morning.

"You see? There's no change in his condition. We haven't had one word out of him since Ned picked him up from the roadside."

The captain leaned over the bed. "Someone must have given him a vicious blow to the head to inflict such an injury. No doubt it was meant to finish him. He isn't one of the Riding Officers though, which was what I had half suspected."

"Perhaps he was mistaken for one of them?" suggested the major. "It was a very dark night."

"I suppose we shall just have to wait until he regains consciousness, if he ever does. Now what about Sir Harry Palmer? He was rather keen to dissuade you from returning to Blakestone. You said he took you up in his chaise after finding you wounded. That seems a strange coincidence to me. Two carriages travelling on that lonely road at exactly the same time? Did you take note of his coachman? Was it the same man who shot you?"

"I'm sorry to say that my brain was not quite as sharp as it might have been at the time. All I can tell you is that Palmer did seem surprised to discover the nature of my affliction."

"Well, surprise is not too difficult to feign and if he had had something to do with the shooting, he was bound to have attempted the pretence. He may have been the man in the hooded cloak. You said you could not see his face. And let us keep in mind the fact that, at the time of the landing, Palmer was away from the house."

"Quite so. I am more than a little suspicious of his motives myself. It seemed strange to me that after his obvious reluctance to assist me in my difficulties, he should then take me to High Dean, especially as I had asked to be taken to my own house. Blakestone was not so far out of his way and one would never suppose that he had ambitions to be a Good Samaritan. Oh, listen, that's Ned's step I hear. We'll make a search of the east tower now. Between the three of us, we must be able to find that missing brandy."

They went out to meet Ned as he came along the passageway. "Good morning to you, Captain. Did you catch up with your smugglers?"

"No, Ned, we did not. They had word of our coming. My guess is, whoever showed that light from the top of the tower also kept watch from up there. Sounds travel easily at night and he may have heard something that warned him of our advance."

"Then it must have been the one they call Eli, for it was he who tipped them the office; we saw the lad in the beechwood," Ned informed him. Then catching sight of the major's face, he frowned and demanded to know what he had been doing to get his face mauled.

"It's nothing. Just a scratch," came the muttered reply.

"Have you been throwing your castors again? I've just seen Sir Harry Palmer and that brother of his who's so fond of the Daffy."

"Have you, indeed?" responded the captain with great interest, "Where exactly did you see them?"

"Riding down towards the village. I thought they must have come from Blakestone," answered Ned, still regarding the major with great suspicion.

Noting this look, the major turned deliberately away from Ned's unwelcome attention and taking the captain by the arm, dragged him off to inspect the ruins, saying, "Come with me, Hal. I'll show you where the smugglers must have hidden that contraband."

When they reached the broken remains of the east tower, the major pointed to two half-demolished walls, vestiges of a small room that had once given access to the tower steps.

"I think this must be where they unloaded the ponies. Yes! Look where these imprints are left in the muddy grass."

"But there's nowhere here to hide anything of size," observed the captain, searching through the scattered rubble, "and you said that there were ankers of brandy on the backs of those animals."

"That is so. There's nothing hidden above ground, I was certain of that last night when Ned and I had a look. We must seek a little deeper for the answer to this puzzle."

He crouched down and began to inspect the solid paving underfoot.

"This stone floor is part of the original building. It was used to be some kind of a fortified manor house several centuries ago. See how worn they are around the base of the stairway? Help me clear some of this rubbish away and we'll see if there's any sign of them having been lifted recently."

With quiet determination they set about the task of examining the large squares of hand-hewn stone. Fortunately, the room had occupied an area of only some few square yards and it was not long before Captain Rowland called out excitedly, "Alex! Come over here! I want you to take a look at this."

The major came at once to kneel beside him. One of the stones was imperfectly laid and an edge was protruding about half an inch above its neighbour.

"Ned, bring me that axe I use for splitting the logs. It will make it an easy matter to lift this."

At once Ned hasted away to fetch it and as soon as he had returned, the major prised up the stone slab using the blade of the axe head.

"Ah! This is something like! I believe we have found a secret chamber. You remember, Hal, that you thought this house held many secrets? Well, it's true. Blakestone is so ancient that such rooms have long been part of its legend. My father once showed us a priest-hole built into the chimney of a fireplace. See? There are some steps under here. Help me move this next stone away."

Together they dragged it aside to reveal a large, oblong aperture with deep steps descending into the darkness below.

"I'll go down and take a look," volunteered the major readily.

"It's deuced black down there: shall I fetch a lantern?" suggested Captain Rowland, peering into the gloom.

"No, there's no need. I've daylight enough to see my way almost to the bottom of these steps, I think."

The major was already on his way down and as he trod carefully on to the second step there echoed the clatter of metal.

"What's that, Alex?"

"I'm not sure; give me a moment."

There followed a brief silence as the major crouched to run his hand over the steps. "It's a tinderbox! How very thoughtful of someone. I must have kicked it with the toe of my boot." He took out the flint and struck a spark from the steel and a light flickered instantly into being.

"You might as well follow me down, Hal. It appears that this is some kind of storage room. It may even have once been an armoury." Captain Rowland eagerly obeyed with Ned clambering right behind him.

"There they are, Hal, exactly as I expected. What a piece of impudence, eh? They obviously know more about my house than I do. I wonder how they discovered this neat little hiding place?" The major pointed at the barrels stacked against the wall. "They must have had some stout lads to carry these down here."

"Oho! Now we have 'em!" chortled

the captain delightedly. "This is quite a find! But I mean to do more than recover part of the contraband. They'll be back to collect these when they think we are off our guard. All we have to do is to keep watch and wait for them to walk into the trap. Those woods of yours will suit my purposes to a nicety. I could hide a whole regiment in there without arousing a whisper of suspicion."

"It'll only take a few strong men to fetch these, Hal. Have you considered that it might be an even better plan to allow them to retrieve the brandy and then follow them from here? That way you have a reasonably good chance of finding the ringleaders."

The captain rubbed his chin thoughtfully. "That's a tempting notion. But I'll have to make sure they don't get wind of this. I can't risk having my net broken when I try to land these slippery fishes."

12

HAVING decided to leave everything as they had found it, the stones were lifted carefully back into place.

"That'll do, I think," declared the captain, dusting down his scarlet coat, "they'll never guess that we've discovered their hiding place. Certainly not when they find the barrels precisely where they left them. Now, Ned, how about a glass of your 'special' before I face that long, weary ride back to Shoreham?"

Ned grinned broadly. "All that brandy just sitting there and you want a bowl of my humble punch?"

"There's nothing humble about your rum punch. That's a royal brew and no mistake! Besides, if I were to drink from one of those barrels, I'd pop off the hooks before I'd downed a second glass. That's genuine firewater: straight from the still. They won't even have had time to add the colouring yet; whereas your famous 'special' is already a masterpiece and I'm a man who can appreciate the finer arts."

"The captain prides himself on having a delicate palate and delights in brushing up his skills, don't you, Hal? But come, we are forgetting our patient, it is time I looked in on him again."

"That puts me in mind of something I meant to tell you, sir," intervened Ned. "Mr Stewart charged me with a message for you. He is going to call on you later this morning to take a look at the stranger, to see if he can put a name to him. As soon as he has finished his business in the parish, he intends to drive up to Blakestone."

"Excellent. I'm hopeful he may be able to identify him as a local man."

They returned to the house and while Ned concocted the brew, the major visited the sickbed. He felt the man's pulse and found it beating a little more strongly now. His breathing appeared to be easier too and the major began to entertain hopes of an eventual recovery.

By the time they had partaken of Ned's sustaining punch, the rector's gig was seen approaching the house. Mr Stewart was accompanied by his eldest daughter, who was looking particularly handsome in a velvet spencer of moss green and a gown of jonquil-coloured muslin, its high waistline circled by a belt of twisted silk, fringed with green tassels. Her shining hair was covered by a close-fitting bonnet of tucked, yellow satin decorated with tiny rosettes of ribbon that exactly matched the green of her little jacket.

The captain hurried eagerly forward to meet the gig as it drew up at the top of the drive. "Good morning, Mr Stewart. Good morning, Miss Stewart. What a delightful surprise." He was at her side in a few quick strides and handed her down from the carriage. "May I say how charming you look in that handsome bonnet, Miss Stewart?" he murmured, his eyes expressing his approbation.

"Thank you, Captain," she smiled blushingly. "I'm glad you admire it. I trimmed it myself, you know."

"Its loveliest embellishment is the face it frames," came the earnest reply.

"What a pretty compliment, Captain

338

Rowland. But I am not come that you might flatter my vanity. Pray take us to this unfortunate stranger who has had the ill-luck to suffer such a terrible accident. Ned told us of him earlier this morning and we are anxious to discover whether he is known to us. And Mama has sent some of her herbal emollients that may serve to ease his pain."

The major was already escorting the rector into the house and offering Miss Stewart his arm, the captain led her after them.

There was not sufficient space to allow all of them into the makeshift bedchamber and so the captain took the young lady to wait in the parlour while her papa attended the sickroom with Major Lacey.

Mr Stewart took one look at the pale, drawn features and gasped audibly. "Good gracious me! It's Tom Shaw!"

"Tom Shaw?" reiterated the major dazedly. "But it can't be, surely? He's on the other side of the world, isn't he?"

"He is certainly supposed to be," admitted the rector, "but that is Shaw without a doubt. I should recognize him anywhere. But how came he here? And who would do this to him?"

"That's what I shall be eager to know. He is the one living person who can help me find out more about Lucius's activities in his last days. We shall also be able to solve the mystery of that paper he gave you and the meaning of his parting words to you. It must be a divine Providence that brought him to my door."

"There's nothing divine about the circumstances in which he has been found. Whoever perpetrated this outrage is nothing short of a devil," muttered Mr Stewart angrily. "It's a wonder he's still alive."

"Yes, I think it almost certain that someone intended to murder him; he was not meant to survive the attack. In view of this, I would suggest that we keep his presence here a secret, at least for the time being. Do you agree?"

"You think he might be in danger of a further assault if it were to become known? Perhaps so." Mr Stewart appeared to ponder over this possibility for a moment or two. "But we have also to consider that we may be running foul of the law. He should not be in England at all and if someone should recognize him, he would be instantly deprived of his present liberty."

"And if that happened, he would most certainly die. I prefer to avoid that responsibility. Time enough to consider the morals of this case when he is fully recovered."

"And what about his wife? Will you tell her he is here?"

"I must think carefully about that. I had better find out how much she already knows."

"That would seem to be the better course . . . " began Mr Stewart but before he could finish, his daughter peeped in at the door.

"Is anything the matter, Papa? You have been so long I feared that the poor man might be worse. Is there anything I can do to help?"

"No, my dear. He is recovering well, Ned has proved a skilful nurse. I think you may safely trust everything to him. Now let us leave this unfortunate fellow in peace; he will need a great deal of rest and quiet if he's to continue to rally his strength."

"Very well, Papa, if you are sure," she answered a little doubtfully.

"Quite sure. He is in good hands; we need not trouble the doctor after all," said her father reassuringly.

"Do you know who he is, Papa?" she asked, as they all left the room and the major shut the door behind him. "I could not see clearly but I thought there was something familiar about his face."

"Your father thought so too. Perhaps the fellow lived here some years ago and has but recently returned to the neighbourhood," intervened the major, unwilling to place the rector in a difficult situation. "He will be better again soon, I'm sure and then he can tell us all about himself."

"No luck then?" interpolated the captain. "Well never mind, I daresay someone will be bound to make enquiries for him sooner or later. Are you leaving now, Mr Stewart? Might I be permitted to ride as far as the village with you? I must return to Shoreham and will be going that way myself."

"Then you will be welcome to accompany us," replied the rector obligingly, well aware that the young captain's request was really directed at his daughter. She certainly looked happy at his answer.

"I'll bring your horse for you, Captain," Ned volunteered, winking slyly at the major behind the captain's back. "I didn't realize you were in such a hurry to leave us."

"Before you go, Hal, there is something particular I should like to say to you," murmured the major in his friend's ear.

"Would you excuse me a moment, Miss Stewart," requested the captain politely, "I have only to fetch my hat."

He and the major returned to the parlour together. "What is it, Alex? Is anything wrong?"

"No. But I thought you would like to know that the rector did identify that man. You'll never guess who he is," he said excitedly. "It's Tom Shaw!"

"Shaw? But I thought you told me he was transported to Botany Bay?" whispered the captain with a puzzled frown.

"He was. Obviously he has effected an

escape; that's why we cannot divulge his name to anyone, nor his presence in this house. I have to protect him from any further harm. You know how much I want to talk to him. Having him arrested now would not be in his best interests nor, I confess, in my own."

"I can see that, Alex. But I hope you know what risks you are taking. In the eyes of the law, the man's a criminal. By the way, I have some information for you. I should have told you earlier but it slipped my mind. You will recall that you asked me to find out who ordered Shaw's solitary confinement? I spoke to Sergeant Roach about it and he remembered the incident because it was quite unusual. Evidently Mr Stewart raised something of a dust over the fact that neither he nor the man's wife were given access to the prisoner. Roach says that one of the magistrates who tried the case had insisted on Shaw's complete isolation from any contact with outside influences. It was feared that an escape was planned, Shaw being suspected of having many associates in the smuggling fraternity. No one was to be trusted to enter his cell, not even Mr Stewart."

"Well, who was it, Hal? Who had that authority?" demanded the major impatiently.

"It was your dear friend and neighbour, Sir Eustace Newbury."

"Newbury! Of course! It was he who had Shaw arrested. Thanks, Hal. It's another piece in the puzzle. You had better go now, Miss Stewart will be waiting for you."

"So she will. Goodbye, Alex. It's been a very interesting morning and well worth the journey — especially now! Keep your eyes and ears open, won't you? I'll be back this evening to begin our vigil. I hardly think they will chance capture by collecting that brandy in broad daylight: not now that you are back at Blakestone."

They went out to find Ned in conversation with Miss Stewart who had given him her mother's remedial ointments and was explaining their efficacies. She glanced up as they approached and held out her hand to the major.

"Goodbye, Major Lacey. I hope you

will not hesitate to send for me or my mama if you should require any help with your patient. Although I do not suppose that we could do more for him than Ned is already doing. I have given him the salves I brought with me. It looks as if you are in need of them also. You have hurt your face, I see."

"Thank you, Miss Stewart. I shall avail myself of your kind gift. Please give my compliments to your mother."

Having made their farewells and watched the visitors depart, Ned and the major went inside.

"What did scratch your face?" asked Ned curiously.

"I was foolish enough to take an undomesticated kitten into my arms."

"Then you deserved to get clawed," commented the unsympathetic Ned, pithily.

"Yes, I did. Now listen, Ned, I've something to tell you about our guest. His name is Tom Shaw and he is that person whose acquaintance I have longed to make, though I never believed I should do so."

Ned gave a low whistle. "Tom Shaw,

eh? Well that's a rare go. What do you intend to do about it?"

"Keep him here till he's well enough to talk. After that, I don't know. I have asked Mr Stewart to say nothing for the time being and he has given me his word."

"What about Mrs Shaw? Oughtn't you to tell her he's here?"

"I'm going to ride over to the cottage after lunch. It will give me time to think what I am going to say to her. And I also want to try to persuade her to tell me where I can find that young cub Eli. I had meant to ask Mr Stewart about him but I quite forgot in all the excitement. You'll wait here, Ned. We must keep a close watch on that brandy. The captain will never forgive us if we let them sneak it away from under our noses."

While the major had been enjoying an eventful and successful morning, Lady Elisa had not. She had ridden away from Blakestone without having accomplished her mission and in a raging tempest of womanly indignation and girlish tears. How she hated and despised that man!

Never in her whole life had she felt so humiliated.

Giving Sabre his head, she raced down the hillside, heedless of nothing but her burning anger. Harry and Alfred would be waiting for her on the road but she didn't care: let them wait. It was their fault anyway; she should have insisted that they go up there this morning. Why should she always be the one to take all the risks? What if Lacey had seen something last night? But if he had, then surely he would have informed Captain Rowland? None of the men had been arrested, so far as she knew; there was no reason to suppose that he had a shred of evidence to incriminate them.

The road was just ahead of her now and she pulled Sabre up sharply. A single horseman was just visible through the trees; she could see the glimmer of a scarlet coat and guessed that it must be Captain Rowland. Unwilling that he should see her, flushed and tear-stained as she knew she must be, she hid among the brushwood.

When he had passed from sight, she slithered down from the saddle and tied the reins to a branch. It was quiet and secluded here; she would rest and take time to regain her composure. She didn't feel like facing the Palmers, they would have to gnaw their fingernails for a while longer. Careless of her riding dress, she leaned her back against a damp, mossy tree trunk, flicking at the overhanging leaves with her riding crop.

Thoughts buzzed in her head like a nest of angry hornets, stinging her with their venom until tears of vexation sprang once more to her eyes. How could he have treated her so! As if she were some slatternly tavern wench! No man had ever dared to use her like that! Not even Harry, who had a reputation for such ale-pot dalliances. He knew too well that she would never permit those infamous liberties. A rake and a profligate he might be but at least he respected her. Like most of the men of her acquaintance, he stood in awe of her temper and wisely kept his distance. Her green eyes gleamed maliciously as she remembered that Lacey too knew better now! How could he and Lucius be brothers? They were nothing alike. Lucius had always behaved with careless affection towards her, as if she were his own sister. She pushed that thought quickly away: not a sister, he had felt something deeper for her. It was merely the difference in their ages that had prevented him speaking his love. They had been so close until *she* came into his life and spoiled everything — pure, angelic Aurelia! But perhaps not so pure and angelic after all. Her relationship with her brother-in-law had been more than friendly. She had flirted with him openly at the assembly rooms; Sir Eustace had been as jealous as a dog with a bone.

And how passionately Lacey had entreated her to stay when he thought that it was Aurelia who stood at his bedside! Had he ever kissed her on the mouth in that odiously intimate fashion? No, not like that. There had been a degradation in that rough embrace to which Aurelia would never have been subjected. He had meant to make her feel like a harlot, seizing on her as if she had been a vulgar street-walker! Hot tears of anger rose and fell. She felt violated, demeaned. Oh, but she intended to make him pay dearly for that insult! Revenge would indeed be satisfyingly delicious! She had only to think of a fitting way to exact it — and what pleasure there would be in devising that retribution. The very thought of it put new heart into her as she climbed up on to Sabre's back and galloped away towards the open fields stretched out below her.

When they reached the road she did not slacken the pace. Instead she set the stallion at the tall hawthorn hedge and with a bounding leap that was all power and grace, he cleared it with inches to spare. A man riding along the field path stayed his horse's steps to watch them. She could not be certain but she thought it was Lacey's servant. However, she did not stop to acknowledge him, preferring to keep Sabre in his stride and so continued in her neck-or-nothing style across the undulating meadows. This was the best cure she knew for cooling her temper and clearing her mind. On they sped, a keen wind rushing in her ears and whipping the blood into her face. Faster and faster, until fields and trees flashed past in a blur of colour; looming hedges and gaping ditches all rapidly disappearing beneath Sabre's flying hoofs. Her heart felt as if it leapt with him and thrilled at every challenging obstacle. At last they came in sight of the estuary and Elisa drew rein, taking great gulps of the invigorating salt air as it blew in from the sea. She was exhilarated, refreshed, her confidence renewed and once more in command of herself. They turned back inland, following the meandering course of the river until they came to a stream that poured its sweet, sparkling waters into the brackish river. Elisa dismounted and kneeling on the grassy bank, washed her face in the clear, cold water. Now she was ready to go home and make her plans. Taking Sabre's bridle she walked him slowly along the edge of the stream to allow him some rest before remounting with the aid of a convenient stile. In the next field there were several men busy with their long-handled scythes, cutting swathes through the golden corn while others followed behind them, raking it into mounds to dry.

One of the harvesters glanced up from

his work and recognizing horse and rider, leaned on his scythe and knuckled an eyebrow.

"Mornin' y' ladyship," he greeted her with a friendly grin, "nice t' see a bit o' sun arter sech a wildsome night." This pleasantry was accompanied by a broad wink.

"Indeed it is, Abel," Elisa replied with an answering smile, "it was so fine a morning that I decided to take a long ride. In fact I have rid all the way from Blakestone."

"Blakestone, is ut?" said he, eyes as bright and knowing as a robin's. "Major Lacey 'ome agin, safe an' sound, is 'ee?"

"Yes, he returned last night. Quite late, I believe it was."

"Did 'ee now? I s'pose 'ee 've found everythin' jest as 'ee left un?"

"I'm sure he did. Oh, by the by, you know that heavy furniture I wanted you to remove to London for me? I have decided to let it remain where it is until a more convenient time presents itself. I'll let you know what I decide."

"Very well, m'lady, you'll know what's best."

Another of the labourers approached, a rake over his shoulder. "Good day to ye m'lady. I was wonderin' if ye moight 'ave bin up t' see Mary? She'm was a-lookin' fer ye this marnin'. Said she 'ad summat to say t' ye an' that if I was t' see ye I was t' give ye that message immediate, like."

"Did she say what it was that she wanted to speak to me about?"

"No, m'lady. But she looked moighty upset t' me."

"Then I had better go by the cottage on my way home. Thank you, Dick and good day to you both."

Elisa turned Sabre about and headed for the field gate that opened into the lane. She wondered what it was that had caused Mary to send such a message. Why should she appear so distressed? It wasn't like Mary to be anxious without reason. A sudden dreadful possibility occurred to her. Could something have happened to Tom? They had tried to be so careful, surely nothing could have gone wrong? The thought alone was enough to urge her into greater haste and it was with a sense of relief that she finally came in sight of the cottage.

Mary came hurrying out to meet her as she rode up to the door. "Thank the Lord ye have come!" she cried gratefully. "I'm that worried I scarce know what I'm doin'. But I daresn't leave the little ones to go lookin' fer 'im meself."

Casting a fearful look all about her, she took Elisa by the hand and drew her into the cottage.

"Peter, take the childer t' play outside. There's somethin' pertic'lar I mus' say t' Lady Elisa."

Dutifully the boy obeyed her, ushering the youngsters out of the door and closing it after them.

"Well, Mary, what is it?" questioned Elisa urgently, noting Mary's careworn face and troubled eyes.

"It's Tom, m'lady!" burst out Mary, almost on the verge of tears. "'E didn't come 'ere last night! And it was all decided that 'e should. I was expectin' 'im and I knows 'e wouldn't let me down, not without a-tellin' me."

She began to wring her hands as though in desperate plight. "What shall I do? Somethin's 'appened to 'im, I just knows it!"

"You mustn't imagine the worst, Mary. It may be that Tom didn't come here because he daren't. There were soldiers on the alert yesternight, perhaps he thought it best to lie low for a while. It's possible he went back with Nick Tranter to avoid the chance of discovery."

"But if that were so, surely Nick would've brought me word b' now?"

"He could be waiting until things quieten down. I saw Captain Rowland riding up to Blakestone, Nick may have seen him too and is merely biding his time. He is always cautious."

"I 'ope you'm right, m'lady. But these last few months 'ave been a drea'ful strain on my nerves. I bin jumpin' out o' me skin every time someone knocks on that there door. Oh, I wish it were . . . "

The door suddenly flew open, startling them both.

"Mam! Theer's a man a-comin' frew th' woods. I fink it's that sojer 'oo lives up at the ol' burnt 'ouse!"

"Oh no! Now what's to do?" groaned Mary agitatedly.

"Mary, I'm going to take Sabre down to the wood at the back of the cottage.

I don't want Lacey to see me here but I'll be close by, you may be sure of that. Find out what he wants with you and then get rid of him as quickly as you can."

"I'll do me best, m'lady. But 'e's the las' person I want t' see right now. I've plenty t' worry me as 'tis."

Elisa gave her a brief hug of encouragement and raced out of the door. She took Sabre's bridle and led him hurriedly out of sight. The moment he was safely hidden in the trees, she crept stealthily back to the cottage.

She arrived in time to hear the major's knock and then the sound of his voice as Mary admitted him into her parlour.

"I hope you won't mind if I interrupt you for a little while, Mrs Shaw, but I would like a few words with you, if I may?"

"What is ut, Major Lacey, sir? If 'tis about them repairs, the men 'ave finished . . . "

"No, it's not that I have come about. It's quite another matter. I am very anxious to speak to that young lad Eli. Unfortunately, I do not know where to find him and hoped that you might be able to tell me where he lives."

Mary stared at him dully. "Eli? What d' ye want with un? 'E 'asn't done anythin' wrong, 'as 'e?"

"I have only a few questions I would like to put to him, that is all. It's nothing to concern yourself about, I assure you. He isn't in any trouble and I mean him no harm. Do you know where he is?"

"I dunno for certain, sir. I mean, I dunno wheer 'e is jest now. Eli comes and goes as 'e likes, d' ye see?" She pulled her shawl tighter around her thin frame and folded her arms to hide her trembling hands.

"Yes, I understand. But he must live somewhere. Perhaps if you could furnish me with his exact direction?"

"'E comes from over t' 'Astings way. I dunno exactly wheerabouts, I've never bin theer meself. Eli only visits if 'e 'appens t' be in the neighbour'ood. I s'pect 'e's gone orf with the fishin' boat. I'll send ye word if 'e do turn up 'ere agin, shall I, sir?"

"Yes, please, Mrs Shaw. I would be grateful if you could do that." He paused momentarily, his keen, blue eyes studying her expression intently. "You see, I know of a man, a stranger, who was found badly injured late last night. I have reason to believe that perhaps this Eli may know something about him and could help me trace any relatives that the poor fellow might have."

He was watching her carefully all the while and her eyes sank before his penetrating gaze, though she was unable to disguise the sudden paling of her complexion. A muscle worked in her jaw and she seemed as though the breath had been knocked out of her. She didn't move or lift her eyes to his; instead she stared blindly at the bare floor as if she couldn't bring herself to look at him. Then at last she spoke, her voice almost a whisper.

"A stranger, ye say? 'Urt bad was 'e?"

"I'm afraid so. The unfortunate man was the victim of a violent assault. He was found not far from here. I don't suppose you have heard anything about it?" he prompted gently, never once taking his eyes from her down-bent face.

When at last she raised her head, the tears were coursing down her cheeks. "Wheer is 'e, sir? I 'ave t' see 'im. I might know 'oo 'e is. Oh, tell me, please, sir," she begged desperately.

"He's up at the house, I'll take you to him now, if you wish," he answered quietly. There was no doubt in his mind that she knew the truth.

"I'll come jest as soon as I've found someone t' take care of the childer," replied Mary, wiping her tears on her apron and striving to calm herself.

"Would you like me to stay with them? Ned will let you into the house."

She was surprised by both the suggestion and the unmistakable kindness in his voice and eyed him wonderingly. "That's very good of ye, sir. Very good of ye indeed."

The back door swung open and Lady Elisa walked into the room. "There's no need to trouble Major Lacey, Mary, I shall take care of the children while you are gone. Go up to the house at once."

"Oh, thank you, m'lady," she said gratefully. "You go along, Major Lacey, sir, I'll be theere direc'ly. Don't wait fer me."

"Well, if you are quite sure?"

She nodded emphatically. "I'll follow ye in a while, I must see the little 'uns settled."

He nodded understandingly and went to the door but, having opened it, he stopped on the point of leaving and turned back towards them. For a moment he stood hesitantly on the door sill as if unsure whether to speak or no. "Lady Elisa, might I have the favour of a few words with you before I go?" he said awkwardly.

Elisa glared at him hostilely. "I don't think we can have anything more to say to one another."

"You may not but I should like to say something to you. Would you step outside with me for just a few minutes? Please."

"Go 'long, m'lady," encouraged Mary briskly. "Can't ye see the Major 'as somethin' pertic'lar 'e wants t' say t' ye?" She gave her a little push towards the door and reluctantly Elisa followed him out, scowling at Mary over her shoulder.

"Well?" she demanded churlishly. "What do you want with me?"

"I know you are angry with me, my lady and you have a right to be. I don't deny it, nor do I deny the fact that I deserve this." He rubbed the livid marks on his cheek. "I should not have allowed my temper to get the better of me, I realize that. But if you would not always be at my throat, we would not fall to such bitter quarrelling. Perhaps if you could try to be a little more conciliatory, we might . . ."

"I? Why must I be at fault? I merely came to enquire after your well-being this morning and was treated like a harlot for my trouble! It is you who ought to be suing for peace, not I!"

"If only you would give me the chance, that is exactly what I am trying to do! I wanted to thank you for your help yesterday but if you are going to be stiff-necked about it then I might as well give up the effort here and now!"

"Well, if it's so much of an effort perhaps you should! I'm sure I couldn't care less! I never expected your gratitude and I certainly don't want it!"

362

"Very good," he said through gritted teeth. "Then I'll bid you adieu, my lady. I'll not waste any more of your time nor my breath!" With that he turned on his heel and stalked away to remount his horse. Elisa threw an angry look at his retreating back before striding to the cottage door and slamming it upon him.

"What are the tears fer?" enquired Mary, glancing at the young lady's face as she leant against the closed door.

"I hate that man!"

"Do ye, m'lady?" murmured Mary, quickly tying on her best, high-brimmed bonnet of plaited straw. "Are ye sartin it ain't somethin' else ye feel fer that young gen'leman?"

"I don't know what you mean, Mary," replied Elisa haughtily.

"Well, ye know, I can't 'elp noticin' the way ye strike sparks orf each other ev'ry time ye meets. An' wheere theere's sparks theere's fire, as my ol' mam used t' say."

"What nonsense you do talk, Mary. I tell you I feel only loathing for that coxcomb!"

"Time'll no doubt prove the sent'ment. Now I'd best be orf t' see what's 'appened t' my Tom." She sighed deeply, shaking her head from side to side despairingly. "I allus knowed it would end up badly for us. Nothin's ever gone right since Tom took up with Sam Frant. My poor, foolish Tom. 'E only ever thought o' us, I know but I jest wish 'e'd kept out o' that business. Will ye stay with the childer till I can get 'ome, m'lady?"

"Of course, Mary. I want to wait to hear what has happened to Tom. I can't go until I know that he is in no danger."

From the window, Elisa could see the major's diminishing figure in the distance and watched broodingly as he disappeared from sight into the far woods.

"Don't let 'em be a trouble t' ye, m'lady. I'll be back as soon as I can," promised Mary, pulling on a pair of much-darned gloves.

"Don't worry. You know they always pay heed to me," smiled Elisa. "Now hurry along, Mary. And would you do something for me while you are up at Blakestone? Would you tell the major that you will try to send word to Eli? I will arrange a meeting for them, it might be interesting and rewarding."

"If that's what ye want, I'll do it," frowned Mary disapprovingly. "But let me warn ye now, m'lady: Major Lacey ain't nob'dy's fool, so don't think t' play yer tricks on 'im. 'E's one 'as got all 'is buttons on, make no mistake about that!"

13

MARY hastened up the hillside towards Blakestone House, her heart pounding more with fear for Tom's safety than with the exertions of the long climb. Her whole mind was bent upon reaching his bedside as quickly as she was able. The major had said Tom was badly hurt, just how badly she did not know and dreaded to discover. Suppose he should die? No, she must not even consider that possibility. Surely the good Lord had not preserved Tom's life in that far-off penal colony, only to let him be murdered on his own doorstep? So occupied was she with her grim imaginings that she remained oblivious to the figure that flitted among the closely grouped trees, keeping pace with her as she drew nearer the old house.

When she eventually arrived at the major's door, it was Ned who answered her knock and took her immediately to her husband's side.

Tom's face was almost as white as the linen on which he lay and her heart lurched wildly as she leaned over him.

"Oh, Tom, what have they done to ye?" she whispered brokenly, stroking his pallid cheek with a work-worn hand.

The major, standing on the other side of the bed, watched her pityingly.

"He will recover, Mrs Shaw, I am certain of it," he assured her with deliberate confidence. "There is every reason to hope that, given time, he will regain his strength completely. Here, feel his pulse. It is quite steady now."

She took Tom's wrist and pressed her fingers to the flicker of life.

"Ah, yes," she breathed with relief, "'tis beating strongly, wouldn't ye say, sir?"

"We are greatly encouraged by it, Mrs Shaw. Your husband has made a vast improvement since Ned first brought him here."

"And God bless ye for it," said she softly, glancing up at Ned who stood beside her and giving him a warm look of gratitude. "Did ye 'ave t' bring the doctor to 'im, sir?" she added anxiously.

"No, we thought it best not to trouble the physician," replied the major carefully.

Mrs Shaw turned her troubled gaze on him. "Then ye guessed from the first that it were my Tom ye'd found?"

He nodded briefly, "I think you and I had better discuss this peculiar situation, don't you, Mrs Shaw? Perhaps you would come into the sitting-room with me where we can converse more comfortably. Ned will stay with your husband."

"Yes," she sighed wearily, "I s'pose it ain't t' be avoided any longer."

They went into the parlour, which at this hour of the afternoon was basking in the warmth of the westering sun, shooting its golden shafts in through the open casement.

"Please sit down, ma'am," invited the major, pulling forward a chair. "Would you care for some tea?"

"No, I thank ye, sir. Don't trouble on my account."

"It's no bother, the kettle's already boiled and I think it would do you good. You've had quite a shock as well as the long walk from your cottage."

It took him only a few minutes to brew the tea and he handed her a cup. She accepted it gratefully, glad of its reviving qualities.

The major seated himself opposite to her, facing the window and waited quietly while she sipped her drink, content to allow her time to compose herself. After swallowing a few mouthfuls of the scalding liquid, Mary eyed him cautiously.

"Well, Major Lacey, sir? What d' ye want to ask me?"

"First of all I must tell you that I didn't know that it was your husband Ned stumbled across last night. I really had no idea who he was until this morning. It was the rector, Mr Stewart, who discovered him to me. But there's no need to be alarmed," he went on soothingly, seeing her frightened look, "Mr Stewart is aware of the need for discretion. Now tell me: how does Tom chance to be in England and how long has he been back?"

"Tom 'asn't escaped, if that's what ye've bin thinkin'," she began, head held proudly erect. "'E were fetched back 'ere by officers o' the law. Leastways, that's what 'e were told when they come fer 'im. They said the charge agin 'im 'ad bin pard'ned and they was sent t' bring 'im t' England. They 'ad a legal paper, prop'ly signed. But Tom says, when 'e got back t' Dover, 'e were taken pris'ner agin. They wouldn't let 'im come 'ome 'cause they said 'e 'ad t' answer some questions. Then they brung 'im ashore when it were dark and took 'im in a carriage to a inn. Well, it weren't much of a place as inns go, just a sort o' 'edge tavern, d'ye see. Miles from anywheeres 'e said 'twas and when they got theere they locks 'im in the cellars. 'Course, 'e were certain somethin' weren't right b' then. If 'e were under arrest they would've took 'im t' the prison like before. Anyways, 'e were left theere till mornin' when a man brung 'im a bit o' bread t' eat. That's when Tom managed t' get away — Tom's allus bin 'andy with 'is fists, like you, sir. 'E's bin back with us since the spring. That's why I 'ad t' take the cottage, sir. I didn't want no'b'dy t' know 'e were 'ere. 'Tis quiet in the medder an' theer's the woods t' 'ide in if they comes fer 'im."

"They are still looking for him, then?"

"Oh, yes, sir!" she replied emphatically. Leaning closer and lowering her voice, she continued, "Tom 'adn't bin 'ome more'n a few hours when they come a-seekin' of 'im. But Tom ain't no fool t' be took agin unawares, an' 'e were lookin' out fer 'em. I were livin' over t' Bar'urst then an' 'ad good neighbours as we could trust. Tom were out that back winder an orf like a scalded cat. One o' 'is pals took 'im in an 'id 'im till they'd gone."

"What did they say to you when they arrived at your door?"

She laughed scornfully. "Told me a right tale, they did. Said 'as 'ow they was Customs' men an' 'ad reason t' b'lieve we 'ad contri-band in the 'ouse. I told 'em they was welcome t' come in an' look fer all the good it'd do 'em. I could tell they was full o' mustard when they couldn't find nothin'. But after that Tom dursen't live with us 'cause 'e were worried fer the childer. 'E's looked after b' good friends and comes to see us whenever 'e thinks 'tis safe. We 'ave plen'y of folks as'll look out fer us. It

371

ain't no way t' live, sir but it's better'n 'avin 'im in Bot'ny Bay."

"This is passing strange," muttered the major, frowning deeply. "There has to be more to this than the poaching of a single pheasant. Are you sure you've told me everything?"

"I've told ye all I knows," she answered simply.

"What about that paper I showed you? Did your husband not mention the significance of that when he returned to you?"

"No, sir. I've never heered 'im mention that. I was a-goin' t' ask 'im about it las' night but 'e never come . . ." Her voice trailed off and she swallowed a sob.

"So he was on his way to visit you and the children when he was attacked?" he probed gently, mindful of her obvious distress.

"Yes, sir. I 'ad bin told t' expect 'im an' I waited up all night but 'e never come."

"From what you have said it seems likely that the men who have been searching for him may have lain in wait for him. And yet . . ." He paused and lifted his gaze to the open window, apparently lost in contemplation of some puzzling thought that had suddenly presented itself.

Mary sat in silence, watching his face and waiting expectantly for him to speak. Then suddenly his meditative expression altered to one of lively interest. The blue eyes narrowed and that hawk-like keenness glittered there once more. In an instant he was on his feet and with a terse "Wait here!" he had gone.

Mary rose quickly from her chair and hurried to the window. She saw him racing across the open stretch of grass that sloped down towards the encircling woods. The sun was in her eyes, impairing her vision and she lifted a hand to shade them from the bright glare. Was that a shadow moving or someone running between the trees? If it was a man, his pursuer was close on his heels.

The major plunged into the woodland a minute or two after his uninvited visitor. Now he stopped to catch his breath and listen for any sound of movement that would reveal the presence of his prey.

He looked carefully all about him, trying to find some clue as to which route the intruder had taken. Had someone come looking for Tom Shaw or was it perhaps one of the smugglers anxious about their precious brandy? Not a sound broke the silence. The crafty fellow must be standing still in order to avoid detection but where? He began to search the underbrush, moving cautiously in a widening semi-circle, pausing every few minutes to listen intently. It was a useless task; there were so many brambles forming dense thickets, it was virtually impossible to have a clear view in any direction. He would have to go back without discovering the reason why this trespasser had come to spy on them.

Perhaps it was as well that Hal had decided to return tonight with some of his men. If they should attract unwanted attention, there was not a great deal that he and Ned could do alone and with an invalid on their hands. It would be wise to bear in mind that Shaw was the object of someone's murderous vengeance. What had the man done to bring so much trouble on himself and his unhappy family? Was it his dealings with the freetraders that had caused his misfortunes? Could it be that he was suspected of an act of betrayal? The smugglers would not let that go unpunished and men had been known to lose their lives in brutal circumstances, once they had been judged guilty of breaking the 'Gentlemen's' code of silence.

When he returned to the house, Mary and Ned were anxiously awaiting him at the door.

"Who was it, sir?" asked Ned, stepping quickly forward to meet him.

"I don't know, I was unable to find any trace of him. But it was a stranger and one who might have overheard something of our conversation, Mrs Shaw. I can't be certain but I believe he might have concealed himself near that open window. I didn't catch sight of him until he attempted to slip away to the woods. I wonder who he was?"

"It must've bin one o' them villains that I spoke of, sir. I knows they watch me, I've felt their eyes on me every time I goes out o' the 'ouse."

"So you've experienced that too, have you?" remarked the major with great interest. "It is a feeling I have come to know well since I returned to Blakestone. Perhaps I now have an explanation for it. And I suppose it must have been the motive for young Eli's attempted abduction, am I right?"

"I b'lieve so, sir. Ye see, Eli's bin 'elpin' Tom, one way an' another, an' they might 'ave sin 'em together mebbe. Anyways, I dunno why else they'd want t' take 'im away with 'em like that. An' I dunno what I'd do without 'er ladyship t' 'elp us, God bless the dear soul. She ain't afraid of 'em, not 'er. Near shot one of 'em stone dead when she caught 'im a-prowlin' roun' the door. They ain't dared come s' close since, not while she's about, an' she comes t' see us every day."

"Indeed? Now I know why I seem to meet her everywhere I go. She has appointed herself your protector."

"Yes, an' I'm glad of it, sir, truly I am. 'Specially for the sake o' the little 'uns. Tom says these men is dangerous an' won't stop at nothin' t' get what they wants." She shivered and clasped her shawl tighter around her. This involuntary action suddenly reminded the major of Aurelia. Even Mrs Shaw's words seemed to echo Aurelia's and brought a mental image of her sitting on the *chaise-longue* at Dovecote Hall, wrapping her arms about herself and saying, "They are unspeakably evil". Except, of course, she had been speaking of Mrs Shaw's husband at the time, or rather, 'people like him'.

The feeling that slender threads of coincidence connected Lucius's sudden death with all these people in some unfathomable way, occurred to him yet again. He needed time to think about everything that had happened in the last few weeks and try to make some sense of it. Above all he longed to question Tom Shaw.

"Ned, I am going to walk back to the cottage with Mrs Shaw. You'll need to keep watch here until I return. You'd better have my pistol at the ready, just as a precaution. I shall be as quick as I can."

"D'ye think Tom is safe 'ere, sir?" asked Mary, concerned at this extreme measure.

"I mean to take no chances, that is all. Tom is as safe here at the moment as he would be anywhere. We shall guard him night and day if necessary. When he is well enough to be moved, I will do what I can to make things easier for you all. Until then, I think it best that you do not come here again. There may have been another explanation for that incident just now, that has nothing to do with Tom's presence in my house. I cannot say any more about that but I consider it prudent that we allay suspicion by asking you to keep away from Blakestone, at least for a while. I shall bring you word of Tom's progress as often as possible. As your landlord, it will not be thought odd if I should visit you at the cottage whenever I happen to pass that way."

"Then 'tis plain ye knows little o' landlords, sir," replied Mary with a wry smile. "But if that's what ye b'lieve, then mebbe ye'd make a good 'un."

"Do you think so?" he responded with an answering smile. "Well, I doubt very much that either of us will ever find out the truth of that."

He walked back with her as far as the stream at the top of the field, where they paused in sight of the cottage door and the children playing outside in the early evening sunshine.

"I suppose I need go no further. I daresay your other self-appointed guardian is watching for you at this very moment."

"That's certain, sir. She'll not desert me. 'Tis strange t' find a grand lady consarn 'erself with the likes o' us, but she do. There ain't a man, woman or child around 'ere that she don't know b' name. But then agin, it ain't often that the gentry leaves their young ladies t' roam the woods an' fields all alone like she's bin a-doin' ever since she were out o' leadin' strings. 'Er pa, Lord Maytland, 'e's a great trav'ller, y'know. There ain't 'ardly a spot on this earth that 'e ain't bin t'. Gone for years sometimes, 'e is. I s'pose that's why 'e brung 'er ladyship up t' be able t' look after 'erself. It ain't made 'er pop'lar with 'er own kind though, they don't like 'er wild ways. Nor they don't like no friendliness between the likes o' us an' the likes o' them, beggin' ye pardin, sir. Though I must say ye don't 'ave no side t' ye either. You an 'er's alike in that respec'. Ye've bin good t' me an' Tom an' I 'opes as ye'll be good t' 'er too. 'Er ladyship ain't got any friends of 'er own kind, 'ceptin' Miss Stewart, o' course, an' we all needs friends sooner or later, as I do know meself. Well, I mustn't prattle on so, yer man'll be lookin' out fer ye an' 'er ladyship'll be wantin' t' 'ear about Tom. Thank ye fer takin' 'im in, sir, an' fer carin' fer 'im. I just 'opes we don't bring no trouble t' yer door b'cause o' it. These is worryin' times fer all o' us but we got t' keep our sperrits up, ain't we? No p'int in givin' in t' worries 'n troubles, eh, sir?"

He wished her good fortune and watched her walk away down the meadow. There was a staunch heart in Mary Shaw. She faced the fates with a brave defiance like most of her class. He had seen many a battle against incredible odds turned to victory by the valiant spirits and sheer tenacity of such indomitable folk.

As he turned to retrace his steps, she

called out to him from the stepping stones. "I'll get word t' young Eli, sir. I'll tell 'im ye wants t' see 'im." Then with a wave of her hand she went on her way.

Elisa came to meet her as she drew near the cottage.

"Was it Tom?" she asked, keeping her voice low.

"Yes, 'tis Tom right enough. 'E's in a bad way but the major thinks 'e'll come through it. I'm not t' go an' see 'im fer a while. Major Lacey d' think 'tis safer."

"Did you tell him everything?" whispered Elisa, aghast.

"'Course not!" answered Mary indignantly. "I just told 'im 'ow Tom come t' be 'ere, that's all. 'E reck'ns those men 'ave bin a spyin' on 'im too. Though why they would be int'rested in 'im I dunno, I'm sure. The major's got nothin' t' do with our troubles."

"Did you give him my message about Eli?"

"Yes, but I didn't like t' do it. Ye got the dev'l in yer eye an' I knows ye mean mischief," grumbled Mary, entering the cottage door.

"I have a score to settle and Eli is to be the means by which I pay him," explained Elisa lightly.

"Well, just ye be careful," warned Mary. "I've already told ye once and I 'ope ye'll 'eed me. Someone was a-lurkin' up at the 'ouse while I was visitin' Tom. The major chased 'im as far as the woods but 'e got away. It might'a bin one o' them vill'ins agin, a-tryin' t' find my poor ol' Tommy."

"Oh? Did Lacey see who it was?"

"No, 'e never. 'E did say as 'ow it might 'ave nothin' t' do with Tom at all. 'E said there was another reas'n why someone could be a-listenin' at the winder."

"Did the major suspect anyone in particular?" asked Elisa, brows drawing suddenly together.

"I dunno, 'e wouldn't say. But I don't doubt it 'ad t' do with Tom."

"Yes, probably," murmured Elisa as if her thoughts were deeply occupied. "I wonder why Lacey should think there may have been another explanation? But don't fear, Mary, we shall ensure that Tom is in no danger."

"The major says 'e'll guard Tom night 'n day. I heered 'im tell that nice Corporal Parrish t' keep a pistol 'andy. I don't think they'd find it easy t' come at Tom while 'e an' th' major's a watchin' over 'im. That Major Lacey's a big, strong man, ain't 'e?"

"Oh, he's strong, I'll grant you. But I think the major is about to discover that mere brawn won't always give him the upper hand. Now, Mary, I really shall have to go home, it's getting late. I daresay I'll have to give my head for a washing when my aunt sees me. I'll call on you tomorrow as usual and don't worry — Dick and Abel will be close by tonight."

On the way back to Dovecote Hall, Elisa had to pass through the village and it was there that she met Miss Stewart returning to the rectory.

"Good evening, Celia," she called, reining in beside her. "You are looking in high bloom, I see. Did Captain Rowland bring that sparkle to your eyes, I wonder?"

Miss Stewart blushed slightly. "Good evening, Elisa. Why should you imagine that gentleman to have had an effect on my spirits?"

"I'll go bail he did!" grinned Elisa. "I saw him this morning, riding up to Blakestone. I'll not believe he came all this way without calling on you."

"As a matter of fact, I saw him up there myself." She went on to explain the circumstances surrounding her visit. "I don't suppose you have heard anything of this have you, Elisa?"

Elisa shook her head. "Not I. And if your father did not know the man then I am certain I would not. But where is Captain Rowland now? Did not your mama invite him to dine with you tonight?"

"Yes, she did but the captain could not stay," replied Miss Stewart looking decidedly disappointed. "He very much wanted to, I could tell, it was just unfortunate that he had important duties to attend to this evening that could not be postponed."

"They must have been extremely urgent indeed if he refused an opportunity to enjoy your company," remarked Elisa, teasingly. "I hope he gave you a satisfactory explanation of them."

"The captain was not at liberty to do so. I must confess that his reticence provoked my curiosity quite considerably. It was obvious that he was being extraordinarily secretive and could only be got to say that he was hopeful of this being a most productive night."

"How intriguing! I wonder what he can have meant? Ah well, we shall just have to wait and see, I suppose. Goodbye, Celia, I must be going. If I am not home by six of the clock my Aunt Wytcherley will be apoplectic."

She did not immediately ride home, choosing to risk Mrs Wytcherley's displeasure by calling on Sir Harry Palmer. He was just returning from the stables when she arrived at High Dean and greeted her late appearance with obvious annoyance.

"Oh, so you've come at last, have you?" he snapped acidly. "Alfred and I waited an half-hour and more for you this morning. What the deuce kept you?"

"Never mind that now," she replied carelessly. "I have something important to say to you. Lacey may well have seen too much last night. I can't be certain but it does seem likely that he and Captain Rowland may be acting upon their suspicions this very night. I have already informed the others of the need for caution and I am come but to warn you. We shall have to bide our time until those items can be safely removed to London."

"Damn it!" he swore furiously. "I can't wait long. I need the money. This is Higgs' fault; I told him to keep them here at all costs. If he weren't such an idle, complaining fellow, he would have prevented their leaving last night."

"It's no good repining now. You will have to wait until we're sure it's safe to move it. I will arrange that myself. You'll get a good price for the rest of the goods, won't you?"

"Yes, yes but the best of the profit is in that brandy! A pox on that fellow Lacey! I knew from the first he'd be an itch not easily scratched!"

Elisa laughed. "Speak for yourself, Harry. I found not the least difficulty in that! Goodnight to you and do try to be patient for once. I'll not have men's lives jeopardized just because you have run yourself aground again!"

So it was that, for three long wearying nights, Captain Rowland and his men waited in vain for the smugglers to reclaim their precious hoard. At last the captain began to despair of their situation.

"It's no use, Alex," he complained to his friend, over a glass of Ned's steaming punch, "they must have learned of our presence here."

"Yes, Hal, it does seem likely, I agree. What do you intend to do now?"

"Well, I can't waste any more time here or I'll have a mutiny on my hands," smiled the captain tiredly. "After tonight, I shall have to admit defeat. Tomorrow I'll get the men to bring the barrels out and we'll take them to the customs' house. At least we will have something to show for our vigilance. That brandy must be worth a good deal of money."

"It certainly is. I confess I am astonished they have not made shift to retrieve it. Those barrels would have formed the most valuable part of that shipment. I fully expected that they would have come back for it by now. But there is another chance. I went to see Mrs Shaw yesterday to tell her that her husband has regained consciousness, although he is in no fit state to be questioned yet, alas. She informed me that this elusive lad, Eli, has finally agreed to meet me tonight on that stretch of beach just beyond the Dower House."

"You mean that same place where those men shot at you?"

"That's right. I assume he selected that particular spot because of its seclusion. I expect he's wary of being seen talking to me in case his friends suspect him of fraternizing with the enemy."

"You couldn't persuade him to do so, could you?" suggested the captain hopefully. "I should dearly like to know who his accomplices are."

"I doubt he'd tell me, even if I dared to ask. I don't want him to know yet that I saw him with the smugglers. Not until you've had your chance to catch them with the evidence. This is my opportunity to find out if he knows anything of this business concerning Tom Shaw and his known associates."

"Well, I shall be wanting to put a few questions of my own once this night is over. I'll not let the matter rest until I've done all I can to put an end to their illicit trade."

It was with mounting impatience that the major awaited the moment appointed for his meeting with Eli. Ned was relieved when the clock eventually chimed the tenth hour and he was left in peace to watch over the sleeping invalid alone.

When the major arrived on the beach, there was no visible sign that he had company. His only option was to wait until the lad decided to show himself. He sat down on a rock at the foot of a chalky scree and gazed about him.

The moon was in its second quarter, throwing a shimmering, silver net across the rippling waves. Innumerable stars glittered like jewels on the velvet of night and far below them stretched the dark, deep-murmuring sea. Slowly the minutes slipped by and yet came no sound to break the vast silence, save only the soft lapping of the water. An hour and more passed until inaction became almost intolerable; he was cold now too and this added to his growing discomfort.

It had begun to occur to him that Eli might well have played him false, in which case that boy would be given a short, sharp lesson when next their paths crossed! He would allow him only ten minutes more before returning to the house.

Then, at the very moment of his departure, the major heard the rattling slither of feet on the shingle and out from the shadow of the overhanging cliffs, stepped the slim shape of a young man.

"Why are you so late? It's long after ten and I've been almost chilled to the bone whilst waiting on your convenience," said the major, much aggrieved.

"I'd a little business of me own t' tend t'," grinned the youth cheekily. "But 'tis done wiv now, an' so I come to tell ye."

"I'm not interested in hearing the details of your questionable nocturnal activities, I merely wish to know more about your uncle, Sam Frant. What can you tell me about his dealings with Lord Cullan? Do you know why he sailed the *Seabird* along the Kent coast on the night he was lost? Has Tom Shaw mentioned anything that might explain what happened to them?"

"'E might 'ave, an' then agin, 'e might not. What's it worth t' ye t' know?"

The major eyed him narrowly. "Don't think to play your games off on me, you young Viking. I'm in no mood for it."

"Well, I can see yer out o' curl, pal, but there ain't no need t' come the ugly wiv me. Didn't I come all this way out o' the goodness o' my 'eart, just t' favour ye?"

A sound like the crack of a distant musket shot made them both turn their faces inland.

"Sounds as if the cap'n's on the scent," remarked Eli coolly.

"What do you mean?" rapped out the major. "Why should you suppose that?"

"I ain't no knock-in-the-cradle," retorted the lad scornfully, "I knowed them sojers was a-waitin' fer us t' bite the worm. Now while they is orf on a wild goose chase frew yer woods, that there brandy is on its way t' Lunnon, free an' easy."

"Then you knew all along," muttered

the major, distinctly annoyed at being thwarted, especially by this impudent puppy. "But just how do you propose to escape notice? The captain will have been watching that brandy with all diligence.

"Can't do no 'arm t' tell ye the lay, I s'pose," shrugged Eli indifferently. "The cap'n's away arter a string o' ponies a-carryin' empty barr-ils while the rest o' our lads is busy collectin' the gen-win harticle." He chuckled richly. "I knowed them sojer boys'd be primed fer action. Arter all them long nights up theer, they'd 'ave 'unted their own shadders if they'd sin 'em movin'! An' the best o' it is — theer's you a-sittin' 'ere s' pretty an' a-gazin' at th' moon whiles they is a-doin' of it!"

Major Lacey found himself torn between a profound dislike of this impudent rascal and a grudging admiration for his sheer audacity. If what he had said was indeed the truth, then he and Hal had been severely roasted.

"It remains to be seen if your plan has proved successful, boy. Captain Rowland is no green young officer. You've certainly made one mistake though — and that's in thinking you could come crowing to me and still escape with your skin intact!" He shot out a long arm to seize the lad by the scruff of the neck but even as he dragged him off his feet, he felt a sudden sharp stab in his ribs.

"Should ye like me t' let some o' that 'ot air out o' ye bellers, pal?" suggested Eli threateningly, pressing the short, thick barrel of a hand pistol hard against the major's chest.

Reluctantly the major released his hold and Eli backed away, only the gleam of his white teeth discernible in his grimy face. "That's better. Ye'll be sensible, won't ye? Stay right wheer y'are an' don't try t' foller me unless ye want me t' turn ye int' a waterin' pot. I'll not be warnin' ye agin, that's sartin."

Slowly he retreated until the darkness swallowed him up.

Fuming inwardly, the major waited till he judged it safe to move and then set out after Eli. There was only one way to go from here and that was back along the dene. Treading softly up the chalky track and keeping in the shelter afforded by the hawthorn trees along the path, he crept relentlessly in Eli's wake.

Once or twice he thought he discerned the crunch of hurrying feet and felt confident that he was gaining on his quarry. He was halfway towards the Dower House when he saw a flicker of light in an upstairs window, as if someone had that moment lit a candle. The gleam came and went in a matter of seconds and all was dark again. Could it be Albert and Tilda not yet abed? But Aurelia had said they were incapable of climbing the stairs now, so it seemed an unlikely explanation. Who then could it be? His attention was snatched by the unmistakable sounds of a frantic struggle. Quickening his pace, he drew steadily nearer to the noise of scrabbling feet. Now he saw two men grappling with Eli, as wriggling and kicking he fought like a demon to free himself from their grip. Even as he watched, he saw the larger of the burly pair of ruffians land a vicious blow to the body and Eli dropped instantly to lie a crumpled heap on the ground. Unceremoniously, they hauled him off into the scrub.

The major also left the path and

ventured across the short, sheep-cropped turf. He had not gone very far when he came to a wooded hollow and peering through the deep gloom saw the men moving down the grassy slope, Eli stumbling between them. Apart from one cursory glance behind them, they were not over-cautious in their going and the major was able to follow them closely without fear of detection. Arriving at a little clearing at the bottom of the dell, they stopped and pinning Eli by the arms, demanded to know where he had hidden Shaw.

"We know ye've got 'im tucked up nice n' cosy somewhere's about, so don't go fer tryin' t' deny it! We knows you an 'e is pals: you an' that swell mort 'oo's s' ready wiv them poppers of 'er'n. An' if ye've 'ad yer fambles on them boxes of ourn, then they'll be fishin' you out o' the sea, ye young cur! Now tell us what ken ye've found fer Tom Shaw an' be quick about it or Skinner 'ere'll show ye just 'ow 'e earned 'isself the name."

"I don't know wheer 'e is, I 'aven't sin 'im fer days. No one knows what's 'appened t' 'im an' I don't know nothin' about no boxes eivver!"

"I think we're goin' t' 'ave t' make this little bird pipe another toon, don't you, Skinner?"

"It'd be a pleasure. An' it won't take me long afore 'e's singin' 'igh an' sweet. I sin rats bigger'n 'im."

"I ain't sin none bigger'n you two, an' that's a fac'," retorted Eli pugnaciously and seemingly unbowed.

"Then ye'll be wishin' ye never set yer peepers on us, ye owdacious . . . "

From out of the darkness leapt an iron-fisted madman who fell upon them with such totally unexpected ferocity, they had not time to defend themselves. The man called Skinner had the knife twisted from his grasp, at the same time buckling beneath a vicious doubler that completely knocked the breath out of him. This was followed up by a sharp and painful jab under the left ear that seemed to explode inside his head and he sank, choking, to the ground.

The second man was forced to free his captive in order to defend himself. With a grunting cry of rage, he hurled himself bodily upon their attacker. The major danced lightly away on his toes, easily evading the swinging punch that had been aimed at his head and the infuriated man momentarily threw himself off balance. Following up his advantage, Lacey closed with his man: fibbed like lightning with right and left, landed a flush hit to the point of the jaw and stood back to watch his opponent go crashing on to his back, arms outflung.

Grabbing the astonished Eli by the hand, he dragged him away, urging him into a run. They had barely reached the top of the slope when a shot rang out behind them and a bullet sang past Eli's shoulder.

"I hope your legs run as fast as your tongue, lad. We're going to have to try to head for Blakestone. Keep close and follow me!"

The major led him out across the downland, only too aware that they presented conspicuous targets while they remained in the open like this. Behind them came the sound of their pursuers leaping through the undergrowth, cursing as they ran.

"Wait a moment!" panted Eli, stopping

to catch his breath. "We can't go t' the 'ouse, Tom's theer! They don't know 'oo you are yet, they'll think ye one o' us wiv a bit o' luck. We'll be able t' draw 'em off."

"And how do you propose we do that? The woods over yonder would be the safest place to hide but those two would have ample opportunity to catch up with us before we got anywhere near them."

"What about the old 'ouse over theer?" suggested Eli, nodding towards the Dower House.

"No, not there, it might endanger the servants."

"Well then, we'll 'ave t' go back t' the beach. I know a way out o' this. Just ye stick wiv me, pal."

Eli plunged off into the darkness, heading for the sparse protection of a small thicket a few yards away.

"Keep yer 'ead down 'n tread soft. They'll kill us fer sure if they ketch sight o' us. Ye've got 'em madder'n a nest o' 'ornets."

As quickly as they dared, they slipped in and out of the shadows, ears pricked for sounds of pursuit. However, it seemed that the others had also realized the value of stealth. There was no telling how close they had drawn and even a gasp for breath might be enough to give them away.

After what seemed like an age, they finally came in sight of the sea and Eli beckoned to the major to follow his lead. Keeping close to the cliff face, they edged towards the promontory of chalkland that formed the perimeter of the beach.

"There's no way out for us here!" hissed the major in Eli's ear.

"Ye can swim, can't ye?" replied Eli with his flashing grin.

"Yes, but the tide's in and it's a long way to the next accessible beach. These cliffs are too sheer to climb."

"Then ye'll just 'ave t' trust me t' look after ye," whispered Eli hoarsely. "Come on, get yer boots off 'n tie 'em round yer waist wiv yer cravat. We'll 'ave t' leave our coats 'ere."

"This is madness! We're like to drown ourselves . . ."

His words were cut off by the shot that ricocheted from the chalk face just above their heads.

"Damn it! They've seen us! Quick, your pistol, lad!"

"Won't do no manner o' good, pal. T'ain't primed, d'ye see?"

With an exasperated sigh, the major bent to pull off his boots. Hastily he tugged off his coat and unwound the long, muslin cravat from about his neck. He tied it round his waist like a sash and thrust his boots through, wishing they were loaded pistols instead of empty footwear.

Now they were both ready and together leapt into the surging tide and waded out until the water was deep enough to support their weight. Another two shots echoed as they struck out from the shore, splashing harmlessly into the sea just in front of their faces and sending sprays of water into the air.

"Dive!" yelled Eli, suiting the action to the words and disappeared beneath the waves. Taking a great lungful of air, the major did likewise and hoped that he would not lose the lad in the darkness. When he eventually came up for breath, he guessed that they were now out of firing range and began to search about for sight of Eli. At first he could see nothing and began to grow anxious. Then, barely a yard behind him, up bobbed the woolly-capped head, streaming water.

"Well? What now scapegrace? On to France, is it?" called the major, mockingly.

"There's no profit in that tonight," came the cheerful reply. "We mus' get clear o' the point. I doubt they'll risk comin' arter us now."

"I should think not. They at least are in their right minds."

"Save yer breath fer the swim. We've a ways t' go yet!"

Eli kicked out again and keeping to the line of the cliff face, headed towards the open sea. When they were well out from the shore, they rested.

"Not far now," gasped Eli breathlessly, "jus' beyond the point."

"Are you sure you know what you are doing?" answered the major, wondering if the lad had the strength to go much further.

"'Course. You'll see. Come on."

They struck out once more, this time

swimming around the point and out of sight of the beach. The major was correct in thinking there would be no landing place for some considerable distance, for the water was lapping at the base of the cliffs. The narrow strip of shingle had disappeared beneath the full tide. However, as he gazed doubtfully towards the lofty, white cliffs, he suddenly spied a small dark shape riding the waves only a few yards in front of them.

"Is that a boat?" he cried gladly.

"How else did ye think . . . we was goin' t' get 'ome?" panted Eli, coming up beside him and pausing again to recover his breath. "Didn't I tell ye t' trust me, pal?"

"I knew of no reason why I should — until now. Here, hold on to me and rest for a while, you're exhausted."

"No! I'm well enough . . . let's keep goin'."

With the means of rescue within reach, the major set off with confidence and his strength being the greater, reached the boat before Eli. He clung gratefully on to the side of the boat and looked back for sight of his valiant companion. Eli was still several feet away from safety and as he struggled wearily onwards, he suddenly seemed to tire and his head sank beneath the waves. Instantly the major swam out to him, gaining his side as he came up gasping for air, coughing and spluttering as he fought for breath.

"Hang on, lad. I've got you. Don't struggle, I'll not let you go." Keeping Eli's head above water with one hand, the major pulled away with his free arm and within a matter of moments had brought the lad back to the boat.

"Hold on tight while I get aboard and I'll haul you up," instructed the major, checking that the boy had a good grip on the bucking vessel. Then he clambered over the side and reached out for Eli's hands. Owing to the lad's slight build, it was a simple matter to pull him up out of the water and lift him into the boat. As the major set him gently down again, he stared at the boy intently for several seconds without uttering a word.

It was Eli who broke the long silence. "My thanks, pal," he croaked feebly, "ye saved my skin!"

"You might have saved mine, were

your claws not so sharp, Eli — or should I say Elisa?" replied the major evenly and stretching out a hand, dragged off the close-fitting seaman's cap to reveal a streaming mass of dark, red hair.

14

"I SUPPOSE I ought to have guessed from the first," continued the major, disgusted at his own gullibility. "Clifton was in the right of it all along. Frant had no relatives, had he?"

"No," confirmed Elisa, seating herself on the wooden bench and pulling on a pair of stout leather shoes. "But he was perfectly happy to acquire a nephew when I suggested it."

"What exactly do you mean?" he demanded sharply. "What do you know about Frant?"

"We'll have that conversation later, Major. For the present we must save our breath for plying these oars. Raise the anchor, will you?"

"You really are the most exasperating female I have ever met," complained the major testily but doing her bidding anyway.

"You must share your views with my Aunt Wytcherley when next you two meet; you and she should get along famously if you were to introduce that theme." Elisa fitted a pair of oars into the rowlocks as she spoke. "You use the other pair," she instructed, drawing them from beneath the seats. "We'll row over to Blakestone Bay. It shouldn't take us more than a few minutes, so they'll never be able to catch up with us."

"How did you know the boat would be here?" he asked, taking the oars and sliding them into place.

"It belongs to Nick, one of the fishermen. I borrowed it earlier. I didn't want to come up through your woods otherwise Captain Rowland might have seen me. This way I can reach Blakestone without exciting attention."

"Is that what you thought? In my opinion your actions seem to have had a positively invigorating effect on those two lobcocks."

Elisa began to pull on the oars, turning the boat about. "Well, they have spent weeks searching for Tom and are naturally feeling more than a little hostile towards me. They once saw Tom and me as we came through the woods but fortunately we both know those woods intimately and easily gave them the slip. I must say that your intervention in that rather unpleasant interview tonight was most welcome."

"They might have been less brutal if you had not insisted on adopting that ridiculous disguise."

"I don't think it in the least ridiculous," she remonstrated indignantly. "It suits my purposes perfectly."

"Smuggling contraband? Yes, I can see that it would. Tell me, my lady, is there nothing that daunts you?"

She wrinkled her brow thoughtfully. "I don't think so . . . well, only one thing but I shan't tell you what it is. Now are you just going to sit there while I do all the work? Or are you going to make shift to help me?"

"I've no objection to that, it will at least keep us warm," he replied amenably and setting his back to her began to ply the oars with long, smooth strokes. As they fell into an easy rhythm, the boat began to skim across the water.

"Tell me," he said presently, "why did you meet me tonight? You could have just left me kicking my heels on that beach."

"I wanted you to believe that you had been outmanoeuvred by a mere stripling. I knew that would be hard for you to swallow. And it was, wasn't it? I could see you were choking on that indigestible bone as soon as I told you how simply you were fooled. Ha! You looked as ugly as bull beef!"

There was a brief silence and she wondered if he was struggling with his temper again. He rested a moment on his oars and then half turning to face her said, "I can guess why you went to such lengths to trick me, Elisa. When we met at Blakestone, my conduct was unpardonable, I confess. I should not have let my anger get the better of me. It was very wrong of me and I must tell you that I sincerely regret it. Indeed, I was sorry for it almost at once and I meant to tell you so when I saw you at Mary's cottage. I offer you my apology now and hope you will forgive me for the lapse."

He did sound truly repentant and after a minute or two's consideration, she decided to acknowledge it.

"Very well, I shall forget that it ever happened. Although you were insufferably arrogant and even Harry would not have stooped so low . . . "

"Now you are revenged, my lady!" he gasped, sounding thunderstruck. "I have my just deserts. I am completely abject."

"That is well. However, in all conscience I too must own that my temper has, upon occasion, led me to express feelings that were best kept guarded. It can be the very devil, I know, especially when one is forced to apologize. Therefore, on the grounds that I may have provoked you a little, I shall accept your olive branch."

"You are most gracious," he declared with obvious amusement. "And I shall in future try to aspire to Sir Harry's splendid example of chivalry."

Elisa chuckled. "That shouldn't be entirely beyond your reach, so take heart. Oh, look, we are almost there."

They renewed their efforts and began to row shorewards. The major shipped his oars as the boat ran aground and he jumped into the surf. Elisa soon followed and together they hauled the boat out of reach of the tide.

"Wait a moment while I put on my boots. I don't want to walk barefoot over this curst shingle. There, that's better. Now let's be on our way," he said, getting to his feet again. They trudged on up the beach until they reached the precipitous cliff path. "This was the means by which Ned and I descended to see your precious brandy come ashore," remarked the major as they began the steep climb upwards.

"How did you know they were there that night? They're usually careful to make no sound."

"Oh, they were wonderfully discreet. It was the spotsman's gun that first alerted us as we came along the road yonder. Then we saw the landing light from the tower."

Elisa laughed gleefully. "That was me! Did you guess? We've always used the tower for the landing signal. It was my idea," she added proudly. "I've adored the view from up there ever since I was a child. You can see for miles around and right out to sea: it's wonderful."

"Yes, I've seen your sketches. I knew you had been up there."

"Did you? Then you'll know how accurately I drew the coastline. It helps to be familiar with all its twists and turns when we are deciding on the most suitable landing points."

"What about that pile of bricks? Did you put them there?"

"I did — with Peter's help. You've seen Peter, haven't you? He's Mary's eldest boy. Sometimes I just cannot escape from my aunt and then Peter has to show the light. We piled the bricks against the wall so that he can stand on them to give a clear signal to the ship. Unfortunately, he slipped on the last occasion and spilt some of the oil from the lamp. I had to scatter some of the bricks to hide the stain: as a precaution. We did not want to arouse any suspicions should it be noticed."

"It was noticed. Hal and I discovered it not long ago. He guessed what it meant, though I have to say that I thought he was letting his imagination run away with him. And now, may I venture to ask you

411

why you tried to shoot me?"

"I will tell you when we get to the end of the path; I need all my breath for this climb," she panted wearily.

When at last they emerged at the top of the cliff, Elisa put a finger to her lips as a warning to keep silent. As soon as she was certain there was no one about, she beckoned him onwards.

"Hurry, I must get to Mary's cottage and change into some dry clothes before I can go back to the Hall. She will find you something of Tom's to wear I expect. Now, as to your last question, the explanation is really quite simple. I had just come from visiting Mary and Tom at the cottage and was going home through the woods, when I heard you and Mr Clifton talking. You were taking the track that led to the stream and I knew there was a possibility that Mr Clifton might call on Mary, perhaps taking Tom unawares. I could have fired into the air, of course, but I thought it would be much more amusing to pay you out for that insult you gave me — in front of Aurelia of all people, too! And under my own roof! So Tom got his warning and I got the satisfaction of seeing you leap into a muddy ditch! But you needn't have worried. I can shoot the pips from a playing card at twenty paces. You were never in the least danger, you know."

"No I did not know," he retorted, singularly unimpressed. "And if ever again you dare to try using me as a means to exhibit your shooting skills, I shall exact my own form of retribution. My thirst for vengeance will be quite as keen as yours, my lady!"

"Oh? What will you do?" she asked interestedly. "Use force to bend me to your will I suppose?"

"No, not that," he answered evenly. "I would merely inform Mrs Wytcherley of her niece's nocturnal adventures."

"What! You would actually stoop to such abominable treachery?" she cried disgustedly.

"Never doubt it. I mean to extract a promise from you this very night that you will refrain from any further nonsense of this sort. Don't you realize that smuggling is not only an illicit but a very dangerous trade? You might well have been foully murdered tonight. Those men were not play acting, they were in deadly earnest. If you will not think of yourself, then please consider how your aunt and your father would feel if the worst had happened. It was pure chance that brought me to your aid; I could just as easily have lost track of you in the dark. Have you so soon forgotten that other incident, that you persist in this foolish masquerade? I should imagine your father would be absolutely appalled if he knew the truth."

Elisa walked on in silence and did not speak again for several minutes. When next he caught a glimpse of her face in a sliver of moonlight, he saw tears glistening on her cheeks. In her ill-fitting seaman's garb, hair hanging in dripping elf-locks and her face streaked with dirt, she looked so wretched and woebegone, that she unwittingly drew his sympathy. He recalled Mary Shaw's words which had explained so much about this singular young woman's eccentric behaviour. She was as unapproachable and unpredictable as a wild creature. Since their first meeting in the storm, she had alternately exasperated and infuriated him. He had never known such an untameable and spirited girl.

When next she spoke, her voice was decidedly subdued. "He would blame himself, I know it. My papa, I mean. If anything horrid should befall me, he would think it all his fault. He has always held himself responsible for my mama's death. She died trying to give him the son he longed for but her sacrifice was all in vain. Poor Papa was left with only me for consolation. I tried my best from the first to show him that I could become a companion to him. But try as I may, I cannot stand in the place of a son to him. He can't take me with him on his travels, you see? Papa says it just isn't the sort of thing that young ladies can do: it wouldn't be seemly. But I mean to show him that I don't care for my reputation: all I want is to be with him wherever he is. When he comes home again, my aunt will tell him that I have sunk quite beyond reproach and then I think he will have to keep me with him. Don't you think so?"

"Don't you think he might be disappointed in you?" suggested the major gently.

"It don't signify. I am sure I have long been a disappointment to him. He needed a son to be proud of: a man worthy to bear his name. Someone like you, Major Lacey," she said rubbing her face with a grubby shirt sleeve. "You're a soldier and an officer. Brave too, I shouldn't wonder, judging by your remarkable ability to pluck me from harm's way. That's the second time you've saved me from a very awkward situation, for which I heartily thank you. I dearly wanted to tell you before how grateful I was but of course, I had to keep my secret. I say, do you suppose you could teach me the rudimentaries of fisticuffs? I especially like that swinging blow to the jaw that I've seen you land."

"That's termed a 'haymaker' in boxing cant. And that's the last and only thing I'll teach you on the subject."

"Oh, but I've excellent bottom and never fight shy," she smiled up at him, a wide infectious grin that would always be reminiscent of 'Eli', even when she was back in her petticoats. He could not refrain from laughing and she began to laugh with him. "You are utterly incorrigible," he said, ruffling her hair playfully. "But I think we could become friends now, do not you? Friends look after each other, just as we have managed to do tonight, so we have already made a start. Shall we make a promise never to allow our tempers to get the better of us in future?"

Elisa gave a delicious gurgle of mirth. "Don't be nonsensical! That's a vow would be broken ere the sun set upon it! But I should like to have you for a friend, I think, so let us shake hands on that."

She wiped her somewhat grimy fingers on her breeches and then they shook hands solemnly before continuing on their way in amicable silence.

Upon arriving at the cottage, Mary drew them quickly inside, astonished to see them together and both in a dreadfully bedraggled state. She found some of Tom's old clothes for the major and hurried Elisa away to change into a set of Peter's homespun garments. They were gone for some little while and the major guessed that Elisa must be telling Mrs Shaw everything that had happened. When they came back into the parlour, Elisa sat on one of the little, three-legged stools by the chimney corner and began to dry her hair. Mary bustled about setting the kettle to boil and laying crockery on the table. The major leaned back in his chair and surveyed Elisa musingly as she bent her tousled head before the flickering flames.

He studied her idly at first, noting the soft curve of her graceful neck and the determined thrust of that almost aggressive chin. Her mouth was perhaps a trifle too wide to be admired by the aesthete but when she smiled it lit up her whole face quite becomingly. "Come here, urchin and I'll dry your hair for you, otherwise Mrs Shaw will never be rid of us."

Without demur, Elisa handed him the cloth and came to sit at his feet, propping her back against his knees. He began to rub her hair vigorously until she protested loudly that she would be as bald as a hen's egg if he persisted in using her head as a scrubbing stone.

"I'd scrub it a lot harder if I thought it would wake up your senses," he scolded. "I meant what I said about telling your aunt exactly what you have been up to. You must promise here and now that you will never again involve yourself with these smugglers."

"Why should I make such a promise to you?" came the muffled reply from beneath the voluminous cloth. "What does it matter to you how I choose to live my life?"

"It matters a great deal to me if you continue to use my property to enact your crimes. You cannot expect me to countenance such nefarious trespassing."

"The major's in the right of it, my lady," intervened Mary sternly as she filled the teapot with steaming water, "'aven't I told you so meself an 'undred times over? It's all very well for the likes o' us t' risk our necks, 'cause we don't 'ave much ch'ice in the matter. Those as ain't got the means o' makin' money t' buy bread, can't afford t' be pertic'lar in 'ow they sets about fillin' the larder."

"Why did you involve yourself in the trade, Elisa? Was it only to test your mettle?" asked the major, freeing her at last from his over-enthusiastic attentions.

She ran her fingers through her rioting curls that, in the ruddy firelight, glowed a golden red like evening sunbeams. Then, tilting her head sideways, she looked up at him consideringly from beneath dark, curling lashes. "Well it wasn't for financial gain, I have never taken a penny of their money. But yes, I suppose you are right, I wanted to show them all that I could do as well as any man," she admitted frankly.

"That's 'alf the truth anyways," muttered Mary, setting the tea on the hearth to draw.

"Mary! Don't you dare say another word!" admonished Elisa warningly.

"Well, it's time the major was told everythin'. I don't like t' speak ill o' the dead as can't answer back but the fact o' the matter is, sir, that your brother put the notion in 'er 'ead in the beginnin'."

"Mary, hold your tongue!" Elisa demanded balefully.

"Be quiet, Elisa. Please go on, Mrs

Shaw," insisted the major, suddenly rousing himself from his admiration of the charming effects of firelight on shining red hair. "I want to hear what you have to say, especially if it concerns my brother."

"Well, sir, I'll tell ye. The late Lord Cullin was in the way of providin' well-paid work for them as was willin' t' take a chance or two and no questions asked. 'E used t' take that ship o' is across t' France quite reg'lar all through the last years o' the war. None o' them Revenue men durst search 'is lordship's vessel. 'Sides, 'e let it be known that 'e liked t' fish these waters at night, just f' sport, an' they believed 'im. More fools them, I say. The lack o' money makes some fearsome 'ungry but the love o' money make others downright greedy, an' that's a fact!"

"I'll not let you speak ill of Lucius . . . "

· "I've no wish t' pain ye, m'dear," continued Mary gently. "But don't ye see 'tis f' the best? Look what's 'appened t' Tom and now theer's you t'night. It's got so's I'm a-sceered t' lift the latch on me door. The thing is, sir, she's 'ad a lonely sort o' life as I told ye, an' yer brother knew it too. It were easy f' 'im t' win 'er affections. A few kind words was all it took an' 'e could be a charmin' cove when 'e wanted anythin'. She'd 'ave flyed t' th' moon an back if it'd pleased 'im t' see 'er do it." She paused to pour out the tea and handed the major a cup. "I 'ave t' tell ye, sir, that this come in on that ship t'other night. But I 'opes it wun't sp'il yer pleasure, 'tis the only kind I got."

The major hid a smile in sipping from the proffered cup. "It tastes quite delicious, despite being steeped in corruption," he assured her.

Mary eyed him perplexedly. "I don't know about that, sir, I b'lieve 'tis growed in Chinee."

"I think you are right. But do go on with your story, Mrs Shaw."

She nodded and offered Elisa a cup which that petulant young woman refused.

Undeterred Mary set it aside and sat down at the table to drink her own. "Well now, wheer was I? Oh, yes, I was about t' tell ye 'ow this all come about.

When 'is lordship needed t' unload the goods, 'e 'ad t' be sure no one were about t' guess what 'e were up t'. So 'e says t' Lady 'Lisa, what a fine joke it'd be if she were t' borrer some ol' duds an' 'elp 'im out b' keepin' watch f' the Preventives: which same o' course she does, only too willin'. An' still does, now them Palmers 'as taken up wheer 'is lor'ship left orf."

"Lucius didn't force me into it. I wanted to do it," interjected Elisa vehemently. "It was wonderfully exciting and really diverting. Especially when we always managed to gull the Riding Officers. I remember that not so long ago, we came upon one of them as we were bringing the goods inland and we had to truss him up like a chicken and take him with us. I let him go when it was safe to do so, of course, but I made certain he would have a good long walk before he could raise the alarm. If ever they questioned me, I always told them that I was Sam Frant's nephew and so no one ever guessed the truth. I never let Lucius down: he was very proud of me, he said so. If only I hadn't stayed so long in London and if Tom hadn't been put under false arrest, I'm sure Sam would never have been lost with the *Seabird*."

"Do either of you know why he did sail her alone?"

"I think Tom do but 'e's not sayin'. I'll tell ye somethin' else though. Tom never poached no bird from Sir Eustace's land. I b'lieve that were done t' get 'im out o' the way. Yer brother were up t' no good. I'eard 'im an' Tom quarrellin' over somethin' 'is lor'ship wanted done, only Tom said 'e wanted nothin' t' do with it. I asked Tom what it were all about but 'e said it were best I didn't know. The very next night Tom were taken up b' Sir Eustace's keepers an' I never sin 'im agin until 'e come back 'ere this spring past. Ever sin' then it's bin nothin' but trouble. First Tom, then Sam an' 'is lor'ship an' all these queer nabs a-prowlin' about Blakestone land. One time, when I were goin' up t' visit ol' Tildy at the Dower 'ouse, I sin one of 'em stop Lady Cull-in's gig. I kep' out o' sight 'cause she don't want me goin' on 'er prop'ty. Threatened t' 'ave me put in prison if she see'd me up theer, she did.

424

Well, this fella asks 'er wheer exac'ly did the *Seabird* go down. Spoke quite rough t' 'er 'e did an' I could tell she were fright'ed 'cause 'er voice were sort o' wobbly when she answered 'im. I don't know why she didn't send 'im orf with a flea in 'is ear f' bein' s' bold with 'is tongue but she never did. Told 'im the wreck 'ad broke up an' come ashore near 'Ythe, over along Kent way."

"She has made no mention of that particular incident to me. I wonder why not?"

"Well, it were some time back, sir, not long after the fire. I durst say she's put it from 'er mind b' now. But there's bin stranger things 'appenin' up theer. The menfolk d' say as 'ow they've 'eered scratchin's an' scrapin's as can't be accounted nat'ral." She lowered her tone and went on mysteriously, "Jem says 'e saw a phant-im up at that 'id-y'ous ol' mess o' bricks, one night when they was comin' by with the ponies."

"Mary's referring to your home, Major," explained Elisa, a quiver of amusement in her voice and her sense of humour suddenly restored. "Some of our men say

425

they have heard seemingly inexplicable sounds but I think it's superstitious nonsense. I've been up there myself on many occasions, day and nighttime and I have neither heard nor seen anything out of the ordinary. Aurelia is there more frequently even than I and has observed nothing odd either. Although I have noticed of late that she has not visited so often as she was used to do. But I put that down to you two having quarrelled the last time you met."

"What makes you think we have quarrelled?" he demanded indignantly.

"I overheard you as I passed the window on my way out," she said with an impish look.

"You mean you listened at the window. But it was not a quarrel. We both have more important things to occupy our time just lately, that is all."

"You mean the sale of the property, don't you? I know Sir Eustace still means to have it. He tried to force Lucius into selling it shortly before he died."

"What do you mean? How did he force him?"

"It won't hurt to speak of it now, I

suppose. Lucius had taken a mortgage on the estate. Sir Eustace arranged it for him through his bank. He must have known poor Lucius would never find the means to redeem it. Financial independence always seemed to evade Lucius's grasp; he never quite understood the principles of accounting. He had a seaman's concept of the ebb and flow of money and even when his pockets were at low tide, he always expected an imminent and timely reversal of fortune. There was no use in my telling him what a fool he had been, it was too late for that; so instead I came up with an excellent scheme for rescuing him from the trap Newbury had set for him. That's why I was in London just at the moment when Tom was in need of friends. Lucius visited me at our house in Bruton Street while I was there. He came to tell me that he could not wait for me to try to solve his problems, as matters had come to a head: Newbury had threatened to foreclose at the end of the month. I asked him what he meant to do to prevent it and he said that an opportunity had recently presented itself whereby he would be able to clear the debt himself. He refused to disclose the nature of the business and could only be got to say that it was wonderfully simple and would pay Newbury out in more ways than one."

"Newbury again! That long-legged spider is at the centre of this web, I'm certain. It was he who gave the order that Tom should be kept in close confinement and I should dearly like to know the real reason why he thought that so necessary."

"I thought as much! And it was his lying gamekeepers who were responsible for Tom's arrest in the first place! Tom told the truth when he said that he had not been poaching that night. He doesn't even own a gun, yet they swore that the bird had been shot."

"That's right, sir. Anyways, Tom couldn't 'ardly 'it the side of a barn on a sunny day in June, never mind a scrawny pheas-int a-runnin' about the woods in the middle o' the night. 'Is eyesight's next t' useless, 'ceptin as far as 'is dinner plate."

"Is that indeed so?" murmured the

major, gazing intently into the dancing flames, his brow puckered in deepest thought. "Tell me, Elisa, did you know who those men were who waylaid you tonight?"

"I only know that they are the same two men who accompanied Tom back to England, because he told me so. They aren't local men, if that's what you mean, though they must be staying somewhere close by because they are always sneaking about the woods. I've tried to warn them off several times with a shot or two to lend wings to their feet but they stick like hounds to a scent."

"I didn't get a clear view of them but it seemed to me that they were not the same men who tried to abduct you when you were walking with Mary."

"No they weren't. We had never seen those two before. But they also were after Tom and demanded to know where we had hidden him."

"You may not have seen them before but I have seen them since — to my cost," he said, rubbing his arm.

"You mean they were the men who

shot you?" she gasped in amazement. "But why you?"

"I stumbled accidentally upon them as they were loading a box of some kind into their boat. They were extremely annoyed that I had taken such an interest in their affairs and I was obliged to take my leave of them without discovering who they were or what they were about. As I rode back towards the lane that runs just beyond the Dower House, I came upon a black chaise waiting under the trees. I stopped to see if I could recognize who it was might own such a vehicle and it was then that a man stepped into my path and threatened me with a pistol. I decided not to further our acquaintance and rode on. I think I may have offended his sensibilities, for he promptly fired upon me for my lack of civility."

"A black chaise?" reiterated Elisa wonderingly. "Harry came along that way in a black chaise, didn't he? But no, I'm sure it couldn't have been him, he has no reason to harm you. At least . . . no, I am certain it was not he."

430

"Did you see nothing as you came along that lane?"

"No, I did not. But then I had not rid all the way on that particular track. I came down through the woods because of the rain."

"You said they were loading a box, did you not?" He nodded. "That's interesting," she continued musingly, "those men mentioned boxes tonight. They were apparently unhappy at the thought that I might have laid my 'fambles' on them. I wonder what it all means?"

The major sighed wearily. "I daresay we shan't discover the answer to any of these questions until Tom is recovered enough to speak. I believe he may hold the only key to this mystery." He got to his feet and held out his hand to her. "Come, Elisa, I'll see you safely to your door. It's time we left Mrs Shaw to her rest."

"There's no need," she said, accepting his assistance, "I am quite used to taking care of myself."

"Well, now you don't have to any more. You have a comrade as of tonight;

we called a truce, didn't we? And shook hands on it, pal."

"So we did. An' pals 'as to look out f' one anuvver, ain't that so?" quipped Elisa saucily, catching his eye with an impish twinkle in her own. They both dissolved into laughter and Mary was quick to note the intimate look that had passed between them and the obvious change in their relationship. Gone was the cold distrust that had been so marked in all their previous encounters. In its place was a warmth and ease of manner that gave rise to the hope that in him she might have found more than a friend.

They made their farewells to Mary and slipped away into the woods behind the cottage.

"How will you get back into the house without being seen?" enquired the major, as they walked leisurely along, side by side.

"The same way I always do: by climbing a tree. There's no difficulty in that. I am provided with my own private stairway to freedom. It is an old sycamore that grows not far from my window and a branch has obligingly grown right up to the sill. It always looks as if it is offering a helping hand, practically inviting me to come out."

He laughed gaily at her daring. "You really are the most amazing creature, I must say. I don't know what the stately dames of London drawing-rooms would make of you."

"They would mark me down as an eccentric, just as you do. Undoubtedly I would get on famously in London. Originals are not considered such a rarity in Town salons. Providing one has the added distinction of being wealthy, of course. Without that I might well end my days incarcerated in Bedlam."

"You are more likely to end your days incarcerated in Newgate! Or dancing a jig at Tyburn."

"They have to catch me first and they won't find that so easy!" she boasted, cheekily.

"Don't be too sure. You were caught easily enough twice before."

"But I have you to rescue me now, don't I?"

"I shan't always be at liberty to do

so. I must rejoin my regiment soon. My furlough is almost at an end."

"Oh, I thought perhaps you might be thinking of selling out. Your tenants are in great need of a landlord who would interest himself in the land."

"I don't think there would be much point in pursuing that interest. I . . . it just isn't practical."

"Completely rolled up, are you?" murmured Elisa sympathetically. "I had begun to suspect as much. Oh, never tell me you made yourself responsible for Lucius's debts?!" she gasped suddenly.

"Well of course I did," he replied a little stiffly. "They naturally became my responsibility when I took over my brother's estate."

"But was there nothing left? What of the money Lucius used to pay off the mortgage?"

"You may well ask! I can find nothing amongst Lucius's papers that would explain how he managed to come by such a sum. That is all part of this whole mystery."

"I wish I could help you. But I've already told you all I know of the affair.

Oh! If only I had insisted that he tell me what he was plotting."

"Never mind. Perhaps Tom Shaw can help us. I hope to be able to question him before I return to London. Who knows? Perhaps you and I may meet again there. Do you go often to Town?"

"Not I. My father and my aunt gave me a coming-out ball in Bruton Street when I was eighteen and I spent the season there. But, as you may easily guess, I did not take. However, although I did not snare a husband, I did acquire a splendid horse and an elegant phaeton, which is far better."

"Then you do not wish to be married?"

"I did wish it very much once," she answered wistfully. "But someone else became his bride. You see, I fell in love with your brother when I was eleven years old and I have never loved anyone else in quite the same way."

"Yes, he seems to have had an extraordinary ability to inspire devotion in the women who have loved him."

Elisa tried vainly to read his expression, she thought she had detected a note of bitterness in that remark.

"I suppose you feel the same about Aurelia?"

"I suppose I do," he said flatly. "First love came to me when I had barely attained my eighteenth year. That is when I met Aurelia. She was just a few months younger; embarking on her first season and as beautiful as a sweet rosebud just unfurling its petals. I loved her on the instant of our meeting and for a time I was convinced that she returned my regard. Eventually I plucked up enough courage to propose to her and she accepted. Shortly after our engagement, my mother fell ill and I had to return to Ireland. Aurelia was enjoying herself so much in London that she did not want to leave and I did not have the heart to insist that she accompanied me. I knew that she would find it deadly dull in Ireland because I could hardly spend time entertaining her while my mother was lying sick. I had met Lucius again in London prior to my departure and I asked him to bear her company while I was away because I thought she might be lonely without me. He had already gained some Town bronze and was quite willing to take her under his wing. It was the worst thing I could have done. Within a matter of weeks I received a letter from Aurelia explaining that she had fallen hopelessly in love with my brother. She said she knew I would understand and would wish them happy." He gave a short, derisive laugh. "But she was quite wrong. I didn't understand at all and was far from wishing them happy, so I left for London immediately. The long and the short of it is, that I had the very devil of a quarrel with Lucius and, I am ashamed to say, I planted him a facer. After that we had nothing more to say to each other. My mother succumbed to her illness and died soon after my engagement had been ended. It seemed that my whole world was tumbling about my ears and I felt that there was little point to my continued existence. An acquaintance of mine had already bought himself a pair of colours and it was his suggestion that I should do likewise, so I took the King's Commission and eventually sailed off to Portugal. There, now you know the full extent of my stupidity."

"I don't think you at all stupid. I

expect you couldn't help falling in love with Aurelia because there is no denying that she is very beautiful. I've seen the way the gentlemen look at her. And when she plays the part of the tragic widow, they all act like besotted schoolboys. But she isn't the helpless female you all seem to think her. I've had plenty of opportunity to observe her since she came to live with us and I know she isn't so heartbroken as she pretends. Someone once remarked how well her mourning gown became her porcelain beauty and since then she has worn nothing but black! Those tears she sheds so copiously whenever she has an attentive audience, they are not the result of deep sorrow. When Lucius married her and when I learnt of his terrible death in that fire, I cried torrents. Enough to know that tears are completely ruinous to the complexion, leaving one with a red nose, puffy eyes and a face like a wrung-out rag. But not Aurelia, oh, dear me no! Aurelia wears her tears like jewellery, to add sparkle to the blue of her eyes. Yes, I know what you are thinking: this is all merely the venomous rantings of a jealous woman. That's what my aunt thinks, she is completely taken in by her. But I don't care how it is construed; I have her measure!"

"I think you wrong her," he said quietly, "she really did love Lucius, even I must admit it. In her heart, she has never been able to come to terms with his death. I cannot even persuade her to leave here and return to London. She insists on remaining so that she can feel near to him. You have only to see how often she visits the family burial vaults to realize just how much she still grieves for him."

"Yes, I've seen her. I can't help wondering why she feels it necessary to spend so much time there and why she is so determined to keep me away. She has always resented the friendship I shared with Lucius; I think it irks her to know how close we were before he even met her. That key is never out of her possession and whenever she enters the mausoleum, she never fails to lock the door behind her. I know because I've tried to follow her on several occasions."

"I think Aurelia suspects that you are

439

trying to spy on her; it seems that her suspicions are not completely without foundation."

"Well, she should not act as if she had something to hide. It is her own fault. Why must she always lock that door?"

"Could it be to keep you out?" he suggested with some amusement. "Aurelia may well regard your . . . ah . . . natural curiosity as something of an intrusion on her privacy."

"Poking my nose in where it isn't wanted: that's what you mean. I couldn't deny that I have been doing that but I can't help myself. I have the curiosity of a cat."

"I can easily believe it. I could name several other characteristics which you share with that particular creature. In fact I am wholly of the opinion that you are more feline than female."

"I know what it is. You think me spiteful because I clawed you and because of what I said about Aurelia."

"Not entirely," he said, pausing to remove an intrusive branch from her path. She slipped past him and found that they were in sight of the lawns that led up to the rear of the Hall.

"Well then, what did you mean?" she persisted.

"Cats are generally spiteful only when they have been treated unkindly. They respond quite differently if handled tenderly." He enclosed her hand in both of his as he spoke and gently stroked the sensitive skin of her wrist with his fingertips.

Elisa stood transfixed to the spot, her heart suddenly beating wildly as she watched him in silent fascination. Then he bent his head and lifting her hand, lightly brushed her wrist with his lips; a kiss that felt like the soft touch of a butterfly's wings.

She watched breathlessly to see what he would do next, her eyes intent on his face. Still keeping her hand imprisoned in his warm grasp, he reached out with his left hand and gently smoothed the wayward curls from her brow.

"Your hair feels like silk," he murmured in a voice so low that he seemed to be speaking his thoughts aloud.

"I should think it feels more like seaweed," she replied, feeling ridiculously awkward and shy. "I haven't combed out the tangles."

He smiled and drew her a little closer. "You're quite a woman, Elisa Maytland. Tonight you have won my deepest admiration. From the moment we met, I sensed there was something extraordinary about you. You've a brave, strong soul in you, my lady. My head has been so shrouded in long past dreams, I have been unable to distinguish reality from fantasy. I don't think I even wanted to. I've tried my best to hold on to fantasy by letting go of my temper whenever you threatened to obliterate my fading memories. I had carried them with me for years as some men carry a painted miniature, thinking the heart could be just as unchangeable as those bright colours. But here's reality." He cupped her face between his hands and his touch again sent excited shivers down her spine. The intensity of her feelings for him and the depth of passion she had heard in his words, somehow made her suddenly afraid.

"You're trembling, Elisa, are you cold?"

442

"I don't think I am. Cold, I mean. But it is very late and I really must be going indoors. The servants will be about soon and I dare not chance being seen in these clothes."

"Yes, it would not do, would it?" he answered softly, reluctantly releasing his hold on her. "Goodnight, Elisa."

"Goodnight," she whispered, beginning to back away towards the house. "I really must go in."

"Of course. But you needn't have feared. I had no intention of risking my skin again."

"You need not have feared either," came the soft reply from out of the farthest moon shadows, "my claws were sheathed tonight!"

15

THE major finally returned to Blakestone to find Ned anxiously awaiting him.

"Thank God you are come home safe!" he exclaimed with obvious relief. "I was beginning to worry that some new catastrophe had befallen you. Where have you been all this time?"

"I'm sorry to have caused you so much concern, Ned. I have been for a swim with Eli."

"What?! Are you run mad?!" ejaculated Ned, astounded.

"I think perhaps I am," replied the major with an enigmatic smile. "I was left too long under the influence of a beautiful moon. Now, what's been happening here while I have been gone?"

"You may well ask," Ned answered, sounding rather disgruntled. "While you've been moon-gazing, those smugglers have escaped with the brandy — right under the captain's nose! He's been well and truly duped tonight and it's made him as cross as a hungry bear. He and his men have been chasing through the woods half the night. Not only did he lose that valuable load of brandy but the smugglers themselves. He was right in thinking he could safely hide in the woods without fear of being seen but so could they — and they know their way about far better than he."

"Poor old Hal! Where is he gone now?"

"He's out looking for you. We were both concerned that you had not returned from the beach."

"Then I had better go and find him. How is our patient?"

"Growing stronger by the hour; you should be able to talk to him soon."

"Excellent news! I'll be back as soon as I've found Hal."

"That might be sooner than you think. Here he comes now."

"Alex! There you are! I have been searching everywhere for you. I was beginning to think you might have drowned yourself."

"I very nearly did. But what's this I've

been hearing from Ned? The fish have wriggled out of your net after all?"

"Yes! Damn 'em! I've been made a monkey of, Alex. We've spent hours running after shadows and just when I thought we had finally caught up with them, all I discovered was a pile of empty barrels left in a clearing. I don't understand it. How did they manage it? They are as cunning as a den of foxes."

"Or a vixen determined to protect her cubs," smiled the major wryly. "Ned, I think our friend is in need of a restorative."

"So are your clothes, by the look of them," replied the captain studying the major's borrowed garments with a critical eye. "Where on earth did you acquire those?"

"Why? Should you like me to give you the name of my tailor?"

"Most certainly! If only to ensure that I avoid him like the plague!"

"If it makes you feel any easier about losing that brandy, then pray insult me as much as you wish. Fortunately, both my tailor and I are men of some mettle."

"Yes indeed, it's called brass I believe. What *have* you been up to tonight, Alex? And what did that elusive young urchin have to say for himself?"

"We had quite a discussion, as a matter of fact."

"Was that before or after you went sea-bathing?" interspersed Ned, busying himself with his brew.

"Ah, now I see," observed the captain with the understanding of the newly enlightened. "There lies the secret of that snug-fitting coat with the miserly length of sleeve."

"Forget my coat for a moment, Hal, will you?" pleaded his exasperated friend.

"Oh, let us consign it to oblivion by all means, at least it will have a properly fitting end."

"Now listen to me, Hal and please do try to be serious. There is something occurring here at Blakestone which is far more sinister than the smuggling of a few barrels of brandy. Whatever it is, it might have cost the lives of at least two men and nearly a third if Ned hadn't chanced across Tom Shaw. This very night, Eli and I almost shared a similar fate at the hands of two men who claim to be officers of the law. Hal, when you return to Shoreham, I would like you to make enquiries about the case against Tom Shaw. According to Mrs Shaw, Tom was given a full pardon by the courts and returned to England in the company of two men who brought a signed order for his release. If possible, I would like to know who these men were and also the name of the signatory on that release document. You should be able to find a record of it at the court where the case was heard. It is my guess that Sir Eustace Newbury set his hand to it."

Early the following morning, as Ned was changing the dressing on Tom's wound, the invalid's eyes flickered open and his lips moved soundlessly as he strove to speak. "Major Lacey, sir! Come at once! He's waking up at last!" cried Ned excitedly.

Within seconds the major was at his side and saw for himself that Shaw was indeed more than just conscious this time and seemed to be making every effort to communicate. The major bent his head to try to catch the first whispered words but Tom's voice was cracked and dry and it was impossible to understand what it was he wanted to say. "Bring some brandy, Ned. We'll try if we can get him to swallow a little. Better put some water with it though."

Ned quickly brought a glass and lifting the man gently from his pillows, they contrived to assist him in drinking a few drops.

It seemed to revive him slightly and this time the major distinctly heard him utter the words, "Mary . . . my Mary . . ."

"Don't worry, Tom. Mary knows you're here and she knows that you are getting better. She's been to see you and will come again now that you are recovering your senses. This is Corporal Ned Parrish, who found you lying in the road. You are at Blakestone House and I am Major Lacey, Lord Cullan's brother."

"Cullan!" croaked Tom, suddenly seeming to focus all his attention on that one word. "Tell Cullan they know! They know! The boxes! They've found the empty boxes!" He began to grow extremely agitated, plucking at the blankets with feeble fingers, his dull eyes seeming to search about the room. "No! Don't say! Not a word! Swear to it! Swear!"

"It's all right, Tom. No one is going to say anything. Rest quietly now, you will be well again soon."

The sick man fell back upon his pillows and closed his eyes again as if exhausted by his efforts.

"He'll sleep for a while now," murmured Ned, "but it's a good sign. Next time he'll probably waken for a little while longer and you'll maybe get a bit more out of him."

"He's repeating the message he gave to Mr Stewart three years ago. He must still be delirious I suppose and my name has triggered some fleeting memory. I wonder what these boxes are that he spoke of just now? Oh well, I shall have to wait until he stirs again. I was going to the Dower House this morning but I think I shall leave that until later. I don't want to be missing when he does feel ready to talk to us."

"He may not be so ready nor willing as you hope," Ned replied dampeningly. "This one's no gabster. Even in his fever he has mentioned nothing but his wife's name. A man whose tongue is that well guarded in sickness will not let it run wild in health."

"Well, if I cannot persuade him to confide in me, I shall see what Eli ... no, Lady Elisa, can do. I think he trusts her enough to speak the truth. Perhaps she may ride over to see him today."

However, owing to the exertions of the previous night, Elisa had slept late into the morning. When she eventually awoke, she stretched luxuriously in the cosy warmth of the wide bed and as she lay drowsily recalling the night's adventures, she smiled happily to herself. Then she lifted her arm and pushing back the sleeve of her thin, muslin nightgown, dreamily studied the blue veins beneath the delicate skin of her wrist. The smile grew more tender and slowly she drew her hand towards her face, pressing her mouth to the throbbing pulse that seemed to quicken its beat with the memory of his touch. She gave a soft crow of laughter. How deliciously foolish this was! Even when Lucius had been alive she hadn't behaved quite so idiotically. But then he had never kissed her. Major Alexander Lacey had. Twice. Now, had that first kiss not been stolen in anger and had the second claimed the place of the first, she might well have been more than halfway to imagining herself . . .

The sound of voices floated up to her open window and she heard Aurelia giving instructions to one of the gardeners.

"Make these into a posy for me, Jarvis. I am going to take them to my husband's tomb. Oh, good morning, Margaret. I was just preparing to drive to the Dower House. It's time I visited the servants to see how they go on."

"How thoughtful you are! I see you have selected some of our loveliest blooms for Lucius. Ah, my dear! I find your devotion to his memory so affecting, so very affecting."

There came the sound of footsteps on the gravel path and Mrs Wytcherley's voice again, upraised in greeting.

"Good morning, Sir Eustace! What a delightful surprise."

"Good morning, ladies. I hope it is not

inconvenient to call at this hour?"

"Not at all, sir, not at all. You are always welcome at Dovecote Hall. Would you care for some refreshment?"

"No, thank you, ma'am. I came to speak a few words to Lady Cullan, if I may," he added courteously.

"But of course. I am sure she will be only too pleased to have your company, won't you, my dear? Now pray excuse me, I must give cook her instructions for the day."

Elisa slipped out of bed and peered through a gap in the curtains. Sir Eustace and Lady Cullan were seating themselves under the sycamore.

"Where is Lady Elisa this morning?" he asked, placing his cane and curly brimmed beaver on a vacant chair.

"I daresay she is already gone out. She is usually an early riser and has most probably gone to see that Shaw woman. Why? Did you wish to see her?"

"No, no," he smiled pleasantly, "I wished only to be certain of our privacy. It is you I came to see."

"Oh? What is it you wish to say to me?"

"Well now, my dear, I think you can guess, can you not? You must know that I have been living in daily expectation of hearing your acceptance of my proposal of marriage. I need not tell you again, I am sure, how eager I am to make you my wife. I have been a very patient man; don't you think it is time you ended my lonely existence and agreed to allow me to announce our betrothal?"

"I . . . I don't know what to say . . ." she began, nervously shredding the petals from a rose.

"You have only to say 'yes'. Surely you cannot mean me to continue in my anguish when you could so easily make me the happiest of men?"

"Please give me a little more time. It's so difficult for me to . . ."

"There isn't anyone else, is there?" he asked pointedly. "I did think Major Lacey something over-particular in his attentions. Is he fancying himself in love with you, I wonder?"

"Only a trifling affection, I think," she said airily. "I am sure it is not serious with him. You know what these dashing young officers are like."

"Then there is nothing to prevent your giving me a favourable answer?"

"Merely my own doubts, Sir Eustace. I do not know if I could ever love you in the way that I loved Lucius."

"I have already said that I do not expect that of you. Enough of affection exists between us to make us tolerably happy, don't you think? And perhaps, in time, you may grow to love and esteem me as much as I love and greatly esteem you."

"Oh, you already have my esteem, Sir Eustace," she assured him quickly. "But I am not so sure that love will . . . "

"Your esteem will suffice. Just give me your promise to be mine before the year is out, or I shall go mad with the agony of this long waiting." He seized her hands in his and began to kiss them fervently.

Elisa, still watching from her window, wrinkled her nose in disgust. How could Aurelia endure it? Surely she did not mean to have him?

"Your answer, Aurelia! I must have your answer!" he entreated her, the passion in his voice quite unmistakable.

"Oh, please, Sir Eustace! Do not press

me for my answer today. I cannot . . . "

"Why? What reason can you have to delay our marriage any longer? I have waited for years, Aurelia, surely you must know there is a limit even to my patience?"

Aurelia appeared to be flustered by his impassioned pleading and tried to free her hands from his grip but he would not release her.

"Very well," she said at last, "if you will have it so. You may make the announcement on my birthday in November."

"You mean it?!" he cried joyfully. "You will be my wife?"

"Have I not said?"

"You will not regret it, Aurelia. I shall restore you to your proper position in society. You shall have your heart's desire. You shall be my greatest treasure, my jewel."

"I hope I can make you happy, Sir Eustace," she answered, a tragic note in her voice.

"You already have, my dearest, now that you are to be mine at last!"

At that moment, one of the footmen

stepped out of the house and Aurelia beckoned him to approach. Elisa heard her ask him if the gig was ready and he replied in the affirmative.

"I'm sorry to have to leave you, sir, but my arrangements were made before I knew of your arrival. Would you please excuse me?"

"Of course. Now that I have your promise, I can bear the separation with hope renewed. When may I call on you again?"

"I am afraid I shall be engaged until the end of the week. Perhaps you could visit us on Friday?"

"Must it be so long a parting? Very well, I shall have to abide by my lady's ruling. *Au revoir*." He bowed over her hand saying dramatically, "And may that hour, my sweet, fly to me on wingéd feet."

Elisa turned away from the nauseating scene with a grimace of disgust. Aurelia must have bats in the attic to have preferred Sir Eustace over Major Lacey. And how mistaken she was in assuming her brother-in-law's affections were not seriously engaged. If Aurelia had been present at High Dean when the major had spoken her name, she would have realized the truth. He was still deep in love with her.

Somehow this thought began to take the proportions of a great cloud of gloom, that gradually blotted out Elisa's happier and more recent memories. The morning had suddenly lost its golden glow.

Later that day, Elisa decided to make her usual visit to Mary. She elected not to go by way of the lane but set out across the open fields so that she and Sabre might enjoy a long gallop. It was a fine afternoon with the sun cocooned in soft, wispy gauzes and the scent of new-mown hay hanging delectably on the balmy air. As they broke from the hazel coppice at speed, Elisa spied a five-barred gate only yards in front of them. Sabre was as eager as she to show his contempt of the puny obstacle and flew over it as easily as Pegasus himself, alighting with the grace of a bird on the other side.

A horseman, who had hitherto been obscured by the high hedgerow, was forced to rein in as the reckless pair sprang into his path.

"Elisa! I might have known it would be you, you madcap girl! Are you determined to break your neck?"

"Good afternoon, Major Lacey," she beamed happily, turning Sabre about and cantering back to meet him. "If I must break my neck, I should prefer to do it this way rather than at the end of a rope as you predicted."

"I should prefer you to keep that pretty head of yours firmly on your shoulders."

"Should you?" she said with a sparkling look from beneath the veiled brim of her black beaver hat.

"Certainly. It would be a pity to lose such a capital capital." He smiled across at her as she rode slowly beside him. "Where are you off to in such a hurry?"

"I'm going to see Mary."

"She is fortunate to have such a caring friend. I've just been to see her myself, to return Tom's clothes and to tell her that he is very much better today. She was the first person he asked for when he spoke this morning."

"He spoke? Why, that's good news!

Mary will be so relieved. Did you manage to get any information out of him?"

"Not yet. But the strange thing is, he muttered something about boxes, empty boxes."

"Did he now? How very peculiar," she replied, her eyes bright with interest. "If only we knew what significance these boxes held, we might begin to understand a great deal more about this entire business. What exactly did he say?"

"He seemed to be trying to tell us that 'they' had found the boxes; whoever 'they' might be. I'm afraid it's all we got out of him before he lost consciousness again."

"Hmm . . . " she murmured, frowning thoughtfully, "I wonder where and what these boxes are?"

"I'm afraid only Tom knows the answer to that, so there's no use in teasing that inventive brain of yours. Speaking of which, I suppose you know that Captain Rowland was deprived of his victory last night? You and your band of will-o-the-wisps led him a merry dance, it seems. You did succeed in outwitting him after all. But you had better hope he does not discover who it was deceived him. He was most unhappy at having lost not only the brandy but several nights' sleep into the bargain. You would be well advised to keep very quiet about your part in that escapade."

"I could not allow him to spring his trap. It cost him only a few hours' rest: it would have cost them a great deal more than that," she said seriously.

"Yes, I know. I must admit that having got to know Mary and her family, I cannot help but feel sympathetic to their plight. And no one has been hurt by their unlawful employ so far as I know."

"These men are all known to me personally, Major, I will vouch for any one of them. They are not murderers like the Hawkhurst Gang, merely men with hungry families to feed," she insisted adamantly.

"Very well. But there are such men hereabouts, Elisa. Someone tried to kill Tom, there is no doubt about that. We might have been lying dead up there on the Downs by now if those shots had found their mark."

She shivered. "Then thank God they

did not! But let's not talk of death and murder on such a beautiful afternoon. Where are you going?"

"I'm on my way to the Dower House. I saw a light in an upstairs window last night that I could not easily account for. I noticed it when I was following you. I thought it rather odd because the servants are too old to climb those stairs and never use them. I thought I'd make sure that all is well."

"How exciting! It sounds most intriguing. Can I accompany you? I can always call in on Mary later, especially as you have already been to see her. May I come?"

"I should have guessed you would be ripe for adventure. But there is probably a very boring explanation and you will wish you had kept to your original plan."

"We may see Aurelia there, if she has not already come away. I heard her making arrangements to visit the house this morning." She glanced askance at him, a furtive and calculating look. "Sir Eustace came to see her just before she left."

"That must have been an agreeable event for her."

"Yes, it was rather." She hesitated briefly before continuing with studied carelessness, "I think we are like to be wishing her joy very soon."

He did not flinch at the news, keeping his eyes firmly fixed on the path ahead. "I hope he'll make her happy," was all he said.

"He will certainly make her very rich."

"Then it's certain she will be very happy. Come, let us see how well you can ride, my lady. That tree up there on the crest of the hill shall be our goal. Shall I give you a head start?"

"It won't be necessary," she cried scornfully. "Sabre shall soon show you a clean pair of heels!"

Gathering up the reins, she urged the stallion into a gallop and they raced away neck and neck across the field.

He pulled Perseus in just ahead of her at the top of the rise.

"By Jupiter! You're a bruising rider, Elisa!" he marvelled, as she came up behind him, swaying gracefully in the saddle while Sabre performed an excited gambado.

"That was wonderful!" she exclaimed

breathlessly, pink cheeks a-glow and eyes shining like emeralds. "We very nearly had you beaten, you know. Another few yards or so and it would have been bellows to mend with your Perseus."

"Never! He's good for miles yet, aren't you, lad?" The major leaned over Perseus's neck and patted him proudly. "We'd prove it too, if we could spare the time. But I don't care to be too long about this business because Tom may wake again soon and I want to be there when he does. Are you ready?"

She nodded and together they rode on towards the Dower House.

There was no sign of Aurelia's gig as they dismounted at the front of the house. "Why don't we ride around to the kitchen garden?" asked Elisa as she tethered Sabre to an iron ring set in the wall.

"Aurelia has given me a key to this door," he explained, producing it from his coat pocket.

"Oh, I see. It's just that she never enters the house through this door herself."

"This is the way she brought me when we came to see Tilda and Albert. That's the room where I saw the light shining: up there."

He went to the door and inserted the key. As before, the screech of hinges almost set his teeth on edge.

"My! Isn't it horrendous?" whispered Elisa in awed accents as she followed him through to the hall. "It looks as old as the Pyramids! No wonder Aurelia prefers to live at the Hall."

"Well, she won't have to live here now, will she? Sir Eustace's splendid mansion awaits her."

He stopped suddenly and peered upwards. A soft scraping noise sounded just above their heads.

"What was that?" breathed Elisa excitedly.

"I've no idea. Unless it's the mice again, of course. Let's investigate."

Together they mounted the uncarpeted staircase, Elisa sweeping up her trailing skirts over her arm to avoid the dusty boards.

When they reached the upper floor, he turned to the right and led her along a dark corridor with a panelled wall on one side and doors set at intervals in the other. A long window at the end of the gallery was securely shuttered, closing out the daylight. They stopped in front of the last door and he tried the handle.

"This must be the room, I think." He pushed open the door and they stepped over the threshold to enter a chamber lit by a casement that faced towards the sea. One of the shutters was broken and a pale light percolated through the dirty glass panes, revealing a few pieces of furniture draped with coarse linen covers. The walls were lined with oak panels, some of which were ornately carved with swags of fruit and flowers and swirling acanthus leaves.

Elisa stared about her with great interest. "How could our ancestors have borne to live in such gloomy style?! I would find this dreadfully oppressive, it would not suit me at all to sleep in such a room."

"Especially as it has no exterior staircase. No doubt that would always be a necessary requirement as far as you are concerned, my lady."

"Unless I could find some other means of escape," she answered ponderingly.

"Isn't this the room where your Aunt Sybil was used to sleep?"

"It may have been. I really don't remember. Why?"

"I met her once or twice: when I was just a child and first came to live here. We got on remarkably well as I recall. Probably because she was inordinately fond of cats," she added with a quizzical smile.

"Or perhaps because she was reputed to be something of an eccentric herself?" suggested the major laughingly.

"Well, whatever the reason, we enjoyed some mutually interesting conversations. Do you know that there is rumoured to be a secret room behind one of these panels?"

"No, I haven't heard that tale myself. But it may be true. My father said there were several such hiding places at Blakestone. These buildings are very ancient and there may have been all kinds of intrigues played out within their walls. Did she mention exactly where this secret room was located?"

"I'm certain there was some trick of opening the panel by means of twisting one of these carvings, though which one I just cannot recall. Wouldn't it be thrilling if we could find it?"

"It might take hours and I've no wish to spend the rest of the day here, thank you. I just wanted to see what was in this room."

"There's nothing of any value. I don't think anyone has broken into the house, if that's what you feared. Perhaps you may have been mistaken about that light. It could have been the moon's reflection on the window pane."

"No, it was a faint, flickering light that moved." He walked to the window and peered out through the rain-smeared glass. "I must have been just over there when I saw it," he went on, trying to envisage the scene again. "The light seemed to pass across the room from here," he indicated the open door, "to this wall where the fireplace is situated. Then it was suddenly extinguished."

"Let me indulge my imagination for a moment. Suppose someone carrying a candle, entered the room through that door and disappeared through another door on this side of the window. Might

468

that not explain the mystery?"

"You are determined to make me look for this secret panel, aren't you? Oh, very well, I shall let you have your way. But only for an half-hour, mind and just to humour you."

"Fiddlesticks! You need not try to keep up the pretence, Major Lacey, I have found you out now. Confess it: you are as eager as I for adventure, is that not so?"

"Adventurous I might be but foolhardy — never!" he said with teasing smugness, as he began to examine the carvings.

"I hope you do not mean to imply that you think me rash." She came to stand beside him, intently studying the wall in front of her. "After all, did you not behave extremely incautiously when you attempted to fight two armed men with only your bare fists?"

"Not in the least. I knew precisely what I was about."

"And what about your audaciously reckless behaviour early this morning?" she said archly.

"What about this morning?"

Elisa traced a carved cluster of grapes

with a dainty fingertip and glanced provocatively up at him. "Wasn't it rather foolhardy to have risked another clawing?"

He watched her guardedly, a little smile lifting the corners of his mouth.

"Ah, but that wasn't foolhardy, was it? That was adventurous. And if you continue to look at me with those bewitching eyes, I don't know but what I might adventure further still . . ." With his right hand still pressed against the wall, he swiftly bent his head towards her upturned face and at that precise moment came the sound of a muffled click as a section of the panelling slid from beneath his fingers.

Elisa gave a yelp of astonishment at their unexpected success. "Oh, my goodness! Look! It is a secret room!"

"Without a doubt," he murmured, equally amazed, and stepped over the wainscoting to enter the dark, little chamber.

Elisa skipped after him. "See! There is a table and two chairs and a candlestick!" she cried gleefully, holding aloft the latter to show him the stub of melted tallow.

"And here's a tinderbox."

The major picked it up and lit the candle end.

"What are you going to do?" asked Elisa, as he held the candlestick in front of him and began to wave it slowly to and fro across the bare walls.

"Just watch the flame."

As he moved along the wall and crossed behind the table, the flame suddenly flickered and almost went out.

"What is it?" she demanded eagerly.

"I think there's a passage on the other side of this wall: if I can find the mechanism to open it up. This room is very similar to one I have seen at Blakestone and probably has another means of escape in case of discovery. Ah, yes! Here it is!"

A soft scraping echoed in the confined space of the chamber and a narrow aperture seemed to suddenly materialize in front of them.

"This is far better even than I had hoped!" exclaimed Elisa delightedly. "Let's see where it leads us."

"I'll go first," he ordered, "you're likely to leap before you look. Now stay close

471

to me and do exactly as I tell you."

"Oh, very well, but please do hurry!"

"Bring the tinderbox then. We may have need of it."

Elisa snatched it up and clutching his coat tails with the other hand, stepped after him into the darkness.

16

"LOOK to your feet, Elisa," he warned, "there are steps circling down but they are very steep."

It was also extremely dark. The tiny candle flame afforded only a meagre light that danced along bare brick walls, thickly netted with dust-laden cobwebs. Down and down they went until Elisa's head began to spin.

"It's like descending into the bowels of the earth," she whispered.

"I think we must be right under the house by now. I wonder how much further we have to go?"

The stairs took another three or four turns and then ended abruptly.

"We're down at last." He moved slowly forward, shielding the candle flame with his hand.

"There appears to be a passageway. Let's see where it leads us."

"I hope it doesn't go on for miles," said Elisa, holding his coat tighter.

473

"Do you want to go back?"

"Most certainly not! This is too exciting! It's just that I wish it were not so . . . so dark down here."

Her heart filled with trepidation but determined to go on, Elisa screwed up her courage and stumbled after him. The musty air grew colder and damper. Now the walls felt wet and slimy as her hands brushed against them. Spidery streamers like sticky fingers clung to her face and made her shudder with horror. She groaned aloud.

"What's the matter? Are you all right?" he asked anxiously, turning to let the light fall full upon her face.

She looked back at him with large, scared eyes and gave a thin, apologetic smile. "I'm sorry, Alex, I ought to have confessed it before. You see, there is something that daunts me. I didn't want to admit to it when you asked me, because it's so stupid and it vexes me to own it. But there's no help for it. I have tried but I cannot overcome the fact that I am absolutely terrified of spiders!"

He stared at her in amazement and

then a slow grin spread across his handsome face.

"Elisa Maytland, the bold, daring leader of an intrepid band of smugglers is actually afraid of a harmless little spider?"

"I know, I know. It is nonsensical and you may well laugh at my expense," she said crossly. "That's precisely why I did not admit to it last night; I knew you would think it vastly amusing."

"Very well, I shan't tease you. But there is a simple solution." He reached out and loosened the veil tied about her hat, pulling it down over her face. "There, you won't be able to feel those long, tickling legs now."

She shuddered again, an expression of dread and disgust on her face. "Ugh! Please don't mention their legs! I can't bear the thought of them touching me!"

"Just keep your head down then and give me your hand."

"Willingly," came the grateful reply as she accepted the proffered assistance.

"I wonder if you really meant that?" he murmured softly and not a little doubtfully, before turning away from her and plunging once more into the darkness.

The spidery horror was forgotten as Elisa's thoughts became wholly occupied with the most delightful daydreams invoked by those gently spoken words and that heart-stopping look in his eyes. She nestled her fingers more snugly in his, heartened and reassured by the strength of his grip. Now she felt no desire to prove her own strength and gladly relinquished all responsibility for this latest escapade. The major had come to her rescue once again and she was beginning to enjoy and desire, his protective presence. It was a good feeling to have the company of a man she could rely on. For once in her life she was at peace with herself: delighting in being a woman and awakening to the wonder of a different kind of power that was both awesome and oddly humbling.

Eventually the long tunnel ended when they came face to face with a solid brick wall. "Oh, no! Surely we haven't come all this way for nothing," wailed Elisa disappointedly.

"Don't worry, there must be a way out somewhere, I don't think this tunnel was built just for concealment. We must look about us for a possible exit."

"Then you'll have to do it on your own. I can't bear to search these dark corners. You never know what may be lurking there!"

"You hold the candle and I'll risk the spiders."

He ran his hands over the brickwork, working methodically from top to bottom but without success.

"I suppose this means I shall have no choice but to face the gantlet," sighed Elisa dismally.

"And let those spiders take another swing at you? I cannot subject you to that, my poor girl. Just lift the candle as high as you can, will you? That's better."

He began to examine the roof of the tunnel and after a few minutes gave a cry of triumph. "Got it!"

"Have you found the way out?"

"Give me one moment and I'll show you," he answered calmly, setting his shoulder to the low ceiling. As he put his weight against it, there came the loud grating of stone on stone and a glimmering square appeared above them.

The major swung himself up through the opening and briefly vanished from Elisa's view.

"Well?" she called impatiently, "What have you found?"

"Pass me the candle and you may come and see for yourself."

In a trice he had pulled her up after him and in the sputtering candlelight, Elisa gazed all around in speechless wonder.

"Oh! We are in the mausoleum!"

"Indeed we are," he murmured, equally surprised and slowly taking in their unexpected surroundings.

A strange half-light filtered down from a stained glass window set high in the domed ceiling and as their eyes grew accustomed to the gloom, they could discern the huge, white marble tombs placed in niches in the walls.

"This is Lucius's tomb," she said quietly, pointing to a plain sarcophagus that contained all that remained of Lucius, Lord Cullan, so long and so sadly lamented by his grieving widow.

Major Lacey came to stand beside her, staring down at the Latin inscription etched into the lid. He had not wanted to look upon it before, there were too many painful memories to be evoked. Now he read his brother's name and titles with a heavy heart, not remembering that final bitter quarrel but seeing again the careless, mischievous companion of his childhood.

Elisa, watching the play of emotion across his features, silently withdrew to an arched niche on the other side of the room to allow him time to collect his thoughts. It was as she waited here that her glance fell upon a bright bouquet of flowers lying against the wall. These must be the blooms that Aurelia had picked that very morning, they were still fresh and fragrant. Elisa stooped inside to pick them up and in doing so, suddenly saw a wide opening in the floor with steps going down.

"Alex! Come over here, quickly!"

"Now what have you found? Not more spiders surely?"

"No, look, some more steps." She pointed eagerly downwards, standing aside to allow him to see for himself.

"This is a day for discoveries, is it

not? I need not ask you if you wish to come with me?" he smiled, holding out a hand to help her down. "Even though this is bound to be as fraught with danger as the last tunnel, simply crawling with spindleshanked arachnids."

"Didn't I tell you that I never fight shy?" she said loftily and boldly placed her foot on the first step.

"That's the soldier, game as a pebble. Come along then, let us see what awaits us at the end of this."

They plunged into the impenetrable darkness below, the major directing their steps as they progressed along yet another dank passage. This time they had to travel some distance until at last they came to a blank wall. Once more he had to search for some means of escape but fortunately recognized the similarity between this and the exit from the secret room. Sure enough, when he finally found the lever, there came the familiar scraping sound and a narrow opening gradually appeared before them.

"Where are we now?" asked Elisa, still clinging tightly to the major's hand.

"We're in the cellars of Blakestone

House itself. Look, there are the wine racks, just as I remember. The fire did not penetrate this far down. It's impossible to reach here from above ground because the old stairway is completely blocked by fallen masonry. It looks as if the upper floors have crashed in upon the rest of the cellar space. See those massive beams and all those bricks? What a terrible mess!"

"Yes indeed it is. But how strange that this part has remained unscathed. It almost seems as if someone had purposely cleared it."

"You're right, let's have a closer inspection."

They moved slowly forward, the major holding high the feebly burning candle. The light barely pierced the thick gloom and it was difficult to see more than a few feet in front of them.

"I think this candle is all but done, it won't last very much longer, you'd better light the tinderbox."

Elisa made to obey and as she fumbled with the box, it slipped out of her grasp and clattered to the ground.

"Oh, bother! Where has it gone? I can't see anything, it's too dark."

"I'll find it. It can't have gone far." He crouched down, holding out the candle to illuminate the stone flooring and cast about in the deepest shadows, edging slowly forward as he searched. "Here it is! It's fallen among these boxes piled against the wall." He reached out to retrieve it and stood up, handing Elisa the candlestick. "I'll light this and then we'll be able to see better."

Soon the flames spurted into life and the shadows receded a little. Now they could see a number of wooden boxes stacked neatly along the wall.

"I wonder what's in them? Shall we take a look?" asked Elisa curiously.

"This one's damaged. Something heavy must have fallen on it, the top is smashed into splinters. Hold up both the lights, Elisa and we'll see what's inside."

Elisa moved closer and the major pulled away the broken wood. In the dancing light of the flames, they saw that the box was filled with small, tube-like rolls of blue paper. For a moment they could only stare at them in mute astonishment. Then the major snatched one up, exclaiming excitedly, "This is

Tom's blue paper! The one the rector gave me!" He tore it open with eager fingers and out into his open palm spilled several gleaming, golden guineas.

Elisa gasped audibly. "Are these all rouleaux of guineas?! But what are they doing down here? If all these boxes contain them, there must be thousands!"

"Many thousands. See, there are twenty in each. This must be Tom Shaw's carefully guarded secret — and probably the reason he is lying up there with a broken head."

"Then these are the mysterious boxes those men were after! Small wonder they were so keen to find them! Who do you think put them here? Tom?"

The major was silently gazing down at the torn paper lying in his hand. "This was Tom's warning to Lucius. A warning that came too late."

"What do you mean? Do you think Lucius was killed for this?"

"I believe so. Don't you see? Lucius paid off the mortgage just before he died. Where would he have got so much money? He was deep in debt."

"It was always low tide with him, I

know. So how in the world would he have accumulated so much wealth?"

"I have no idea. He borrowed ten thousand pounds from me while I was out in Spain."

"Ten thousand pounds?"

"Yes," he gave a short laugh. "I had no use for it at the time and Lucius desperately needed it for some mad scheme that was supposed to change his fortunes. Perhaps it did and this gold is the result of it."

"No, I don't think so," she murmured pensively. "But what are we going to do about all this?"

"Well, we can't move it alone, that's certain. It will have to remain here for the time being. And I'm hoping that when Tom recovers, he will furnish us with some explanations. Now, let's go back to the horses."

"Oh dear, must we go back the way we came?" she groaned reluctantly.

"I'm afraid we have no choice," he said pityingly. "At least, I don't think we have. Wait here a moment while I take a look over there. In my father's day, there was used to be a trap door that opened up to allow the barrels to be lowered down to the cellars. I had quite forgotten about it until now."

After some minutes searching, he called out to her to come to him. "There it is up there. If I pile up some of those boxes I should be able to reach it. Then we'll have to hope nothing heavy has fallen on to it from above."

He managed to drag some of the boxes across the cellar and piled them up until he could get his shoulder to the trap door. To his surprise it lifted easily and as it opened, the scent of the sweet early evening air breathed in upon them. He turned and held out his hands to Elisa who nimbly climbed up after him; then he swung himself up through the hole and reached down to pull her into the welcome light. As she came up through the door, he gazed at her as if some thought had suddenly struck him.

"What is it? You look as if you've seen a ghost," she said.

"I once imagined I may have done. That night you hid the brandy in the old tower. Someone came up out of this very door, only to scuttle back like one of your dreaded spiders as soon as he saw me. What a chuckle-head I am not to have realized sooner."

"Didn't you know who it was?"

"It was far too dark to see clearly. That's why you crafty smugglers chose that particular night, isn't that so?"

"A moonless night is a smuggler's delight," she answered saucily. "Is that how you knew where we had hidden the brandy? Did you see us put it down there in the old armoury?"

"Not exactly. As I said, it was dark. But Hal and I found it the next morning. That's why you came to visit me, didn't you? You wanted to know if I had seen you."

"Harry asked me to find out. He was afraid you had escaped his house in time to see what was happening. I wasn't sure if you already knew about the armoury. Lucius showed it to me years ago and I knew it was possible that you also knew the secret."

"Palmer should have come himself. He had no business sending you on such an errand."

"It saved Harry from another broken

nose. And I had a salutary lesson into the bargain. You made me realize that I had put myself so far, beyond the pale, I was in danger of losing my own self respect."

He looked at her with contrition in his blue eyes and placing his hands on her shoulders, gazed into her face as if memorizing every detail. "Elisa, when I kissed you that day, it was not done with any kind intention. I meant to hurt you because I was angry with you. You never seemed to give me a chance to get to know you better and though I could not admit it to myself, I very much wanted that opportunity. These last two days I feel that you and I have drawn closer. We have become good friends, haven't we?"

She nodded. "Yes, we are friends now. I knew we would be one day, I felt it that night in Mr Stewart's garden, when you were looking up at the sky. Do you remember what a beautiful evening it was? And that thrush singing in the pear tree? I just knew your feelings were the same as mine, it was in your face. Suddenly I sensed that we were kindred spirits and I wanted so much to have you for a friend. But then, when I had plucked up the courage to speak to you, your face altered and the mood was broken. You weren't at all interested in me, it was Aurelia you were really thinking of, wasn't it?"

"I thought I was still in love with her," he admitted frankly. "You see, I made the mistake of believing that because I cared for her so much, she must surely feel exactly as I did. I never doubted it. But lately I have begun to realize that her thoughts and her desires were far different from mine. She isn't at all the sort of person I imagined and wanted her to be. I have been deluding myself for all these years and it is only now that I have forced myself to face the truth. Aurelia has never loved me as once I loved her. For her it was merely the brief infatuation of a young girl enjoying her first romantic encounter and did not stand the test of time. In my youthful ignorance I enthroned her in my heart like some unattainable goddess. It has taken a lovely, spirited, flesh and blood virago to shatter the foolish illusion. You're real and exciting; I like being with you, you make me feel happy and I enjoy your company. Elisa . . . do you think . . . "

The question was never posed because just then Ned appeared, standing on the ruined portico and looking all about him.

"Oh, there you are! I've been wondering what kept you so long. Where's Perseus? I couldn't see him in the stables."

"No, we left the horses at the Dower House. I must go at once and bring them back," called out the major and taking Elisa by the hand, helped her over the rubble towards the west wing.

They were pleased to learn from Ned that Tom had recovered sufficient strength to take a little gruel earlier on and if only they would be patient a while longer, he might rouse again soon.

"Then do you think you could ride to the Hall and tell my aunt that I shall be late home, Ned? Just say that I am staying to keep Mary company, she won't think it strange. She knows I frequently do so even if she does not like it. I'll stay with Tom. I must be here when he wakes up to hear what he has to say."

In a fever of impatience, Elisa sat by Tom's bedside, her eyes never straying from his thin face. It had grown dark by the time he showed signs of wakening and Elisa was beginning to think that she would never get to speak with him that night. However, when he opened his eyes, she was thrilled to see that he had recognized her and gave her a weak smile. "M'lady, 'Lisa, what're ye a-doin' 'ere?"

Elisa called excitedly for the others and was soon joined by Ned and the major.

"Tom, are you well enough to talk to me?" questioned Elisa, leaning nearer his face. "We have found the gold. Do you know how it came to be at Blakestone House?"

"Ye've found it? All o' the gold?" he whispered hoarsely.

"Yes, all of it. Major Lacey and I discovered it this very afternoon. Do you know anything about it? Whose gold is it?"

"I'll tell ye all I know if ye'd give me a sip o' that brandy, sirs," promised Tom, indicating the bottle still standing on the table.

490

The major readily complied with his request and when Tom had been fortified with a sip or two, he began his tale.

"That gold is ol' Boney's gold. Leastways it was meant to be, cause 'e paid f' it. Don't ask me 'ow 'tis done but yer brother un'erstood it all. Boney needed the gold t' pay 'is army."

"'Twas some 'ow supplied by merchants in Lunnon a-raisin' bills on forr-in banks an' discountin' an' prem'ums an' the lord knows what else besides. Me an' Sam couldn't make 'ead nor tail o' any of it. But the smugglin' folk all knows about Boney's gold. 'Twas taken over t' France quite reg'lar when Boney was Emperor. Used t' be smuggled out o' the port o' Deal and rowed across the Chan-nil."

"Surely not? All that gold taken across to France in a rowing boat? Impossible!" Elisa said in disbelief.

"Ah, but they was guinea boats."

"Guinea boats? What are they?"

"Forty-foot galleys, they was. Pulled over t' them Frenchies by two dozen o' the best oarsmen in Kent."

"But what of the Revenue cutters? Wouldn't the smugglers have risked capture and the loss of the gold?"

"Not they! No ship could 'ope t' ketch 'em, not with all sail laid on, they couldn've. Didn't I telled ye they was the best? Boney would've bin a-countin' of 'is gold jest five or mebbe six hours after that gold left English shores. Dependin' on 'ow the seas was a-runnin', o' course."

"And this was done regularly, you say?" intervened the major in astonishment. "But that is beyond belief!"

"Smugglin' gold was a 'ighly prof'table business, sir. Why, a single guinea'd fetch as much as thirty shillin' durin' the war."

"But what had my brother to do with French gold?"

"Well, sir, ye've t' remember that 'e 'ad got 'isself into a mort o' debts an' was bein' 'ard pressed t' pay up. 'E 'ad bin a fool, there ain't no denyin' it. So 'e comes t' me an' Sam Frant an' tol' us 'is lay. Ye see, sir, me an' Sam 'ad bin in the way of 'elpin' 'is lor'ship bring a barr-il or two from over the water now an' agin. But smugglin' a bit o' baccy an' brandy is one thing an' smugglin' French gold is another. 'Owsomever, 'is lor'ship 'ad struck a bar-gin with them Lunnon merchants t' bring the gold down 'ere an' then sail it along the coast t' the guinea boats a-waitin' at Deal. But I s'pose the sight o' all that gold 'ad bin too much f' 'im in is pre-dicamint an' e' tol' us 'e never meant f' it t' get int' Boney's 'ands. Accordin' t' 'is lor'ship, if 'e was t' keep the gold out o' sight at Blakeston' an' load the *Seabird* with boxes full o' stones, an' then scupper 'er at sea, why, no one'd be the wiser. But I didn't want nothin' t' do with that, I can tell ye. I know them Lunnon folk, they'd cut ye throat as soon as look at ye. 'Sides, I got Mary an' the little 'uns t' think on, so I says no to it. Then 'e shows me this roll o' guineas an' puts it in me pocket. 'Theer's more wheer that come from', 'e says. Well, we 'ad a bit of an argu-mint an' 'e said as 'ow e' couldn't carry it orf unless I 'elped 'im. But I jest daresn't risk it f' the sake o' me fam'ly, so I gives 'im back the gold. Then Cull-in comes t' the cottage wheere we was livin' an' 'e tries t' pe'suade me t' join 'em. Says that 'e an' Sam 'as already spent some o' the gold an' so they got t' carry it

493

through or else they be dead men. So I says I'd think about it, jest t' get rid o' 'im, 'cause Mary were gettin' suspicious. Anyways, the followin' night we 'ad t' go over an' collect a few barr-ils an' a bit o' tea an' when we 'ad tucked it away safe 'n sound, 'is lor'ship gives me a guinea for me trouble. 'An' remember', says 'e, 'there's more wheere that come from if ye changes yer mind'. Then orf I goes 'ome with the money in me pocket. That's when them Lunnon men got me. Caught in their trap I was like a 'elpless rabbit an' theere wasn't no gettin' out o' it neither. Well, then they searches me pockets and out comes the guinea piece. They seems t' be very in'erested as t' 'ow I come by it but I never telled 'em 'oo give it me. Whiles I was a-sittin' in that pris-in, the magistrate Sir Eust-iss come t' see me. 'E asks me about the guinea an' 'e says if I don't tell 'im wheere it come from, things is goin' t' go very bad with me. That's when I starts t' wonder if it's all on account o' that gold that they've gone t' sech troub-il to put me away. But I can't tell Sam nor yer brother what's 'appened 'cause

494

I ain't allowed t' see nob'dy, d'ye see? Then I finds a bit o' paper in the linin' o' me coat an' I sees as it's the paper orf that gold yer brother tried t' give me. So when I gets a chance t' speak t' Mr Stewart I slips it t' 'im as a warnin' f' Sam an' Cull-in. But when I come back 'ere a couple o' months ago, I find out I was too late. They must've caught up with 'em after all an' they was both done fer. Then those fellas as brought me back 'ere starts gettin' nasty an' askin' about the gold an' wot I've done with it. They said they 'ad found the wreck o' the ol' *Seabird*. It'd taken 'em years but they 'ad sent down divers to fetch up them boxes an' all they found was a pile o' stones scattered on the seabed. Theere weren't a guinea in sight. I knowed they wouldn't bel'eve me an' that if I didn't tell 'em wheere it might be, then I was never goin' t' see Mary an' the young uns ever agin. So I got out o' that cellar as soon as I got the chance. An' I've 'ad t' lay low ever since."

"Until they found you in the lane and almost killed you," said the major grimly.

"Oh, that weren't them, sir. The vill'ins as done this t' me weren't those Lunnon men. As I went down I 'eard one of 'em call out a warnin' that someone was a-comin' an' then I knowed it weren't them. They wasn't ony o' our lads though, I knows all o' them pretty well. All I can tell ye is, that one were called 'Toby'."

"That was the name of one of those men who tried to kidnap me in the woods!" cried Elisa.

"Tom, you haven't yet mentioned Daniel Prescott," said the major suddenly. "How does he come into this?"

"I dunno about 'im', sir, 'ceptin 'e was a drinkin' pal o' Sam's. 'E weren't one o' the brother'ood. 'E wasn't born an' bred 'ereabouts, d'ye see. 'E'd only bin 'ere f' a year or two."

They were interrupted by Captain Rowland who came hallooing at the door and Ned went to let him in. He was surprised to find them all gathered at Tom's bedside and even more amazed when they explained the reason why.

"This is more fantastic than a fairytale!"

he exclaimed. "You're not gammoning me, are you?"

"Come and see for yourself, Hal, if you don't believe it."

"By all means," he agreed with alacrity and snatched up his hat again. "Now is a good time, I think. Oh, by the way, I've left my men watching the road and just came to tell you that you were right about Newbury. He did sign Tom's release. Those law officers came down from London saying they were Bow Street Runners and had received information that proved Tom's innocence. Sir Eustace says he had no choice but to clear Tom of the charges against him, especially as the men he had employed as gamekeepers had left his employ without a word. He says he is appalled that they had apparently perjured themselves."

"You have spoken to him then?" asked the major, taken aback.

"Yes, he came in as I was making my enquiries and asked me why I was so interested in the case. I'm afraid I told him Mr Stewart was anxious on Mary Shaw's behalf to know how Tom was faring. I also asked him if he knew where Tom had been taken when the officers brought him back to England but he said he had not troubled himself to find out. As far as he's concerned the matter is closed."

"I see," muttered the major, stepping out into the cool night air. "Said they were Runners, did he? I wonder if he bothered to check their credentials?"

"We could write to Bow Street ourselves," suggested the captain as he waited for the major to light the lamp.

"I suppose neither of them was called Toby?"

"No, definitely not."

"Then Tom was right. I think we are dealing with two separate cases here. Now tread carefully, Hal, I don't want you falling into my cellars."

"I shouldn't object if you can assure me you still have some of your father's vintage claret hidden down there."

"That would be worth more than mere gold to you, wouldn't it, Hal?" he grinned, opening up the entrance to the cellar.

"How are we to get down here?" asked

the captain peering in by the light of the lantern.

"The same way we got out. You'll have to stand on those boxes."

"What boxes? I can't see anything."

"Here, let me, I'll show you." The major knelt beside him and then slithered on to his stomach to lean down through the opening, holding the lantern as far down into the dark void as he could reach. Back and forth swung the golden glow but all in vain. The boxes had gone.

17

"**B**UT who has taken them and how could they have disappeared in just a few hours?" asked the captain, more than a little perplexed and beginning to wonder if his friend had dreamed up the whole.

"I've really no idea, Hal. All I can tell you is that they were there this afternoon. I saw them with my own eyes. They cannot have vanished into thin air, so the only logical explanation is that someone has taken them out through the tunnel I told you of. In which case they are either in the mausoleum or at the Dower House. I think I will put my money on their being taken to the house but I'll take the key to the mausoleum anyway. There is a spare one amongst the items the lawyers gave me. Come on, Hal, we'll get the horses and ride over there at once."

They hurried back to tell the others what had happened and Elisa insisted on accompanying them.

"No, Elisa, I think Ned should go with us, it might be dangerous," argued the major, unwilling to place her at risk. Despite her furious protests, the men all agreed she should remain at Blakestone with Tom and they eventually rode away without her.

The Dower House was in darkness when they arrived and all they could hear was the soughing of the wind in the firs and the distant murmur of the sea on the shore. "Ned, wait here with the horses," whispered the major, "Hal and I will look inside the house. Stay out of sight and keep your eyes and ears open."

They dismounted and headed for the rear of the house: the major did not want those ancient hinges screaming out a warning.

Tilda and Albert were already abed and the major knew that, hard of hearing as they both were, they would not be easily roused. He was forced to resort to house-breaking and entered through an unlatched casement in the kitchen. Hal slipped in after him and they crept stealthily up the servants' stairway to the main hall. A branch of candles was standing on a side table, still burning brightly and softly lighting the carved staircase. There was another gleaming at the top of the stairs as they continued to climb up towards the first floor. This had not been visible from the outside of the house because the shutters were all firmly closed.

They had to tread lightly on the bare boards and progress was necessarily slow. Not a sound could be heard anywhere and the house seemed to be utterly deserted. The major paused at the door of the far bedchamber and gently turned the handle. The door swung inwards to reveal an empty room.

"Look, Hal. That's the sliding panel, just as Elisa and I left it this afternoon," hissed the major. "Let's take a look inside."

As they approached the secret room, he noticed that the heavy curtains were now drawn across the window so that tonight there would be no danger of showing a light. He directed Hal's attention to the strip of wainscoting and they both stepped warily into the candlelit room. They could see the entrance to the winding staircase was also open and a rush of cold air fanned their faces as they peered down into it.

"Shall we investigate?" whispered Hal excitedly.

"If we do, we must risk showing a light. Better get one or two of those candles, I suppose." He was just about to fetch them when the scrape of feet echoed from far below.

"Someone's coming along the tunnel! Quick! We mustn't let them know we're here." Slipping swiftly out of the room and into the bedchamber, he showed Hal where to hide and they hurriedly concealed themselves in the window embrasure behind the floor-length curtains.

After a few minutes they heard footsteps coming up the stone steps. The movements seemed slow and awkward and there was the rasp of laboured breathing.

"Wait on, Toby," panted a hushed voice, "rest easy, pal. Set it 'ere on this table whiles I ketches me wind. 'Tis a mercy this be the last of 'em. We've earned our money t'night, I'm damned if we 'asn't."

"Well, if ye'd made a better job o' gettin' rid o' Tom Shaw, we wouldn't be a-shiftin' this load in such an 'urry. Now get a-movin', will ye? The ship'll be 'ere ony minut'."

"I be the one as found out wheere e'd got t', bain't I? If I 'adn't a-follered 'is missus we'd still be a-lookin' f' 'im. I should've tried t' get a shot at 'im wheere 'e lay. I could've shut 'is bone-rattler f' good."

"They 'ad 'im too well guarded. 'Sides, our gen'leman rackoned 'e weren't fit t' shoot the gab, leastways, not for a long while. Come on, take 'old o' this 'ere box an' let's get out o' this plaguey ol' ken."

There came the soft scrape of the closing panel and the two men stepped out into the bedchamber. Through a tiny chink in the curtains, the major recognized one of the men who had accosted Elisa near Mary's cottage. The other was certainly one of the seamen from the longboat and between them they carried a stout box.

Signalling to Hal to remain silent, the major waited until they had gone downstairs and then crept after them. The men left the house through an unlocked window in the dining-room and disappeared into the garden.

"They are going down to the shore. Tell Ned to hide the horses and I'll keep these two in sight. Come after me as soon as you can and I'll meet you there. We'll see what we can do to stop them making off with the gold."

"Then do be careful, Alex. And don't try anything on your own. I just wish I had brought my men along with me."

He went off to fetch Ned and the major followed in the wake of the two seamen.

As they made their way to the seashore, the men were joined by another who came to meet them.

"Come on, Toby. We're all a-waitin' on ye. We got t' be away on the tide."

"These boxes is damned 'eavy, Vose! I'm a-sweatin' like a pat o' butter in J'ly."

"Oh, stop yer moanin', we've all 'ad

t' take an' 'and, ain't we? 'Ere, give it t' me."

Off they went again, hurrying along the chalk path until they arrived on the beach. A small cutter lay at anchor a short distance out and a longboat was just pulling away. The major screened himself from their view by stooping down behind a rocky outcrop. As he peered down on to the beach, he saw a cloaked figure emerge from the other side of the rocks.

"Bring the boxes down immediately and look lively! We've little enough time as it is!"

"Aye, aye, sir, we're a-comin'."

It was now that the major noticed a small cave cut into the cliff at the back of the scree where he had sat the night before. More men appeared at its entrance and he saw that they were all carrying the boxes of golden guineas.

Suddenly, a shot rang out from the clifftop and a voice bellowed down to the men on the beach.

"Stand where ye are, me brave lads! Unless ye wants a ball o' lead in yer gizzards!" The men stopped in their tracks and looked fearfully upwards.

"It's Skinner!" yelled someone. "Skinner's found us!"

A flash of flame and another shot echoed, this time from the beach and the shadowy figure on the cliff whisked out of view.

"Got 'im! 'E's got Skinner!" shouted Vose triumphantly. Hardly had he finished speaking when a volley of shots exploded from above and the men let fall the boxes and scrambled into the rocks for cover. The sailors in the longboat pulled quickly away and headed back for the safety of the ship.

"Arm yourselves fools and go up there after them!"

"But sir! The gold!"

"Leave it here! We'll settle with Skinner and his crew first! We've not come this far to give it up now!"

The major looked anxiously about him, hoping that Ned and Hal were out of the firing line. He crouched lower as the men ran past his hiding place and began to swarm up the cliff.

Within minutes came the sound of a ferocious battle as the two factions clashed on the grassy slopes above. It would be hopeless to try to intervene alone and armed only with a single pistol, so the major was at something of a loss to know what to do for the best. He began to edge his way inland, in search of his companions, knowing that they must be close by. He had not gone far when he saw a troop of red-coated soldiers marching along the path just ahead of him. As they drew rapidly nearer he saw the captain at the head of the column.

"Alex! What on earth is happening now? It sounds as if war has broken out again."

"They're fighting over the gold; two opposing parties seem to be laying claim to it. I was this very moment wishing for a band of bold Grenadiers. Come on, Hal, let's show 'em what disciplined fighting men can do!"

The captain gave the order to march in battle order and away they went. When the soldiers of the line advanced over the brow of the hill, a cry of panic arose from the smugglers. Some had already fallen and lay hunched and motionless in the windblown grasses. Others were engaged in hand-to-hand combat, fighting with bare fists or knives, while the rest took to their heels and ran in all directions.

It did not take long for the soldiers to end the affray and soon all that remained to be done was the rounding up of those combatants still on their feet.

The cutter fled the scene without firing a shot and was fast disappearing on the horizon. As the prisoners were herded together and surrounded by the King's men, the major searched the grim faces, looking for the ringleaders. Skinner was not among them, neither was the man in the cloak, nor could they be found among the dead and wounded.

"How did you manage to bring your men here so quickly, Hal?" asked the major as the captain came up with him.

"That was Lady Elisa's doing. I don't know how she thought of it but she took a lantern to the top of the tower and signalled to my men. I had left them patrolling the coast road and my sergeant decided to venture as far as your woods. It was he who saw the light from the tower and thinking it might be the smugglers again, came straightway to investigate. Lady Elisa sent him to the Dower House to aid us and that's where Ned and I heard them coming."

"Where is she now?"

"I left her at the Dower House. She came with my men to show them the quickest way."

"Then knowing Elisa, she'll be straining at the leash by now. I'd better go and tell her all is well here."

"She was mad as fire that you left her behind," warned the captain with a broad grin, "you'd be wise to keep your guard up!"

"Thanks, Hal. I shall bear that in mind when I enter the ring. I think I shall wait until she's sparring for wind before attempting to close with her!"

He set off up the path and drawing near the house saw Elisa running towards him. "Alex! Thank heaven it's you! It's Aurelia! She must have been in the house when I arrived with the soldiers. She had on a long cloak with a hood but I caught a glimpse of her face as she turned her head. I had just gone in to see if the servants were frightened by the sound of the guns and as I was about to go down to the basement I heard a noise at the end of the gallery. I saw Aurelia rushing upstairs and when I came back towards the hall, a man came out of the dining-room and leapt up after her. It was that awful man called Skinner, the one who threatened me with a knife last night. Aurelia went into the secret room and escaped down the stairs. She must not have had time to close the outer panel because he went in after her. Then I heard him kicking at the panelling in the secret room and he has broken it down. They have both gone into the underground passage. What shall we do?"

"Go after them as quickly as we can. Where are the horses? We'll try to catch them at the mausoleum, they will have no choice but to go that way."

Moments later they were riding like the wind along the steep road towards Blakestone. Upon reaching the mausoleum on the brow of the hill, the major threw himself from the saddle and raced up the steps to the colonnade. He had barely reached the top when a loud report reverberated from inside the building. The huge doors were shut fast and it was with considerable relief that he remembered he had brought the key. Elisa came up after him and as the doors swung inwards, the major strode quickly through.

A branch of candles had been placed on one of the tombs and the eery light fluttered down upon a dark shape sprawled grotesquely across the entrance to the second tunnel.

Feeling sick with apprehension, they approached the body lying concealed beneath a thick cloak. Elisa stood rigidly waiting while the major knelt silently beside the still form and slowly reached out a hand to pull back the cowl.

A bloodless face with wide, unseeing eyes that stared in awe upon eternity, was pillowed against the cold, marble floor.

"Lucius!" gasped the major with incredulity, his head reeling with shock as he gazed down at his brother's ghostly features.

Elisa knelt beside him, her eyes fixed on Lucius's face in a kind of numbed trance. It was some while before either of them spoke, each feeling as if they were caught up in some strange, fantastic nightmare.

"It cannot be Lucius," whispered Elisa faintly. "It just isn't possible."

"I don't understand it myself," he muttered beneath his breath, still stunned by the appalling discovery. "How could this happen? What's been going on here?"

There was a sudden movement in one of the shadowy recesses and now Aurelia stepped forth into the light. Her face, though pale, was calm and composed and her voice remarkably steady as she addressed them.

"It's really quite simple, Alex. You see, Lucius wasn't killed by the fire. But he is dead now. This time there is no second chance."

She came to her dead husband's side and looked down at him, sighing pityingly. "My poor Lucius, his careful plans and efforts all for nothing."

"Who shot him? Was it Skinner?" demanded the major, rising to his feet and seizing her by the wrist.

She wrenched her arm angrily away. "Of course it was! And you brought him down on us! You've ruined everything! Everything! Why did you have to come back here?!"

"Where has Skinner gone?" persisted the major, ignoring her outburst. "Tell me now, Aurelia, before I shake it out of you!"

"He escaped down the steps. Yes! Go after him!" she shouted spitefully. "Perhaps you'll kill each other!"

Elisa glared at her disgustedly. "I always thought you were playing a part! You have known from the first that Lucius was alive and yet you let us all go on grieving for him. It was despicable of you! But it seems you have laughed in the face of fate for too long. You are both well served!"

She did not stay to listen to Aurelia's retort but snatched up a candle and started after the major realizing full well that he was in a fearful rage and therefore might be driven to act recklessly. So anxious was she for his safety that the terrors of the dark tunnel were forgotten as she hastened towards the cellars, cupping the candle flame in her hand. On this occasion, the passageway seemed even longer and she sighed with gratitude when she saw that the entrance to the cellars had been mercifully left unsealed. Now she would be spared the necessity of fumbling in the darkness for the latch. Glancing up as she stepped through the aperture, she could see that the trap door was still as Hal and the major had left it but this time there was a ladder leaning against the opening. She gathered her hampering skirts more tightly around her and discarding the candle, began the climb upwards. Emerging into the black ruins above, she searched anxiously about for some sign of the men.

At first she could see nothing but then the sounds of a struggle reached her ears and she scrambled over the rubble towards the gutted rooms on the north side of the house. Now she saw the major wrestling with Skinner who at that moment was sent flying backwards by a mighty blow to the jaw. He lay stunned for a second or two and shaking his head, got groggily to his feet. As the major lunged at him again, the man stooped quickly and picked up a length of wood, striking out at his opponent with vicious force. The major stumbled slightly, warding off the blow with a raised arm but he recovered himself immediately, seeing which Skinner turned and leapt away into one of the damaged rooms.

"Alex!" screamed Elisa in sudden terror, as the major went in after him, "Don't go in there! It's too dangerous!"

Her heart in her mouth, Elisa sprang as fast as she could over the fallen debris until she arrived at the fire-blackened doorframe. Just as she was about to go in herself, there came an horrific cracking noise like the sound of forked lightning and suddenly the whole ceiling caved in, crashing down upon them.

Blinded and choking on the thick clouds of dust which rose high in the air, Elisa fell back against the outer wall, gasping for breath.

"Elisa!" called a voice out of the darkness. "Elisa! Are you hurt?!"

"Captain Rowland! No, I'm safe but Alex is in there!"

In a trice came the captain to her side, closely followed by Ned holding a lantern.

"Alex went in after the leader of the gold smugglers. A man named Skinner. He killed Lucius and Alex is out for revenge. Please help me find him!"

"Of course! But you must wait here. These walls are liable to collapse if we are not careful. Come on, Ned, follow me."

They covered their mouths with their handkerchiefs and went to look for the major. As the dust slowly settled, they picked their way over the fallen plasterwork and began to search among the wreckage for some sign of life.

"Look, Ned! Over here! Quickly!"

The captain leant down and clawing at the rubble with his bare hands, managed to dig his comrade out.

To his amazement, the major's eyes opened and a slow smile curved his lips as he blinked up at them. "Who needs to enlist to find excitement, eh, Hal?" he spluttered, trying to get to his feet.

"Certainly not you," chuckled the captain, helping him up.

"Aye! He leads trouble about like a dog on a string," scolded Ned. "Haven't I told you that all along? It's as well he has the luck of the Irish!"

"Unlike that gallowsbait, Skinner. Part of that wall came down on him and now he's done for."

"I'll get some of my men to dig him out. Let's get you into the house and we'll see if you've any bones broken."

Before they could move, Elisa had come up with them and threw her arms tight about the major's waist.

"Oh, Alex! I thought you were dead!" she exclaimed with a little catch in her voice, her face pressed against his dusty coat.

He smiled lovingly down at her, tenderly stroking her gleaming red hair.

"I must own that it was extremely foolhardly of me," he admitted, leading her out into the fresh night air, while she still clung to his side. "What a pair we are, Elisa!"

"Didn't I tell you so?" she murmured softly. "We were made for each other, Alex. I think I have known that since the first moment we met."

"I remember," he replied, eyeing her fondly. "You standing in the rain wearing that adorable little hat with the dripping wet plumes, ruffling your feathers at me like an indignant chick unjustly evicted from its nest."

"It wasn't a nest it was a saddle and it was you who tumbled me from it. It made me out of reason cross and I was very sharp with you."

"Like a mouthful of lemon! But I have since discovered you to be a very sweet girl after all."

"Take care! I shall remind you of that the very next time we quarrel," she warned playfully.

"Must we quarrel?"

"Inevitably. But only think how we shall enjoy our reconciliations," she said, snuggling into him and giving him a coquettish smile.

"I'm sorry to have to break in on your love-making," ventured the captain, as they neared the major's quarters. "But I ought to tell you that Lady Cullan is inside waiting for us. We found her sitting on the steps of the mausoleum as we rode back from the beach. I think she wants to speak to you, Alex."

"Good. I certainly want to speak to her too," he said curtly, his face taking on a grim expression.

Aurelia was sitting in the parlour, staring pensively into the leaping flames but she looked up as soon as she heard them enter the room.

"Oh, it's you, Alex. I might have known. It's not the first time you have inconveniently come back from the dead."

"We Laceys take a deal of killing, do we not? Perhaps you'd explain just how my brother managed to arise like the phoenix from the ashes of Blakestone?"

"Why not? It hardly matters now," she said inconsequentially, "I suppose Shaw has told you how Lucius planned to steal the gold?" He nodded. "We knew he would. That's why, when Lucius found out that Shaw had returned to England, he had to try to keep him quiet. If he should have fallen into the hands of Skinner and his murderous crew, it would have been all up with us."

"They already knew Lucius had stolen the gold," intervened the major sternly. "They had sent divers down to the wreck and found only stones in place of the gold. Lucius must have realized that they

520

would not leave all that wealth lying at the bottom of the sea. It was obvious they would make every possible attempt to recover it."

"Lucius had hoped that by the time they did find out, we would be far away. We had planned to go to America and start a new life there."

"Then why didn't you? Why wait three years?"

"Because of the fire, why else? We hadn't planned on Blakestone being burnt to the ground. Lucius had concealed the gold in the cellars and when the house was destroyed, all the boxes were buried beneath tons of fallen masonry. It took him all this time to recover it. We would have succeeded if it hadn't been for you. Skinner was the leader of the men who had been hired to bring the gold from London to Blakestone. He was not happy to have lost a substantial fee and when you came to live here, he thought you had come to claim the missing gold. He couldn't believe you would have chosen to live in such squalor unless you had good reason. He has been watching your every move since you came here, hoping to see where the gold was hidden. Lucius had to stop all the excavation work in the cellars, just when it was almost completed too! You were happy enough to stay away for all these years, why must you live to spoil everything for us?!"

"And you always knew that Lucius was alive?" he questioned insistently.

"Of course I knew! That's why I had to dampen your pretensions and those of that loathsome creature Newbury. For three long years and more, I have had to hold him at arm's length. I had planned to use you as an excuse to cry off but it became unnecessary when we decided to take what gold we had and sail for America. We meant to go tonight but for you and Skinner. You might have favoured us, Captain Rowland, and got rid of him sooner. But he escaped your soldiers and followed Lucius back to the Dower House. We tried to evade him by using the secret tunnel but we weren't quick enough. He caught up with us in the mausoleum and shot Lucius in the back. I hid behind one of the tombs and he went on to the cellars thinking that I was ahead of him."

"How did you know about those tunnels? I never did."

"Those secrets were traditionally imparted to the eldest son of the house. Lucius received the documents relating to them on the day he attained his majority."

"Is that how Lucius survived the fire?"

"Yes, he escaped through the cellars."

"Then whose remains lie in the mausoleum?"

"Daniel Prescott's. He was well known to Frant and when Shaw was taken up for poaching, Lucius was desperate to find someone to take his place and help them load the *Seabird*. Prescott happened to be looking for a chance to make some extra money by participating in a little smuggling and asked Frant for work. Lucius had no time to find anyone else better known to him and took him on. They told Prescott that he would be required to assist in loading some contraband goods on to the *Seabird* and to keep quiet about it. But he began to ask too many questions and Frant became suspicious. As soon as the boxes were loaded, he dispensed with Prescott's services and he and Lucius took the vessel out together. Unknown to them, Prescott had managed to conceal himself aboard the *Seabird* and it was Frant who discovered him breaking into one of the boxes. He called out to Lucius to come down and help him but before Lucius was able to overpower the man, Sam Frant was shot dead. Then Lucius had no choice but to scupper the *Seabird* and make his own escape in the tender."

"He left Prescott to drown!?" exclaimed Elisa.

"What else could he do? Prescott knew the gold was not on board. Lucius left him there and came back to Blakestone the following day. He told me what had happened and that we must be sure that everyone supposed Frant to have sailed off by himself. I went ahead to the wedding feast and Lucius remained alone in the house to change his clothes. We had arranged for all the staff to be out of the house while Lucius got the gold safely away to the Dower House. As things had turned out, he had no one to assist him and so was forced to leave it where it was until he could devise another plan for its removal. While he was upstairs

524

getting ready, Prescott suddenly appeared at the door. He had been rescued from the water by some fishermen and brought safely to shore. But he came to blackmail Lucius saying that he knew all about the gold and wanted a share in it. Evidently he had all along been in the employ of those faceless men who had supplied the gold for Bonaparte. When Lucius heard that Prescott had been spying on him, he knocked him down and as the man fell, he spilled the candles from the table and the curtains caught fire. By the time Lucius had got the better of Prescott, the room was well alight and Lucius couldn't quench the flames. He ran to fetch help but Prescott regained his senses and came after him. A violent struggle ensued during which they both tumbled down the stairs and Lucius hit his head so sharply that he lost consciousness for a time. When he eventually roused himself, he found Prescott lying at the bottom of the stairs with his neck broken and almost the whole of the upper floors were ablaze. By this time, we had all hurried over from Barhurst and Lucius called down to us to keep out of the house. He said he would try to take shelter in the cellars if he could get out no other way. That's when I knew he would survive because he had shown me the secret passage just prior to hiding the gold. I slipped away while the others fought the blaze and hurried to the mausoleum. I was so relieved to see Lucius there waiting for me. He told me about Prescott and we decided it would be wiser for Lucius to hide at the Dower House until we knew how things would turn out. I met him there the next morning after being told that Lucius's remains had been discovered in the house. This seemed almost providential because now Lucius could escape all recriminations from the men involved in smuggling the gold out of the country. All I had to do was play the distraught widow and plead ignorance of everything if anyone should question me. As soon as things had quietened down, we would retrieve the gold and make our way to America. Alas for us, it was not to be that simple. Lucius struggled for months trying to dig the gold out but it was an impossible task alone. So he decided to hire some help from the smuggling fraternity. Frant had always been responsible for getting the contraband away to London and had used the same trusted men each time. They didn't know Lucius, he had made sure that only Frant and Shaw knew about his using the *Seabird* to smuggle goods. So he approached them as an old comrade of Frant's saying that Frant had recommended them for their discretion. He went under an assumed name, naturally and offered to pay them in gold if they would help him recover some boxes of valuable contraband. He said that he and Frant had secreted them in an underground tunnel at Blakestone just before the fire. He explained the need for extreme caution because a rival group were searching for the goods, knowing that Frant's death had left the contraband uncollected. He gave them an advance payment and they agreed to help him. However, when one of the boxes was brought out broken, they soon realized the truth and Lucius had to promise them half the gold. But at least it made them determined to see the job through and fight to keep the gold if called upon to do so. It was thanks to them that he managed to retrieve the boxes so quickly tonight after you two had chanced upon them. Lucius was staying at the house to oversee the work and in order to keep you, Alex, from disturbing him unexpectedly, I had to give you the key to the front entrance. Lucius would always know when you were about because of the terrible noise of those hinges. Clever, wasn't it? He saw you and Elisa go into the secret room and followed you down the tunnel. It didn't matter though, we had decided to go tonight anyway because things were becoming too risky; what with you and Shaw and then Newbury this morning forcing me into a public declaration of our marriage. I had to agree to that because it was imperative that I did not arouse his suspicions. He had already questioned me closely about Lucius's having paid off the mortgage so easily. That's why Lucius said I must feign complete ignorance of all our financial dealings and act the empty-headed little fool."

"It was Lucius who asked you to agree to an engagement?" interposed the major swiftly.

"Yes. I didn't like to play that part but Lucius was adamant that Newbury should have no reason to doubt that I was anything other than a grieving widow. I tried to divert Newbury's attention elsewhere. As a matter of fact, Elisa, I tried my best to persuade him that you were a better catch but somehow, he could not be got to agree to it. I could find nothing in your favour that would recommend you to him, not even your money was enough to convince him that he would be striking anything but a very bad bargain."

"I would not have had him if he had begged me on his knees. You'll have to take him now though, won't you Aurelia?" she said scathingly. "I wish you joy of each other."

"Will I? I wonder what makes you think that? It may surprise you to learn that I have quite different plans."

"As long as they do not include your remaining with us, I don't really care what they are. Why didn't you stay at your own house in the first instance?"

"We feared it would bring too many unwanted visitors to the house. The servants' presence and their being so old and deaf provided me with an opportunity to visit frequently without arousing anyone's suspicions. They even slept peacefully through all that disturbance tonight! Then, later on, when Lucius had to find help, it was necessary because we didn't want the men to guess our secret. They thought me in ignorance of their excavations which I must say suits my purpose very well now that things have gone awry. Mind you, living there would have been preferable to having to tolerate your ill-temper for all these years."

"In that case you need not stay a moment longer, need you?" snapped Elisa with acerbity. "My father has written to tell me he is coming home again very soon, so you may make your excuses to my aunt and take yourself off this very night!"

"Don't worry, Elisa. There's nothing to keep me here now. Besides, enduring your distempers is one thing but witnessing your love-sick moonings is quite another.

That I could not stomach! As for you, Alex, if you mean to have her, I think your inevitable misery will be ample recompense for having robbed me of my happiness."

"And your ultimate disappointment shall be mine. As to your happiness, I shan't ask you which was your greatest loss, I doubt you could answer me truthfully."

"You always did have difficulty in accepting my answers, didn't you, my poor deluded boy?" she murmured disparagingly. "Goodbye, Major Lacey, or must I now call you 'my lord'? You may as well agree to Sir Eustace's terms, Lord Maytland is certain to look for you to bring a little more than a worthless title to the marriage." She arose proudly erect and went to open the door. "On the other hand, a girl with such a worthless reputation will get no better match," she added maliciously as she turned to go.

At that, Elisa was across the room in a trice and slapped her so hard that she almost fell back into the arms of one of Captain Rowland's enlisted men who had that moment left Tom's sickbed.

531

The major swiftly seized Elisa round the waist and lifted her back into the parlour before she could follow up her advantage. The captain hastily stepped forward and instructed the soldier to escort Lady Cullan back to the Hall. Recovering her dignity, her ladyship swept away with the young man hurrying dutifully after her.

"Phew!" gasped the captain, slamming shut the door. "I had sooner face a regiment of Scotsmen armed to the teeth than two women in a temper!"

"What did you think of that haymaker I landed, Alex? I think I had it right, don't you?" smiled Elisa triumphantly.

The major set Elisa back on her feet, shaking his head despairingly. "I need never complain again that life after war is dull, Hal."

"There's not the least likelihood of that!" he agreed wholeheartedly.

"She'd better be gone when I get home," warned Elisa, still bristling.

"I'm certain she will be. I think she intends to stay only long enough to pack a few essentials and then take herself off to an inn for the rest of the night."

"How can you know that?" asked Elisa, puzzled by his air of certainty.

"Just a few days ago I saw her most precious luggage being loaded into a longboat. I know she has not forgotten about it, that's how she has managed to maintain that calm exterior. But let's not speak of her. We have more important matters to discuss. What's to be done about Lucius?"

"He really is dead this time?"

"There is not the least doubt of that any more, Hal," confirmed the major, "I saw him myself. He is lying stone dead in the mausoleum."

"Then I suggest that the best solution would be for Ned and I to go up there now and lay him to rest. After all, he already has a tomb waiting for him. No one else need know about this. Lady Cullan said that not even his own men knew who he really was and she won't want her part in this to be made known. It will have to be thought that the ringleader escaped. At least we have the gold, which will stand me in good stead with my superiors, especially after my disappointment over that brandy. What do you say, Alex?"

"Thank you, Hal, I would be grateful. This has been an ugly enough business as it is. But I think I must explain matters to Mr Stewart and to Tom Shaw, I owe them that."

Ned and the captain left immediately and the major was alone with Elisa.

"You know, Elisa, I have a strange feeling that we still do not know the whole story. I am convinced Newbury has played a part in this. It's my guess that it might well have been he who supplied Lucius with the gold while he was in London. You remember that Lucius told you that he would be able to pay Newbury out? I think Skinner and Prescott were in Newbury's employ. But we'd never manage to prove it, he will have made sure of that. War produces not only men who stand on fine principles but those who sit on fat profits. Newbury probably knew that Lucius would be tempted to steal that gold. He has already told me that he was aware of my brother's financial problems and my guess is, that's why Prescott was set to spy on him. It was more than coincidence that Tom was wrongly accused of poaching just after Lucius had paid off his mortgage. No wonder my brother was so determined to allay Newbury's suspicions to the extent that he allowed Aurelia to agree to an engagement. Perhaps Newbury had not only an eye to Lucius's property but to his wife also. If my brother had not disappeared in that fire, Skinner or one of his cronies would have been lying in wait for him one dark night. I believe they were all entangled in Newbury's sticky web."

Elisa shivered involuntarily. "What a horrid thought!"

"I'm sorry, my dear. You'd best go home now, you must be exhausted. The last two nights haven't exactly been uneventful, have they?"

"No, not exactly," she agreed slipping her hand into his. "But at least we've enjoyed spending them together."

He lifted her hand to his lips and kissed her fingers reverently. "I hope you will soon give me your promise to spend all our nights — and days together. And if I weren't coated in all this dust, I would show you just how enjoyable they could be. When does your father mean to be home?"

"The day after tomorrow," she answered, her eyes reflecting her joy as she gazed adoringly back at him.

"Then may I call on him in three days' time to ask his permission to pay my addresses?"

"I shall tell him to expect you. He will be so surprised! I'm sure he has long since given up hope of seeing me married. You won't change your mind will you?" she added anxiously. "After all, three days is a long time and gives you ample opportunity to reflect upon my deplorable faults."

"There is not the least fear of that, I have quite made my mind up to have you. As to your faults as you call them, I have grown to appreciate the fact that they would be a valuable asset to a soldier's wife. And if you are content to accept me as I am: irascible, pig-headed and poor as a church mouse, then I think we shall rub along tolerably well together, don't you?"

"I don't see why we shouldn't be blissfully happy — at least for most

536

of the time! Who could ask for more? Meanwhile, I shall spend my hours contemplating my good fortune. I couldn't have wished for a finer husband and I shall be immensely proud to be a soldier's wife. Now I suppose I shall have to leave you for a while. I'll take a look at Tom before I go, I left him in the care of that young private but I don't think he relished the task."

Tom was sleeping soundly when they went in to him and Elisa was able to return home happy in the knowledge that he was making a good recovery.

Three days later, a handsome Hussar officer, resplendent in all his regalia, arrived at Dovecote Hall and was received most graciously by Lord Maytland and his lovely daughter. Elisa had solicited Miss Stewart's help in dressing for the occasion and was looking remarkably elegant in a high-waisted morning gown of sea-green silk with long, tight-fitting sleeves and a high neckline trimmed with a small, white ruff. Her red curls had been brushed until they gleamed and her large, green eyes had never shone more brightly.

Lord Maytland was a tall, lean, well-looking gentleman with twinkling eyes and a ruddy complexion. It was obvious from the deep colouring of his skin that he was used to being out in all weathers. He shook hands heartily with the major remarking cheerfully, "So you're the young warrior bold enough to want to take this impudent scapegrace to wife? I admire your resolution, Major Lacey. I never thought there lived a man so valiant."

"Don't worry, sir, with your permission, I intend to keep her to a vow of obedience."

"And I shall see to it that I am constantly cherished," interjected Elisa determinedly. "But for now I shall leave you two to get better acquainted but don't be too long about it. I have waited two whole days to see Major Lacey and I am anxious to remind him of my finer qualities."

When the door had closed behind her, Lord Maytland invited the major to be seated and offered him a glass of wine.

"If it's all the same to you, sir, I should like to get straight to the heart of the matter before I accept your hospitality. I must tell you that I am deep in love with your daughter and if you have no objection to it, I am come to ask for her hand in marriage. However, I am in honour bound to tell you that I have only an officer's pay to support her and the rather meagre revenue that my estate provides. I realize it must seem very presumptuous of me to aspire to . . . "

Lord Maytland raised a hand to silence him. "Major Lacey, I really cannot allow you to continue," he said gently, "it would be most unfair of me."

The major eyed him doubtfully. "My lord, I am sure if you would allow me to state my case, you might . . . "

"There's no need to say anything more, Major. You see, I understand your circumstances only too well. Please do sit down, we will both be much more comfortable."

He indicated a convenient chair and waited until the major was seated before relaxing himself. Then pouring a glass of wine from the decanter at his elbow, he handed it to the major with an apologetic smile.

"I haven't always been a man of means myself, Major. My fortune was built upon some daring and very precarious speculations." He helped himself to some wine and rested his head on the back of his chair, his eyes twinkling more brightly than ever. "Indeed, in all honesty, I have to say that many of them have been undeniably reckless. I suppose Elisa has not mentioned the purpose of my visit to South America? No? Well then, allow me to enlighten you. I was obliged, through unfavourable circumstances, to take immediate and desperate steps to place my financial affairs on a safer footing. An exciting business venture presented itself that proved to be a somewhat lengthy expedition but which finally led to the acquisition of a very lucrative gold mine. I now find myself in the extraordinary position of being something of a Croesus."

"I see," said the major flatly, "then, of course, this alters my case."

"Indeed it does," he agreed, watching the major's crestfallen expression. "But there is no need to look quite so dejected. Let me explain matters to you as they now stand. Elisa has told me of your brother's death and I offer you my sincere condolences. It seems that his untimely passing has left you in a most difficult situation. I believe he had borrowed a substantial amount of money from you which he was unable to repay?"

The major nodded briefly, feeling too bitterly disappointed to reply.

"He did not inform you, I think, that he gave that money into Elisa's keeping?"

Now the major looked startled out of his misery. "Elisa?! He certainly did not!"

"My daughter knew that I was in need of a business partner to help me finance my latest project and she, being as headstrong as her father, invited Lord Cullan to invest ten thousand pounds in the scheme. You will forgive her, I am sure, for having such an unwavering faith in her papa's abilities and naturally she was unaware that your brother had petitioned you for the money. She did it with the best of intentions, desiring to help me and Lord Cullan at one and the same time. So you see, Major, with your brother's death, you and I became equal partners in the venture, which has happily resulted in a considerable increase in wealth for both of us. There, sir, you need have no more qualms about taking Elisa off my hands. You have my blessing to wed the chit as soon as you wish; I shall advise her to name the day immediately, before every spinster in the neighbourhood decides to set their cap at you."

The major leapt joyfully to his feet and seizing Lord Maytland by the hand, shook it vigorously, his whole face alight with relief and excitement.

"Thank you, Lord Maytland! This is wonderful! And naturally I am delighted that I shall now be able to do some good here and keep my wife in some style. May I go and tell her the happy news?"

"She already knows: I told her when I arrived home yesterday," beamed his lordship, reclaiming his aching hand.

"Oh, not that! I meant the news that we have won your blessing!"

"I think you will find that she is not surprised at that either. But go by all means, my boy, we shall have plenty of time to discuss business later."

The major ran out of the room in search of Elisa and found her waiting outside the door.

"Elisa! You must come with me into the garden at once! I have something very particular to say to you," he insisted, dragging her by the hand and ignoring her indignant protests. They stopped beneath the old sycamore tree and he took possession of both her hands. "Elisa, you remember the day you came to Blakestone and I treated you so cruelly?"

"I remember many such days," she sighed sadly. "Which one in particular are you referring to?"

"You know very well what I am referring to," he answered sternly, drawing her into his arms. "I gave you your first kiss, didn't I?"

She nodded, smiling up at him.

"I thought I did. Well, ever since that day I have very much wanted to kiss you again. A proper kiss this time, not one snatched in anger. May I, Elisa?" he entreated humbly.

"I wish you would," she answered

eagerly. Now she surrendered to his lips willingly, standing on tiptoe, her arms encircling his neck while he embraced her even tighter, crushing her close against his chest. When she eventually opened her eyes, she felt deliriously happy, the blood racing through her veins and her heart pounding with excitement.

"I need you, Elisa," he whispered earnestly, his cheek pressing hers as he held her safe in his arms. "Will you marry me?"

She drew back her head and looked into his eyes, her own wondrously tender. "Oh, Alex! If I am to be your wife, I swear I shall never go climbing trees again!"

"And I shall promise to make certain you won't ever want to," he murmured in a low voice, "and this is how I mean to discourage it."

BUTTERFLY MONTANE
Dorothy Cork

Parma had come to New Guinea to marry Alec Rivers, but she found him completely disinterested and that overbearing Pierce Adams getting entirely the wrong idea about her.

HONOURABLE FRIENDS
Janet Daley

Priscilla Burford is happily married when she meets Junior Environment Minister Alistair Thurston. Inevitably, sexual obsession and political necessity collide.

WANDERING MINSTRELS
Mary Delorme

Stella Wade's career as a concert pianist might have been ruined by the rudeness of a famous conductor, so it seemed to her agent and benefactor. Even Sir Nicholas fails to see the possibilities when John Tallis falls deeply in love with Stella.

CLOUD OVER MALVERTON
Nancy Buckingham

Dulcie soon realises that something is seriously wrong at Malverton, and when violence strikes she is horrified to find herself under suspicion of murder.

AFTER THOUGHTS
Max Bygraves

The Cockney entertainer tells stories of his East End childhood, of his RAF days, and his post-war showbusiness successes and friendships with fellow comedians.

MOONLIGHT
AND MARCH ROSES
D. Y. Cameron

Lynn's search to trace a missing girl takes her to Spain, where she meets Clive Hendon. While untangling the situation, she untangles her emotions and decides on her own future.

TIGER TIGER
Frank Ryan

A young man involved in drugs is found murdered. This is the first event which will draw Detective Inspector Sandy Woodings into a whirlpool of murder and deceit.

CAROLINE MINUSCULE
Andrew Taylor

Caroline Minuscule, a medieval script, is the first clue to the whereabouts of a cache of diamonds. The search becomes a deadly kind of fairy story in which several murders have an other-worldly quality.

LONG CHAIN OF DEATH
Sarah Wolf

During the Second World War four American teenagers from the same town join the Army together. Forty-two years later, the son of one of the soldiers realises that someone is systematically wiping out the families of the four men.

THE TWILIGHT MAN
Frank Gruber

Jim Rand lives alone in the California desert awaiting death. Into his hermit existence comes a teenage girl who blows both his past and his brief future wide open.

DOG IN THE DARK
Gerald Hammond

Jim Cunningham breeds and trains gun dogs, and his antagonism towards the devotees of show spaniels earns him many enemies. So when one of them is found murdered, the police are on his doorstep within hours.

THE RED KNIGHT
Geoffrey Moxon

When he finds himself a pawn on the chessboard of international espionage with his family in constant danger, Guy Trent becomes embroiled in moves and countermoves which may mean life or death for Western scientists.

NURSE ALICE IN LOVE
Theresa Charles

Accepting the post of nurse to little Fernie Sherrod, Alice Everton could not guess at the romance, suspense and danger which lay ahead at the Sherrod's isolated estate.

POIROT INVESTIGATES
Agatha Christie

Two things bind these eleven stories together — the brilliance and uncanny skill of the diminutive Belgian detective, and the stupidity of his Watson-like partner, Captain Hastings.

LET LOOSE THE TIGERS
Josephine Cox

Queenie promised to find the long-lost son of the frail, elderly murderess, Hannah Jason. But her enquiries threatened to unlock the cage where crucial secrets had long been held captive.

THE LISTERDALE MYSTERY
Agatha Christie

Twelve short stories ranging from the light-hearted to the macabre, diverse mysteries ingeniously and plausibly contrived and convincingly unravelled.

TO BE LOVED
Lynne Collins

Andrew married the woman he had always loved despite the knowledge that Sarah married him for reasons of her own. So much heartache could have been avoided if only he had known how vital it was to be loved.

ACCUSED NURSE
Jane Converse

Paula found herself accused of a crime which could cost her her job, her nurse's reputation, and even the man she loved, unless the truth came to light.

THE WILDERNESS WALK
Sheila Bishop

Stifling unpleasant memories of a misbegotten romance in Cleave with Lord Francis Aubrey, Lavinia goes on holiday there with her sister. The two women are thrust into a romantic intrigue involving none other than Lord Francis.

THE RELUCTANT GUEST
Rosalind Brett

Ann Calvert went to spend a month on a South African farm with Theo Borland and his sister. They both proved to be different from her first idea of them, and there was Storr Peterson — the most disturbing man she had ever met.

ONE ENCHANTED SUMMER
Anne Tedlock Brooks

A tale of mystery and romance and a girl who found both during one enchanted summer.